A Winter Garden

A Novel

David A. Ross

Published by Open Books 2012

ISBN: 0615708161
ISBN-13: 978-0615708164

CHAPTER 1
MIXED DUMPLINGS

In his pocket, Doran Seeger fingered a roll of banknotes (money he fully intended to lose at tonight's poker game) as he walked after sunset across the fabled Charles Bridge on his way to Prague Castle. In truth, he'd never had much luck at card games—or other circumstances governed by chance. Which was not to say that serendipity hadn't played a fundamental role in his destiny. Quite the reverse was true—at least since he'd given up his all-too-conventional life in America and cast his proverbial fate, like a fallen leaf, to the winds that blew over European terrain. That was nearly ten years ago, and while he'd never really accomplished anything approaching full cultural integration in Europe, he did now exist within a certain zone of comfort.

During the first few years of his expatriation, he'd drifted from city to city—Amsterdam, Geneva, Rome, Paris, Munich, among others—trying in each location to find cause to remain and put down roots. But each stop on his continental march had proven, for one reason or another, inadequate. He considered the possibility that perhaps this particular period of his life was simply ordained for itinerancy: it seemed to him as likely a possibility as any. In fact, the closest he'd come to finding a suitable home was during his first summer as a wayfarer. On the Island of Corfu, he'd encountered a nurturing environment, an agreeable local culture, and a totally unexpected romance with a Dutch woman named Alarice Van Zyl, who had come to Corfu on a summer long holiday with her younger sister. But the affair had faltered as summer turned to autumn, and the Van Zyl sisters returned to Rotterdam to care for their ailing mother.

For a time Doran carried a torch for Alarice, hoping for an eventual reunion on Corfu. He might easily have gone to the Netherlands to be with her, but he sensed—probably correctly—that the vivacity of their relationship emanated from particular circumstances at a particular locale. For a while they corresponded faithfully, but the ecstasy of everyday contact dimmed over time, and the letters grew more and more infrequent. And while Doran had never intended for the affair to end by default, that was indeed the way it had ended.

Serious romance had not found him since that first summer in Europe, and while he'd made many friends across the continent, a definite void existed in his life concerning devotion and commitment. A man without love was not complete: this he readily acknowledged, while the sad realization of his circumstance brought him no closer to fulfillment.

In retrospect, he sometimes wondered why he'd chosen not to pursue the affair with Alarice. There was no denying the fact that the connection they'd experienced that summer on Corfu was very special—an all-too-rare occurrence in Doran's life to date. For he was not a man inclined to frivolous love. Nor was he likely to expose his vulnerability as a matter of course. Certain events in his past had put him on guard, and his defenses often had to be broken down by degrees. It took a kind and patient heart to draw him out of reticence, yet when he was finally able to trust the intentions of a woman, the love he returned was unconditional.

Yet even in the absence of a romantic union, he did not exist in a social vacuum. Since coming to Prague he'd made many friends, some of them more or less influential in the city's cultural revival since its liberation from totalitarian Communist rule in 1989. Primary among his circle of friends was Scarlet Ponton.

Doran had met the audacious Colombian girl shortly after his arrival in Prague. Happy to have the counsel of another expatriate, he'd accepted one invitation after another to accompany her to bars and nightclubs and cultural events. Perhaps each had assumed that a romantic relationship might blossom out of familiarity, but it had simply not come to pass. Neither held the other accountable for the absence of romantic passion; instead each came to value, somewhat protectively, their platonic friendship.

At only twenty-six, Scarlet was fearless in the realm of commerce, time and again risking family money on outrageous business schemes that somehow always seemed to succeed. Coming to Prague immediately after the Velvet Revolution, she'd been the first to import drinkable coffee into Czechoslovakia. And shortly thereafter she'd hatched a plan to buy paintings from disenfranchised Ukrainian painters and import them into Western Europe. On a whim, Doran had gone with her to Kiev to buy canvases. Scarlet purchased the artwork with currency only slightly less soft than the rubles the artists so desperately needed. Sometimes she traded jeans or denim shirts for paintings. Back in Prague, or Berlin, or Frankfurt, she connected with German buyers flush with money and eager to acquire the spoils of a fallen system. Needing an occupation, Doran stuck with her as she tutored him until he was ready to go on buying trips alone.

He also counted Jan Storic among his friends in

Prague. A former dissident, Storic now worked as an administrative secretary in the Executive Office at the Castle. As a long-standing member of the resistance organization, Charter 77, Jan had known Havel for years. Like his friend, the president, Jan was a playwright. Two of his plays had been critiqued by Havel's wife Olga, and eventually performed at the Magic Lantern. In the political realm, he had served Charter 77 not as an idea man, but as a facilitator, and, as most Czechs, he held the new president in high esteem. But his feelings went beyond loyalty. He saw the president as a new type of leader for the free world—a politician committed to real civility. And he saw himself as part of a liberating fraternity.

Also invited to tonight's slightly illicit poker party was Vasil Basso, a thirty-two-year-old writer and rock singer whose star was rising in the Prague underground. As an artist, he too had endured the repression of the Communist regime, and he found this renaissance of creative freedom invigorating, though somewhat daunting. Vasil also knew Havel from the wine bars. He'd encountered the future president on many occasions, engaging him in philosophical discussions concerning literature and politics. Doran was not always inclined to agree with Vasil's particular vision of a liberated society, (anarchistic yet completely civil; altruistic yet somewhat protective of its cultural identity), but he certainly admired the poet's sense of resolve, and his stamina.

It was Jan Storic who had negotiated the terms of their entrance to Prague Castle, then to the inner offices of the Czech president himself. (A somewhat effortless arrangement, Doran concluded, and so unlike the fate of Kafka's frustrated Land- Surveyor, K). Their presence here tonight was not *officially authorized*, though under present circumstances, *Securité* was not likely to intervene.

For tonight the entire country held its breath and prayed for its ailing national hero, the poet and president Vaclav Havel. This unlikely head-of-state, Doran agreed, embodied the qualities for which a true leader should stand: truth, fairness, humanity, and genuine political decency. The dramatist and poet turned politician now stood upon the worldwide stage, symbolizing hope for politically oppressed people everywhere.

Recently reborn, the current incarnation of the Czech democracy was still somewhat fragile, and after years of totalitarian repression, the Czechs had good reason to question its efficacy. Their caution was not merely the result of cynicism and fear; it was a condition resulting from years of necessary social withdrawal. Reticence and anonymity had become the passkeys to survival.

During November 1989, Doran, along with the rest of the world, had watched in amazement as a critical mass of solidarity was reached throughout the Communist block. Wenceslas Square filled with key-rattling students, workers, clergy, and journalists, and a once obsequious proletariat, suddenly emboldened, demanded the immediate abdication of a government turned not only against them, but also upon itself. As the Soviet stranglehold on Eastern Europe lost its autocratic grip, the multitude in Wenceslas Square grew by the day. Russian soldiers with drawn automatic weapons quickly moved in to ensure order, but the Czech demonstrators only belittled the once-feared commandos by placing flowers in the barrels of their guns.

Meanwhile, Gorbachev sequestered himself inside his villa on the Black Sea; he would take no calls from the Russian *intelligentsia*. Soviet military tanks did not rumble through the Prague streets as they had in 1968. The secret police were now powerless in the face of the citizens' quorum. The Communists slunk away hoping only to save their necks. Not a drop of blood was shed in the Velvet Revolution, and Vaclav Havel, a long-suffering dissident who embodied the conscience of a stifled society, became president of the reformed Czech-Slovak Republic. These thoughts and others occupied Doran Seeger's mind as he entered Prague Castle.

Once inside the complex, a security guard escorted him to the president's inner offices, for it was there that tonight's poker game was to take place. Already present were his three friends: Scarlet Ponton, Jan Storic, and Vasil Basso. Doran shook hands first with Jan, then with Vasil. Scarlet kissed him warmly on the cheek and queried, "Did you bring your money, Seeger?"

"I brought enough to bankrupt the three of you," he said.

"Now that's American confidence for you," Vasil laughed.

Storic offered a beer as Doran sat down at the already prepared poker table. "Any word yet on Havel's condition?" Doran asked the presidential secretary.

Storic's face showed the concern he surely felt for his friend and his president. "It's too soon," he answered. "We won't know anything for a few more hours. Pavel Kahout promised to call as soon as Havel is out of surgery." Jan took a seat at the poker table, and laying his palm on top of the deck of playing cards, he invited the others to take their places as well. So the game began at this unlikely time and place, as the four friends waited for word of Havel's prognosis from Vienna.

Though hardly an aficionado at cards, Doran was holding his own after two hours of play, winning a pot every so often and hedging his bet on weaker hands. It was Storic's turn to deal, so he shuffled the cards, defined the game as five-card draw with no wild cards, called for the ante, and dealt a new hand. One by one, Doran routinely collected his cards: first, the king of hearts; then the ace of spades; another king; a third monarch… He waited in utter disbelief as Storic methodically dealt the final card of the hand. Was it possible that he might receive a second ace? Surely the odds against being dealt such a fortuitous hand were astronomical. Finally, he received his fifth card: the ace of clubs. An ace-high full house! It was certainly the best hand he'd ever drawn directly from a dealer. Realizing that over his boyish features a poker face would probably look ridiculous, he nevertheless tried to remain placid.

Rubbing reddened eyes, Vasil Basso drew two replacement cards from the deck to augment his weak hand and regarded the female member of the group. Scarlet declined replacement cards. Of course Doran also refused cards, instigating a friendly but predictable showdown. Storic took three cards from the deck and immediately folded. Assessing tonight's poker losses, he laughed ironically, for he was somewhat accustomed to ill fortune and personal mediocrity.

"What time is it anyway?" Vasil Basso wanted to know.

"Eleven-thirty," answered Storic.

"What's taking so long?" Basso asked in an irritated voice. He arranged the cards in his hand, his long fingers moving nimbly but nervously. "Why doesn't Kahout call?"

"It's complicated," said Storic. "He'll call when they know something."

"The waiting is terrible," Vasil grumbled.

"Play your hand," said Scarlet. "The game will occupy your attention."

Basso indulged her, increasing the pot by twenty-five crowns. "I can't help thinking about him lying in that operating theater. I get a vision of overpowering whiteness. God only knows what they're doing to him."

"He's getting the best of care," said Jan Storic. "It's not like he's here in Prague. Or in Moscow. He's in Vienna, Vasil. They have every imaginable medical miracle in Austria."

Basso was hardly consoled.

Scarlet Ponton's wager was considerably more aggressive than Basso's: one hundred fifty crowns. Her expression, though, was one of abdication. She directed her comments to Jan Storic, whom she'd known since first coming to Prague just days after the Velvet Revolution: "How can a doctor warm the lungs of a man who has spent months in a dark, wet prison cell?"

"This is not the president's first operation. Nor will it be his last. For Havel, it is one more trial in a long line of spiritual tests," said Storic.

Scarlet's look conveyed disregard. "Jan, the truth is that the man is dying—perhaps by degrees—but he's dying. And I don't know if I should break down and cry or be sick or just give up hope."

"You're not Czech," observed Vasil Basso. "So why such depth of feeling, Scarlet?"

She brushed the black, curly hair from her round face. "So many reasons," she said. "Of course there is my capital investment. But that's almost beside the point. There's a spiritual element as well."

Doran Seeger's reasons for living and working in the new Czech Republic, on the other hand, were far more coincidental. As an American, his political convictions were less than resolute. At forty-nine, he had now fully mortgaged the certainty of a materially comfortable future, only to borrow the soul of a gypsy.

Doran matched Scarlet Ponton's bet and raised the stakes another one hundred fifty crowns. Which drove Vasil out of the contest immediately. "You can't be serious, Seeger," said Scarlet.

Doran did not answer; he did not flinch. "It's your bet, Scarlet," he said simply. "But take your time."

"I'm ready to play now," she said confidently. And she laid down another one hundred fifty crowns.

Doran held his cards close to his chest as he recounted the day the American president had visited Prague. "Together, Clinton and Havel walked slowly across the Charles Bridge as the reporters and cameras followed. And I remember thinking: Clinton's teeth are so white and straight! And his mouth is so wide! His lips were flapping like a banner in a gale as he outlined the conveniences of a very peculiar kind of democracy, a democracy that ultimately separates classes with the precision of a centrifuge: a democracy called the Market Economy. And all the while Havel walked with his hands clasped behind his back, listening, listening, listening. His head was bowed, and he exhibited that characteristic, pensive expression he often has on his face, as he extracted the unfeigned intent concealed in the silence between Clinton's words."

"Heady assessment, Doran," said Jan Storic.

Doran shrugged. He looked straight into Scarlet's black eyes and said, "I have to call for your cards now."

"Of course," she said, and laid down three queens.

"Ah! Very good, Scarlet. Very good indeed! But not good enough, I'm afraid." He gloatingly revealed the full house.

"I don't believe this!" she consternated as he drew the chips to his position. Laughing, she suggested, "Now you can buy us all breakfast, Seeger."

The midnight bells in a hundred spires began to chime as they cleared away cards and coins. The telephone rang, and Jan Storic jumped up to answer it. Offering neither salutations nor small talk, he conversed quietly with the caller, listening more than speaking. His brow was furrowed; his fingers worked the receiver. Thanking the caller, he hung up the phone and turned to his friends in the presidential anteroom: "That was Pavel Kahout. Apparently, the surgery went well. But Havel is not out of danger. He'll be in intensive care for several days—maybe weeks. The doctors will be able to form a prognosis in forty-eight hours. That's all Kahout knows. So we wait. We wait."

At night, Prague was magical. From the time of his arrival in the city Doran had felt the nocturnal mystery of its cobbled streets and narrow alleyways, the fascination of its unscathed architecture resplendent throughout a complex history, the allure of a newly free society and a critical generation hardly aware of its reconstituted potential. Walking with Scarlet and Vasil on his way home, all three paused, as if on cue, halfway across the deserted Charles Bridge. Gazing across the river, Doran contemplated the bright spotlights that illuminated the Castle's exterior and reflected upon the black water of the Vltava. And though he had deliberated upon this scene a hundred times or more, his emotions were dramatically affected each time he stopped to consider his presence at this site.

The *Prazsky hrad*, or Royal Palace, was actually a collection of galleries, halls, towers, cathedrals, gardens and residences. It's architecture spanned more than six hundred years, including styles as diverse as Romanesque, Gothic, baroque, and renaissance. And its favorable position in the Hradcany district near the Vltava River was equaled only by its venerable place in history. Once the domicile of Bohemian princes and kings, it was now the seat of government in the Czech Republic.

On the right bank, the lighted towers of the Bethlehem Chapel and the Old Town Hall served as beacons on the way to the *Staronamesti*, or Old Town Square. The trolleys were not running after midnight, and few cars passed in the darkened side streets. Walking in front of the clock tower, they went through an archway and turned up the grand pedestrian mall known as *Vaclavske namesti*, then to the right along Vodickova Street, leading to the location of the New Town Hall. Doran's second floor apartment was located in an early nineteenth century building that stood at the intersection of the New Town Hall Square and a tributary street called Navratilova.

Reaching the door to the foyer, they paused in shadow before Doran took out his key. Overhead a sliver of moonlight filtered through a few wispy clouds in the indigo sky. Certainly spring was not long in coming, but tonight Doran could see the vapor from his breath. "I'll brew coffee," he told his friends. "Come inside awhile."

The American turned the key in the lock and the door opened onto a dimly lighted, musty foyer. All three moved quickly inside and the heavy door closed behind them.

Having been away the entire day, Doran collected the mail in his box. From it he took a single letter with a rather surprising return address. It read: *Van Zyl: Lagos, Portugal.* He knew surely the name, if not the locale, but the handwriting was not familiar. Climbing the spiraling stairs with his guests to the second floor, he tapped the envelope against his free hand and speculated silently about what news it might contain.

Unbolting the double lock on the door of his apartment, Doran directed his guests inside ahead of him. The apartment was noticeably cold, for the building's furnace was anything but reliable. But most everyone in the Czech Republic was sadly accustomed to such inconveniences; in fact, it was far better now than it had been before the revolution. All three kept their coats buttoned to the neck as Doran tossed the envelope onto a table and began fiddling in vain with the old-fashioned thermostat.

"Would you mind brewing the coffee, Scarlet?" Doran asked.

Rubbing her cold hands together, the Colombian girl went to the kitchen and measured the dark blend into the basket. She filled the pot with water and set it to boil on the stove. When the brew had sufficiently percolated, she called for Vasil and Doran to join her at the table.

Such a centrally located, old-city apartment was a rare find indeed for a foreigner, but Doran had come across it serendipitously, like so many circumstances in his life since he'd left the States, and rented it, modestly furnished, from a Czech doctor who was currently in residence at a hospital in Budejovice. The apartment itself consisted of a parlor, a kitchen, a bedroom with a sleeping loft, and a combination bathroom/laundry room with a separate toilet. The fixtures and furniture were standard Communist issue: a tragically comical 50's-style orange and black vinyl dining booth installed in one corner of the kitchen; metal cabinets with industrial-looking handles;

linoleum floor and countertop, once matching but now yellowed. Modular shelving covered the length of one wall in the parlor. The doctor had taken away the television, but a small radio that received only news and classical music remained. Besides a black vinyl sofa, an old wooden rocker, and a frayed, wing-back chair, there were several mass produced, veneer-covered accent tables that were manufactured to look modern, but looked, to Western eyes, only pathetic. The carpet was slightly shabby; the walls needed paint—not desperately, but noticeably. And the doctor's bed was made of a four-inch-thick piece of foam rubber, cut to size and laid over a plywood foundation. A heavy, antique armoire stood in one corner of the bedroom. A matching dresser was placed near a window that looked out to a central courtyard. There, children often played ball while women hung wash to dry in the breezy alcove.

The building was surely timeworn, though the advantages of living in the area known as the *Nove Mesto*, only blocks from Wenceslas Square, were obvious. Numerous cultural events played at theaters and concert halls year round and were within easy walking distance of the apartment on Navratilova Street—venues such as the now famous Theater on the Balustrade, the Semaphore, and the Café Slavia, where intellectuals and artists still gathered each night to fashion the philosophical bearing of a society in rebirth. A nearby language school offered Doran the opportunity to meet other foreigners who, like himself, were trying to learn enough of the Czech language to facilitate their own particular needs. He often visited the office where the English language newspaper was published and even wrote a few articles fashioned to aid recent American or British or Australian expatriates now living in Prague. Or sometimes he would loiter at the American Bar just off the *Staronamesti* to drink beer or wine and see who might turn up. The nineteenth century apartment's old-world charm was undeniable. The large parlor window overlooked Navratilova Street, where a rather animated café with summertime outdoor seating attracted gatherings that not long ago were forbidden by the Communists. Up the street, near the New Town Square, ran red trolleys with clanging bells. A nearby outdoor market offered everything from tasty homemade foods to clothes, household staples to handicrafts.

Doran knew that his time in Prague might well be limited; still he took the initiative to personalize his rented living quarters. He hung paintings that he'd acquired in the Ukraine on the parlor's walls, and covered the floor with hand-woven rugs from Slovakia. Books and magazines in Czech, English, and German were scattered about the apartment, and various clippings of personal interest were taped to the refrigerator. On one of the of the kitchen walls he'd hung a handwritten recreation of Vaclav Havel's peculiar typo-gram entitled, 'ALIENATION,' a picture-poem in which a maze of intertwining asterisks were initiated with the possessive, 'MY' and concluded with the somewhat dubious concept of 'SELF.'

"The genius of Havel's literary talent was realized by intellectuals and working people alike," said Vasil Basso, referring to the enigmatic poem on Doran's wall, "but his morality and his sense of conviction, and especially his philosophical depth, were largely overlooked outside Czechoslovakia. I believe his rise to the presidency took other world leaders completely by surprise. I'm sure many refused to take him seriously. After all, a poet as president! Yet the fact that a once-jailed dissident was able to assume a position of national leadership in today's singular political hierarchy is a powerful message to elitist governments concerning the final authority of public will."

Scarlet related: "I was traveling outside Colombia for the first time in 1990, and Prague was so alive that summer. It seemed everyone in Europe had come here to celebrate the end of totalitarianism. From May through September, the momentum continued to build and people poured into the city, but the Czechs themselves were slow to join their own party. They looked stupefied by the obvious wealth of Western Europeans—by cars and clothes and jewelry. Nevertheless, there were parties in the street, celebrations with ethnic music and dancing and food. On my second day in the city, I was crossing the Charles Bridge when a girl handed me a free ticket to a staging of 'Audience' and 'Private View' at the Semaphore Theater. I'd never seen one of Havel's plays, so I decided to attend. It was incredible! And the theater was magical! Have you ever been inside the Semaphore, Doran?"

"Never," he answered attentively.

"Just off Wenceslas Square," she continued, "the theater is built three stories underground. Symbolizing resistance to censorship, of course. All the actors and directors who worked there for free during the 60's, 70's, and 80's have autographed the walls: Kirk Douglas; Shirley Temple Black; so many others. The Festival Theater Company's production was enthralling. Sitting in the audience, I became aware that I was taking part in something tremendously important, and I concluded that I was presently in the most free and open society on earth. Somehow I knew I'd better start learning Czech and find a way to make a living, because I wanted to be nowhere else."

"So, Scarlet the entrepreneur was born," said Doran.

Scarlet laughed. "First I used family connections to import coffee. The coffee here was terrible—full of grain. The idea seemed natural enough, but the bureaucratic problems were monumental," she said, shaking her head. "It was a nightmare. Regulations galore! The old system of commerce was not fully unraveled. That took time. I became frustrated, but I stayed with it."

"And the entire country is glad you did," Doran observed as he sipped the rich Colombian brew.

"Eventually I went to St. Petersburg. Just to have a look," Scarlet continued. "From there I went to Moscow.

Finally, I ended up in Kiev. There I was introduced to a group of artists. Their circumstance was regrettable. They were accustomed to all kinds of subsidies—the Soviets were essentially underwriting their entire profession—and I quickly recognized an opportunity. These creative people were desperate to make a living in a society where prices were spiraling out of control. They were starving while the Russian Mafia flourished by stealing cars."

"And when you saw the quality of the work, you knew you could sell the paintings in Europe."

"I risked little to find out. A few D-marks purchased five paintings. I went to Berlin and immediately tripled my money. I knew I had something. But I never imagined the scope of the demand. Not for six more months. By that time I'd been in and out of the Ukraine more than a dozen times. Each time I arrived with more hard currency in my pocket, and each time I left with more paintings than the time before. The artists with whom I dealt told their friends. Soon I was shipping canvasses by rail in specially constructed wood crates. If I failed to show up in Kiev when expected, they would write to me in Prague, imploring me to buy more artwork. Of course, that's about the time I met you, Doran. And you know the rest of the story. You helped write it!"

It was true: there were countless opportunities for venturous people in the recently liberated Czech Republic, and many expatriates were making sizable fortunes. With Scarlet Ponton's help, Doran had carved out a niche for himself.

The three friends talked until four in the morning, mostly speculating about the future of the Republic should President Havel not recover from his illness. Vasil Basso enucleated the political background; Scarlet Ponton offered vision and unbridled enthusiasm. True to character, Doran listened quietly, filed away the information and opinions offered, and reserved judgment.

Once his friends had gone, Doran undressed and lay

upon his bed. Though tired, he could not sleep. Impatient with his insomnia, he rose. He went to the kitchen for a snack but changed his mind. He looked out the parlor window. The first light of dawn was in the sky, but Navratilova Street was deserted. Going room to room, he paced circles around his discomfiture. Then he noticed the letter he'd tossed aside earlier that evening.

Turning on a light, he stared at the envelope. The return address was quite curious. The letter had come from Portugal. Alarice lived in Rotterdam, and he'd not heard from her for nearly a year. That fact aside, the handwriting was definitely *not* her familiar script. Finally, he unsealed the envelope and removed the letter.

15 March, 2001

Dear Doran,

Dag! *I'm sure you are surprised to hear from me. I hope you are well. It's been nearly ten years since we parted on the dock at Corfu Harbor, yet it seems like only yesterday. What a summer it was!*

Of course you know that Alarice and I returned home to the Netherlands. Mother was quite ill with Parkinson's disease. She underwent fetal transplant therapy, but in the end it was not successful. Her death was very hard on my father. His health declined as well, so Alarice (always my dutiful sister) chose to remain in Holland to administer his business. I, on the other hand, could not remain at home—not after that glorious summer on Corfu. The university never appealed to me, so I worked for a while and saved all my money. I knew that traveling was in my blood. I landed first in Malaga, Spain, then Morocco. I even went to Senegal for a while! Each time I ran out of money I went back to Rotterdam to work with

Alarice in Father's business, but I guess it's true—at least for some people—that once estranged, philosophically speaking, you can never really go home. I now reside in Lagos, Portugal.

Alarice told me that she corresponded with you for a time. I know she was ecstatic to receive your letters. When I last inquired about you, she told me that she'd not heard from you for a very long time. I was afraid that we'd lost you forever. Then something extraordinary happened.

Here in Lagos, I met a young man from Ukraine. His name is Alexi Stolaroff. We live here in Lagos together. He is an artist. His father, Vladimir, is also an artist still living in Kiev. When Vladimir told Alexi that there was an American man in Kiev buying paintings and importing them to Western Europe, we asked his name. Imagine my surprise when he said Doran Seeger! Apparently, you've bought several paintings from Alexi's father. Of course Vladimir had your address in Prague. For a time, I considered whether or not to write to you. But life is so short. And good friends are rare. So I write this letter in hopes of reconnecting, Doran.

But that is not the end of my story. The relationship between Alexi and me is tentative. I am considering a break-up. For me, Lagos has run its course. I need to go somewhere else, and the thought of returning to Rotterdam chills me to the bone. I hear Prague is a splendid city. I look forward to coming there in the near future. I will look you up when I arrive.

Until then, good luck to you, and I remain,

Your loyal friend,
Gisela Van Zyl

Doran laid the letter on his lap and smiled. His remembrances of Gisela Van Zyl were fond ones indeed. On holiday with her sister in Corfu, she'd seemed an impetuous teenager, though the tone of her letter now suggested the similarly gracious approach of her older sister. Apparently, Gisela had grown into a mature young woman.

Considering that their parting on Corfu had been wholly circumstantial, Doran wondered to himself why he'd ever stopped communicating with Alarice. And he also wondered whether Gisela had shared his current whereabouts with her sister. In any case, Gisela's letter had calmed him, and he was quite happy that contact had been re-established between himself and the Van Zyl sisters. As the morning light spread over the city, Doran knew he would now be able to sleep.

CHAPTER 2
PLASTIC PEOPLE OF THE UNIVERSE

Even in wintertime the sun shone nearly every day in Lagos. Located along the Portuguese south coast, the waters were Mediterranean rather than Atlantic. Morocco was a short ferry ride away, and often the siroccos blew from North Africa to warm the beach towns and fishing villages of the Algarve. The Canary Islands and the lush oasis of Madiera lay further to the southwest.

Lagos was largely a tourist destination, but it was the off-season, and the town was quiet except for housewives buying produce at the outdoor markets, or laggards idling over cups of espresso.

Arriving as a summertime tourist, Gisela Van Zyl had never intended to stay long on the Algarve; she'd meant only to have an extended holiday on the south coast of Portugal, and then return home to Holland once her money was spent—a routine she'd certainly practiced to perfection. But one thing had led to another. The offer of a job in a dress shop, along with the fact that she hated winters in Holland, had convinced her to stay as summer turned to autumn and most of the tourists went away.

Telephoning her sister Alarice in Rotterdam, she explained the situation.

"It's so lovely here, Arissa. Sunshine everyday, sea breezes, and flowers everywhere. And I just can't face another cold, rainy winter in Holland."

"I knew it would come to this," said her sister. "Ever since our trip to Greece ten years ago, I've known that you would eventually leave Holland forever."

"Who said anything about forever?" Gisela postured.

"There's no need to justify your decision, Gisela."

"I'm not justifying, Arissa. But I don't want you to feel as though I'm deserting you. Or the business…"

"Gisela, darling, you've never really had an inclination for business of any kind."

"That's true," she conceded. "You've always been the serious one."

"For me, it's a way of life," explained the older sister. "For you, it never will be."

Silently, Gisela acknowledged the truth in her sister's assessment. "I have a job in a shop," she related. "And I've rented a lovely apartment that overlooks the sea. I've furnished it with wicker chairs and colorful prints and painted pottery."

"You see? You can't help yourself. You've got a full-blown case of wanderlust. If it's in your blood, you must get it from mother. I'm more inclined to take after papa." Alarice sighed as she thought of her parents, both deceased.

"I miss them terribly, Arissa. Especially mother."

"She left this world far too young," said Alarice.

Gisela agreed. "I know she was looking forward to her retirement. I think she might have liked to travel or teach."

"But of course papa was all business. He was never inclined to venture out."

"But I believe that mother's inclination, deep down, was different. After all, it was she who encouraged you to go to Greece that summer. And it was she who cajoled you into taking me along. Remember? My God, if she'd only known what she was instigating. In me, I mean. Look how things have turned out."

"Oh, I think she knew your nature, Gisela. I remember her telling me not to keep too tight a rein on you. Even then. Even when you were only nineteen."

"It seems like all papa ever did was work."

Alarice sighed. "And look at me," she lamented. "I'm following right in his footsteps. Sometimes it seems as if he's looking over my shoulder. But I can't escape my nature any more than you can escape yours, Gisela. So everything's just as it should be, darling. No need for you to fret over me or over the business."

"Still, I can't help indulging myself in a little bit of guilt."

"I'll send you some money," said Alarice.

"Thanks," said Gisela. "It will probably help."

"Now don't forget to telephone me," implored Alarice.

"I'll call at least once a week," Gisela had promised.

Shortly after deciding to remain in Lagos for the winter, Gisela had met Alexi Stolaroff in the lending library at the English Church. Finding Russians on the Algarve was hardly common, and Gisela was intrigued. They were the same age. They were both expatriates: she from Holland, and he from the Ukraine. She had no particular profession, but he was a painter. He spoke English well, as did she, and they'd gone to a café and talked over drinks for hours.

Over the course of the next few weeks she'd run into the young painter on several occasions. Meeting in front of a news kiosk, Alexi had told her that he was being evicted next day from the studio where he worked and lived. "I don't know what I'm going to do," he said in frustration. "I can sleep anywhere, but I need a place with good light, so I can paint."

Gisela considered the young artist's dilemma, but only briefly. "My place has beautiful light; perhaps you could paint there," she'd offered.

Expressing profuse gratitude, Alexi had accepted the invitation to stay at her apartment, and moved in immediately.

In the beginning their affair had been filled with the romance and daring of an artistic lifestyle, and the delight of new love. They lived life by a different clock: Alexi often painted throughout the night, so they might linger in bed until noon, falling in and out of slumber, and making love. Sometimes they drank champagne for breakfast, or ate their dinner at midnight.

Gisela had always considered herself an iconoclast, but she knew that Alexi's sense of rebellion far exceeded her own; and even though Gisela's personality was a strong one, still Alexi occupied a dominant role in their relationship, a dynamic with which Gisela was not always at ease. Within a month of their first meeting he had literally taken over her apartment, his canvases and paints and brushes and bottles of turpentine occupying every modicum of empty space. Only their bed was spared his clutter. Everywhere else—even the bathroom— contained the muddle of Alexi's life and vocation.

But that was not the worst of it. Alexi liked having things his own way, and he had a bad temper when crossed. And he drank. He drank far too much. She would often haul seven or eight empty bottles of Stolichnaya to the trash along with the rest of the household refuse.

After living together only a few months, Alexi's once compelling, nonconformist personality had become the sole source of Gisela's anxiety, and she found her tolerance severely tested by his habits and his idiosyncratic personality. He was self-centered, sometimes loutish, and perpetually inconsiderate of her needs and feelings. To Gisela, it seemed that Alexi was maniacally compulsive about everything he did, a personality trait thoroughly contrary to her own nature. Yet she was undeniably drawn to him as well, so she walked a precarious line between obsession and instinctive caution.

And though she'd never intended it, Alexi had become a fixture in her home, and in her life as well. Now, Gisela often felt like an intruder in her own apartment—the bright and pretty apartment overlooking the sea that she'd furnished with wicker chairs, colorful prints, and painted pottery. And as the months passed she found herself spending more and more time away from home—especially cherishing the morning hours as a time to reconnect with her more private self, a time to recapitulate and analyze, and a time to plan.

Working on a difficult canvas for days, Alexi had been drinking continuously, not stopping to eat or sleep. His clothes were stained and filthy, and he smelled from not having bathed for days. Gisela knew well to leave him alone during such fits of creative frustration, and she'd gone to bed that night without so much as a kiss or a kind word.

But in the early hours before dawn she had awakened to the unmistakable sounds of destruction. Alexi was on a rampage, slashing canvases, fracturing easels, hammering palettes, and spreading his red anger over everything. Still in her nightgown, she bolted out of bed and ran into the parlor—or rather the room that had once been the parlor and now served as Alexi's studio—only to see an expression of torture on her lover's face. She screamed at him to stop, but instead he picked up a tray of paints and flung it at her. Gisela ducked away as the tray crashed against the pristine white wall, spreading primary colors in a random mosaic.

"What's wrong with you?" she yelled.

"It's shit!" he barked. "It's all shit!"

"What are you talking about?"

"Look! It's plain to see!" he bellowed as he took up a knife.

"What are you doing?" Gisela pleaded.

Alexi proceeded to slash yet another canvas from end to end, and then kicked out the legs that supported the easel with the severed canvas.

"You're drunk!" Gisela scowled.

Alexi laughed pathetically. "Of course I'm drunk. It's the Russian way."

"This is bullshit," Gisela retorted.

"It's *all* bullshit, isn't it?" Alexi muttered. Then he threw up in the middle of the parquet floor.

Gisela ran back into the bedroom and slammed the door. Trembling from anger, and terrified to come out of the bedroom, she dressed hurriedly to the sounds of Alexi's riot. After fifteen minutes she heard a heavy thud, and then it was suddenly quiet in the parlor. Peeking out through a crack in the bedroom door, Gisela saw that Alexi had passed out cold on the floor in his own vomit. Unmoved to revive him, she ran from the apartment in disgust and took refuge at a nearby café. There she'd passed the early hours of the morning drinking coffee and smoking, and considering how to be rid of the brutish Russian painter once and for all.

Indeed, this was not the first time Alexi had turned aggressive. Neither was it the first time he'd driven her from the apartment to seek refuge and peace. In fact, two weeks earlier, under similar circumstances, she'd written a letter while sitting at this same café—a letter to her longtime friend Doran Seeger, a letter indicating her intention to leave both Alexi and Lagos and come to Prague. In retrospect, Gisela acknowledged that her letter to Doran had perhaps been written speculatively, yet in light of Alexi's most recent outburst she was now glad she'd taken the initiative to contact her sister's former lover.

Ten years ago, Doran Seeger had proved to be what she least expected of an American. He was thoughtful and he spared his words. But when he spoke, his opinions often reflected an obvious consideration of the ideas of those around him. At the time Gisela had entertained the unspecific notion that the laconic American was trying to escape an undeclared demon, though the affair with her sister, as well as their experiences in Greece as a threesome, had seemed to draw out his more hopeful side, and to somehow revitalize and heal him. She herself had been involved with a Greek boy all during the summer holiday, so her core appraisal of her sister's lover was mostly based on casual observations, which were supplemented by her own conjecture. Though later she had learned more about him through conversations with her sister, and by reading a collection of letters sent to Alarice after their return to Holland, letters her sister offered to share with her. The letters determined Doran's essential timeline, though the intermediate details of his life remained sketchy.

Gisela remembered their parting on the dock at Corfu Harbor as if it had happened only yesterday. The night was black, but the lights from the two ferryboats docked in their berths illuminated all three faces. It had been a very emotional time, and each had seemed to be searching for something not yet recognized. Indeed, they were already old friends. They were friends of the best kind. And they'd hugged and kissed and promised to write letters at Christmastime, and to return to Corfu the following summer. But even as they made their promises each had known that it would be impossible to recapture the splendor of that wonderful time.

Unforeseen events had imposed themselves upon sincere intentions. Returning from Greece, Alarice had become predictably involved in circumstances at home in Rotterdam; while Gisela's own course had taken one unexpected turn after another—a trend that, to her, now seemed redundantly defining. Immersed in the vicissitudes of her own life, she'd thought only occasionally of Doran Seeger, but as she sat quietly sipping coffee, and contemplated abandoning both Alexi and Portugal, Gisela guessed that she and Doran had always shared a common nature, (though at nineteen she had been too young to recognize it), and she could not help wondering just what diversity a fast moving decade had offered him. Perhaps he would answer her letter. Or perhaps they would reconnect in Prague.

Alarice Van Zyl was nothing short of flabbergasted when she learned that her sister Gisela had discovered, quite by accident, the whereabouts of Doran Seeger.

"One chance in a million," she said to Gisela calling from Portugal. "Who would think that your Ukrainian boyfriend, whatever-his-name-is— "

"Alexi."

"Who would think that he'd lead us back to Doran?"

Gisela taunted her sister with playful repartee: "Spooky, huh?"

"It's just so unlikely."

"He's living in Prague. I'm sure of it."

"And when are you going there?"

"Not soon enough."

"Then it's really bad between you and Alexi?"

"I can't pack fast enough."

"Do you want to come home for awhile?" Alarice asked.

"I'd rather go to Prague."

"I hear it's beautiful there," Alarice sighed.

"It was never bombed during the War," informed Gisela. "And fifty years of Communism saved it from automobile pollution, because there were very few cars."

"I haven't heard from Doran… I can't even remember how long it's been."

"This is really odd," Gisela began.

"What's really odd?"

"When we were in Greece, and you met him and started whatever it was that you started…"

"Yes?"

"I didn't think much of him. And I couldn't understand why you liked him so much."

"There's no explaining the chemistry between people," Alarice concluded.

"No lie! If I understood that, I wouldn't be in the trouble I'm in now. But my present situation aside, I found that the more I thought about Doran, and about the way he was—or is—the more I liked him. Or at least I appreciated him."

"He was kind and gentle to me."

"To me, he seemed lost."

"That too…"

"Anyway, it should be interesting."

"Maybe you might convince him to come to Holland for a visit?" Alarice suggested.

Gisela chuckled. "I think that's your cause, Arissa."

"It's been ten years," Alarice observed.

"And that in itself is a little overwhelming," said Gisela.

Alarice only sighed.

Indeed, it had been tens years since she'd taken her last holiday, since she'd spent an enchanting summer on Corfu—her one real adventure to date! And it had been ten years since she'd met Doran Seeger and fallen in love with him while touring the Cyclades. But that wonderful summer, as well as their affair, had ended so abruptly.

For just as she and Doran had returned to Corfu from a romantic cruise of the Aegean Islands, Gisela had informed her that she'd been told by their father that their mother was seriously ill with Parkinson's Disease, and that he'd suggested they return home at once. Alarice had not wanted to leave Corfu. And she had not wanted to end her affair with Doran Seeger. Nevertheless, she'd gone home to Rotterdam. For a time she held out hope that Doran would come to Holland to be with her. Instead, he chose to drift through Europe that winter. She received his letters from Munich and Paris and Sicily. Though not once did Doran offer to come to the Netherlands.

Maude Van Zyl had died the following spring. At the height of the tulip season in Holland, the girls buried their mother and consoled their father, barely taking time to reconcile their own loss.

Consumed by overwhelming grief, Frederick Van Zyl lost interest in just about everything, particularly his business. Such a disposition was decidedly out of character for the lifelong entrepreneur, and the change in his personality came as a complete surprise to his daughters. Each, in her way, tried to redirect his perspective, but the widower stubbornly resisted all efforts. In the months following his wife's death, Frederick began to neglect not only his affairs, but his personal hygiene as well, allowing his once meticulously trimmed hair to grow wild and unkempt over his ears and shirt collar, and often forgetting to shave for days at a time. He bathed only after his daughters insisted. And his once profitable import-export business teetered on the edge of bankruptcy. Had Alarice not taken control of the firm, the prosperity resulting from a lifetime of effort would surely have been lost.

Ten years... Where had the time gone? Gisela had worked at her side all during that spring and summer, while Frederick continued to decline.

"Papa stares vacantly out the window for hours on end," Alarice lamented to her younger sister. "What is he thinking? What is he feeling? Does he expect Maude to come riding around the bend on her rundown bicycle, her thumb poised on the warning bell attached to the rusted handlebars, her frumpy sweater buttoned unevenly over her chest, and her faded scarf covering her head? He mutters to himself. He's losing his will by the day. It's so sad, Gisela."

"I don't know how much longer I can stand to watch him falter," Gisela said somberly.

"Yes, he's failing," Alarice assessed. "Steadily and quickly. We're going to lose him, too."

Gisela felt a lump come into her throat. "Then you don't think he'll come out of this?"

Alarice shrugged. "Who knows? But I don't think it's

likely."

"Maybe Dr. Voorwinkle can give him something for the depression."

"Why put him through that?" Alarice asked.

"I don't know. There are drugs for depression."

"But there's no cure for a broken heart, is there?"

"Since when have you become such a fatalist, Arissa?"

"I'm not. But look at him!"

"I can barely bring myself to look at him."

"I know. I want to do something to help him. But maybe there's nothing to be done," said Alarice.

The following November, Frederick Van Zyl followed his wife to the grave. He died without a sound while sitting upright on a straight back chair and staring out his parlor window at the pouring rain. Returning home from work for lunch, Gisela had found him with his hands neatly folded on his lap, his lips slightly parted as if unexpectedly silenced in the middle of some unknown utterance. His pale blue eyes were wide open. She sighed as she covered his legs with the wool blanket that had fallen away. Then she telephoned her sister to come at once.

Both parents dead within thirteen months: once unthinkable, it was nevertheless true. Each sister sought to redefine her life as an orphan. Alarice had her own apartment in the *Cubiswohnung*; she'd lived there ever since graduating from the university at Leiden. And she had long ago immersed herself in Frederick's business affairs. But Gisela was hardly so well grounded. She continued to live in her parents' apartment even after Frederick's death. And she worked faithfully at her sister's side. She was barely twenty-one, and she was indeed too young to have suffered such a loss. But fate was irrevocable, and she diligently tried to immerse herself in the life that her father had wanted for her—no doubt a life that her sister lived at the expense of her own happiness. Of that Gisela was certain. Yet one was obliged to respect the wishes of the dead—especially one's parents—and there were certain well-defined obligations to uphold. Time and again Gisela imagined her father's taciturn face charging her from the grave. She desperately wanted to honor his memory, yet the drudgery she felt day by day as she processed orders and detailed shipments ultimately evoked her true nature—the vagabond personality that Maude so astutely suspected when she had implored Alarice to take her to Greece.

For Alarice, her one attempt at escaping such a life, subconscious as it surely was, had been subverted through circumstance. She was socially particular; this much she understood of her character. Doran Seeger had found her sitting contemplatively upon a giant sunflower, her back turned toward him as she stared out to sea. A mirage-like pyramid floated upon Ionian waters. A solitary island near the horizon...

And like an ultramarine jewel, the tranquil sea ebbed and flowed between its blue-green and violet moods. Centuries ago, mythological superstars had populated these isles, self-absorbed in the hemisphere of Creation. Had she, herself, descended from Zeus and Dione? Such a notion seemed entirely possible, for here time was irrelevant.

Aboard the ferryboat *Poseidon*, Alarice had watched moonbeams skip across the waves as Doran lay sleeping on the narrow bed opposite her. It was very late, but she could not sleep. The ship rocked from side to side, but the motion of the ferry boat did not disturb her equilibrium nearly as much as did the gentle man sleeping on the berth opposite hers.

On their first night in Athens, Doran had been robbed. After midnight, they'd lain upon a large flat stone in the Agora at the foot of the Acropolis. They'd meant only to rest a few moments, but they'd fallen fast asleep in each other's arms. When they awoke, Doran had discovered that his wallet was missing. They scoured the ground near the stone where they'd slept, but the wallet was nowhere in sight. Luckily, the thieves had profited little, and when they returned to their hotel room Doran was philosophical about the crime. "I left a funny little note inside my wallet for a potential thief," he told her as she washed her face and brushed her hair in the bathroom. "It informs him that the leather is coated with a slow-acting, iridescent ink."

"Just like Houdini," she'd laughed.

And as she came out of the bathroom wearing only her bra and panties, Doran sat at the foot of the bed. So smoothly, she sidled beside him, tenderly rubbing his back and neck. She pressed her soft cheek close to his, and her warm breath coaxed him out of concealment. In a moment his hand was on her bare thigh. The fine hairs on her lithe arm rose under his touch. Their lips brushed lightly together, then they kissed fully.

At Paros Island they'd toured the interior by Jeep, visiting the towns of Naoussa and Lefkes. They swam at golden beaches and sunbathed naked on top of stone ledges by the sea. They tramped through the Valley of the Butterflies, falling to the ground amidst thousands of cornflowers to make passionate love under a perfect sky.

Mykonos was something else: giant pink pelicans scolding sybarites as they nursed hangovers in cafés at noon.

On the Island of Naxos, they'd visited the Temple of Dionysus, walked the streets of the Kastro, and made an excursion to the ancient mountain village of Chalkia. There they met an amiable Greek man who offered them a drink called *raki*.

"What's *raki*?" Alarice asked.

"*Po, po, po*! You don't know about *raki*? *Ohhh… Ahhh…* Listen! When the treading of the wine grapes is finished, what remains in the vat is never thrown away. It is put into a special jar called the *harani*, and then it is boiled to practically nothing. The end product of the distillation is called *raki*!"

The old man's clear moonshine was pure poison, and Alarice recalled fondly the little poem he'd recited for them:

> *"We're making wine*
> *So come and help,*
> *Stand in the vat*
> *And tread the grape.*
>
> *And if our grapes are trodden*
> *By one as sweet as you,*
> *Then this year's wine will surely be*
> *As sweet as honeydew."*

In the shade of a plane tree they drank *raki* with their host until a downpour drove them indoors. When the bus bound for Chora arrived, they thanked their host for his hospitality and climbed aboard. And as the bus pulled away, Alarice remembered, they had watched through a dust-covered window as the happy Greek danced the steps of a well-practiced, traditional dance.

At the wayward side of Santorini they'd discovered Perissa beach, (an eight-kilometer-long stretch of black sand), a dramatic mountainside, (on top of which were the ruins of ancient Thira), and the seaside village of Kamari, a place so picturesque that one might want never to leave. And Alarice had met Professor Dumas at the archeological excavation site of Akrotiri. She'd always loved archeology, and offered to work for no pay. Professor Dumas had taken her on, and the hot days of August had passed with her going off to sift sand at the dig, while Doran rode across the island on a rented scooter to swim and jog along the expansive black sand beach. Around four o'clock she would return from the site looking filthy but happy. Brown as cinnamon, Doran would come riding up by six. They would shower together, and then make love as the siroccos came in from northern Africa. She remembered the long white curtains in front of the terrace doorway blowing gently in the breeze, and the air coming into the room to cool their torpid bodies.

And each evening they arrived at the Oasis Bar before sunset. Over glasses of luscious Santorini wine they watched as the star-like lights of Thira Town rose. In the sky, streaks of violet light intimated the coming change of season, but unaware of their impending separation, they basked in the warm currents of late summer.

In the cool darkness of the Eden Restaurant in Athens, a four-blade fan whirled overhead as Doran told her, "I'm considering *not* going home."

Silently, Alarice totaled the sum of the past month's experiences. "The idea of staying in Greece is very tempting," she conceded.

"After seeing how happy you were working at Akrotiri, it's difficult for me to imagine you back in Rotterdam, working in your father's business," he said.

"Are you suggesting I stay here with you?"

"Surely our feelings for one another are grounded here."

They had arrived back at Corfu on the morning of Aphrodite's funeral. The mother of their friend Modestos had passed away only the day before their return. That was the first bit of bad news. Gisela's break-up with Spiro was the second. Learning of Maude's illness was the final shock. With Gisela, they sat at the back of the church as the Thromos family mourned the loss of their matriarch.

That evening, as the sun was going down, Alarice had found Doran sitting alone on the beach. She sat beside him and wrapped her arms around her knees. For a time they shared silently the sights and sounds of a place where they had first come to know one another, and fallen in love. Together they lay on the warm sand and talked in whispers.

"What happens to *us* when the light of Hellas fades from our memories?" she had asked.

"Sometimes a choice is no choice at all," he replied.

Anxious for rapprochement, Alarice conveyed an alternative. "Why not come back to the Netherlands with me? We'll take all the beautiful memories of this summer with us."

"Or you could return here once everything is resolved…"

Through her tears, Alarice saw the evening's first star appear, and no longer able to deny the reality of the impasse, she fervently wished that blind Eros, his arrows dipped in fire, would never leave her heart.

And as they stood waiting at the dock, the lights of two ships bound for different ports illuminating their sad expressions, Alarice found herself swept out to sea and thrown over waves, swallowed by troughs until she was finally washed ashore on an all-too-familiar solitary island.

Now, ten years later, she caught her breath as she realized the impact of that glorious summer. Time had dulled the ache of their parting, just as it had led her back to the life she'd managed to briefly forget—a life of credits and debits. A life, perhaps, for which she was meant.

CHAPTER 3
ANNOUNCING THE END
OF THE WORLD

"Stolaroff has five new canvases," Scarlet Ponton told Doran. "And he's collected two dozen others from his artist friends in the Ukraine." Along with their friend Vasil Basso, they sat at the underground wine bar *U kocoura* (located in *Mala Strana*, or small town) after midnight. Nearby and settled upon a hilltop in all its luminary magnificence, Prague Castle prevailed over the venerable Czech capital.

"Are you planning a trip to Kiev?" Doran asked.

"I can't go. My mother is arriving from Colombia the day after tomorrow," Scarlet explained.

"How is your money situation?" he asked her.

"Renting shop space and buying computers has left me a little strapped," she confessed. "But I can afford some of the paintings," she said. "What about you?"

"Right now I'm fairly flush," he told her. "I can probably pay for twenty canvases, if you can cover the others."

"Yes, I think that's workable," she said.

"I presume you want me to make the trip?"

Scarlet smiled. "Don't worry, I'll make it worth your time and effort."

Doran nodded and turned to Basso. "Want to take a little vacation, Vasil? I could stand some company."

"A trip to Kiev?" Basso shook his head skeptically. "No, thanks."

"Where's your sense of adventure?" Doran baited.

"Not in Kiev," said Vasil drolly. "Besides, my band is booked through the end of the month."

"The Plastic People are playing at the *Roxy* in Prague Center tomorrow night," Scarlet confirmed. "And Vasil assures me that it's going to be a very curious show." She raised her black eyebrows as she regarded the perspicuous musician. "Maybe you'd like to come with me, Doran?"

"Sure, I'll come."

"Good. The concert is at eleven-thirty. I'll come by your apartment around ten. We can go for a drink before the show begins."

Doran turned to Vasil Basso. "For better or for worse, it looks like I have a date," he said to the sallow-faced poet.

Vasil smiled as he extinguished his cigarette. "You could do worse," he concluded.

Scarlet socked him playfully on the shoulder. "Notice I haven't asked you out, darling."

"An unfortunate omission on your part, Scarlet," he said.

"Or perhaps the province of feminine insight," she bantered.

"My dear Scarlet, may you wonder for eternity."

"I'm far too young for you, Basso," she retorted. Her penetrating gaze openly mocked Vasil's insincere advance. The lights in the bar were turned low; nevertheless her full face glowed with confidence.

Smiling wryly, Vasil regarded Doran. "Apparently Scarlet does not understand the many advantages of dating a mature man," he conjectured.

"Experience over beauty, I agree," said Doran.

"Give me a break!" she laughed. "Either one of you would take a younger lover in a heartbeat."

"May God spare me that," wished Vasil. "And may He spare Doran as well!"

"I don't believe you," Scarlet challenged. "Not for one minute!"

"Of course a younger woman has certain charms," Vasil allowed. "But there remains a question of depth."

"Are you saying that younger women are necessarily superficial?" she asked, incredulous.

"Present company notwithstanding," Doran conceded.

"Yes, there *are* exceptions," said Vasil.

"Unless I'm uninformed, neither of you has had a recent invitation from Claudia Schiffer," she taunted. "Nor from Madonna!"

"Very busy women," observed Vasil.

"I heard that Schiffer's with that oddball TV magician, Copperfield," said Doran.

"Not that she'd know either of you are alive," said Scarlet.

"A low blow," said Vasil.

"Tit for tat," she said.

"You're one in a million, darling."

"This is too much!" she huffed.

"Don't take Basso too seriously," Doran implored her.

"You should talk, Seeger. You're a co-conspirator!"

"Hardly," he said.

"It's getting late," Scarlet concluded. "And I'm sufficiently drunk." She pushed her chair away from the table.

"And I suppose you're late for a rendezvous with your *younger* lover?" teased Vasil.

"Don't go blind fantasizing about me, Basso," she cautioned.

"A low blow," said Vasil.

"Tit for tat," she said

Doran stood up as well, though it was apparent that Vasil intended to remain at the wine bar a while longer. "I'll walk with you," Doran offered her.

"No need to go out of your way," she said dismissively.

"You know I don't mind," he said.

With lips full and red, Scarlet smiled. "*Gracias, amigo*," she said. She draped her red cape over her shoulders and took his arm. Together they headed for the door.

As they walked across Old Town Square and past the astronomical clock tower, Scarlet talked about the purchase she had recently made of twelve computers, her intention being to open an internet café in central Prague. They also discussed the progress of their business dealing in Russian art.

"Scarlet, I have no doubt that someday you'll be a rich woman," said Doran.

"I seem to have a knack for recognizing opportunities that other people miss," she said. "But I don't do it for the money," she laughed. "I think I just like hatching schemes."

"Importing paintings from the Ukraine was an inspired idea, Scarlet. And it's proven to be a real gold mine," he said.

"But I don't know how much longer we can continue," she speculated. "Either the supply will dwindle, or the market will dry up." She shrugged nonchalantly. "What good thing lasts forever?"

"I guess you have a point," he allowed.

"Don't worry, Seeger," she said. "You're a terrific partner. You're honest. And you're not afraid to take risks. Whatever I decide to try, you can consider yourself included."

"Seeing that I have no work visa, I appreciate the offer," said Doran.

"I know that sometimes I give you a hard time," she said, "but I really like you, Seeger."

Having left Scarlet at the entrance to her apartment, Doran made his way through the city center toward his home. So many nights he'd walked the empty streets of Prague after midnight, after drinking and socializing at the wine bars with expatriate friends and Czechs alike, and the city had never failed to charm him. With its spires and quaint streets, its bridges and antique street lamps, old Prague tantalized his sense of fantasy and gently nourished a once demoralized spirit.

Which was not to say that he was free from the pain of his particular disenchantment, or the resulting cynicism. Such feelings had originated at least in part from a growing realization that he'd been co-opted by his own government, having been employed to design guidance systems for so-called smart weapons in return for substantial redress. Neither he nor his co-workers had been told the specific applications of the systems they were designing, and apparently no one thought to question authority—an absence of insight or courage that ultimately had had devastating consequences the night the bombs fell on Iraq. Throughout the televised air raid on Baghdad, Doran had purged into the toilet, though he'd not been able to rid himself of remorse. Indeed, the deaths of two hundred fifty thousand Iraqis weighed heavily on his conscience—not to mention the resultant deaths of half a million children under the age of five who might have lived full and productive lives had it not been for subsequent sanctions on food and medicine imposed after a wholly conditional armistice. And though he knew that it was pointless to personally shoulder blame, or to try to understand all the particulars of the politics at play, he could not help harboring resentment at having been used as a pawn by more powerful players in such ruthless international intrigues. While Doran had never really intended an extended stay in Europe, neither did he want to return to his former profession or way of life in the

States. Certainly, importing art from Eastern Europe did not fully satisfy his creative tendencies; but it did provide him a living in *black* money, which was necessary since he did not have legal standing outside his own country. And it was fair to say that he felt far less co-opted in the Czech Republic (or anywhere else in Europe for that matter) than he had in the U.S.A.

Just where he was headed, now almost ten years after the fact, remained to him a mystery. Indeed, a rather curious position for one nearly fifty years of age. And there also remained for him the nagging issue of atonement and recompense for deeds done (whether intentional or not) that were counter-productive to peace and the greater humanitarian cause—at least that was his particular notion of balance and justice. Certainly his time as an expatriate had offered him a measure of self-forgiveness, yet a lifetime deserved a more noble defining deed, did it not?

As he turned the cobbled corner onto Navratilova Street, Doran walked with head lowered in thought, so at first he did not notice the shadowy figure huddled in the doorway of his apartment building. Though as he moved closer the silhouette of a young woman became obvious. He knew the occupants of his building by sight, and even in dim light it was clear to him that the loiterer was distinctly out of place. He was not alarmed by her presence, only curious, and possibly concerned for her welfare. He called out a greeting and asked if she was looking for someone particular.

"Doran, is that you?" she inquired.

He squinted his eyes, trying to see more clearly in the weak light. "Gisela Van Zyl!" he said as a smile spread over his expression.

Wrapped in a jacket far too light for the chilly weather, Gisela rose from her crouched position in the doorway. "I've been waiting here for you since eight o'clock," she said.

"Why didn't you telephone me?" Doran asked as they

kissed cheek to cheek.

"You never sent me your number. All I had was your address."

"I had no idea you'd come so soon," he said.

"I hope it's not a problem," she ventured.

"No. No problem at all. In fact, I'm delighted you're here!"

"Well good!" she said as a shiver moved over her body.

"You look frozen stiff," Doran observed. "Come inside."

Gisela nodded enthusiastically as she picked up her bag. "I thought that maybe I had the wrong address," she said.

"If you'd only written to tell me when to expect you," said Doran as he turned the key in the lock.

"You know how it is," she said shyly. "I mean, I wasn't exactly sure when I'd arrive. I stopped in Barcelona. Also in Nice. It's a long way here from Lagos."

"And from Corfu!"

"Yeah, no kidding."

"But now you're here."

"And come what may!" she said.

"So you're not planning to go back to Portugal?"

"Never would be too soon," she said decisively.

"Prague is fantastic," he informed her. "Everybody's here. And I mean *everybody*!"

As Doran turned on a light inside his flat, Gisela laid down her bag and looked round the parlor. "Nice apartment," she complemented. "It's really big!"

"I was fortunate to find this apartment," he told her. "Vacancies are rare in the center of the city."

"My apartment in Lagos was half the size of this place," she measured. "And of course after Alexi moved in with all his crap, I was relegated to a corner."

"Alexi is Vladimir Stolaroff's son?"

"Right!"

"And also your most recent antagonist…"

Gisela laughed ironically. "I lost all control of the situation," she explained, "and it simply became unbearable."

"Sorry to hear it," Doran consoled.

"Strangely enough," she analyzed, "I don't feel any remorse at leaving him."

"None?"

"No," she shrugged.

"Well, I guess that's good," Doran judged.

"I mean, you'd think that after living with a guy for over a year... But he was such a bastard, Doran. He doesn't deserve a single tear. And apparently I'm not inclined to shed one!"

"Always the sentimental one—that's how I remember you, Gisela."

"All sarcasm aside, Doran, he was very cruel to me."

"Not physically, I hope."

"It was coming to that, I have no doubt."

"Then you were right to leave."

"I know I was."

"And it looks like you're traveling light," he observed.

"I had to get out as fast as I could," she said somberly.

"So, why didn't you go home to Holland?" Doran asked. "To your sister."

"Alarice wanted me to come. But Rotterdam is not right for me—never has been."

Doran nodded, for he understood convictions of this kind—convictions as inevitable as they were vague. "So, take your time," he advised. "Even as your next step is right in front of you, it's not always obvious. I know this from experience, Gisela."

"I'm not even sure why I came to Prague," she said. "But your hospitality means a lot to me, Doran. I don't know how to thank you."

He waved off her gratitude. "My home is your home. I'll give you a key."

She smiled. "You're too much."

"You still look chilled. How about some coffee?" he suggested.

"Yes, thank you."

"My business partner is Colombian," he told her as he put the pot to boil. "She imports the finest beans," he bragged.

Over coffee at the kitchen table, Doran considered the appearance of the younger Van Zyl sister. As a teenager Gisela was tall and angular; but as a young woman her body had filled out nicely, looking now much as Alarice had looked ten years ago. And her hair, once dyed rebellious black and cropped short, had grown in full and returned to its natural, soft brown color. The craze of silver jewelry she'd worn as a girl had been replaced in maturity with a tasteful gold bracelet and matching earrings. Her clothes were stylish and sexy, and her make-up, also once exaggerated, was now flattering in its simplicity. Of course there were obvious differences between the Van Zyl sisters: where Alarice's eyes were warm and sentimental, Gisela's wide violet gaze conveyed a venturous nature; and where Alarice's body language expressed a relaxed confidence, Gisela's posture hinted at some irreconcilable peril. Though this concealed desperation—whatever it was—did not diminish her appeal, nor did it make her unapproachable. In fact, Doran had always found Gisela's implicitness rather compelling. Studying her long, steady fingers as they traced counter-clockwise rings around the rim of her coffee cup, or watching the tip of her tongue move slowly over her full, parted lips, Doran was unexpectedly prompted by an all but forgotten fascination.

And though the light that shone from the overhead fixture in Doran's kitchen was mostly inadequate, Gisela tended to see her host in very different terms. Over time, she had developed the capacity of seeing both objects and people—especially people—in their own particular radiance. Emanating from Doran Seeger's profile, she perceived a vibrant ring of neon blue light, receding progressively into shades of violet, and then disappearing altogether. Her own aura burned red as the rising sun and advanced in prismatic increments into the yellow gradient of the color spectrum. Alarice's predominant color was rose; Alexi's aura glowed sickly green.

Gisela had become well accustomed to seeing the world in such affected terms, though she attached no specific interpretation to her perceptions. To each individual's blush, her reaction tended to be emotional, not rational. She remembered perceiving the aura of Spiro Thromos, her summertime lover on Corfu, as being white-hot and fading to watery blue; and she'd understood instinctively the steady retrogression of his practiced bravado into fundamental insecurity. Her mother's brilliant white light had conveyed to Gisela a keen and precise intelligence, while her father's deep umber emanation had somehow foreshadowed his grim fate. Now, as she absorbed herself in Doran's cerulean light, she was most careful to refrain from quantifying the expression, for she was deliberately inclined to allow circumstances to define themselves naturally.

"Would you like to see the rest of the apartment?" Doran asked as they finished drinking coffee.

"Sure," said Gisela.

Doran led his guest through the parlor as he explained, "I'm afraid there's only one bedroom, but as you can see there is a loft. Normally, I sleep down. If you're not opposed to sharing a room, you can have the loft."

"Any place is fine with me," Gisela allowed. "If you'd rather have your privacy, Doran, I can bunk on the sofa."

"I'm sure that the loft will be more comfortable," he said. "But the choice is yours."

"Then I'll sleep in the loft," she decided.

"I have extra sheets and blankets," he offered.

"You're the perfect host, aren't you?"

He smiled at her. "You're a special guest, Gisela. How

many pillows do you prefer?" he asked.

"Two?" she ventured a little hesitantly.

"Two it is!" he confirmed.

Together, they moved toward the bathroom. "The hot water is fickle," he explained. "Especially in the morning. High demand, I suppose."

"I can adapt," she offered.

"And the heat is rather sporadic," he told her. "This is a *good* night."

"So I guess I should wear my flannels," Gisela proposed.

"Flannels?"

"You know, pajamas!"

"You have flannel pajamas?" Doran queried.

"Just kidding, Doran."

"You must be exhausted after traveling all day," he speculated.

"I'm tired, but I'm excited to be here," she said.

"Well, I guess I'll just get the bedding now," Doran said, and he went into the parlor. Gisela trailed behind. From a bureau drawer, Doran collected sheets and pillowcases. Then he moved to a closet for a blanket. "This should do it," he estimated. "You'll be quite comfortable, I think."

"It's very late, isn't it?" Gisela said.

"About half past two, I believe," said Doran.

"I hope you don't have to get up early tomorrow morning," she said with concern.

"Not really. My only job is importing art from the former Soviet Union. I'm leaving on a buying trip in a few days, but until then, I'm yours. What would you like to do tomorrow?" he asked.

"I'm sure I'll sleep until noon. But then I'd love to see the city," she answered.

"Of course," said Doran as he went to make her bed. "I'd love to show you the sights."

Gisela smiled contentedly as she watched him climb the

ladder leading to the loft. She watched as he smoothed sheets, spread her blanket, and encased her *two* pillows. "You're really too much, Doran," she reiterated as she began to unpack her bag.

"I'm just happy that you wrote to me. And I'm equally happy that you decided to come to Prague."

"Yes, I'm beginning to think that it was a fortunate decision," Gisela confirmed.

When each was finally ready for bed, and the lights were turned out and silence prevailed, Gisela lay fully awake in the strange bed, considering her fate. The reunion with Doran had been pleasant though a bit awkward, she thought. And she found it curious that at no time during their conversation had he asked about Alarice. She'd always presumed that they had been deeply in love. Though neither had been inclined to extend the relationship over the ensuing ten years. That in itself she found curious. But of course each affair of the heart had its particular dynamics. And she was certainly no expert at maintaining a relationship. For years she had implored her sister to find someone—anyone! Even so, Alarice had chosen to molder in Rotterdam doing business, going to movies, reading books, and sleeping alone.

Likewise, Doran had kept his distance once they left Corfu, and Gisela could only speculate that there was more to their particular story than she knew. Why else would two lovers purposely separate themselves from one another? She could not help seeing their circumstance as tragic, but in the end she concluded that it was none of her business. Nevertheless, she was grateful for Doran's unconditional hospitality. And she was strangely interested in getting to know her sister's former lover—this time as an adult herself.

Next morning, they ate breakfast at a café on Wenceslas Square before Doran conducted Gisela on a walking tour of central Prague. From Old Town Square, with its Romanesque, baroque, and gothic architecture, they moved down the fashionable Pariska Boulevard toward the old Jewish Quarter. They visited the fabled Jewish cemetery, and then wandered through the *Mala Strana* to see the green-domed Church of Saint Nicholas. Smiling, Doran told her, "Old Saint Nick is the protector of wayfarers. He's the only saint to which I have a connection." "Ah," she said. "Then maybe he'll watch out for me, too."

By early afternoon, the buskers had gathered on *Karlovy Vary*. A city landmark since its construction in the thirteenth century, the bridge served not only as an overpass for people moving from one bank of the Vltava to the other, it was also Prague's principal venue for street performers. They paused to watch gypsy musicians, ethnic dancers, and mimes.

"Long ago, this bridge was the scene of Knight's tournaments," Doran relayed. "Can you imagine it?"

"To me, all that stuff seems untouchable," Gisela said as she leaned against a buttress. She lit a cigarette and looked whimsically upriver. "What about the statues?" she asked.

"There are seventy of them," he told her. "The most famous is of Jan Nepomuk—the one with the halo of stars above his head."

"And what's that about?"

"It seems that Jan Nepomuk was a priest during the time of King Wenceslas. Apparently, the queen chose him as her confessor, and admitted a series of affairs. But when the priest would not compromise his commitment of confidentiality, King Wenceslas had him drowned in the Vltava. The story claims that a golden circle of light appeared immediately afterward in the water, confirming Jan Nepomuk's martyrdom. Hence, the gold-starred halo over his statue!"

"Perhaps it's because I'm not Catholic," said Gisela, "but Sainthood always seemed such a futile reward."

"No doubt, most of them never had the best of it in

this life," Doran acknowledged.

"And this is all very beautiful," Gisela sighed. "The river, the bridge, the spires…"

"More than a hundred of them," Doran informed.

And he could see that Gisela's concentration was divided, and a hint of melancholy defined her expression. "Lay your hand upon the crucifix at the base of Father Jan's likeness," Doran suggested. "It is said that your fondest wish will come true."

Gisela examined the crucifix but she did not touch it. "Maybe I'll have to come back another time," she said. "When I have a specific wish in mind."

"Well, I'm sure the statue is not going anywhere," Doran said.

"No, I suppose not."

"Are you hungry?" he asked.

Gisela shrugged. "I guess so," she said.

"Let's get a sandwich or something," he suggested. "I know a place close by."

At a small café just off Wenceslas Square, they lunched on ham salad sandwiches and pilsner beer. Sensing Gisela's unease, he found this reunion awkward at times; yet he was willing to afford her whatever time she needed to feel whole again. Personal reconstruction, he understood, was a highly personal matter, each individual rebounding in his own way. Gisela, too, was aware of her particular discomfiture, and as much as she might have wanted this to be a happy and carefree time—a new beginning for herself, as well as a renaissance of her friendship with Doran Seeger—she was neither able to hide her sadness, nor able to affect her mood.

"I have plans to see a concert this evening," he mentioned. "Perhaps you'd like to come along?"

"What sort of concert?" she asked.

"My friend Vasil Basso has a band called Plastic People of the Universe. They're quite original."

"How so?" Gisela asked.

"Their shows tend to move outward from the music, encompassing burlesque and dance and mime. And whatever else they dream up to make a statement. They're very popular here in Prague."

"Sounds interesting."

"My friend Scarlet is picking me up around ten o'clock," he informed.

"I wouldn't want to impose on your date," Gisela recoiled.

"It's nothing like that," he assured her.

"Are you sure?"

"Of course I'm sure. Scarlet is my business partner and my friend. Nothing more. Why not come, Gisela?"

"Okay," she said, and smiled for the first time since they'd sat down to lunch.

As previously arranged, Scarlet called for Doran at ten o'clock. Doran introduced Gisela to his business partner, and each in turn marveled at the unlikely coincidence of Gisela's affiliation to the Stolaroffs, and to Doran. "I know it's an ever smaller world," commented Scarlet, "still the infinite network of connections never ceases to amaze me. It's such a dramatic game we play; there must certainly be some higher intelligence maneuvering the pieces."

Gisela's eyes widened at the presumptuousness of Scarlet's bold analysis, but she refrained from comment. To Gisela's eye, Scarlet swam in a pulsating aura of fiery red. Surely the god Aries ruled her disposition. And though she herself radiated a ruby red energy, Gisela knew immediately that their spiritual temperaments were decidedly different. Scarlet ruled whichever domain she entered—not through a commanding or aggressive force, but rather by an intrinsic cogency. Gisela's power was far subtler, for in maturity she had tried to cultivate (contrary to her natural tendency) the art of self-restraint.

At a bar adjoining the Roxy Theatre, they had drinks; and over vodka martinis it was suggested by Scarlet that

Gisela accompany Doran on his upcoming trip to Kiev. Sighing in skepticism, Gisela balked. Though she might have enjoyed traveling to Kiev, the very idea of meeting Alexi's father under present circumstances seemed to her quite inappropriate.

"So you've never met Vladimir," said Scarlet.

"No," she confirmed.

"He's a teddy bear," Doran evaluated.

"Hardly like his son," said Gisela sarcastically.

"Has Vladimir ever seen a photograph of you?" Scarlet inquired.

"Not to my knowledge," said Gisela.

"Then why not go incognito?" she proposed.

"What do you mean?" asked Gisela.

"Well, if Doran were simply to introduce you as somebody else, then Vladimir would be none the wiser, right?"

Gisela cleared her throat. She glanced at Doran and smiled her understated smile. "I'm not usually inclined to such deceptions," she said to Scarlet.

"But aren't you curious, Gisela? Ah, to be a proverbial fly on the wall!"

Gisela considered Scarlet's query, as well as the proposed intrigue. "Of course I'm curious."

"Then why not go along with Doran? I know he'd welcome your company," said Scarlet.

"No doubt about that," confirmed Doran.

With a quizzical look on her face, Gisela turned to Doran. "Is Kiev so distasteful?" she asked.

"It's not that," he said. "But I've made the trip a number of times." In fact, Doran liked Scarlet's plan, and he hoped Gisela could be persuaded to come to the Ukraine with him. "Kiev is a very interesting city," he appraised, "so why not see a few of the sights. And once I take possession of the paintings, we'll go directly to Cologne, where a pre-arranged buyer is waiting to purchase them from me."

"I think you should go, Gisela," determined Scarlet. "After all, Doran is willing to pay your ticket and hotel." Scarlet nudged her business partner's shoulder to prompt him, and Doran quickly agreed that he would cover Gisela's expenses.

"I'll think about it," said Gisela as she finished her martini.

"She'll end up going with you," Scarlet concluded to Doran.

"I hope so," he said.

Gisela regarded each of them with eyebrows raised.

The Plastic People always attracted a distinctive crowd if not a distinguished one, and tonight the Roxy was packed with the band's loyal followers, as well as many uninitiated curiosity seekers. In truth, their shows had become notorious throughout Prague for their ribald poignancy, and tonight's presentation promised to be no less penetrating. As the house lights were turned down, and the stage was illuminated in three thousand watts of shocking white light, each spectator held his breath in anticipation of the performance.

Emanating from the massive array of loud speakers, a bone-jarring hum amplified the crowd's collective tension by degrees. And just as the subsonic vibration reached what seemed to be a critical resonance, Vasil Basso himself appeared at center stage wearing a blood red suit. His face was painted a ghastly shade of white, his hair was blackened and slicked back, and his features were hideously distorted by make-up. Boldly, the vampire proclaimed: *"I have come tonight to announce to you the End of the World!"*

Indeed, out of humanity's crisis rose a sonorous chord, a haunting harmony, a combination of musical tones at once compatible and mismatched, a permutation that was familiar yet irreconcilable: the questionable chord resonated pure religion. From a once dark society came an even darker vision. Here in Prague, Armageddon was hardly an impending allegory; the creative voice of the Czech people had been strangled for so long that finally it called out, red-faced and resolute, *Insanity No More*! So, who better to see a cause equally insidious?

"The World Bank has burdened the poor with unsupportable debt!" went Basso's litany. *"And as the Global Masters feed like carp on squandered spiritual capital, the dissidents gather again outside fortified walls! Here in Prague! In Den Haag! In Genoa! In Berlin! In Seattle!*

"The Goblins of Globalization think we doth protest too loudly, but once all the small fish have been consumed, the barracudas will have no choice but to cannibalize each other. So again we rattle our keys!"

"What diatribe!" Doran remarked to Scarlet.

"Not my angle," she conceded. "But maybe dissent is a hard habit to break."

"Christ, I'm just trying to survive emotionally," said Gisela.

The chaotic music gathered momentum, as the Plastic People mimed the interplay of the moneychangers. And gathered in groups around rustic tables, spellbound spectators drank vodka and smoked and waited for a cue that remained safely in the future. Because for most the message was provisional: by day the rats ran dutifully upon their wheels; at night, numbed by exhaustion or boredom or terror, they drank or drugged or fucked to forget their pain. The god of materialism determined the course of their lives; and it was no doubt a demanding god, if indeed a nebulous one. Yet, life was a day-by-day affair, and the fascia of normalcy prevailed. And the anarchistic model lacked the definition necessary for wide embrace. So the Plastic People of the Universe went about their business of incitement, subliminally scratching a persistent itch, and courting a critical mass.

"Basso may look like a crazed demon," said Doran to Gisela, "but he's really a tender soul."

Gisela shrugged and rolled her eyes. "It's all so desperate," she said.

"Yes, I think that's the intended message."

"I can't live that way," she said.

"With an arrhythmic heartbeat?"

"Right! I'd burn out in no time."

"But doesn't one burn out anyway?" he asked rhetorically.

"I don't know."

"Bullshit!" Scarlet proclaimed. "Even if they have a point, it's too late. The wheel has already turned. It's an old story, and a repetitive one. Basso is eating himself alive. Better to run with the big dogs," said Scarlet the entrepreneur.

"Or simply withdraw from all of it," suggested Gisela.

"I've been looking for that island for years," said Doran.

"It doesn't exist," said Scarlet.

"Maybe it does," said Gisela hopefully.

"No, there is no panacea," Scarlet reiterated. "Whether we like it or not, it's a dog-eat-dog world!"

"Well, Scarlet, you can perceive it that way if you like, but I believe there are still places where people are unaffected by all the bullshit," she maintained.

"And maybe it's better to understand that the rat race is all-inclusive," said Scarlet.

"Such ominous issues!" Gisela charged. "My own needs are simple ones, and too much consternation just gives me a headache."

"And perhaps there is a balance to be struck," Doran refereed.

"Always the fulcrum, aren't you, Seeger?" said Scarlet.

"Am I?"

"You play both roles equally well."

"That's just survival," he said.

"And maybe it's the reason you can't find your island," she surmised.

But Doran knew that it was not that simple. For he'd played the game, and he'd withdrawn from it, too. Each stance exacted a price. What he searched for (if indeed it were to be found at all) existed on a plane far less tangible. Loss of commitment had become his fate, not necessarily by choice. But the object of one's commitment remained all-important: this he understood by default.

As did Vasil Basso and his *Plastic People*...

The music rumbled through the halls of the Roxy for the better part of two hours, each musical number augmented by costume changes and diabolical theatrics and revival meeting rhetoric, and finally, after two o'clock in the morning, the show came to a close. Muscles taught and teeth bared, the crowd filed out in charged-up amazement, and Scarlet remarked: "So they've done it again!" referring of course to the dynamic performance given by Basso & Company.

It was very late, and they were tired. All three walked, with feet shuffling, to Scarlet's apartment. Bidding her companions good night, Scarlet again advised Gisela to consider accompanying Doran on his trip to Kiev.

"I'll think about it," Gisela promised.

CHAPTER 4
KIEV

By the time Doran and Gisela left for Kiev, word had come from Pavel Kahout in Vienna that the Czech president, Vaclav Havel, would recover from his most recent surgery. To Doran, as it was to his friend Scarlet Ponton, and to the Czech citizenry at large, this news was personally reassuring. Lacking precise political allegiance, Doran agreed at least in part with Vasil Basso's assessment of world politics. He knew that in the modern world money meant power, and power necessarily expressed itself in domination. In some circles it was believed that Havel represented a fading hope for reputable and responsive government. No doubt, the results of Vaclav Havel's resistance had been far more severe than mere expatriation; nevertheless Doran Seeger, a long-time itinerant, considered himself no less compromised than the Czech playwright turned president. Doran believed passionately in the sanctity of the individual, and he also believed at least in part in a nebulous and pervasive force that sought to undermine free will for its own self-seeking purpose. Havel's vision was penetrating—unapologetically so—that much was obvious to anybody who read his plays. And his honesty was not only refreshing, but it rendered hope as well. His continued presence on the world's political stage was perhaps essential at this time— at least to those with an analogous perspective. And though his conviction was not vociferous, Doran Seeger counted himself among those who held such a viewpoint.

As the train rolled through the Moravian countryside, Gisela remarked, "I really don't know what I'm doing here." She lowered her eyes to contemplate a naked finger—a finger once adorned by a friendship ring given to her by Alexi Stolaroff.

"Just consider it a pleasure trip," Doran suggested nonchalantly.

"A pleasure trip with a few weird caveats," she contended.

"Hey! It's not everyday that a person has the opportunity to visit Kiev," he said sarcastically.

"How did you become involved in selling paintings?" she asked.

"Simple," he said. "I needed money. And Scarlet's offer addressed the problem."

"And it's worked out well for you?"

"Better than I ever would have imagined," he said.

"So you like it?"

"It's only commerce," Doran evaluated. "And I'm not thoroughly convinced that the trade is always equitable. When the Communists were kicked out of power, the rug was pulled out from underneath most of the artists, because they were accustomed to receiving sizeable government subsidies. Many artists suddenly found themselves in dire financial straits, and they were forced to sell their paintings at a fraction of the real worth. And it remains so to this day. It provides Scarlet and me with a golden opportunity, speaking from a capitalist's point of view. But I can't say I'm completely comfortable with the arrangement. And these trips to the Ukraine! Let's just say that I could find more pleasurable ways to spend my time."

"I'm not sure how I feel about meeting Alexi's father," Gisela said.

"Of course it's up to you. But I rather like Scarlet's idea about visiting Vladimir incognito."

"I don't know if I'm comfortable with that either," she said.

"If you like, you can stay at the hotel while I negotiate the sale of the paintings."

"I don't know. I'll think about it," she said.

Indeed, the interior of the Pullman was familiar to Doran, as was the passing scenery, for he'd now made the trip to Kiev more than twenty times. The black money he earned was both substantial and welcome, though the trips to the Ukraine and the subsequent expeditions to Berlin, or Brussels, or Maastricht had become mundane.

Doran recalled the first time he'd exported paintings from the Ukraine into Germany. Having crated the canvases for rail transport, he'd arrived in Berlin speaking little German and having virtually no knowledge of the city or where he might market the paintings. Customs formalities had gone smoothly, and he'd rented a cargo van and hired a porter named Karl, who'd accompanied him first to the Kurfurstendamm, then to an open marketplace in the Breitsheidplatz. Having little success at selling the paintings at either of the first two venues, Karl had directed him to a quarter known as the Tacheles, once the site of a luxury department store that had now become a multi-cultural, self-governing housing project populated by fifty squatting artists. In front of a repertory cinema called the *Camera*, he'd set up shop on the sidewalk and sold all the canvases within two hours. With a pocketful of Deutsche Marks, Doran had returned to Prague, considerably richer and no less amazed by the success of the endeavor. And after paying Scarlet her commission, he was immediately ready for another buying excursion.

On his second trip to Kiev he used the profits from his first venture to purchase twice as many canvases as he'd bought the first time. This time his chosen marketplace was the Grande Place in Brussels. Amidst the grandeur of seventeenth century architecture, he set up a makeshift stall near the flower vendors, and again the commerce was successful beyond all expectations. Scarlet's commission was incidental, so once more Doran parlayed the profits into a larger stock of paintings. (By this time Vladimir Stolaroff had told many of his artist friends about the Colombian woman and the American man who came regularly to Kiev to buy his work; he'd offered to negotiate the sale of their paintings as well, and now he too was part of the commercial pyramid). Doran took the paintings acquired on his third trip to Maastricht, a commercial center in the southern part of the Netherlands, and there he sold the canvases at the daily small wares market. At Berty's Café on Vrijhofswtraat, he counted his profits as he contemplated future buying trips.

But even as his fortune stockpiled, Doran had eventually come to regard the buying excursions to Kiev as monotonous. He seldom took time to enjoy Kiev; nor did he linger in the city where he sold the paintings. It was a commercial operation start to finish—in-again, out-again! Prague was his home now. There he had friends.

Yet something important was missing—a problematic circumstance, though one hardly difficult to define: the persistent illusiveness of romantic love in his life. Though his chosen lifestyle was no doubt eccentric, his existence was a satisfying one—with a single exception. Now, sitting across from Gisela Van Zyl, Doran was inclined to recall his relationship with her sister Alarice. And while his affair with her was nearly ten years in the past, he was nevertheless compelled to consider its implications.

What a glorious summer they'd shared, first on the Island of Corfu, and then touring the Cyclades! Lying naked in one another's arms on sandy Grecian beaches, they'd fallen in love. At least it had seemed so at the time. But a forced separation had cooled their fire. In retrospect, Doran had come to question not only the veracity of their feelings for one another, but also the very possibility of lasting love ever entering his life. And whether or not the absence of such a lasting love was an omission he could tolerate remained an open question indeed: chemistry did its part concerning the opposite sex, but at forty-nine, especially considering the void left by past affairs of the heart, Doran was not even certain he was capable of such unyielding devotion.

Gisela, on the other hand, was feeling profoundly dislocated. Unlike Doran, she found no difficulty falling in love, though the security of a rightful home had persistently eluded her since leaving Rotterdam shortly after her father's death. She'd wanted to travel, and in fact she had made itinerancy her primary credo. Yet, the many changes of geography she embraced had imparted to her a restless spirit as well. At nearly twenty-nine, she needed to establish some sort of foundation, though she knew not where to begin. She'd come to Prague on the run, seeking refuge—or something as yet undetermined. And as she rode through the Moravian countryside, Gisela felt as though she might have been anywhere on earth—or no place particular! Doran Seeger was her longtime friend, yet after years of only sporadic contact he might as well have been a stranger to her. After a period of mutually thoughtful silence, she asked, "Doran, don't you miss your life in America?"

"My life in America?" He was surprised by her question.

Gisela shrugged. "Yes, your home."

"I've been away from the States for nearly ten years," he recounted.

"That's a long time," Gisela agreed.

"Why do you ask?" he wanted to know.

"No particular reason," she dismissed.

"Ten years ago," he began, "my life in America seemed to fall apart all at once. My father got himself into trouble. Alcoholism. He became quite ill. I took a leave of absence from my job and went to Texas to try to help him. But it was too late. He kept sliding downhill. And to make matters worse, he had a habit of disappearing every now and then. Without a word. For days at a time.

"Meanwhile, my girlfriend unexpectedly took my father's cue: she disappeared as well, leaving our house abandoned. Only a basement full of lab equipment for me to dispose of."

"Lab equipment?"

"She fancied herself an amateur chemist."

"Curious."

Doran nodded. "And of course I had friends," he continued. "But as I grew older, it seemed to me that those relationships became more and more conditional. These days, Americans are drawing some very fine lines. Competition is often brutal and extends well beyond the traditional marketplace; it permeates family, friends, and acquaintances. Cooperation and true empathy, on the other hand, are progressively viewed as personal weakness. The value implicit in simple humanity is lost. But it's all very subtle, you understand."

He paused to light a cigarette. Exhaling smoke, he retraced the steps of a well-remembered path.

"In time, my father died. After his funeral, I decided not to return to my job. For reasons of conscience."

"What was your job?" Gisela asked.

"I was involved in making guidance systems for the U.S. Defense Department."

"Oh…"

"Anyway, I decided to come to Europe for an extended holiday. Don't ask me why; to this day I couldn't tell you. I flew to Amsterdam, drifted through Germany and France, gadded about in Switzerland and Italy, and finally landed on Corfu. Of course it was there that I met Alarice. When word came that your mother was ill, and you and Alarice had to return to Rotterdam, I was deeply disappointed. But of course I understood the situation first hand.

"Originally, I'd planned to go back to the States. As I'm sure you remember, the three of us stood on the dock at Corfu Harbor waiting to leave Greece. I watched the two of you board the ferryboat bound for Venice. I was supposed to take the other ship—the one leaving for Brindisi. But I never boarded that ship. Perhaps I knew deep down that I really didn't want to go back to America. And of course there was the appeal of Greece. That summer was sublime.

"Anyway, I tried to stay on Corfu for the winter. But Modestos had left for Cyprus—a two-year posting with the Greek Army. And all the summer visitors went away as well. It just wasn't the same. And I was pining for Alarice, too. By November, it began to rain buckets. It rained for days on end. Finally, I couldn't take it anymore, so I left for Italy. I wound up in Taormina, Sicily, rooming with a Cuban lawyer. We were the only foreigners there. And the *pensione* had no heat!"

Gisela was rapt as Doran detailed his history.

"After Sicily, I tried living in Rome for awhile. That was no good: too expensive! Paris was even worse. I went to Munich for a time. Finally, I came to Prague. Shortly after arriving in the Czech Republic, I met Scarlet. She was a lifesaver. She knew so many people. I made some friends and rented an apartment. Then I became involved in the art export business. And here we are! Up to date!"

"I think I might like to visit America," Gisela said.

"Really? That surprises me," said Doran.

"Why?"

"I don't think you'd like it."

"Because you don't like it?"

"I never said I didn't like it," he backtracked. "I was simply having problems fitting into the grand philosophical scheme."

"And Europe suits you better?"

"I suppose it does."

"And do you consider Prague your home?"

Stroking his chin, he pondered her question. "I've made a life for myself in Europe," he explained. "Yet it's an evolving lifestyle. I guess I like that."

"But do you feel at home?" she persisted.

He again considered her poignant inquiry. "I can't say that I truly feel at home anywhere," he answered.

"Yes, I understand," said Gisela. "In that respect, we're not unalike. I too have lived as an expatriate. It seems as though we desperately want to escape aspects of our nationality, yet I'll always be Dutch."

"No matter where I choose to live, I'll always be American."

"Right! But I can't help believing that each of us has a more authentic identity."

"Each person has many identities," said Doran. "I think we're talking about cultural identity here."

"No!" she protested. "I'm talking about another type of identity. Something much more elemental."

"I think I follow you," said Doran. "Though I'm not sure that one's elemental identity has anything to do with where he chooses to live."

"Environment *must* play a part!" she maintained. "Otherwise why would we put ourselves through the difficulties of moving place to place?"

"For me, it's not that simple. Nor is it that desperate," said Doran.

"I've been bumming around for the better part of a decade now," recounted Gisela. "And I have to admit that I'm a bit worn out. I need to feel grounded somewhere."

"And what is your first impression of Prague?"

"It's beautiful… It's exciting…"

"But…"

Gisela swallowed her discomfiture. "Yes, you read me well, Doran. Prague is *not* my elemental place."

"You've determined this after only a few days?"

"I think it's probably something one knows immediately—instinctively."

"Perhaps you're right about that," he allowed.

"For me, it's always that way."

"So, what's next?" he asked.

Gisela rolled her eyes. "God, I don't know. I have to think about it. I really have to think about it. I have to gain a sense of my internal geography first. Do you know what I mean?"

"Yes, I think so."

"It's not an easy process."

"Of course not."

"So, I'll take my time. As you've told me, there's no hurry to leave."

"Certainly not!"

"So maybe you're stuck with me for awhile, Doran."

"A terrible fate," he joked.

"Somehow I knew you would understand all this."

"I stopped defining what I *do* and *do not* understand a long time ago," he said. "I'm like a pinball: I've been ricocheting off the bumpers ever since I left the States. Probably before that."

"At least you feel comfortable with your life in Prague."

"Relatively speaking," he qualified.

Having passed through Hradec Kralove and Rybnik in the Czech Republic, the train crossed the border into Poland, and now they were approaching the station at Krakow. Gisela stood up to stretch her legs; Doran fished through his jacket pockets for another cigarette.

"I don't remember you smoking," said Gisela.

"A habit that living in Europe has imparted."

"May I have one too?" she asked.

He offered her the pack. She took a cigarette and placed it between her lips. He held out his lighter for her.

"I think I'll stand in the corridor for awhile," she said

as she opened the compartment door.

Doran nodded as he inhaled.

The long train screeched to a halt in the crowded terminal at Krakow. From a corridor window, Gisela watched as passengers disembarked and boarded the train. Within moments people carrying luggage were moving through the corridors in search of vacant seats inside the compartments. They had traveled in privacy from Prague all the way to Krakow, (a pleasant circumstance on a long journey), but from the volume of passengers presently boarding the train, Gisela surmised that she and Doran would soon be sharing the compartment with other travelers. She returned to her seat in order to make it easier for those boarding the Pullman to pass through the corridor.

And it wasn't long before two well-dressed young men, each looking slender, gray, and humorless, entered the compartment. Each placed his suitcase on the overhead luggage rack, though they kept their identical, black attaché cases close at hand. Settling into their seats, they had a brief exchange in a Russian dialect that Gisela, (with her recent but limited indoctrination in the Russian language), could not understand. Neither man greeted Gisela or Doran.

"Putin's cousins," Doran remarked under his breath.

Gisela smiled sardonically.

The train remained in the station at Krakow about twenty minutes before resuming its journey eastward. It was a foggy day and the Polish landscape appeared in chiaroscuro, as though shrouded in a cold and damp dream. Not having traveled in Eastern Europe, and considering her recent experience with Alexi Stolaroff, Gisela found the atmosphere intriguing. She placed her hands on her lap and looked out the window, though from time to time she glanced from the corner of her eye at the two stoic Russians. Their presence imparted a tension, previously absent, into the small compartment.

Doran remained more nonchalant. Having made this journey on several other occasions, he was quite accustomed to encountering Eastern Europeans and Russians. He regarded the two men with only mild curiosity. Sallow-faced and severe, with cropped hair and steely eyes, they were probably Russian businessmen conducting commerce in Krakow. Not an uncommon occurrence. Though he was vaguely aware of an unspecific suspicion they conveyed. Or perhaps it was only curiosity. As westerners, he and Gisela no doubt appeared somewhat out of place. But whatever the reason for their stilted quiescence, Doran judged it inconsequential. Quietly, he drew Gisela back into conversation. And assuming that neither Russian understood English, they talked as though they were in the company of deaf-mutes.

As the train continued toward the city of L'viv in the Ukraine, they talked for the first time about Alarice, and about her situation back in Rotterdam. In truth, little had changed for the elder Van Zyl sister during the past ten years. In spite of a long held desire for romance and diversion, she persisted in a lifestyle that was defined by repetition, seemingly for its own sake. "I really wish she'd sell that infernal business," Gisela consternated. "Maybe then she'd spread her wings and fly."

"It's not that easy for her," Doran assessed.

"Why not?" Gisela said in well-meaning frustration.

"She's burdened with an over-exaggerated sense of duty," he surmised.

"But it doesn't have to be that way," Gisela implored.

"Perhaps not for you. And not for me, either… But Alarice has her own agenda—obviously."

"She's not very happy," Gisela concluded.

"It's always difficult for an outsider to judge such things," said Doran.

"But I'm her sister! And I know her better than anyone else!"

"When she's ready, she'll make her move," said Doran.

"She'll never budge," said Gisela.

"Don't be too sure," Doran advised.

"I don't know how she stands it, year after year, transaction after transaction. Arissa is a lovely person, kind and warm. But she purposely locks herself inside a deep-freezer. She smothers all her best qualities in routines."

"Not an uncommon practice," said Doran.

"But life can be richer than that. It has to be!"

"People can only move according to their nature," Doran conjectured.

"Well maybe one has to struggle against his nature. If his nature is slowly but surely destroying him…"

"Gisela, you can't presume to impose your own values on your sister."

"I know. I know."

"I must tell you," Doran related, "that when you and Alarice went back to Rotterdam to help your father care for your mother, I never thought Alarice would remain there indefinitely. I fully expected that after the situation was resolved, we would reunite on Corfu. I thought we had a future together there."

"I figured that you would end up coming to Rotterdam."

"As a couple, we were connected to that place—Corfu. And while I can't really explain the dynamics of it, I nevertheless came to realize that it was true."

"Pardon me, Doran, but that sounds a bit like a cop-out."

"We both had free choice," he said.

"And neither of you chose to trust the love you felt."

"Circumstances always offer many roads one can travel down. As you well know, Gisela."

"Whenever Arissa told me that she'd received a letter from you—and I have to tell you, Doran, that she let me read some of those letters—I always wondered why the two of you chose to remain apart. I just couldn't understand it. So I figured that there was probably something between you—something that I was unaware of—that prevented a reunion. And I was sad for both of you."

"As I said before, Gisela, one can only move according to his nature."

"I guess I don't follow you."

"Alarice and I were connected by the heart, but neither of us could sustain the affair on pure sentiment. Our individual natures demanded different courses. Our efficacy as a couple, I believe, was somehow reliant on that place. Greece! Hellas! Corfu in particular. And once that environment was taken away, there seemed nowhere to go. It's difficult to explain. But I know that she felt it too."

"I think Arissa held out hope," said Gisela.

"As did I—for a while. But then there's hope against hope, isn't there?"

"If you say so, Doran. I'm certainly no expert. And I don't hold anything against you. I only wondered."

Traveling through dense forests of bare trees, and past unplanted farms and brown pastures, they stopped briefly at one backward-looking hamlet after another. To Gisela's eye, each of these rural communities appeared grimmer, more impoverished, and more hopeless than the last. Here a rough and dour peasant existence was maintained, and the economic disparity between Western Europe and Eastern Europe became all the more obvious.

Beyond the city of L'viv, the landscape remained shrouded by the last of the winter snow. Arriving only recently from the Algarve, the mere sight of the frigid countryside sent a shiver through Gisela's entire body. She laid her jacket across her lap and drew her arms across her chest for warmth; and the sense of displacement that she'd first felt in Prague grew by degrees.

Out of the corner of her eye, she watched the two Russian men. Since entering the compartment they'd spoken hardly a word. Sitting opposite one another, they did not read, or snack, or smoke. Each maintained a rigid, angular posture; each conveyed a Griseldan expression: to Gisela they appeared as if they were opposing profiles carved from stone.

Yet, even in their enforced silence, they seemed to advise caution. The aura emanating from the man sitting directly to Gisela's left was the color of a weak sunrise viewed through a cold, winter haze. The other man's spectral character was revealed in a rather low frequency orange glow—the color of ginger root, or nuclear fallout. Had she been riding alone in the compartment, Gisela might have collected her luggage and moved to another seat, but Doran's presence, and his detached attitude, lent her a measure of tolerance for the situation. She smoked another cigarette and listened to the train's wheels clatter over the tracks.

Partly the result of the icy environment, (inside and outside), and partly the result of her reunion with Doran Seeger, Gisela's thoughts migrated to a warmer climate: the ephemeral Island of Corfu. There she'd spent the summer of her nineteenth year, (first in the village of Kondokali, and then on the western shore at Glyfada), and a magnificent season it was! Like her sister Alarice, she too had fallen in love that summer; and as Alarice cultivated what Gisela then had judged to be an unlikely relationship with an unremarkable American, Gisela was herself swept off her feet by Spiro Thromos, the son of their Greek landlord, Modestos. Ironically, each relationship had failed by summer's end, but the dreamy remembrances of sunny seaside days passed at Paliokastritsa and Ypsos, and balmy nights spent at Taverna Loyiza Hara-Theou, remained firmly fixed in her reminiscence, Modestos Thromos—or 'Takis' as they'd come to call him—being the glue!

For Doran, too, the reunion with Gisela Van Zyl rekindled memories of the summer they'd spent on Corfu. He recalled not only the warmth of the Grecian Isles, (both climatic and cultural), but the affection and tenderness of a new love, as well as the camaraderie of many new friends. Diakatos Leonidas and Katerina Ginny from Taverna Loyiza Hara-Theou; Matthew Niven and Brandon Harrison, two good-natured Australians who arrived at the *taverna* every night to sip ouzo and play cards until the wee hours; Markus and Petra Äastrom, a brother and sister from Sweden who occupied the flat below them in Kondokali Village. And, of course, Modestos Thromos! A chance meeting at Corfu Harbor had inaugurated a fortuitous friendship with the retired army captain. Day by day, throughout the summer, Takis had shown Doran the many splendors of Corfu Island; and by his generosity and unqualified acceptance, he'd won a special place in the heart of the itinerant. Even after ten years, and over many miles, Doran felt the unfailing vitality of Modestos' friendship. "I support all things," Takis had once told him.

"What are you thinking about?" Gisela asked Doran off-handedly.

"I was thinking about Corfu," he replied.

"Funny, so was I," she said with a far-away expression on her face.

"I was thinking about Modestos," he further related.

"An extraordinary man!" said Gisela.

"One of the most amiable men I've ever met," remarked Doran.

"You knew him better than I did," she surmised.

"A matter of age," he determined.

"And gender," she added.

"Probably so."

"Still, he was very kind to me—especially when he learned about my mother's illness. You and Alarice were away touring the Cyclades; and after my break-up with Spiro, I was alone in the apartment at Glyfada. When Modestos learned about my mother's condition, he visited me each day. He brought me fresh eggs and homegrown vegetables. He was never presumptuous or intrusive, but in his own way he let me know that I had a friend I could count on. I suppose I overlooked his insight at the time, but in retrospect I've come to appreciate his sensitivity and good will. And what a sweet, sweet man!"

"He was all energy," Doran remembered.

"A catastrophe waiting to happen," Gisela laughed.

A smile came to Doran's lips, too. "When Takis was around, anything could happen. But for every problem he created, he solved ten. And it was all so good-natured!"

"And how he could eat!" Gisela exclaimed.

"No kidding. Sitting down to dinner with him, his portions were twice what anyone else ate."

"And he finished his dinner in half the time!"

"If everybody could live as Modestos lives…"

"A bit schizophrenic, perhaps."

"But so animated! And so alive!"

"A great guy!" said Gisela as she yawned and stretched away her sedentary stiffness.

So it was in retrospect and reconnaissance that Gisela passed the journey—remembering aspects of a spectacular summer spent on Corfu, and cautiously monitoring the actions (or inactions) of the two Russian businessmen. The train passed through the town of L'uts'k, then Rivne, and finally Zhitomyr before the man sitting to her left leaned her way and said in a low voice, "Pardon me, but I've heard you speaking English. Where do you come from?"

Gisela was certainly surprised by his overture, and she was further surprised to hear him speaking English. "I come from the Netherlands," she told him. "And my friend is from America."

The man regarded Doran. "America? How curious to encounter you here!"

Doran acknowledged his inquiry: "Presently, I live in Prague."

"I understand many Americans live in Prague," he said.

"It's true," Doran confirmed.

"Why is it so?" the Russian wanted to know.

"It is a vibrant city," Doran explained. "And many opportunities exist there."

"But certainly there are opportunities in America," he assumed.

"Of course," said Doran. "But Prague is wide open. The establishment is virgin."

"Yes, I understand," he said. "It is the same in the Ukraine."

"As it is everywhere in Eastern Europe," Doran evaluated.

Now, the other man entered the conversation. "Why are you traveling in Ukraine?" he asked. Though abrupt, his tone was not accusatory.

"Business," Doran said simply. "I deal in art."

"Ah!" said the first man. "What kind of art?"

"I buy paintings from artists in the Ukraine to sell in Western Europe."

"Interesting. And how is the market for this artwork?" he wanted to know.

"Quite good, really," said Doran.

"How long have you been dealing in Ukrainian art?" the second man asked.

"About two years. Though my partner has been operating longer," he told him.

"And how do you acquire the paintings?" the first man queried.

"We've established a network of artists," Doran related. "It's well-established now."

"Indeed," said the inquisitor.

"A capitalist!" proclaimed his partner.

"Call it whatever you like," said Doran with a shrug. "But I'm not the principle entrepreneur. My partner has an uncanny ability to recognize unexploited opportunities."

"So you are only the facilitator?" presumed the first man.

"More than that," said Doran.

"And what about you?" the other man addressed Gisela. "Are you also an art dealer?"

"No," said Gisela, "I'm only along for the ride." Mildly

uncomfortable with the conversation, she shifted her weight on the seat.

"Is this your first time in Ukraine?" she was asked.

Gisela nodded, though she felt decidedly uneasy with the barrage of questions. She wished the conversation would end. But Doran was inclined to small talk.

"And where do you come from?" Doran asked.

"Kiev," he was told. "We are also businessmen."

"In what line?" Doran inquired innocently.

"We collect debts," announced the second man, who was without question the more dour of the two.

"I see," said Doran.

"Do you work for a bank?" asked Gisela.

Doran coughed conspicuously as Gisela's gullibility was shining like a star.

"No, we collect private debts," the first man explained.

At once Doran suspected duplicity; and he was given immediately to speculate that these two men were probably part of the infamous Ukrainian mafia. Suddenly, he felt stupid for revealing the nature of the business he conducted—not to mention compromised! Solicited through a seemingly innocent, off-hand conversation, they had cunningly gained considerable information regarding his private affairs, information that in retrospect might have been better not divulged. Still, they were aboard a train, a public conveyance. What could happen? He determined that the best tactic to employ was probably a measured withdrawal from the conversation.

But Gisela now seemed intrigued by the nefarious nature of their business. She wanted to know more about their presumed activities. "And what happens if the debtors don't pay?" she wanted to know.

The two men regarded one another; apparently trying to determine which one might answer her question, and what he might say. Finally the first man revealed, "Once, my friend here shot a man. It happened in Tallin."

Gisela's eyes widened. "Obviously, he was not

apprehended by the police."

"Obviously not," came the reply.

"I didn't kill him," the goon qualified. "I only shot him in the shoulder," he said without conscience.

Suddenly recognizing her unwise passage into territory better left unexplored, Gisela tried to swallow her unwariness. "I could never shoot someone," she said.

The perpetrator only shrugged. The other man offered a rationalization. "A creditor has the right to be repaid. And if a debtor cannot pay, or if he refuses to pay, there is no choice. Enforcement becomes *necessary*. This is nothing new, you understand."

"I'm glad I don't owe anybody money," she determined.

"Don't misunderstand us," the racketeer implored. "We're actually fair-minded fellows."

If one were only on their right side, Doran concluded.

After another uneasy hour spent with the two Ukrainian *businessmen*, the train at last arrived at Kiev. Making its way slowly over a maze of interlacing tracks and switches, it finally came to a screeching halt at the city's main railway terminal. Doran and Gisela bid their acquaintances good-bye as they collected their bags and prepared to disembark. The two thugs followed closely as they proceeded up the narrow platform.

Drawing Gisela close to him, Doran intended to make a speedy exit in whichever direction the debt collectors chose not to take. Gisela, too, felt the imperative need to lose the two goons, and she implicitly followed Doran's fast track. Making their way through the crowd on the platform, they headed directly for the terminal. Doran periodically looked over his shoulder, as did Gisela, to determine if they were in fact being followed. The debt collectors were not far behind as they, too, marched toward the station's main hall. By luck or by resourcefulness, they managed to elude their nemeses by the time they entered the building. Or so it seemed.

"They were utterly creepy," Gisela remarked as they caught their breath in front of a tobacco kiosk.

"And probably dangerous," said Doran.

"Do you think they had evil plans for us?" she asked.

"Who knows? But I had no intention of sticking around to find out."

"Sorry if I was too obvious," said Gisela.

"You? I was the idiot. I was the first to open my mouth. I might as well have told them that I was carrying a large sum in my wallet to buy the paintings. I might as well have flashed the money in front of their eyes. Christ, I can't believe I was so susceptible."

"I don't see them anywhere," Gisela said as she continued to survey the large public hall.

"Good!" said Doran, relieved but not vindicated of his error in judgment.

"Let's get out of here," Gisela suggested. "Where can we find a taxi?"

"There's a queue just outside the terminal," said Doran. "Follow me!"

With Doran holding fast to Gisela's sleeve, they made their way to the other side of the terminal. Outside, the weather was cold, and Kiev looked bleak beneath a dome of gray. In front of the station, the human commotion abated some, but still many people scurried about. Walking toward the taxi queue, Doran put up his hand to signal for a ride. A car pulled forward to meet them. But just as they reached the taxi, one of the Ukrainian triggermen approached from the periphery. Reaching the car first, he held open the door for Doran and Gisela. "So we meet again!" he said with a derisive smile on his lips.

"Sorry, this one's ours," said Doran.

"Perhaps we could share it?" he suggested.

"I'm sure it would be out of your way. We're headed all the way across the city."

Another blunder?

The hit man paused. He regarded the driver and said

something in Russian. The driver answered perfunctorily. Neither Doran nor Gisela understood a word. Then the G-man turned to Doran and said, "As you wish, my friend. I told the driver not to rip you off."

"Thanks," he said. Though he remained dubious. He probably should have yielded the taxi without question and moved off, but the instinct to stand his ground had prevailed, and he'd thoughtlessly argued for the ride. Now, he had no idea what exchange might have taken place between the goon and the driver. Or what arrangement might have been made. Should they get into the car? Or should they walk away? It seemed somehow too late for retreat.

With his free hand, Doran motioned Gisela into the car. Clutching his overnight bag, he slid in beside her. He took a deep breath and regarded Gisela without uttering a word. But he didn't have to say anything. She understood perfectly that the situation was tenuous. She knew trouble when she saw it. Trouble had an unmistakable radiance— like the telltale burn after a radioactive explosion. She shuddered slightly as the mobster waved the cabby forward.

Within minutes they were moving along with traffic up Khreshchatik Street, Kiev's tree-lined main boulevard. Straight ahead, the five green minarets of Saint Andrew's confirmed their direction. And though Doran knew the route to the Hotel DNIPRO well, and even as he determined that they were proceeding correctly, still he resisted a sigh of relief. Something was not right. Trying to resist his own paranoia, he turned to look out the rear window. "Shit!" he cursed under his breath.

"What is it?" Gisela said desperately.

"There's another taxi right behind us. Guess who's riding in it."

"No way!" She turned to look.

"What do you think?" he asked.

"It's them. No doubt about it."

"I think we're in trouble," Doran said gravely.

"Just because they're in the taxi behind us doesn't necessarily mean they're following us," she offered hopefully.

"What do you think he said to the driver?" Doran asked.

"I don't know."

"Well, I don't think it had anything to do with giving us a fair deal."

"Yeah, you're probably right."

"Do you know enough Russian to ask the driver where he's taking us?"

"Then you don't think he's taking us to our hotel?"

"I have my doubts."

"What are we going to do, Doran?"

"Can't you talk to him?"

"I don't know enough Russian to ask where the bathroom is!"

"This is a busy street. There are plenty of people around. Maybe I can get him to stop the car and let us out."

Gisela shrugged. "May as well try."

Doran leaned forward to address the driver. "Hey, Buddy! Friend! We want to get out. Stop here! Stop the car! Understand? Stop the car! Stop here! Stop now!"

There was no response from the driver as he regarded Doran in the rear view mirror. And before reaching the Hotel DNIPRO he turned off Khreshchatik Street onto a tributary road and sped up.

Doran flew backward from the G-force. A look of deep concern spread over his boyish features. "I think he has prior instructions," he told Gisela.

She too was in a panic. "What do you think they're going to do to us?" she asked.

"Probably rob us," he said. "Let's hope nothing more."

"That one guy said that the other guy shot somebody," she reminded him.

"We'll cooperate. That's all we can really do," Doran offered.

"Alexi told me about shit like this," she ruminated.

As it became ever more obvious that the cab driver had no intention of taking them where they'd asked to be driven, Doran decided to try a different tactic. From his wallet he took one hundred Deutsche Marks. From the back seat he leaned forward and carefully placed the money on the center console where the driver could easily see it, and in a very low voice he said simply, "Hotel DNIPRO, if you please."

The driver palmed the bill and answered glibly, "Different route, Mister."

Doran sat back in the seat and sighed deeply.

"Nice try," said Gisela.

"For all the good it did," he replied.

"I've gotta tell you, Doran, I'm pretty scared."

"Let's not panic. Let's stay cool. That's all we've got."

The driver turned onto a road paralleling the river and headed for a complex of dilapidated warehouses. The multiplex seemed to be deserted. The taxi containing the two thugs followed close behind.

"I think this is it," said Doran. "The moment of truth."

"What are we going to do?" Gisela asked.

"Let's see what they want," he counseled.

The driver turned up a narrow passage and stopped in a blind alley to await the arrival of the collaborators. Long ago abandoned, the aggregate of industrial buildings seemed the perfect place for criminals to do their will. No doubt, thought Doran, we will be left destitute. And hopefully not dead!

Tracing the course of the first taxi, the car containing the Ukrainian *businessmen* arrived directly. Neither Doran nor Gisela made a move to get out of the car.

The two gangsters got out of the taxi and approached. The more amiable of the two opened the rear door and motioned them out, while the more sinister one held a handgun close at his side. Doran slid out first. He made no challenging gesture. Gisela followed, her knees threatening to buckle from fear.

"So sorry to inconvenience you this way," said the goon in mock apology.

"I suppose I should have expected this," Doran said.

"I presume you're carrying a substantial sum of cash to purchase the artwork," he said.

"You can have the money," said Doran. "Just don't hurt us."

"Hand over the money—all of it! If you cooperate, violence won't be necessary," he promised.

"Okay," said Doran.

"Don't move your hands," he instructed. "My colleague will take your wallets."

"Whatever you say," Doran agreed.

The man with the gun moved toward him. Pointing the barrel straight at his ribcage, he reached into Doran's pocket and took out his wallet. He quickly rifled its contents, holding up a wad of banknotes for his partner to see. "Is that all of it?" he said curtly.

"Yeah, that's all I've got," Doran confirmed.

The gunman handed the taxi driver several bills. He also gave him the leather wallet as a bonus. Then he took Gisela's wallet as well.

"Sorry we can't offer you a ride," said the spokesman.

Doran shrugged. "We wouldn't think of imposing," he said.

"Then move toward the wall, please," they were instructed.

"Wait a minute!" Doran protested.

"Don't worry," he was consoled. "In a moment, it will all be finished."

"What are you going to do to us?" Gisela pleaded.

"Just move toward the wall," he directed.

"You said you wouldn't hurt us. Just take the money. We won't go to the police."

Both men found Doran's statement rather funny. "Here the police are not interested in such things," he was told.

"Then there's no reason to harm us," he postured.

"The wall! Please!"

Slowly, Doran and Gisela followed instructions.

"Now, put your hands on the bricks and spread your legs apart," they were told.

"Why are you doing this?" Gisela whimpered.

"Count slowly to one thousand before moving away from that spot," commanded the thief.

"Whatever you say," Doran acceded.

"Start counting now!" came the troublesome voice.

"One, two, three…"

"Count slower. Begin again."

"One… Two… Three…"

"That's better."

"Four… Five… Six… Seven…"

They heard a car door slam, an engine start.

"Eight… Nine… Ten…"

A second engine turned over.

"Eleven… Twelve… Thirteen…"

Both cars drove away, and they were left alone in the dank alleyway. Their bags, too, were lost.

"We'd better sit tight," Doran suggested.

"I think I peed my pants," Gisela said shakily.

"One thing at a time," said Doran.

"I thought they were going to shoot us!" Gisela stammered.

"But they didn't. Now, let's just wait here fifteen minutes. The greater the distance between them and us, the better."

"Then what?"

"We start walking, I guess."

"Where are we?" Gisela asked.

"I'm not exactly sure," he said. "But we can follow the river to the center."

"Maybe somebody will help us," she hoped.

"We must contact Vladimir," Doran determined.

"We don't even have coins for a telephone call," Gisela observed.

"We'll think of something," Doran consoled.

"I feel ridiculous wetting my pants," she said. "And I'm really cold!"

"Let's try to reach the center before it gets dark," said Doran.

"Okay."

And they set off to find the road that ran alongside the river. After a forty-minute walk, they reached a commercial district, and Doran entered a hotel as Gisela waited outside, embarrassed to be seen in wet pants. He explained to the English-speaking desk clerk that he'd just been robbed and needed to phone a friend.

"Shall I contact the police?" asked the clerk.

"No," Doran instructed. "I only wish to call my friend to pick me up."

"Very well," said the clerk. He handed Doran the phone.

But realizing that Vladimir's number was in his wallet, and that his wallet was now in the possession of the accomplice taxi driver, Doran hung up the receiver. To the clerk he turned once more for help. "Do you have a directory?" he asked.

"Do you read Russian?" the clerk inquired.

"No," said Doran.

"What is the name? I'll look it up."

"Thank you. The name is Stolaroff. Vladimir Stolaroff."

"Very well."

The number was easily found and the call was made. Doran explained to Vladimir what had happened, and the artist told him to wait outside the hotel, and that he would send a friend with a car at once.

"Sorry to impose this way, Vladimir," Doran

apologized.

"Unfortunately, this sort of thing happens often in Kiev," said the painter. "At least you and your friend are safe!"

They waited outside the hotel for nearly an hour before Vladimir's friend arrived. Gisela's pants had now dried, but she was convinced she could smell urine in her midst. The ride to Stolaroff's home on the outskirts of the city took forty-five minutes, and it was a long ride indeed, since Vladimir's friend spoke neither English, nor German, nor Dutch. To make matters worse, his car was without heat, and Doran and Gisela huddled close together in the back seat. Through the city they went, past the university and the Kyjevo Pecherska Lavra, (the Great Bell Tower), and past the bronze statue of Sholom Aleikhem, and another of Panikovsky, The Great Beggar, at the corner of Proriza and Khreshchatyk. Moving from the city center to the suburbs, the streetlights were lost and blackness prevailed, and they drove through the darkened countryside in silence.

Finally, they reached Vladimir Stolaroff's home—a place Doran knew well from past visits. A rustic, timbered house with a thatched roof, it stood in a small clearing surrounded by large pines. Inside, the lights were lit, and wood smoke plumed from the chimney. As they got out of the car, Vladimir stood waiting in the open doorway.

"Thank you for sending a car," Doran told the artist.

"Of course, of course," said the burly Ukrainian as he ushered them inside the house. "A most unfortunate incident. Terrible!"

"Their only interest was money," said Doran.

"They had a gun," Gisela added.

Stolaroff regarded Gisela, and Doran stuttered to introduce her.

"This is my friend…uh…she is simply called Z," he said.

Vladimir shook her hand. "You come also from America?" he asked.

"No," she answered, making a mental note of the name Doran had given her. "I come from the Netherlands."

"Your welcome to my country was most ungracious," said Vladimir, "but you are safe in my house."

"Thank you for rescuing us," said Gisela.

Stolaroff turned to Doran. "How did it happen, Seeger?" he wanted to know.

"My own stupidity," Doran confessed. "We met them on the train. They engaged us in conversation and I revealed far too much. Outside the station, they commandeered a taxi driver to take us to an out-of-the-way place—some abandoned warehouses near the river. I'm afraid we made an easy target."

Vladimir shook his head in disgust. "In Kiev, as you unfortunately now know from experience, crime is out of control. The police are useless, as many of them are in league with the mafia. And the situation seems to grow worse by the day!" He showed them to a seat on a comfortable sofa near the fireplace and gave them each a drink of brandy. Refreshing his own glass, he took a seat opposite them.

"We never had such problems when the Soviets were in power," he continued. "Of course we had many other problems—issues of social freedom, and, of course, the *gulags*... Brutal though Communism often was, at least there was order. This is something altogether different: this is chaos! No saints were the Communists, but I would welcome back Gorbachev and his crew with open arms!"

With her two hands wrapped round the brandy snifter, Gisela regarded their host with a particular curiosity. The father, it seemed, had contributed few of his traits—neither in physique nor personality—to his son. Where Alexi was tall and thin, almost gaunt, Vladimir was short and robust. Alexi's demeanor conveyed an unmistakable intensity of purpose and conviction, like a bird of prey;

Vladimir was affable and homey, his temperament being more like that of a zoo-kept walrus. Yet there was something familiar in the father's eyes—a poignant quality that Gisela readily recognized but could not define specifically. Vladimir's aura radiated rich amber light.

"The thieves took everything," Doran explained to Vladimir. "They even made off with our luggage. So purchasing the paintings on this trip is now out of the question."

"Nonsense," said Stolaroff. "We all have too much invested in this endeavor. I will lend you what you need for your return, and you will take the paintings with you as arranged. You can send me the money when you return to Prague. Or we can settle up on your next buying trip."

"I appreciate your trust, Vladimir, but our operation is not so lucrative that we can stand a set-back like this one."

"Then you've lost everything?"

"No, not everything," said Doran. "But the loss does create a serious problem."

"This is unfortunate," said the painter. For he had collected works to be sold from numerous artists, friends and acquaintances spread out over a vast territory.

"I know this puts you in a difficult position," Doran recognized. "And I'm truly sorry."

"It's not your fault, Seeger. The important thing is that neither of you was harmed."

"When I return to Prague, I'll see that you're compensated for your effort. And for the inconvenience this incident has caused. Perhaps Scarlet will have some idea how to rectify the situation," he offered.

"Scarlet is a very resourceful woman," Vladimir acknowledged. He finished his brandy and stood up. "Surely you must be hungry and tired," he said. "Tonight I can offer you something to eat and a warm place to sleep. Tomorrow we will discuss this problem."

Vladimir graciously offered Doran and Gisela his own bed, but when they explained to him that their relationship was one only of friendship, he gave them blankets and pillows to make a cozy sleeping arrangement in front of the hearth. Doran slept in his clothes, but Gisela took off her soiled pants.

Lying upon fleece rugs, and wrapped in wool blankets, they recounted the unfortunate events of the afternoon. Doran was angry about the theft, but he was philosophical as well. This was *not* the first time he'd been robbed.

As Gisela lay beside the fire, she shivered more from nerves than from cold. It was true that she'd lost only her luggage—a few articles of clothing and her *toilette*—but her sense of security had been severely compromised. Never before had she worried about such things as she traveled from place to place. Such occurrences were not common, which rendered the assault all the more poignant. She too felt angry, but moreover she felt fortunate that neither she nor Doran had been harmed.

Sleep came grudgingly for them both. And on several occasions one or the other awoke to the strangeness of an unfamiliar room. Sometime before dawn the last embers of the fire went out, and Vladimir's parlor promptly took on the obstinate chill of Ukraine's lingering winter. They huddled close together and talked in whispers.

"Doran?"

"Yes?"

"Are you awake?"

"I'm awake."

"It's freezing in here."

"I know."

"May I come closer to you?"

"Of course." He put his arms around her trembling body.

"I don't know where I am," Gisela whimpered.

"You're here with me. We're in Vladimir's home. And you're safe," he consoled her.

"And I don't know where I'm going."

"The journey itself is our home," he told her.

"Do you really believe that, Doran?"

"I think I do."

"Sometimes I wonder if I can find the courage."

"The courage to continue without a grounding?"

"Yes," she whispered. She moved even closer to him, and only the blankets wrapped round their bodies excluded tangible contact.

"We continue because there is no choice except oblivion. And oblivion is unthinkable. So we continue… Somehow, we find courage. Or, in our angst and our default, courage finds us. That's how it is until the end."

"Some people never seem to face this dilemma," she said.

"I think everyone faces it, Gisela. We see the brave faces of friends and foes alike. All the while, terror is kept well out of sight. Some mask the fear with bravado. Others hide in the shadow of faith. And we continue. We continue."

"I only want a place with light. And warmth."

"A place called Paradise?"

"Nothing so auspicious as that," she qualified.

"Then what?" he asked.

"A place I can call home," she said.

"The journey itself is our home," he told her.

"Do you really believe that, Doran?"

"I don't know."

Next morning, Gisela asked Vladimir if she could launder her jeans, and the host showed her his facilities and gave her two artist's smocks that she fashioned into a knee-length skirt to wear while her pants dried on a line. After a short tour of his grounds, the artist cooked a breakfast of potato pancakes and cured ham. Over strong tea they recapped the events of the previous day, and Vladimir outlined a timetable for their return to Prague. After breakfast, they viewed the paintings that Doran had come to purchase.

"The quality is superb," Doran acknowledged.

"Thank you," said Vladimir. "And I will convey your approval to my colleagues."

"I can't say when I'll return to purchase the canvases," Doran informed.

"I understand the circumstances," said Vladimir. "But I have confidence that something can be arranged."

"I hope you're right," said Doran.

"I believe that there is a train leaving tonight for Prague. If you are inclined to return at once, I will arrange a ride to the station."

"We should return as soon as possible," said Doran.

"Very well." Vladimir reached into his pocket and laid some money on the table. "Take this for your fare," he said.

"Thank you," said Doran. "I'll send you a draft as soon as I get beck to Prague."

"It's nothing, my friend."

"And as for the purchase of the paintings…"

Vladimir waved him off. "We'll see what Scarlet Ponton has to say about it," he determined.

Though Doran knew that most of his capital was lost, and that this might well be his last trip to the Ukraine to buy paintings.

From the Kiev railway station, Doran had telephoned Scarlet to convey the bad news and to inform her of their plan to return immediately to Prague. So when the train arrived in the Czech capital at six o'clock the next morning, she was there to meet them. Offering each a kiss of welcome, she asked, "Are you both all right?"

"We're okay," Doran confirmed.

"What happened?"

"There were two Russian men in our compartment. They asked a lot of questions. And I was too stupid to realize what they were up to."

"Christ!" said Scarlet as they walked up the platform toward the terminal. "The two of you might have been killed!"

"There was a moment or two of uncertainty," Doran related.

"And they took everything?"

"They even stole our clothes," said Gisela. "Then they left us in an alley."

"What did you do then?"

"We walked to the center. I telephoned Vladimir from a hotel," said Doran.

"Did you contact the police?" Scarlet asked.

"I didn't see any point in it," he said.

"Just as well," said Scarlet. "And what about Vladimir?" she asked.

"He sent a car for us. We stayed overnight at his house. I explained to him that it might be difficult for us to raise more money for the paintings."

"What did he say?"

"He is convinced that *you* will come up with something."

"Me?"

Doran shrugged. "He has a high opinion of you, Scarlet."

When they reached the terminal they entered a café, and over coffee they discussed the situation further. After Doran and Gisela had recounted the details of the robbery again, and after failing to reach a solution regarding the purchase of the artwork, Scarlet dropped a little bomb of her own.

"I hate to have to tell you this, Doran."

Over the rim of his coffee cup he looked quizzically at her. "What is it?" he asked.

"Well, you were not the only robbery victim during the last forty-eight hours."

"What are you saying?" he inquired.

"The computers were stolen," she said.

Incredulous, he asked, "When?"

"The night before last," she related.

"Same as us."

"Yes."

"How?"

"A break-in," she said.

"And they're gone?"

"The thieves left me a note apologizing for the inconvenience," she said sardonically.

"How thoughtful of them," said Gisela.

"Did you call the police?" Doran wanted to know.

"Of course."

"And…"

"They're not very hopeful of recovering them. Apparently, there are countless fencing operations for stolen electronics in Prague."

"I can't believe it," said Doran. "What are the odds of both of us being robbed on the same day?"

"Astronomical, I suppose. But that's little consolation now."

"We're really tapped out, Scarlet," said Doran.

"It looks that way," she said dourly.

Doran sighed ironically.

"Yesterday, my mother arrived from Colombia for a visit," Scarlet told them. "She suggested that I go to New York for a while."

"Why New York?" Gisela asked her.

"Our family has an apartment there."

"Are you considering it?" Doran asked.

"I think it might be a good idea," she said.

"Prague is so full of promise," Doran assessed.

Scarlet's expression was full of anguish. "I don't want to leave you high and dry, Seeger."

"You don't owe me a thing, Scarlet," Doran dismissed. "If anything, I owe you for the opportunity you provided me!"

"While it lasted."

"Scarlet, you need to do what you think is best," said Doran.

"Let's get out of here," she said as she stood up. "If we talk about this any longer, I think I'll break down and cry."

Once outside the terminal building, they went their separate ways.

In the chilly hours before dawn, Doran sat contemplatively at the kitchen table drinking the last of his Colombian coffee. Clad only in his bathrobe, he weighed the implications of his current situation, as Gisela slept on the loft in the bedroom.

Circumstances often change without warning, he thought to himself. So naively we believe that we have arranged our affairs neatly, and that everything in our domain is under control. We tell ourselves that we've anticipated potential pitfalls, and that we've insured ourselves against catastrophe. Ignorant in our complacency, we begin to believe that we are untouchable. But like a broadside accident, the catalyst seems to come from nowhere. Time and again we are dumbfounded by the imposed order of chaos.

The ancient Greeks saw chaos as the essence of all creation, and even their gods were not particularly inclined to impose order on the universe. Only mortal men seemed to need the comfort imparted by method and sequence. To this Achilles' heel, Doran was hardly exempt. Most men see themselves as nouns, he thought. I seem to be a verb.

Indeed, it was something immutable for which he searched. Mathematics offered pi. Navigation employed the Prime Meridian. In physics, the speed of light functioned as an absolute. And, as he well knew, directional cartography and range finding measured the inverse speed of sound in the Doppler effect. Still, no compass had yet established a magnetic constant in his personal life.

Growing up in the suburbs of Houston, Texas in the '50's and '60's, his childhood had been a normal one—

with the sole exception of having an alcoholic father. An above average student in high school, he'd excelled in math and science, though athletics—not academics—took up most of his time and energy. College had provided him the opportunity not only to learn job skills that were in high demand, but also to avoid service in Viet Nam.

Out of college he'd gone immediately to work in the private sector as an engineer. On-the-job training multiplied his skills and eventually made him a sought-after commodity; and a progression of jobs had eventually landed him in the heart of the American Defense Industry. Though unaware of it at the time, he'd given his talents to the task of developing a guidance system for the Cruise Missile, an endeavor he now deeply regretted. The experience of seeing his work subverted for the purpose of mayhem not only tormented his conscience, but also soured his opinion of the government for which he'd toiled.

One thing had led to another: a strange relationship with a girl in Boulder, Colorado, (a pseudo-scientist who had persuaded him to turn over classified Defense Department data on propulsion); the disappearance and subsequent death of his father; a somewhat spontaneous excursion to Europe from which he'd failed to return home. He'd spent the past ten years drifting from country to country, from one situation to another.

With renunciation had come a degree of deliverance. Certainly he was happier selling art in the Czech Republic than he'd been making killer missiles in the U.S.A. And, in general, Europeans conveyed less social duplicity than Americans—an unanticipated cultural difference that also offered Doran respite. Yet his progress seemed somehow backward. Most men his age, whether they lived in the States, or whether they lived in Europe, had well-established lives. They had families, and homes, and careers, and money. He had none of these things. Instead, his assets totaled a collection of diverse experiences. By default he had managed to alter his course, while never having replaced his old credo with a well-defined new one.

Now, with his bank account seriously diminished to compensate Vladimir Stolaroff, and with Scarlet gone away to New York, and their quasi-business left in shambles, Doran was forced once again to evaluate his situation. Departures and arrivals were no doubt a well-rehearsed scenario in his life, but was he really ready to make yet another ad hoc change? His tenure in the Czech Republic had been both pleasant and rewarding, and though his means of support had been literally stolen away by thugs in a bleak, dead-end alley in Kiev, he would, with the help of friends like Storic and Basso, surely be able to turn up something in the way of an occupation were he to remain in Prague.

But perhaps maintaining his residency in the Czech capital was really not the issue at all. Indeed, Gisela's unexpected arrival seemed to intimate the renewal of something beyond their friendship. Her presence invited Doran to revisit a very different chapter in his experiential log—one profuse with hospitality and warmth. One filled with the sweet urgency of romantic love. And while he understood that conditions in the past did not necessarily portend events in the future, still Corfu had rekindled his sense of optimism in a way unlike any other place. The temperate, cerulean waters of the Ionian Sea; the Apollonian sunsets beyond the horizon at Glyfada Beach; the stars of the southern sky, so near that one might reach out his hand and pluck them from the firmament, gathering them as sparkling specks of divine light to warm the hearts of an already affable race!

And Doran recalled other, less tangible, aspects of life on Corfu: the housewives (*nikokiri*) flinging open their windows at sunrise to hang the bedding out to air, and singing as they washed down doorsteps with stiff-bristled brushes and pales of steaming, soapy water; and the village barber in Kondokali, who opened his one-chair, cubbyhole shop only after dark, and who strangely refused on three separate occasions to cut Doran's hair; and how the Corfiot children declined to knock at the door of a grandparent, preferring instead to stand below the window and call, regardless of the time of day or night, '*Babou*! *Babou*!'

These were the lasting impressions of Corfu; and these qualities and others called home its wayfarers and its prodigal sons time and again. Yet Doran was not a native Greek. What influence had this island or this culture over him?

In all honesty, Doran had been overwhelmed by the generosity of those who themselves had so little. Time after time he was offered a basketful of fruit, a pastry, or a bottle of homemade wine. In winter, when he was ill with a chest cold, his landlady, Tasoula, had boiled leaves of camphor and eucalyptus and made him inhale the vapors. Each morning she brought him tea with honey and lemon until his cough subsided. Modestos himself had made Doran an offer that seemed conspicuously openhanded: '*Everything okay*?' he'd inquired. Feeling lighter than air, and on top of the world, Doran answered, 'Takis, what could be wrong?' To which Modestos tendered, '*If you need something, I will try to help you.*' At the time Doran remembered thinking: Even had Greece not been favored by the gods with physical beauty, still he would return again and again, for it was the people of Hellas that made this land so beguiling!

But he had not returned. Instead, he'd stumbled through Europe for nearly ten years, engaged in one false start after another. No doubt, Prague had been the most sociable of these experiments, though now it seemed to be slamming its door in his face, too. Greece, on the other hand, had not expelled him. Inexperienced in European ways, he'd sought out the lessons learned only through integration, leaving Hellas of his own choosing. In retrospect, it was perhaps a superfluous decision, though at the time how could he have known? Even so, he thought, life advances along a forward timeline, and only a fool tries to retrace his steps.

Doran's feelings for Greece and for its people were fond ones indeed, but such feelings now seemed distant, if not oblique. He had come to regard the past as only a dream, sometimes splendiferous, and other times—most times—wanting.

And he sometimes pondered the question of where he might be at the time of his own death. Where indeed? He'd lived his entire life treading perimeters, eyes wide open and yet still blind. Never had he come close to a nexus point. Indeed, if he possessed a nuclear identity, it was one yet to be realized. And as time stole away potential, the answer to his hypothetical question seemed stunningly irresolute: far from home…

As Doran poured himself a second cup of coffee, he heard Gisela in the bathroom. Uncharacteristically, she was up and about before dawn. The apartment was quite chilly, and Doran could see not only the steamy vapors from his cup of coffee, but also those from his own breath. Apparently, the building's boiler was once again functioning in a tenant *modus operandi*. So be it. Visions of Mediterranean warmth and splendor had, for the moment, caused him to pay the chill no heed. He rubbed his palms together and blew on his fingers, then wrapped both hands around the ceramic mug to impart its warmth to his flesh. With a blanket wrapped round her, Gisela wandered into the kitchen. "You're up early," Doran observed.

"Nightmare," Gisela related as she sat down opposite him.

"Sorry to hear it."

Gisela shrugged. "Ever since the robbery, I've had unsettling dreams," she said.

"Replaying the event?" he asked.

"Not exactly."

"Feeling threatened?"

"I've been living a rather threatening existence for some time now," she asserted.

Remaining receptive, Doran asked, "Would you like coffee?"

Gisela nodded and pulled the blanket closer to her body. "It's freezing in here," she said.

"The coffee will warm you," Doran said. "I'm afraid it's the last of the Colombian," he told her.

"And Scarlet has gone to New York…"

"I guess all good things eventually come to an end," said Doran with resignation, but no specific regret.

Gisela consciously evaluated his quintessence as he prepared her drink. In the days since the robbery, Doran's aura had changed. The spectral gradient that he emanated, once violet and latently spiritual, had first gone orange, and then modified itself into shades of umber. And though she knew not how to precisely interpret the prismatic array coming from one person or another, she did intuit that the change she noticed in Doran's aura was hardly for the good. This morning, she observed, the colors he emitted had again mutated, this time symbolizing in luminescent terms his present emotional and spiritual condition. His light was ultramarine; it's conveyance, one of warmth and cogency. His improved condition put her at ease.

"I telephoned Alarice yesterday," she said as Doran put her drink before her.

"Is she well?" he asked nonchalantly.

"She's fine," said Gisela. "I asked her to send me some money," she conveyed.

"The robbery wiped you out?"

"More or less," Gisela confirmed.

Doran shook his head with compunction as he again sat down at the table. "She works very hard to maintain your father's business," he speculated.

"Fact is that the business is more profitable than ever with Alarice at the helm."

"To her credit," said Doran.

"Of course half the business belongs to me. On paper, anyway," explained Gisela. "But Arissa and I have an arrangement. Since she's inclined to remain in Rotterdam and act as administrator, she pays herself accordingly. But the company earns far more than either of us needs. She puts my share of the profit into an escrow account, and then disperses money as I need it. Sometimes I feel a little uneasy with the agreement, but my sister assures me that she is content with it. What can I do?"

"No need to do anything, I suppose," said Doran. "You're fortunate to have a ready-made means of support."

"I've never seen myself as a trust fund baby. Or anything like that."

"Still, there's no need to apologize for good fortune," said Doran.

"Yes, I guess I'm lucky," Gisela concluded.

"I'd say so," Doran judged.

"What about you?" Gisela asked. "I mean after the robbery."

"I'm not destitute," said Doran. "But my finances have been in better shape."

"And of course Scarlet has gone to New York."

"As we've said."

"And that more or less finishes your career as an art dealer."

"I could continue if I had fresh capital," he speculated.

"What's the possibility of that?" she wanted to know.

"Slim to none," he had to confess.

"Tough situation," she concluded.

"Not so bad. I've learned to live on very little."

"You've been thinking about Greece," she said abruptly.

"What makes you think that?" he asked.

"It's only natural since I've arrived back in your life. And through me, Arissa as well!"

"I suppose so," Doran allowed.

"I've been thinking about it too."

"As you say, it's only natural."

Gisela sipped her coffee as she pensively surveyed a horizon beyond their present locale. It was one colored very much like Doran's newfound aura. "What would it take to convince you to go back?" she finally asked.

"Go back?"

"To Corfu."

"Why would I want to go back to Corfu?" he asked.

At once, they both laughed out loud. For the answer to his rhetorical question seemed absurdly obvious. "It's really beautiful there," said Gisela. "Remember?"

"Sure I remember!"

"But it's more than that."

"The place has certain qualities," he recounted.

"Exactly!"

"I was thinking about it as I sat here shivering and drinking the last of my Colombian coffee," he admitted.

"And Scarlet has gone away to New York."

"As we've said."

"What about it, Doran?" Gisela postured.

"Go back to Corfu? You and me? Together?"

"Why not?"

"That was ten years ago. Circumstances were different."

"Yes, that was ten years ago. And circumstances *were* different."

"What would Alarice think?" he posed.

"That was ten years ago, Doran."

"Still, I haven't forgotten."

"Nor has she, I'm sure. But…"

"Corfu? You and me? Together?"

"Just as friends," she assured him.

"Yes, just as friends."

In the days following their early morning chat, several more such discussions took place; and while Doran was not diametrically opposed to returning to Corfu, he nevertheless needed further encouragement to leave Prague. To that task Gisela was equal, for she had known ever since arriving in the Czech capital that neither the city nor the North in general was her cup of tea. Having lived in the Algarve, she craved not only the climatic warmth of the Mediterranean, but also its social conviviality. Further, she knew that such a change of venue would benefit Doran as well.

So, rekindling the memories of their shared experience in Greece, and proposing a new set of possibilities as well, Gisela eventually persuaded Doran that a self-styled change of climate was in their mutual interest. And once the decision to return to Corfu was made, the perpetual itinerant sold the few possessions he did not wish to transport, (including the paintings in his personal collection), and prepared to leave Prague for a return engagement in Hellas.

CHAPTER 5
A MALODOROUS RETURN
TO KONDOKALI

They might have liked to travel to Greece by train through Zagreb and Belgrade, for it was the most direct route; however, the recent civil war in the Balkans had rendered that option impossible, as many bridges and connections had been destroyed during the fighting. So the unlikely companions went first to Vienna, then to Venice, Italy. From Venice, they took an overnight train to the Adriatic port of Brindisi. There they boarded a ferryboat for the ten-hour overnight crossing to Corfu.

Approaching Kerkyra at dawn, the twin fortresses, each in its own rite normally visible long before docking, were obscured by dense fog. Such an advance differed markedly in tone from Doran's first arrival on the island, as ten years ago he'd approached Corfu at dusk, in the midst of a strident Ionian light that had brought him close to tears. Likewise, the melodrama of Gisela's first landing at Kerkyra contrasted this morning's placid afflux. She recalled being herded along with other disembarking passengers into the ship's hold, where the temperature was unbearable, and the aroma of several hundred crates packed tight with live stinking chickens loaded on flatbed trucks had nearly made her swoon. This morning they were in port and secured before they'd ever laid eyes on dry land, and the only drama was that of trying to determine their bearings in the soupy atmosphere once on the pier.

"I have a telephone number," Gisela told Doran.

Doran looked at her curiously. "You kept Modestos' number?" he wanted to know.

"Not for Takis," she explained. "For Spiro."

"Still carrying a torch?" he baited.

"Hardly. We wrote for a time. I always meant to continue the correspondence, but you know how that goes."

"Even if we telephone, it's doubtful they will remember us," Doran conjectured.

"I don't know about you," she teased, "but I'd like to think I cast a stronger impression than that."

"Ring them if you like," Doran conceded.

From a pay telephone Gisela dialed the number of the Thromos household, but she received no answer. No matter, she thought. She was well accustomed to unplanned arrivals.

Hauling many more bags than was customary for normal tourists, they moved up the pier until Doran spied the Hotel Atlantis. By this familiar landmark he knew the way to the center of town. Crossing Zivatsianou Street in front of the harbor, they moved up a tributary boulevard leading to San Rocco Square in the center of New Town. There they boarded a bus that took them out of the city proper, along Corfu's major northbound highway, and around Gouvia Bay. Within fifteen minutes they reached the outskirts of Kondokali village.

The sights were familiar as they began the trek up Christopher Street, leading to the commercial center. Lined with tall Cyprus trees, the lane remained shady and cool as the sun burned away the morning fog. Simple houses painted pink or ochre hid behind lush Mediterranean vegetation, and a welcoming committee composed of three unleashed dogs fell in step to escort them into the village.

Past the *tavernas* and nautical shops they walked, past the bakery, the barbershop, and a butcher's shop displaying strings of sausages, three skinned hares, a bovine carcass on a meat hook, and the dismembered head of a pig, (to Gisela it seemed to be smiling), sporting comical, oversized yellow sunglasses. Red bougainvillea adorned the whitewashed walls of the primary school, and a fountain splashed clear water over its three tiers in front of the Navigator's Bar. From the belfry of the Orthodox Church rang ten chimes, (the bell actually sounded more like a Chinese gong), and the marble sidewalks gleamed in the silvery sunlight. Yet many of the tourist shops were boarded up, Doran noticed. And considering the season, that seemed odd indeed.

"Pension Aphrodite is one hundred meters ahead. Perhaps we'll find Modestos there," Gisela speculated.

"If he's not there now, he'll turn up sooner or later."

"Right!"

"If we have to wait for him," Doran proposed, "we can have breakfast at Restaurant Pericles."

"Good idea. I'm starving!"

But as they came closer to the neighborhood of their fondly remembered *dhomatia*, a rather putrid odor permeated the normally sweet air. "What's that smell?" Gisela rankled.

Doran winced as he caught a whiff of the offending odor. "Sewage," he remarked.

"It's horrible!" Gisela complained.

"Greek plumbing is notoriously bad," Doran remembered.

They walked a little further up Christopher Street, past the closed-up Onari Nightclub, and then turned up the narrow lane that led to Pension Aphrodite.

There they caught first sight of their old friend Modestos Thromos. Beneath the leafy grape arbor in the *dhomatia's* walled-in garden, he stood. In his hands he held a plumber's wrench and several remnants of rusted-out pipe. A vexed and confounded expression shone in place of his typical, good-natured smile.

Seeing Doran and Gisela at the gate, Modestos was more than happy for the opportunity to abandon his cause. Moving toward them, he beamed, "My friends, my friends! Why did you not telephone me? I would have met you at the port." And still clutching the bits and pieces of his plumbing catastrophe, he leaned forward to kiss each of them on the cheek. Then, looking down at the degraded elements in his rust-stained hands, and shaking his head in utter disgust, the Greek ruminated, "Now I have big problem. *Po, po, po!*"

So much for the notion that they would not be remembered, Doran conceded. Indeed, Takis welcomed them as if they were long-absent cousins. "Why do you stay away from Kerkyra so long?" he implored.

"Yes, it's been too long," Doran agreed. "How are you, my friend?"

"Growing old," Modestos resigned with a chuckle. Modestos took him by the arm and led him to an excavated sewer pipe. "Smell! Smell!" he implored.

"Sewer gas," Doran determined. "We smelled it as we walked through the village."

"Too many lines coming into the main one," Takis determined. "Big problem! Too much shit!"

"Perhaps a wider pipe is needed," Doran conjectured.

"Yes! But my government won't fix," said Takis. He laid down the rusted pipes and turned up his palms. "Big problem, big problem…"

Yet, in spite of the sewer gas leak, the *dhomatia's* garden was every bit as lovely as Doran remembered it: the flagstone patio, the whitewashed staircase with its old-style balustrade, the profuse bougainvillea climbers. Perhaps Modestos measured time by the graying of his temples, or by the stiffness in his joints, but these surroundings, both natural and man-made, seemed more or less timeless to Doran, and he was quick to acknowledge Gisela's wisdom in initiating their return to Corfu. Because here prevailed the inherent and unmistakable feeling that no matter what might go wrong, a good life, an elemental life, was not compromised.

"Where is your sister?" Takis demanded of Gisela.

"She's in Holland," Gisela answered.

"Why does she not come with you?" Takis implored.

"She is working," Gisela answered.

"I remember that one," said Modestos referring to Alarice. "Always reading book. Very quiet."

"That's my sister," said Gisela.

"Too much serious, that one!" determined Modestos. "Not like you, eh?" He grinned broadly at Gisela, and she somehow knew that his recollection of her time with Spiro was behind the smile.

"No, not like me," she conceded with a touch of embarrassment.

"As you like," said Takis as he washed his hands under an outdoor spigot. "Anyway, how long will you stay here? Maybe all summer long, eh?"

"Actually," said Doran, "we were hoping you might know of an apartment for us to rent long term."

Takis' eyebrow rose in consideration. "Long term? How long?"

"Hard to say," Doran postured. "Maybe one year. Maybe longer."

"You like to stay one year? Okay. Maybe you like to rent my mother's old apartment?"

Doran and Gisela looked at one another in silent recognition of what they presumed to be good fortune. For surely Aphrodite's apartment was the best of all the flats in the complex. Quite pleased, Doran said, "That might be perfect."

"Come have a look," said Modestos. "If you like the apartment, I make you a good price. You are my friends!"

And you are a good man, Modestos, thought Doran to himself.

So up the stone steps they marched to view the apartment where Aphrodite Thromos had lived until her death at age ninety-three. Standing on the small covered balcony, Modestos turned the key in the lock and motioned his guests inside. The old-style, double doors opened onto a long narrow alcove. The walls were painted yellow, and a long runner with a modern design in primary colors covered the floor. At the end of the antechamber was an antique credenza with a matching writing desk. Above the desk was a colorful theatrical poster showcasing the celebrated Greek actor, Thumios Karakatsanis, in *The Death of Aristophane*. Smiling, Modestos conveyed his pride in the apartment. "Step inside," he invited. "See the rest of the apartment. I think you will like it."

Beyond the alcove lay a spacious rose-colored room with a parquet floor and a high, pine-paneled ceiling. A stained glass divider defined separate sleeping and sitting areas. In the parlor, a large rug of Greek design covered the parquet tiles, and two easy chairs, a TV, a small stereo, and an empty bookcase made the living area seem at once intimate and homey. The bedroom area was furnished with twin beds, an armoire, and a mirrored dressing table. On the wall above the beds hung a large framed picture of the *Three Graces* at leisure in a beatific mythological setting. Modestos pulled back the curtains, opened the window, and pushed back the shutters. A vivid, chromium light poured into the room.

"Very bright!" Gisela commented.

Takis was inclined to reminiscence. "As you know," he said, "my mother, God rest her soul, lived in this apartment for many years." He crossed himself with two fingers and cleared his throat before continuing. "Yet in all the years she lived here, never once did she open the shutters to the light of day. After her death, I opened all the windows to let in the sun. It took one full year for her sadness and grief to disappear!"

Though Modestos alluded to Aphrodite's sorrow, Gisela could not help wondering if his true reference was not to his own particular melancholy, or apprehension, or uneasiness. Or to a well-concealed insecurity. As far as Gisela was concerned, the Greek was an open book filled with enigmas. His personality literally overflowed with good-natured intensity and enthusiasm for life. Invariably, it drew others to him as a bee is drawn to pollen. Yet sometimes that same intensity made her want to take cover. An indigo border around his sunny, pre-eminent aura intimated something withheld. Whatever the source of her caution, it remained undefined, and she was above all inclined to accept his gracious hospitality. For perhaps the modicum of reticence she felt originated in her own personality, not his. After all, it was she who came from a society modeled on reservation, and sympathy notwithstanding, she could not help but acknowledge the veritable chasm of cultural awareness between Northern Europeans and Greeks.

Together they inspected the fitted kitchen. Floral print wallpaper brightened the room's aspect, and a semi-circular table was placed in front of the window, which looked down upon the grape arbor that sheltered the walled-in garden from the southern sun. Upon a marble countertop, a two-burner, propane stove was provided for cooking. The refrigerator was small but adequate. Modestos flipped on a switch that activated the hot water heater and showed them the fuse box.

The large bathroom located just off the kitchen, he explained to them, was multi-functional. It was equipped with a particularly large basin to facilitate not only personal grooming, but clothes laundering as well. A drying rack occupied the space opposite the wide-open shower stall.

"As you know, there is a small problem with the plumbing," said Modestos. "But, if I'm lucky, I will have it repaired in no time at all."

Doran was amused at how fast a 'big problem' had become a trifle, but optimism, he knew, was Modestos' nature. Hopefully, plumbing was one of his acquired skills. He glanced at Gisela to ascertain her initial opinion of the apartment, and she returned his inquiry with a confirming smile. "Yes, the rooms are very nice," Doran complimented. "How much per month, Takis?"

"For you, my friend, only sixty thousand drachmas per month. Not so much to pay, eh?"

Doran mentally computed the conversion. "No, Takis, not so much."

"Then you are welcome to stay as long as you like. And if you need something, Takis will help you!"

Plainly remembering Modestos' unbridled hospitality from his previous visit, Doran knew that the promise was not a hollow one. And prompted by the Greek's unqualified offer of help, he briefly considered a particularly imminent personal dilemma: his American passport was due to expire soon. Without a valid passport, life in Europe would be difficult, and he sincerely hoped that Modestos would be able to guide him through the bureaucratic maze he anticipated. Though that problem was better dealt with in the future. Now he was concerned only with unpacking his belongings, settling into the apartment, and finding a meal. If indeed his appetite could survive the malodorous environment of Kondokali Village.

After eating breakfast on the patio at Restaurant Pericles, Doran and Gisela had a short walk through the village. While many things endured just as they remembered them—the blue- domed Orthodox Church, the venerable Taverna Rankios, and Fedra's Nightclub—some notable changes were evident, too. To both Doran and Gisela the village appeared just a bit tawdry and time worn, a carcass picked over and left by scavengers moved to a more fruitful feeding ground. Supermarket Spiros, a once thriving enterprise, was now boarded up. As was the Panorama Bar and Katerina's Boutique. Fallen brush and debris blocked the entrance to the Tip Top Restaurant, and the grimy windows of the deserted Scania Sail Shop offered graffiti artists a backdrop for clever drawings and messages. Such was the fate of a tourist destination now out of favor.

But there was also a conspicuous new development in Kondokali Village. On Gouvia Bay, where once a crude wooden dock harboring the boats of local fishermen defined the water's edge, a brand new, up-to-date harbor with slips to host three hundred yachts and cruisers was now situated. The development included a chandlery, a public swimming pool, a laundry, a modern supermarket, and a café; and to further enhance the complex, the Kondokali Bay Hotel, a luxury resort complete with a *faux* floorshow, Bingo *auf Deutsch*, and a first-run movie parlor, had been built on the peninsula adjacent to the marina site.

From the pier, looking past the tall masts of the moored boats and clear across the blue waters of the bay, the entire Northeast coast of Kerkyra could be seen—the nearby verdant hillsides, as well as the denuded summit of Mount Pantocrator. In the distance lay the tall mountains of a nether land, if no longer forbidden, then still forbidding: Albania.

And as they walked along the quay, Doran silently read the names of the docked boats: Saving Grace, Steel Pulse, Blue Moon, Pathfinder, Cloud Nine, Another Story. Atop the masts fluttered the flags of various nations: Great Britain, Holland, Italy. These yachts were apparently home to their inhabitants, and Doran could only conclude that each boat's name suggested some aspect of the owner's situation.

At the end of the pier they met an old fisherman named Napoleon. Sitting on the edge of the dock, he cast his handheld line into the water again and again with little result.

"Before the marina was built," he lamented, "Gouvia Bay was full of fish. And the fishermen of Kerkyra understood the natural cycle. You see, a particular wind coming off the mountains of Albania altered the water's current, bringing thousands and thousands of fish into the bay. It was magnificent! We had only to put out our nets to catch many kilos. But since the marina was built, everything has changed. Now we catch only a few small ones. Nothing important."

He coughed deeply as he dashed out a hand-rolled cigarette and coiled his line in resignation.

"The marina is very modern," he went on. "The boats come here from every country in Europe. Even from America! It's true! I know this because I see the flags on each mast. And who can blame them?" he reasoned. "Kerkyra is a beautiful island. So instead of fish, we now catch Euro-money. And this they call progress!"

He stored his tackle inside a plastic bag and prepared to leave. "You are nice people," he said with an ironic smile. "I mean you no disrespect." He shook hands with each of them before moving up the pier with his paltry catch.

Passing again through Kondokali Village on Christopher Street, they noticed an advertisement scrawled on a chalkboard in front of the Navigator's Bar. It read: "Karaoke at 21:00; Live Greek Music at Midnight!"

"Sounds like fun," Gisela remarked. "Want to come here for dinner tonight?"

"Sure," Doran agreed.

But now they needed rest, as three day's travel, along with the overnight crossing from Brindisi to Corfu, had left them feeling quite exhausted.

Back inside their newly rented apartment, Gisela had a shower as Doran sipped a soda. Once Gisela came out of the bathroom, he too took the opportunity to shower. When he returned, she was already asleep on one of the twin beds. He put on his underwear and dried his hair with a fluffy towel. Not immediately ready for sleep, he settled into one of the easy chairs and put up his feet. He drank the remainder of his soda as his mind wandered.

Behind the stained glass divider Doran could see the diffused image of Gisela's body as she lay on her back upon the bed. Her figure was full and her legs were long. Her feet were big and narrow, and her hands were folded over her breasts. Her chestnut curls fell over the pillow revealing a smooth neck and tiny ears. She was not a classic beauty, as was her sister, though for the moment Doran found himself transfixed by her overall aspect. His offhand interest, cavalier as it were, surprised him, and he promptly dismissed his consideration as inappropriate. Beside the fact that she was twenty years younger than he, she was also the sister of his former lover. Any involvement he might endorse with Gisela could only end badly for everyone concerned. Not that he'd ever considered such an advance. His momentary musings were relegated strictly to fantasy, and though pleasant enough, such imagery seemed somehow selfish and frivolous. He purposely directed his attention elsewhere.

He wondered how Scarlet was getting along in New York and decided he would telephone her to let her know that he'd left Prague and gone to Corfu. She would no doubt be surprised by his impulsive move, but her own retreat from the Czech capital had been no less spontaneous.

Lost in thought, Doran reflected upon the enigmatic name of Basso's Rock band: *Plastic People of the Universe*. Indeed, he himself embodied Vasil's metaphor. As did Scarlet. And Gisela. Invariably, plastic people molded easily to new situations. Plastic people readily adopted new habits and new philosophies. Truly, he'd never modeled his personality on the notion of pliancy, yet variation had become his governor. Such a tendency required blind faith—a condition not germane to his personality, but one that had over time imposed itself upon him by necessity and through practice.

Exhausted from travel but unable to sleep, Doran chased the ghosts of his past. He traced the pivotal incidents and influential encounters of his personal history from childhood to the present moment. But was the sum necessarily a total of its parts? How odd it seemed to him that one might know every minute detail of a lifetime yet remain inconclusive and without relative direction regarding one's essence and destiny—a veritable stranger unto oneself!

Though he had to admit that drifting had its high points as well. Spontaneity offered experiences that otherwise might have been missed, and a free and easy lifestyle, he reasoned, possibly rendered him an agent of some greater if nebulous universal influence. He moved from the apartment to the garden, and the warmth of the sunshine seemed to reassure him after a cold Prague winter.

CHAPTER 6
CHASING FIREFLIES

After sunset, Doran and Gisela dressed in casual clothes and set out for the Navigator's Bar. Strolling along Christopher Street, they were but two of many who were out and about after a day of sun and seaside fun. At Restaurant Pericles, sunburned tourists, as well as locals, dined *al fresco* on prawns, or mussels, or roasted lamb. Glasses were raised time and again to punctuate the evening meal. "*Yamas*!" called a Greek man in a sailor's cap. "*Salute*!" proposed a Dutchman to his companions as he downed an entire glassful of red wine.

And as they passed Fedra's Nightclub, a debonair bartender called out to them, "Good evening, my friends! Welcome. Please, come inside!"

Doran returned the proprietor's good-natured smile and explained, "We're on our way to a restaurant for supper."

"As you like," said the bartender with a nod. "Then come later for a drink. On the house!"

"Thanks," Doran acknowledged.

Further along the road they passed the Cava Golden

Gate. There, wine and brandy and *raki* were sold straight from the barrel. Next door to the *cava*, red bougainvillea climbed the white washed walls of the Gerekos Fish Restaurant, and from a wide-open, arched doorway at Taverna Lithari came the sound of bouzouki music. Doran and Gisela stopped to watch as two men danced arm-in-arm, stomping out the joy of yet another day. No doubt it was a dance they'd danced a thousand times or more, yet their enthusiasm seemed to proclaim: *This is the first day of the world! The first day of our lives! So together we dance!*

Above the marina, a full yellow moon rose against the backdrop of an infinite sky. Passing a small park, Doran and Gisela watched as children played on swings and slides. Young fathers sat together on benches, conversing casually and twirling worry beads as they supervised their children.

"When I left Corfu ten years ago," Gisela recalled, "I was certain that I'd never forget the spirit of the Greek people. But I did forget."

Doran agreed: "How could one really sustain such an approach once away from this place?"

"I wonder why we've waited so long to return," Gisela asked rhetorically.

"So often we don't trust what we know," said Doran.

En route to the Navigator's Bar they'd walked a mere two hundred meters, yet it seemed as though they had passed through another world—one that was now foreign to their northern sensibilities, yet one distantly familiar in memory. Or was it something else, something more elemental? This country, and this village in particular, seemed to evoke a thoroughly natural, if latent, attitude of fraternity and good will.

Though it differed significantly in character from the Greek establishments in Kondokali, somehow the Navigator's Bar did not seem out of place—mostly due to the fact that it was owned and operated by an Englishman from Liverpool and a Belgian from Antwerp for the benefit of the large population of British and Benelux expatriates living aboard yachts in Gouvia Marina. Written on a chalkboard was the menu for a traditional Sunday lunch: roast beef, mashed potatoes and gravy, mushy peas, and Yorkshire pudding; and posted on the pub's door was a placard with a decoupage of an old-time movie advertisement billing Charlie Chaplin as *The Adventurer*. In the plate glass window was a detailed model of a Clipper ship under full sail. Tonight, Ian McCann, a Scottish folk singer from Glasgow, was to be the host of the karaoke sing-along. Doran and Gisela went inside the pub, moving, as it were, from Greece to England as they crossed the threshold. "Well, what do you think of this?" Doran mused.

Gisela only laughed. "I suppose tourism makes places like this inevitable," she said. "But let's stay. It seems friendly, and the karaoke will be fun."

"Whatever floats your boat," said the American

The inside of the pub resembled an establishment that might well have been exported from Greenwich or Haarlem, its interior trimmed in dark wood, the décor displaying a decidedly nautical theme. Behind the well-stocked bar stood a tall, sallow-faced English girl with long, chestnut-colored hair and thin, pursed lips. She drew pints of Boddington's or Amstel with a deft hand as she conversed with the familiar patrons not in the Queen's English, but rather in some northern dialect.

Indeed, English was the language of choice at the Navigator's, as most conversations revolved around boats, and the sailing life in general: or about former military careers—SAS, British Intelligence, the Faulklands War; or about British politics; or family members still in the UK. Doran observed that many of the people in the pub seemed to know one another quite well; and as newcomers, he and Gisela were regarded with only passing interest.

They dined on lamb chops and roasted potatoes and

salad; and as they ate their dinner, the pub grew gradually more crowded with would-be pop stars intent on showcasing their vocal talents at the karaoke. Apparently the weekly sing-along was a popular diversion. Some of the more regular singers were dressed up for the event, emulating idols of a by-gone era: Bobby Darin, Leslie Gore, Jerry Lee Lewis, and Elvis Presley. Yes, Elvis was alive and well and living on Corfu! Though in this incarnation he spoke with an Albanian accent. Doran watched in amusement as each singer earnestly analyzed the song list to remember forgotten lyrics and recapture faded melodies. Just after ten o'clock, Ian McCann kicked off the festivities with his own rendition of *Mack The Knife*.

At the end of the song, everybody clapped and cheered as McCann welcomed the crowd and encouraged singers to submit their requests. The pub's two owners—a convivial Englishman dressed in black and white checkered pants and a sloppy T-shirt, and a Belgian Ponce in an ill-fitting suit—circulated among the tables taking orders for drinks. Doran stayed with wine, but Gisela graduated to ouzo and water.

"Not exactly Vasil Bassso's Plastic People of the Universe," Doran evaluated.

Gisela smiled. "Hey! To each his own!"

"Here! Here! So welcome back to Corfu!" he saluted, raising his glass.

"Yes, it's good to be back, isn't it?" said Gisela as she downed half her drink. "And come what may!"

"Better be careful," Doran cautioned. "That stuff goes down easy, but it packs quite a wallop."

"I'm ready to have some fun," said Gisela.

Doran only shrugged as a Leslie Gore look-alike stepped up to the microphone. "My God!" said Gisela. "She's wearing a hair extension!"

"All part of the show, I guess," said Doran.

Gisela giggled as she drank the ouzo with little regard for consequence. The liquor slid easily down her throat before exploding in her belly. "This is a kick!" she laughed as the intro- music to a hit song from the early sixties began. A moment later, the girl with the hair extension was wailing away.

> *"It's my party,*
> *And I'll cry if I want to,*
> *Cry if I want to,*
> *Cry if I want to,*
> *You would cry too,*
> *If it happened to you…"*

As the song ended, everyone again clapped enthusiastically, and the MC took the microphone to praise what was by all measure a feeble effort. "Who's next?" he encouraged. "Come on now, write in your requests and step onstage. Don't be shy. It's all good fun!"

Next up was a well-dressed, middle-aged guy with a chiseled face and Chia Pet hair. "Okay," said the host. "Let's have a glorious hand for Richard—to sing a big hit from the sixties, *Big Bad John.*"

The words to Jimmie Dean's melodramatic mining song flashed across the teleprompter, as the amateur delivered the heroic story in all seriousness. And each time he reached the song's refrain, the audience vociferously joined in the chorus: *Big John…Big bad John!*

"This is hardly what I expected to find on Corfu," Doran remarked to Gisela.

"In their own way, these ex-pats are simply making a home away from home for themselves."

"An exercise with which each of us has some familiarity," Doran observed.

Stony-faced Richard finished his ode to the legendary mining martyr as the two waiters made their rounds to take orders for drinks. Gisela freely called for another ouzo, as Doran paced himself with the glass of wine already before him.

Onstage, Ian McCann swilled a pint of beer as he queried the audience, "Who's here from England?" Most of the revelers raised their hands, and a round of applause was given. "And who's here from Holland?" implored the host. Far fewer hands went up, Gisela's included, but still the Dutch were well represented. "How about Germany?" inquired the MC. Still fewer hands were raised, but proudly so nevertheless. And noticing that Doran had not put up his hand in response to previous promptings, the karaoke host turned to him and asked, "What about you, mate? Where're you from?"

Not knowing exactly how to answer McCann's question, Doran simply said, "I'm from America."

"Out of this world, mate!" laughed McCann.

The MC hushed the audience before introducing the next singer: "Ladies and gentlemen," he declared in an affected, sonorous voice, "Elvis has entered the building!"

A passionate cheer went up as a young man dressed in a white suit ornamented with glittering rhinestones moved toward the stage. McCann waved his free hand in the air to encourage the applause. "A warm welcome, if you please, for our friend Orestos, to sing the late Elvis Presley's winsome ballad, *Are You Lonesome Tonight*? Ladies and gentlemen, the king of rock and roll!"

As an Elvis impersonator, the debonair Albanian immigrant was flawless: indeed, the voice was impeccable, his movements were evocative, and the attitude he projected seemed to summon Presley from the grave. With eyes closed, he crooned into the microphone, wringing unbridled emotion from each lonely heart. "Isn't he marvelous?" said Gisela as she finished her second ouzo.

"An Albanian Elvis imitator? Never in my wildest imagination! But he'd probably take Vegas by storm," Doran laughed.

And as the song came to a crescendo, the audience called out the singer's name: "*O-res-tos*! *O-res-tos*! *O-res-tos*!" Perpetually in character, the counterfeit bowed graciously before walking off stage.

"Ladies and gentlemen, Elvis has left the building!" declared McCann. Though the fervent ovation did not subside for several more minutes.

Just after midnight the karaoke came to an end with a rousing rendition of *I Wanna Have Sex on the Beach*! sung by two Dutch girls, arm-in-arm. Their pantomimed antics instigated the well-soused crowd to frenzy, as nobody doubted the sincerity of their decree. Gisela had downed four drinks in two hours, and she was feeling no pain whatsoever. Doran was high as well. Though an inclination to measure his mirth had left him in far better control than his companion. He wandered outside for a breath of fresh air, as Gisela engaged a Greek man with an infectious smile in conversation.

The night air was balmy and a light breeze blew off Gouvia Bay. The moon had now moved behind Mount Pantocrator, so a thousand stars shone brightly in the black sky. And even after midnight Christopher Street was still quite active, as revelers seeking nightlife went from bar to bar. Doran looked inside the Navigator's through the plate glass window. Gisela was still with the Greek guy, who at twice her age seemed thrilled to have her attention. He had a healthy, golden complexion, a fit, compact body, silver hair and big teeth—magnanimous teeth as white as the whitewash on the walls of the Orthodox Church. They sat opposite one another, eye to glassy eye, talking in whispers.

Certainly this village was not the Kondokali that Doran remembered. But that was ten years ago, and memory was a fickle mistress. Anyway, change seemed to be the one thematic constant that defined his experience, so he was not inclined to judgment—at least not right now. As an itinerant he'd learned the art of patience: he preferred first to gather data, then summarize his impressions subconsciously; for he knew that ultimately a growing anthology of encounters and experiences would fashion his prevailing opinion. He walked back inside the pub, though he did not approach Gisela and her newfound companion. Instead he took a seat at the bar and ordered a brandy.

Drinking beside him was an English couple, (over sixty by their appearance), who immediately engaged him in cordial conversation. In a voice so low that it was difficult for Doran to hear each word over the barroom din, the man observed, "You're new here, aren't you?"

"I arrived just this morning," said Doran. "But I spent a summer here ten years ago," he explained.

"Right-o! Come back on holiday then?"

"Hopefully something more," said Doran.

"Bloody good!" he said raising his glass. "Cheers!"

Doran, too, lifted his glass to toast. "*Yamas*!" he said.

"You're American, aren't you?" asked the Englishman.

"Yes," said Doran, "but I've not been back to the States since I left ten years ago."

Nodding in instant camaraderie, his newfound drinking companion said, "That's like the missus and me, you know. We left England seven years ago. Went back once, but it was no use. Same old life back there, you understand. Corfu suits us well."

"A special place," Doran agreed as he sipped his brandy.

"My name is Philbar Cullinain," the Englishman offered.

"Doran Seeger. Pleased to meet you."

Cullinain turned to his female companion. "And this is m'better half," he said.

"Dazey with a *z*!" she informed as she put out her hand for Doran to shake.

"Where're you staying, mate?" asked the Englishman.

Doran motioned toward Gisela, who was now shamelessly kissing the Greek stranger full on the lips, before explaining, "Gisela and I are longtime friends. In fact, we met here on Corfu ten years ago. We'd not seen one another for many years… Until we recently reconnected in Prague… Ironically, our lives seemed to reach some sort of apex at the same time. One thing led to another, and after considering our options we decided to give this place another try. We've rented a small apartment in the village. From a Greek friend—a man we first met when we came here ten years ago. Maybe you know him: Modestos Thromos?"

"Can't say I know him," Cullinain confessed. "Mind you, we have a few Greek friends here. But in the end it always proves a bit difficult. Too many cultural differences. That's just the way."

Not knowing how to respond to such an analysis, Doran nodded politely before glancing once more over his shoulder at Gisela and her new friend. Lost within the reverie of yet another smooch, they were obviously both quite drunk. No matter. Doran suspected that after Gisela's difficult break-up with Alexi, and after her less than stellar experience in Prague—not to mention the fiasco in Kiev—she likely needed to let her hair down. By no means did he intend to be her chaperone. And as the kiss gradually lost its passion, and the flirtatious couple separated, the Greek smiled broadly while Gisela giggled in silly drunken amusement.

Philbar Cullinain told Doran that he and Dazey lived aboard a boat moored at Gouvia Marina. "Most of the ex-pats are sailors. And the marina is a secondary village—a satellite, if you will, of Kondokali. Our boat's called *Overdraft*. We're docked just opposite the Maestro Café. So feel free to come around anytime for a drink. You're always welcome."

"It's a small village," said Doran. "I'm sure we'll run into one another again."

"Cheers!" said Cullinain as he again lifted his glass.

Even after the karaoke crowd had dispersed, the pub was by no means empty or subdued. On the stereo, Sting begged a far too ardent schoolgirl, *'Don't stand, don't stand so, please don't stand so close to me*!' In a darkened corner a Korean girl, short and compact, danced with her mismatched, six-foot-six partner, who was know simply as Thirsty Harold. A longhaired Dane wearing soiled pink pants played chess with a fellow countryman who smoked one hand-rolled cigarette after another. A demure Pakistani sold bootleg CD's at the end of the long bar. A middle-aged Frenchman with a gray ponytail was accompanied by not one, but two beautiful women.

With visions of better things to come, Gisela's foxy admirer had bought her yet another ouzo. Not that she needed further encouragement. She was already drunk beyond remorse. Though Doran doubted that she could follow through with the flirtation. At this point he wondered whether or not she could even stand without falling flat on her face. Well aware of Gisela's condition, the bartender asked Doran if he'd like her to call a taxi to take them home.

"Well, we're not driving," he said. "And from the look of it, I'm not sure whether or not she'll be sleeping in her own bed."

"Good point," said the bartender. With raised eyebrows she smiled benignly.

"I'll speak with her," said Doran. "Let's see what she has in mind."

With no intention of placing himself between the couple, Doran approached his friend. "Everything okay?" he asked her.

"Splendid!" she said. "This is Spanos."

Doran turned to the Greek, who was obviously not threatened by his presence. "Hello, Spanos," he said.

"Hello, my friend!" said the Greek. His smile was indeed winning.

"I think I'm just about ready to head back to the apartment," he told her. "If you want to stay awhile longer, the bartender says she'll call a taxi for you."

"I'm thoroughly ripped," said Gisela. "I'd better come

119

along."

"Why leave now?" Spanos implored. "Have another ouzo. The night is young!"

Gisela smiled. "What would your wife say?" she teased.

"My wife is away in Germany," he beamed.

"All the more reason for me to go," she laughed.

"*Sagapo*, Chicitita! I love you!"

"You're wasted, Spanos!"

"No! Spanos no drunk. Everybody Spanos' friends. *Sagapo*! *Sagapo*!" The Greek's eyes rolled back in his head as he fell face first onto the tabletop.

"I guess that's that," said Doran.

Gisela giggled as she too staggered.

"What about that taxi?" Doran queried.

"No taxi," said Gisela.

"Do you think you can make it home?"

"Sure!" she proclaimed.

Outside, the nighttime air was warm. A gentle breeze continued to blow off the water. Doran put his arm around Gisela's waist to steady her as she walked, and Gisela laid her head upon his shoulder and sighed wistfully. "I don't want to go back to the apartment yet," she said. "I want to go to the beach."

"The beach?"

"Kondokali Beach."

"On the peninsula? Next to the big hotel?"

"Nobody will be there at this hour," she said.

"Probably not."

"What do you say? Come with me!"

"Do you think you can walk that far? I don't want to have to carry you all the way back to the apartment."

"Of course I can walk that far. I'm not *that* drunk."

"You had quite a few ouzos."

"I'm fine," she assured him.

"All right," he said.

With the lights of the Kondakali Bay Hotel as a beacon, they set out along Odos Irithos, en route to the local beach. Gisela's steps were slow and uncertain, and Doran regulated his stride to accommodate her impaired gait. From time to time they held hands, or walked arm-in-arm, or stopped to admire a prolific grove of eucalyptus trees cast in silhouette against the backdrop of the night sky. Carried upon the damp night air they could hear the distant sound of Greek music: bouzoukis and accordions striking out happy melodies over an accompaniment of chords played on guitar. "*Opa! Opa!*" cried the musicians again and again, as the sound of plates smashing on marble floors defined a particular rhythm.

It was after two in the morning when they reached the beach, and just as they'd expected, nobody was around. Across the bay they could see the shrouded lights of the harbor, but on Kondakali Beach itself—a small cove of sand and two or three grottos protected by a verdant escarpment on two sides—only the flickering lights of fireflies punctuated the otherwise perfect darkness.

"Look!" Gisela called gleefully as she wobbled over the uneven sand. "There must be thousands of them!"

"When I was a kid back in Texas, we called them Lightning Bugs," said Doran. "My sister and I captured them in jars."

"Why?"

"Once the twilight had gone, we pretended the jars were lanterns to light our way."

"What a charming memory!" said Gisela.

"A shame such innocence disappears as we grow older," he said.

"Oh, but it doesn't have to disappear, Doran! Really, it doesn't!" Without embarrassment she stripped off her clothes and went running into the swarm, bobbing and jumping and spinning in drunken rapture.

"You're one-in-a-million, Z!" Doran called after her. He sank to the sand and lay back to gaze into the starry sky.

"This is magical!" she called from the other end of the

beach. "Take off your clothes and join me!"

"You're drunk as a skunk, Gisela!" he proclaimed.

"And you're not?"

"Not as drunk as you are!"

"This is like dancing naked among the stars," she squealed. "Give it a try, Seeger!"

"I'm not so sure the gods want to see me naked," he hedged.

"Don't be such a curmudgeon, Doran!"

"Is that what I am to you, Z?"

"If you don't strip and shine, I'll come right over there and peel you myself!"

"Really?"

"It's a promise, boy."

What choice did he have? Apparently Gisela meant business. So he watched as she whirled in dizzy amazement among the tiny pulsating phosphorescent lights, and he kicked off his sandals, unbuttoned his shirt, and slipped out of his jeans. He stood naked against the night, the sentient air wrapping itself around his body like a cloak. And he ran barefoot over the sand towards a girl he'd once known—a girl now grown into a woman—the sister of his former lover.

Together they ran after the pulsating points of light, randomly changing direction to pursue each flash of illumination: flailing, laughing, never really hoping or expecting to capture or hold on to such a beacon: a scatty, frolicsome pursuit; two souls chasing the white radiance of eternity. Finally out of breath, they joined hands and stood amidst the firefly firmament. The surf washed gently upon the shore. The prolific beachside vegetation exhaled pure oxygen. The atmosphere hummed with energy.

Gisela sighed as she trembled against a sudden chill. Doran put his arms around her. In an embrace as familiar as it was anonymous, they exuded a glowing white aura, a benign light not unlike the pulsing hue emitted by fireflies at dusk.

And the stars swirled overhead: tiny points of light in the vast blackness. Giddy, drunken stars shining in heaven's ebon vault. At the edge of the world the ground beneath their feet became unstable. Aphrodite sang her eternal song to Poseidon. "This is impossible," she murmured. "Yet, it's inevitable," he conceded. Drawn into the abyss, they kissed passionately.

The light of day broke with total candor, and after having slept only three hours Doran rose reluctantly to confront the veracity of an untimely and superfluous encounter. Gisela lay naked and uncovered on the bed beside him, her tawny hair falling over her pillow in disarray, her expression suggesting perfect detachment. And though his remembrances and impressions remained hazy, and his personal forecast somewhat unsettled, the sight of her lean and muscular body—her rounded shoulders, her globular breasts and fleshy thighs, her big hands and feet—initiated within him a plethora of emotions ranging from delight to self-recrimination.

In drunken reverie they had stripped off their clothes to chase fireflies, and finally dizzy and out of breath they had turned to face one another, only to be drawn together by a force neither had suspected or acknowledged. Doran's first reaction to the soft wet kiss from Gisela's supple lips was one of surprise, and he'd nearly turned away. But the insistence of her passion had rendered any resistance futile. So instead of rebuffing her advance, he put his arms around the small of her back and pulled her closer. A second kiss followed the first. Her firm round breasts pushed against his chest, and her smooth torso caressed his belly. Lost in the ecstasy of a compelling embrace, they sank to their knees. They lay upon the cool sand as trembling fingers sought out secret places. And Doran recalled that Gisela had murmured softly as he moved over her. A few feet away the sea lapped gently against the shore. And then he was inside her, and she drew him deeper and deeper into her mystery.

But her unexpected passion had not ended there. Like a wrestler executing a reversal, Gisela had flipped him onto his back and straddled him, her physical strength coming as a total surprise to him. And she stared out to sea as she moved up and down upon him, rotating her hips in rhythmic abeyance to her agonizing desire. Doran knew that she would willingly have come before him had it so happened, but their climax was simultaneous. Just as he reached his climax, Gisela clutched her breasts and arched her back. Her leg muscles constricted and she shuddered as a wave of pleasure washed over her body. Once they'd relaxed, they waded into the sea chest deep to cool their fire.

As a younger man he'd been easily coaxed into sumptuous pools of affection; he'd swum there often and freely. But he'd learned through experience that awkward dependencies often developed far too quickly for his liking. And this particular connection certainly had its own set of peculiar circumstances. Of course, he'd been quite drunk, as had Gisela. Still, the sense of abandon that each had shown seemed to address not so much a momentary lapse of judgment, rather a longstanding, if well-concealed, desire. This in itself was troubling, for Doran knew that certain knots, once taught, were difficult to untie.

He showered, shaved, and dressed as Gisela slept. Leaving the apartment, he closed the door quietly so as not to disturb her. At Restaurant Pericles he sat at an outdoor table beneath a leafy eucalyptus tree to cultivate the tranquility so necessary for his various ruminations. He ordered a much-needed cup of coffee. The Nescafe cleared his head but rumbled in his stomach. Still, all things considered, he probably felt better than he should have felt. Gisela, he suspected, might not fare so well. And sometime during the much-abbreviated night—perhaps shortly after he'd fallen asleep—he'd heard her in the bathroom. She was obviously in distress, and he'd called out her name. "Okay, okay," she'd answered. Understanding that his presence might only contribute to her humiliation, he'd chosen to preserve her privacy at such a moment.

Just how Gisela might feel in retrospect about their passionate and serendipitous encounter remained uncertain, though before the day was out, he understood, they would have to face one another. Such a realization, even more than his memory of the incident itself, contributed to Doran's pervasive uneasiness. The situation was sopping with poor judgment, if not drowning in duplicity. He'd neither sought nor courted Gisela's affections. Nor had she invited his—at least not openly. Doran might have demanded from himself a better-defined sense of compunction, his relationship with Scarlet serving as a well-heeled model. They had fortunately avoided the so-called dirty deed as each in time became aware of certain impediments. Gisela, too, was presumably savvy enough to know better. Yet, the fundamental chemistry between them was apparently quite volatile, and even well practiced restraint had not stopped the boulder from falling off the mountain. And once it began to roll momentum was everything. How might they justify their indiscretion, if indeed justification was even necessary? And how might they proceed, precluding the possibility that their actions had not finished the friendship once and for all? Whether such morning-after impressions were bittersweet and guilt-ridden, or infatuated and enthusiastic, Doran knew that a bumpy road lay before them.

Before returning to the apartment, Doran shopped for a few groceries at Supermarket Trofo. He bought bread and milk and butter and eggs, pasta and tomatoes and salad, vegetables and orange juice, a bottle of wine. He also bought bath towels and cleaning supplies, shampoo and hair conditioner, soap and disposable razors, and a package of aspirin. In bright morning sunshine he walked back to the apartment off Christopher Street with two heavy sacks in his arms.

Unpacking the provisions in the kitchen, Doran listened for any sound that might indicate that Gisela was awake, but he heard nothing. Behind the room divider she lay inert upon her bed. For a moment he considered slipping out of his clothes and crawling into bed beside her, but he quickly banished such a notion, the dismissal coming as much from his own uncertainty as out of consideration for her condition. Moving quietly through the apartment, he took time to re-organize his belongings. He smoked several cigarettes. He reset his wristwatch. He checked the telephone for a dial tone. He examined his about-to-expire passport. Sitting at the desk located in the long alcove, he wrote a short letter to his sister in Las Vegas informing her of his whereabouts.

Shortly after noon he heard Gisela stir. He did not intrude. Twenty minutes passed. He focused his attention on the ticking of the wind-up clock atop the credenza. He lit another cigarette. He wanted to call out her name. He wanted to say something meaningful to her. But any sentiment he might express seemed inappropriate and graceless. To Doran, no circumstance seemed worse than interpersonal ambiguity.

Finally, he heard her up and about, and he peeked around the door leading to the salon. Nude and bent forward, Gisela rummaged through her still-unpacked bag looking for her bathrobe. Her hair was disheveled, her complexion pallid. He noticed that her hands were afflicted with a slight tremor. Not finding the garment for which she searched, she cursed under her breath then padded off to the bathroom, still naked.

Doran remained in the alcove. He heard water running in the bathroom as she washed her face, brushed her teeth, and combed her hair. When she returned to the salon, he called out to her, "Are you okay?"

She grumbled an inaudible reply.

"Are you dressed? Can I come in?" he asked.

"Of course," she allowed.

He moved tentatively through the half-open doorway into the salon. She was standing before the mirror wearing only her bra and panties. "Rough morning," he assessed.

Turning from her reflection to face him, her expression was mordant, though tolerant. Though she'd scrubbed her face vigorously, her color remained ashen. "Give me a cigarette," she said. He retrieved the opened package of Marlboros from the alcove and handed her one. She had to strike her lighter several times before it ignited. She inhaled the first puff and rolled her eyes before expelling the smoke. Between her fingers the cigarette quivered. "How long have you been up?" she asked.

"Several hours," he told her.

"You bought towels."

"Yes."

"Thanks."

Doran shrugged. "I bought groceries as well. Nothing much. But if you're hungry…"

"I can't even think about food," she groaned.

"That bad, eh?"

"I puked twice last night," she drolly informed him.

"I heard you in the bathroom. I didn't want to intrude."

"Thank you," she said sarcastically.

"I warned you about drinking too much ouzo."

"Please, no lectures."

"Okay. Anything I can do for you?"

"Bring me a glass of water," she requested.

"I'm not so sure you want to drink water," he cautioned.

"Why not?"

"Ouzo hangovers are strange. If you drink something—anything—you'll be sick again."

"Great!"

"Gisela, we have to talk," he said seriously.

"About what?"

"About last night."

"What about it?"

"What do you mean, what about it?"

Her look was both vague and inquisitive. She sat on one of the chairs, drew her knees up to her chest, and wrapped her arms around her bare legs. "What's to talk about?" she asked.

"You know... Last night... On the beach..."

"What beach?" she said.

"You don't remember being at the beach?"

She shrugged sheepishly.

"We were chasing fireflies," he recalled.

"Fireflies?"

"Yes. At Kondokali Beach."

She shrugged again.

"What *do* you remember?" he asked.

"I remember the karaoke sing-along. And that crazy Albanian in the sequined suit who impersonated Elvis Presley... And I remember kissing that funny little Greek guy," she said. "What was his name?"

"Spanos."

"Right."

"After we left the pub we walked to Kondokali Beach," he prompted her.

"If you say so."

"Gisela!"

"What?"

"You honestly don't remember, do you?"

"You're making all this up," she accused.

"Why would I do that?"

"I don't know."

"Check the clothes you were wearing last night for sand," he suggested.

She cocked her head to dismiss his suggestion. "Are you sure I can't have a drink of water?" she said.

"You'll only be sick again. Take my word for it."

"I'm *so* thirsty."

Doran found the shorts and the blouse she'd worn the night before. A little perturbed, Gisela watched as he shook sand onto the floor. "I told you we were at the beach last night," he said.

"I don't remember much of anything," she said.

"You must remember something," he implored.

"I'm afraid not," she said.

"Then this is worse than I thought," he ruminated.

"What's worse than you thought, Doran?"

"I don't know how to tell you—"

"Tell me what?"

"Sex! On the beach!"

"Oh, yeah, I remember that stupid song they were singing at the end of the karaoke."

"Gisela, you're being obtuse."

"What are you talking about?"

"Last night we made love on the beach."

For a moment she was silent. She puffed on her cigarette then rested her chin upon her drawn-up knees. "In your dreams, Seeger," she said.

"You really don't remember?"

"What sort of game are you playing, Doran?"

"No game."

"This isn't like you, Seeger."

"I'm not spinning tales, Z."

"I don't like what you're implying," she said.

"I'm not implying anything. I'm telling you what happened."

"No, it didn't happen. I would remember."

"We walked to the beach. You stripped naked and went running into a swarm of fireflies. You made me strip too. And we made love in the sand, Gisela."

"I have such a hangover," she moaned.

Doran didn't know what to think of her denial. And it seemed pointless to discuss the issue further—at least for now. He took a moment to gather his composure. "Would you like an aspirin?" he said finally.

"Do you have aspirin?" she asked.
"I bought some this morning."
"Give me three," she said.

Gisela had feigned ignorance with such conviction that she nearly believed her own denial. But of course she did not believe it. She knew perfectly well what had happened. She remembered leaving the Navigator's Bar and walking under a dome of swirling stars to Kondokali Beach. And she remembered shedding her clothes as if they were ablaze and running naked down the shoreline towards a thousand tiny points of light, a thousand neon ballerinas dancing and whirling in mid-air. And she remembered all-too-well calling ecstatically for Doran to strip naked and join her. Then and there she had known what would happen. She'd known... But she'd refused to consider consequences, for she wanted only to feel the warmth of his body as it pressed close to hers, and she'd wanted desperately to feel the electricity of his touch as he explored each forbidden recess of her body. She felt desperate to cast off the emotional scars of her recent past, and she so wanted to lose herself in the arms of a man she trusted, a man who would be kind and gentle to her, a man with whom she shared a likeness in attitude and approach—a friend in kind! But now, after the fact, she could not openly acknowledge the act. Not to Doran; and certainly not to her sister Alarice!

Under present circumstances, Gisela could not remain inside the apartment, so she showered and dressed and set out with no specific destination in mind for a walk. At the village bakery she bought a small crusty loaf of bread. At a second shop she bought a soft drink. Then she headed along a twisting road leading into the low hills behind the village.

The ascent was gentle as she walked past pastures with grazing goats or sheep, through groves of olive trees shading pretty houses painted ochre or pink, along a stone wall covered by blooming geraniums. Taking an adjacent footpath as a shortcut, she encountered a farmer who gave her a cup filled with freshly picked raspberries, then offered to show her his pig. To be cordial she had a look at the sow, and together they praised its plumpness. And before she said good-bye and went on her way, the farmer loaded her arms with ripe kumquats.

Around a steep switchback, the road turned from asphalt to gravel. In the distance she heard the bleating of lambs and kids, and the braying of donkeys. Swallows swooped overhead, finches twittered in the low branches of the Cyprus trees, and an Exaltation of Lark sang in a nearby meadow. An opening in a verdant hedgerow led her into a long-ago-abandoned citrus grove.

Through long grass Gisela wandered among orange trees and lemon trees until she came upon the ruins of a small cottage. No doubt once the rustic home of a bucolic Corfiot, the roof of the house was now partially collapsed, its broken tiles cluttering the hardened earthen floor. The window shutters were still whole and in place, though the warped door was now off its hinges. Outside the front door of the cottage grew a lemon tree with a wide canopy, and underneath the tree stood a dilapidated, sagging wagon, one wheel broken and nearly off the axel.

From a tree heavy with ripened fruit, Gisela picked an orange and sat near the old wagon in the long grass. She peeled off the rind and tasted a single section. Delighted by the sweetness, she ate the rest of the fruit as juice ran over her fingers and down her arm. Once the orange was eaten, she broke the bread. The inside of the loaf was still warm from the baker's oven, and it smelled of yeast and butter. The crust was crisp and firm, but the inside was soft as cake. She ate several pieces before lying back on the grassy loam.

A *secret garden*, she thought to herself. A place where silvery light filtered through pale leaves and fell upon shadowy ground: an idyllic place! A place to think; or not think at all: a place where she might come time and again to ground herself. And she seemed to understand instinctively that she should say nothing about this hide-away to anyone, for more than ever she needed a place of refuge: a place to define issues; a place to reassess; and a place to determine appropriate riposte…

For the events of her life had seemed recently to unfold with unsettling rapidity: the tumultuous break-up with Alexi and her subsequent flight from Portugal to Prague; her curious reunion with Doran Seeger; the trip to Kiev and the robbery; and finally her return to Corfu. She did not regret leaving Alexi and she did not miss him; though she did lament the fact that the life she'd once envisioned in Lagos had never materialized. Last night's encounter with Doran, though seemingly vital at the moment, had been in retrospect quite myopic; and she could not help wondering just what he might be feeling, not only concerning the incident itself, but also about her denial that it had ever taken place. Whatever his reaction to her refutation, such a disclaimer had at the time seemed to be the only way out of an impossible situation.

After leaving the secret garden, Gisela did not return immediately to the village. Instead, she hiked further into the hills; and at the end of a particularly long ascent a magnificent vista opened in her wake. Below her position, Kondokali village lay midway around the arc of Gouvia Bay. On a peninsula to her right was Corfu's deep-water harbor, as well as the city itself, which was dominated by the ancient twin fortresses. And to her left stretched Kerkyra's northern coastline, with its succession of hospitable resorts tucked neatly into successive coves, and its fundamental villages and pastures and farms embellishing the mid-highlands, and finally the summit of Mount Pantocrator looking petulantly down upon the whole of the northern isthmus. Across the bay rose the stark-looking mountains of Albania. But it was the water that most affected her, its deep azure tranquility acting as a fluidic mirror.

Just look at this place, she told herself. Look at the sea, look at the mountains, the shoreline, the olive groves, the pastures, the flowers! Feel the implications of the undulating terrain! Hear the echo of antiquity! And the light! The light! Sun and sea and land—I am here! Now, I am dancing in a contemporary circle; I am dancing to the ancient music of this place, Hellas!

Yes, the dancing! Dizzy dancing among the flickering, random lights of fireflies, *in naked beauty more adorned*. To touch the light is to extinguish it, she thought, but to whirl and whirl among shimmering intimations of radiance is sheer ecstasy. For the essence of existence is revealed not in stasis, but in perpetual motion. The process is axial, yet ever-changing. Dancing among fireflies, Gisela knew not where the next flash of light might appear; yet the randomness of each beacon had only amplified her sense of delight.

Ultimately the vital impact of sensation held more weight than any imparted philosophy. *Upon this bank and shoal of time*, her life's intrigues and inconsistencies and uncertainties fell away like the clothes she'd shed last night on the beach; and once again Gisela stood naked in the sentient garden.

CHAPTER 7
A TRIP TO OLD PERITHEA

During his first week on Corfu, Doran paid a visit to the American Consulate for advice concerning his soon-to-expire passport. There the consular informed him that simple re-issuance was doubtful due to the fact that he'd not returned to the U.S. for nearly ten years. "The law states that any American citizen living abroad must 'touch American soil' every seven years for his national status to remain valid," the consular explained. "Of course the seven year law is largely symbolic; and it may even seem outdated, or a bit arbitrary, considering the present-day realities of the business world. But institutions are slow to adapt, and in your case the law is likely to be cited."

"So you're telling me that my passport is not likely to be re-issued simply because I've not been back to kiss American ground?"

"Fundamentally correct, Mr. Seeger."

"Before coming to Europe I worked for a number of years as an engineer in the private sector on American Defense Department contracts," Doran postured. "And during those years, the government had no better servant than me."

"Your situation is ironic, Mr. Seeger. But your work history is probably inconsequential. Of course you can make your application at the embassy in Athens. It can't hurt to try."

"The real irony is that I'm not particularly interested in renewing my American passport. Truthfully, I'd much rather obtain documentation from the European Community. After all, I've lived and worked in Europe for nearly ten years!"

"Do you have proof of residency?" asked the consular.

"Nothing official," Doran conceded.

"Then I'm afraid that obtaining a European Community passport might prove quite difficult. And once your American passport expires, technically speaking, you become a Stateless person. Certainly you want to avoid such a dilemma. And the best way to do that is to return to the United States and take the necessary steps to renew your documentation."

"But I have no wish to return to the U.S.—at least not now. Nor do I presently have the means to do so anyway."

"At any rate, your problem is certainly not insoluble, but I strongly suggest that you don't ignore it. Without a passport your mobility will be severely limited. Not to mention inconveniences in dealing with various local agencies: banks, utility companies, et cetera."

"What about a Greek passport?"

"By presenting yourself to the Greek authorities, you'll of course expose yourself as an illegal alien."

"Surely the Greek Government doesn't want the headache of dealing with a so-called Stateless person."

"They could deport you."

"Is that likely to happen?"

"Present status notwithstanding, you are an American citizen. And the Greek attitude towards the United States has always been a bit fickle. On one hand, there are probably as many Greeks living in the U.S. as there are in all Greece. And the U.S. is certainly well remembered for its role in the Cyprus conflict, as well as for its commitment to protect and defend Macedonia. Yet, contradictions remain. The recent NATO bombing of Serbia—of course led by the United States—deeply angered many Greeks. The inevitable result of similarities in culture and religion, you understand. At any rate, the relationship between the two countries, politically speaking, is always a bit ambiguous. And you have to remember, too, that a certain amount of ethnocentrism is, at present, politically fashionable—not only in Greece, but in Europe as a whole! I know it's difficult, Mr. Seeger, but you must consider all the circumstances. I think I'd be inclined to take the path of least resistance."

On the short bus ride back to Kondokali village, Doran considered not the implications of his political status, rather the various impressions left on his consciousness during his first week on Corfu. Yes, he'd now grown accustomed to the clanging of the church bells each morning at half past eight, as he'd also become familiar with the call of Yiannis the fishmonger, who arrived on his motorcycle each morning at nine o'clock sharp to peddle fresh sardines and squid from the bike's side cart. He was now well acquainted with the smells of cooking that came from Fedra Koukourous' kitchen at the noon hour, as he was also tuned in to the sounds of Euro-pop music that came from the next door apartments of the Venetti family each day after the siesta was finished. At night, Fedra's husband Mikalis could be heard for blocks calling out, "*Opa!*" as he danced around flaming clay pots to *Zorba's Theme*. Across the road from Taverna Lithari lived an old toothless woman who kept chickens inside an abandoned storefront and pushed a shopping cart through the village, collecting bits of cast-off cloth, which she used to patch holes in her timeworn dress. Each evening children played in the park until midnight; and after sunset idlers congregated outside the *cava* to drink beer and bemoan their particular fates. Indeed, Kondokali village was not as it had been ten years ago: the once prolific tourists were now all but gone; and the society had returned, albeit in modern dress, to its cultural roots. And that was fine with Doran: the elemental nature of day-to-day Greek life seemed to suit his temperament well. Though he was not so sure what effect it might be having on Gisela.

In fact, he'd not seen much of his new roommate during the past week—not since their drunken encounter on Kondakali Beach, and her subsequent denial of the same. Apparently Gisela had quickly initiated her own rhythms and activities, often leaving the apartment before he awoke, and not returning until late at night. And Doran was one day surprised to see that she had cut her hair short and dyed it red. With her new look had come a fresh persona—one that he had to admit was quite foreign to him. At this point he could only wonder what strange destiny might come his way as a result of coming to Corfu with her.

Of course sex had complicated everything. It was never good when it was casual. But the irony was that it never seemed casual until the morning after. Especially when drink was part of the mix. So he was now forced to deal on his own with the aftermath, complicated though it seemed to be. And it certainly seemed incongruous that an act of such total intimacy had ultimately created utter resistance between them. But that was certainly the case.

Returning to the house on Christopher Street, Doran found Modestos at work in the garden, sweeping up fallen leaves from the overhead arbor. "*Yasou*, my friend!" called the Greek as Doran came through the gate. He stopped sweeping, wiped sweat from his forehead, and took a package of cigarettes from his shirt pocket.

"Hello, Modestos," said Doran.

"Takis clean everything," he said as he struck a match. Then he offered Doran a cigarette, too.

"Thanks," said Doran as he took one from the open pack.

"Everything okay?" Modestos inquired as he struck a second match and held it out.

"A small problem," Doran related as he exhaled the first puff.

"What problem?" asked Modestos.

"This morning I visited the American Consulate. About my soon-to-expire passport."

"What do they tell you?" Modestos wanted to know.

"Apparently, it will be difficult to get a new one," he said.

"I don't understand, what is the problem?"

"I've not been back to America for almost ten years."

"Maybe they don't remember you, eh?"

"Something like that," said Doran.

Together they sat in the shade of the grape arbor. "Anyway, I believe it is not so difficult to take a new one," said the Greek.

"American or Greek?"

"Maybe you like to take a Greek one," said Modestos.

"At this point in my life, it would seem to make more sense," said Doran.

Modestos nodded thoughtfully. "Perhaps I can help you, my friend."

"How could you help?" Doran queried.

"Perhaps it is only a matter of speaking with the right person. If you like, I will ask my friend, who has another friend, who has a brother, who has an uncle, who works in government… Understand?"

"Not really," Doran smiled.

"Never mind. If I learn something helpful, I will tell you."

"Knock yourself out," Doran invited, and Takis cocked his head at the unfamiliar idiom.

"Anyway, maybe you like to come with Elena and me to the north side of the island?"

"When?" Doran asked.

"Tomorrow morning we go to a place called Old Perithea—the oldest village on Corfu. High on the mountain. Not so many people living there now. Only a few shepherds. And one man who keeps bees. We go there to buy the best honey. You like to come with us?"

Remembering the many extraordinary food-finding missions that Modestos had conducted ten years ago, he said, "Sure, Takis. I'd like to come with you."

"What about the girl, Stella?"

"I don't know," said Doran. "But I'll ask her."

"Okay! I will pass here tomorrow at eleven o'clock. If you still like to come along, be ready then."

"Okay," said Doran.

To Doran's surprise, Gisela was indeed interested in going along on the trip to Old Perithea; so at precisely eleven o'clock, they waited together in front of Pension Aphrodite for Modestos and Elena to arrive. The hour came and went with no sign of Takis. "Greek time," Doran commented, and Gisela smiled knowingly.

Doran was happy to see that for the first time in more than a week Gisela was in a relaxed and familiar mood. As the change had seemed to come out of nowhere, he watched her closely for signs of duplicity, but found none; and he was indeed relieved to see the re-emergence of her former personality. Not inclined to tempt fate with an obtuse comment, he hoped the repercussions of their so-called incident were now behind them.

"I've discovered the most extraordinary place," she told him.

"During the course of your travels last week?"

"Yes. In the low hills above the village, there is a hedgerow that lines the side of the road. At a particular spot, there is a hole in the shrubbery. One day I happened to tumble through it, like Alice in Wonderland!"

"And there you met the March Hare?"

"Thankfully, no. But beyond the hedge there is a magnificent sloping grove of orange trees and lemon trees. There is also an abandoned cottage—very old—and an old wagon, too. I call it my secret garden. I've gone there nearly every day this week to read and write in my journal. There's something nourishing, or renewing, about the place, Doran."

"You'll have to take me there. Unless you're keeping it as a private sanctuary."

"If I were," she said, "I would never have told you about it."

"Maybe one day next week we could take a picnic lunch and spend the day there," he suggested.

"Yes, I'd like that," Gisela said. She folded her hands and lowered her eyes in thought. "We do need to talk," she added.

Once Modestos and Elena arrived, any semblance of tranquility was immediately lost. The Greek jumped out of his car with an exaggerated sense of urgency—as if he were late for his own funeral—and tossed their daypacks into the trunk. He held open the rear door for Gisela, and Doran slid in beside her. In effect, Takis seemed to materialize in the driver's seat and throw the car into forward gear even before Doran had slammed the rear door shut. Off they went, bound for the north side of Corfu Island, Takis consternating in Greek about a delivery truck blocking the road, as Elena fiddled with the radio tuner searching the dial not for Greek folk songs, but for Euro-pop music.

"Just like old times," Doran commented under his breath to Gisela. Again, she smiled.

Up the northern coastline they drove, through the resort villages of Gouvia and Dassia and Ypsos. On the left rose the verdant foothills leading to Mount Pantocrator; on the right, the sea shone like an amethyst. Around dangerous curves Modestos honked his horn but gave no ground. They passed an ancient church, a roadside vendor selling sprigs of rosemary, and an ancient wall of stone draped in heliotropic splendor. After Ypsos, the road ascended quickly, and they parked on a cliffside that overlooked Nissaki. Across the water, Corfu Town was visible in the distance. Further along, they stopped for coffee at a lovely little cove called Kouloura. There a picturesque marina sheltered fishing boats and small pleasure craft; and the view from the wharf was of a vast mountainside covered with yellow flowers.

"Not with all the money in the world can a man buy such beauty!" commented Modestos. Doran nodded. And Gisela could not help but agree. "The whole world has gone crazy for money," Modestos lamented. "But in the end, money is useless. It cannot buy happiness or peace of mind."

Again, Doran agreed.

"Let me tell you a story about Onasis," Modestos offered. "Of course you know Onasis!

"When Ari was at the pinnacle of his wealth, and at the peak of his veracity, too," Takis began, "the multi-billionaire shipping magnate called a news conference for all the journalists in Greece. He told them that he had decided to offer a sizeable prize to anyone who could guess the actual worth of his worldly possessions. Onasis himself probably had no idea of the true number; still, considering the prize, many people ventured a guess. But not one Greek was able to put a value on his diverse holdings. Finally, a Sicilian with a very audacious nature came to Onasis and said: '*Signore* Aristotle, I know precisely how much you have in this world.' Ari was skeptical but he conceded, 'If you tell me accurately, my friend, then the prize is yours.' So the Italian made Onasis give him a piece of paper and a pencil, and he drew out a rectangle that measured exactly one meter by two-and-a-half meters. 'There!' he said. 'This is how much any man owns of this earth!' Of course the prize was his."

Doran and Gisela both smiled as they drank their

coffee, while Elena only looked distracted.

"There is another story about Onasis," Takis offered.

And his audience of two gave their rapt attention.

"Apparently, when Aristotle Onasis was on his deathbed, he'd become so ill that he could no longer open his mouth. His jaw was frozen shut. So he asked his doctor for a piece of paper and a pencil and wrote out a message: 'If you can open my mouth,' the message read, 'and bring me a cup of olives and a bit of bread, I will give you all my money!' And the doctor took the pencil from Onasis and wrote his answer: 'Now, only God can open your mouth.' This is a true story!" confirmed Modestos.

"I'm sure there are a hundred stories about Onasis," Doran said.

"*Po, po, po*," said the Greek. "Ari was a very rich man—probably the richest man in the world! But most Greeks do not love money too much. If the heart is bursting with kindness and generosity," Modestos surmised, "then it is not so important that the pocket is full."

Doran nodded his agreement as he lit a cigarette. "Still, the material life is a struggle for some," he said.

"*Endaksi*. But in the end, the marble has the final word."

"The marble?" said Gisela.

Takis smiled. "*Nai*, this is the way. You see, there once was a great debate held between Marble and Gold—to determine which one was more important. Gold was allowed to speak first, and Gold pompously maintained, 'Surely I am most important. Kings wear me around their fingers, and the *papas* where me around their necks. Without me, you can do nothing. I am everything!' And then it was Marble's turn to speak, and Marble replied, 'What you say about the kings and the priests is true, my friend, but in the end everybody comes to me—even you!' So, money is never the measure of a man. Money is only money."

"I was once a slave for gold," Doran bitterly admitted.

"Not that I really wanted money. But I was ignorant and easily led, and I helped make bombs and other weapons of war, and the American Government gave me money—lots of it! The money was supposed to numb my conscience and pacify my guilt—a rather convoluted sort of justification, I think. But when I saw the results of my work, I was forced to break my chains."

"The Americans are always anxious to send their planes, it seems. F-16's, F-17's, B-1 bombers. Very powerful, indeed! Now the Serbs know all about it. But what is really gained?" wondered Modestos.

Back in the car, they drove further north to a sheltered beach called *Agios Spyrodon*. Standing on the shore, the ambiance was sublime: the Ionian Sea, deep blue even as it met the distant horizon; and Mount Pantocrator casting its pervasive shadow over forested ground that sloped ever so gently toward the northern coastline. Modestos prepared a primitive fishing line and motioned for Doran to follow him up the coastline. Together they walked to a place where the sandy beach gave way to a rock-covered jetty. There they waded hip-deep into the water, and the Greek put out his lure. "Now is not the right time for catching fish," he admitted. "But maybe today I am lucky. We'll see."

Meanwhile, Elena had taken Gisela in tow and led her into the water. With a small knife in one hand, and two plastic bags in the other, she scraped sea urchins off the rocks. After harvesting two-dozen creatures, she handed the knife to Gisela and implored, "You try now!"

Gisela took the knife and bent low to locate her quarry. Finding a colony of urchins on a large flat stone, she tried to pry one away with the blade, but failed. She tried a second time, but again came up empty-handed. After several more unsuccessful attempts at scraping urchins from the rock to which they clung, Gisela handed the knife back to her tutor for another lesson in technique. Elena was only too happy to oblige. She reached into the water, her face just above the surface, and deftly scraped up another creature. "Not so difficult," she said as she handed the knife back to Gisela.

This time Gisela was able to bring up one of the black spiny creatures. She handed it to Elena, who, disregarding the sharp quills, promptly pried it open and scooped out the eggs inside with her finger. She put the fish row in her mouth and assessed the flavor: "Very tasty!" she smiled. "How many do you want to take home? At least twenty," she suggested.

"Twenty?" Gisela asked dubiously.

"No less," Elena advised. "Very tasty on dark bread," she said.

"Like caviar," said Gisela.

"*Nai, nai,*" Elena smiled. "Costs nothing," she laughed.

And as Takis reeled in one small fish after another, he said to Doran, "Not so important—only food for cats. But in October we return to this beach for fishing—you and me! We come here very early—to surprise the fish! Or maybe we sleep on the beach and wake up before the sun comes up. That way, catching many. Very tasty! No pay for food."

Each now carrying a plastic bag filled with sea urchins, Elena and Gisela waded back to shore. Elena instructed the novice concerning cleaning and preparation; and Gisela commented that Modestos could probably devour everything they'd harvested at a single sitting.

"Takis like too much!" Elena confirmed. "But no eating now."

"Why not?" Gisela queried.

"Problem Takis... Very bad stomach," she explained.

Modestos and Doran remained in the water long after the women had gone ashore. "As you know, my friend," Takis' monolog continued, "there are many opportunities on Corfu to obtain fresh food. From the sea we take fish. If you come to the right place at the right time, catching many. Also, many olive trees! Ten trees for every person on Corfu! I have a small grove on the mountain—about forty trees. Old ones. This winter I will put out the nets. If I am lucky, catching many olives. The best ones for eating; the others I save for the press. Very good oil—no chemicals! Understand?"

Doran nodded. He remembered well Modestos' passion for fresh food.

"And when the rain begins—around the end of October or the beginning of November—it is possible to grow many vegetables."

"During winter?"

"The best time," Takis confirmed. "No need for irrigation."

"Where do you grow vegetables?" Doran inquired.

"I have some ground near Kondokali," Takis explained. "Very good ground—about one thousand square meters. I will take you there. Maybe tomorrow."

"I'd like to see it," said Doran.

"When I was a boy," Takis explained, "my father grew potatoes on this ground. *Po, po, po*! And onions! And *kukia*, too!"

"What's that?" Doran asked.

"*Kukia*? Long beans. Very tasty."

"So every winter you grow a vegetable garden?"

The Greek sighed wistfully. "I like to make a farm," he said. "But Modestos now growing old. Sometimes very difficult."

"Maybe I could lend a hand," Doran offered.

"You like too much this work?" Modestos queried as his eyebrows rose.

Doran shrugged. "What else do I have to do?"

"*Nai, nai*! You help me by preparing the ground and digging some holes. I buy everything we need. If we are lucky, the rain will come at just the right time, and we will take many vegetables. We divide the harvest by two. No pay for food. Understand? Maybe we sell potatoes at the street market in the town. We'll see. Anyway, I am happy that you like to help me, my friend."

Apparently a bargain had been struck.

Having rejoined the women, a few minutes were given to admire Takis' catch, and to remark over Elena's and Gisela's harvest of sea urchins, then they were back inside the car and heading up the twisting road leading to Old Perithea.

In springtime, Corfu was resplendent with blossoms of many varieties: lilies and lantana; cherry blossoms and mimosa flowers, and the fragrant yellow blooms that covered each acacia tree; emerging bougainvillea in red or white or orange; blue phlox; clover; geraniums and ruby begonias. Halfway up the slope of Pantocrator, the road ended where the ancient village began.

"Old Perithea is the oldest village on Corfu," Modestos reiterated to Doran.

But that hardly made sense. "Why didn't the first Corfiots make their settlement by the sea?" he asked.

"Danger from pirates," said Modestos.

And it was at once obvious that from their elevated position one would no doubt have seen the advance of an approaching ship long before it arrived at Kerkyra.

Walking into the village over uneven cobbled roadways—streets that were at most meant for a crude cart, if not the hooves of a donkey, or a goat, or a human foot—the foursome examined the ruins of several buildings: an old church, a stable, a mill, a public washing house. Battered walls and fallen roofs told a tale of times past, and spoke also of endurance. On the wind, a carillon so melodious that it gave Gisela pause—bells tied round the necks of goats grazing a sparse mountainside pasture. She listened for a time to the music of this mountain, Pantocrator. "So," she said, "I guess nobody lives here anymore."

"Only one man," said Takis. "Theofano, the beekeeper."

"I don't see a single house that looks even remotely

livable," Gisela remarked. "Where is he?"

"He lives at the top of the incline," said Modestos.

Doran smiled. "So that's why you wanted to come here, Takis—for the honey!"

"The best *meli* on the island. Perhaps in all Greece!"

Within a few minutes they reached the village heights, and there the beekeeper's hives surrounded his shack. For a moment all four remained still and quiet, breathing the perfumed air and listening to the incessant buzzing of the worker bees. The sky was perfect, the land severe yet forgiving. As they stood before the decrepit stone hut where the apiculturist lived and worked, Modestos called out the beekeeper's name. "*Ela! Ela*, Theofano!"

Dressed in dungarees and a long-sleeved shirt, a bucolic man emerged from the shelter. "*Yasou*, Modestos! *Yasou*, Elena!" Theofano moved toward them with his arms outstretched, and Takis and Elena both kissed the bearded apiarist cheek to cheek, as if he were perhaps an uncle or a cousin not seen for a long time. When the voracity of the greeting subsided, Modestos introduced Doran and Gisela. "My friend from America," he said with his hand placed over Doran's heart. "And the Queen of Holland!" he said of Gisela. Doran bowed slightly, and Gisela shrank from embarrassment.

"I have special *meli* for you, Takis," said Theofano. "Very special indeed!"

Modestos' eyebrows rose in query.

"Wait here," he instructed. "I will bring you a taste."

Theofano crossed the yard where the hives were arranged like gravestones in a cemetery. Through a dark swarm he walked, fearless among the whole host. With a stick he collected honey from a particular hive, and then walked nonchalantly back to where the foursome was standing. He offered Modestos a taste of the honey. "The bees here—my bees—know only the innocence of this mountainside. Like Adam and Eve in the Garden—before the Serpent came to tempt the woman!" He cleared his throat as Takis handed the stick to Doran to taste. "But the man had to find out which *meli* was the sweetest taste, eh?" Theofano laughed then licked his fingers one by one.

"We buy two jars," Modestos proposed to Doran. "I pay two thousand, and you pay two thousand. That's enough!"

Doran agreed, so the honey was brought out, each ceramic jar containing a full kilogram! "In Holland," Gisela remarked, "the crock alone would have cost twice the price. And the taste is incomparable."

Leaving the beekeeper to his work, they began their descent toward the village entrance. Modestos and Doran walked ahead, as Elena and Gisela strolled more casually through the vestiges of time. Takis talked enthusiastically to Doran about harvesting chestnuts in autumn. "Not so difficult to find an untended grove," he said. "We go together in the early hours. I shake the tree, and you catch the nuts. Many kilos! And then, and then... We roast the nuts over hot coals. Very tasty!"

"And we pay nothing," Doran verified.

"*Endaksee!*"

Conversation between Elena and Gisela, though at times a bit halting due to language difficulties, took quite a different bearing. "Stella, why do you not telephone Spiro?" Elena wanted to know. Gisela had no sufficient answer. She shrugged and waited for her former boyfriend's mother to continue. "Spiro tells me that he would like to see you again. Maybe you telephone him, Stella? Maybe make a date?"

"I'd like to see him again," Gisela said. "Tell Spiro that I'm sorry for not calling. Tell him I'll call soon to make a date."

"*Poli kala,*" said Elena, satisfied that she'd adequately delivered her son's message, and achieved the desired response.

The drive back to Kondokali went not along the coastal road and through the tourist centers, but over the mountains, through one venerable village after another. Here time had a different quality; urgency was unknown. Old men loitered in cafés over cups of coffee and conversation, as their wives sat in front of doorways doing needlework or rocking contented babies upon their knees. In Messaria an old woman dressed head-to-toe in black led a burdened donkey down an alleyway; and in Troubetas village a farmer stood by the side of the road selling onions and garlic and freshly-cut herbs. Doran was personally glad to see that even though many changes had taken place during the course of his ten-year absence, still some of Corfu's more charming aspects—its fundamental villages and agrarian culture—remained unaffected. For it was the simple and happy life of these village people—not beach bars or *souvlaki* stands or charter cruises—that made Corfu a special place. Riding in the back seat of Takis' car, Doran held Gisela's hand as they drove over narrow roads and around countless dizzying switchbacks.

When at last they reached Kondokali village, they thanked Modestos and Elena for a wonderful day and went through the garden gate and up the whitewashed steps to their apartment. Feeling tired from the sun and sea and mountain air, Doran went immediately to have a shower, but Gisela had something else entirely on her mind. She rummaged through her belongings to find her address book, and as soon as she heard the water running in the bathroom, she was out the door and heading up Christopher Street, bound with intent for the Demos Gift Shop. There she meant to use the metered telephone to call the Thromos household before Modestos and Elena arrived home.

"Hello, Spiro. This is Gisela Van Zyl."

"My mother told you that I wanted you to call me?"

"Yes. How are you, Spiro?"

"I'm fine, Gisela. But I have many things to tell you."

"No doubt. It's been a long time since we've seen one another."

"Ten years," he confirmed.

"No small measure for change," she said.

"Perhaps we could meet somewhere for coffee and conversation," he suggested.

"I'd like that very much. You name the time and place."

"Do you know the Liston?" he asked.

"Yes, in the Old Town."

"The Café Capri is easy to find," he said.

"When?" she asked.

"Tomorrow?"

"What time?"

"I prefer four o'clock, if that's okay with you."

"I'll be there at four, Spiro. I can't wait to see you."

"Until tomorrow, Gisela. And thank you for telephoning me."

"See you then," she said and hung up the phone.

Gisela paid her bill and then sauntered back up Christopher Street, remembering fondly and in vivid detail the ecstatic days and nights she'd spent ten summers ago with a debonair and volatile Greek boy, Spiro Thromos. He'd been her first lover, and the affair had ended badly, abruptly. But time had smoothed the rough edges left by silly tantrums, and now the only memories that remained were pleasant ones. On the telephone he'd seemed older, more mature. Certainly that was to be expected. But she had sensed something else, too. Something unfamiliar. Nevertheless, Gisela was anxious to see her old friend.

CHAPTER 8
BLIND MAN'S BLUFF

Occupying the north side of the Esplanade in Corfu Town, the Liston was a two-block long arcade on a tree-lined, marble-paved square built by the French in the early nineteenth century. Handsome, multi-storied buildings, ornamented at ground level by an impressive portico and decorated with Venetian lanterns that hung in each archway, bordered the west side of the square. In each arcade was an identical café, one distinguished from another only by the sign above its doorway: Café Kriti; Café Venecia; Café Ionian. Opposite the Liston was the cricket field, (a hold-over from the time of British occupation), which was flanked by the Museum of Asian Art. At Café Capri, Gisela sat in the shadow of the stone portico and sipped a cappuccino as she waited for Spiro to arrive.

It was a sunny afternoon, and a sublime breeze blew off the waterfront. The summer heat had not yet begun. Nor had the steady flow of tourists from Northern Europe. The atmosphere remained casual as Corfiots strolled along the Esplanade, or sat at tables placed beneath the trees that lined the east side of the Liston, nursing drinks and chatting.

As she waited for her friend to arrive, Gisela wrote a few sentences in her journal. Though it was a lengthy memoir, the log was certainly not formal; it served only to document her private thoughts and reflections—impressions taken over a ten-year span of time. Ironically, some of the diary's first entries described her first encounters with Spiro Thromos. With a sense of nostalgia, she now read the words she'd written ten years ago.

'Perhaps someday I will be reading these words back in cold, gray Rotterdam, but I doubt it. I love traveling—it's so much fun! Greece is very special…

I've met a Greek boy named Spiro Thromos. He is the son of the man who owns the apartment we've rented. He is handsome and clever, though not particularly serious—a perfect summer romance, I think. Ha! He should be so lucky. But I'm hoping to see him again.'

Memories of that dramatic summer ten years ago flooded her mind.

"Let's swim naked," Spiro had coaxed.

To the boy's obvious amazement, she'd stripped off her tight shorts and tank top. On a fine beach at Sidari, the moonlight shone on her hair and silhouetted her figure against the sandy cliffs. Spiro, too, had shed his clothes as if they were on fire, and clasping hands they went running into the shallow surf until they both fell forward from the resistance of the tide. The chilly water was shocking at first, but each warmed to the other's slippery embrace. They kissed over and over again as they bobbed up and down with the waves in the glimmering luminescence.

And they'd swum in the private cove as the night grew full. Feeling astonished by the depths of their peculiar closeness, they teased, then touched. Wriggling free from Spiro's embrace, Gisela dove beneath the surface. Spiro followed. Once they surfaced, their game began again. Finally fatigued, they came ashore and lay on the beach where the shallow spurge of the surf could wash away the sand from underneath their wet bodies.

The night was warm, and they'd fallen asleep in each other's arms. At sunrise they awoke to the sound of a simple Greek song sung by a passing fisherman.

Yet even then she'd known that her relationship with Spiro was provisional.

Divided loyalties: a circumstance with which Gisela was awkwardly familiar. It was not uncommon for her to have one relationship in decline, another concurrent but fluctuating in commitment, and still another on the distant horizon and active largely in her own sense of possibility. And such a perspective was not wholly relegated to her love affairs; it pertained to other aspects of her life as well. For instance, she was continually torn between her predilection for travel and a sense of shirked responsibility to her sister and to the business they mutually owned. She was likewise uncertain of her bearing as an expatriate opposed to an inbred loyalty to her native country. Yet these were contradictions with which she'd learned to live, and they did not seem to compromise her wider-held sense of integrity. She cut through ambiguity like a Windjammer in a gale, bouncing over waves and taking on water, but always emerging from each storm into sunlight, undamaged and with a new heading. She fixed each unmarked course with determination and resolve. If navigation was her weakness, then resiliency was certainly her deliverance.

Absorbed in reminiscence and personal assessment, Gisela did not at first see her former lover advancing along the Liston. And even had she been watching for him, she might easily have overlooked him; for the young man that now approached her was a dramatically different person than she'd known ten years ago. Her mouth fell open in dismay as she regarded the once confident and slightly audacious *kamaki*, his steps now tentative as he tapped at the ground with the white cane of a blind man. His eyes hidden by dark glasses, and his head inclined at an ungainly angle, he seemed to struggle to navigate a course that he'd no doubt traveled hundreds of times as a seeing person.

In a voice quite louder than her natural tenor, Gisela called out to him. "*Ela*, Spiro Thromos!" At once he cocked his head to gain a sense of her bearing. Gisela rose from her seat and went to guide him to her table at the café.

"Hello, Stella. It's good to see you," Spiro said.

She put her hand upon his shoulder. "Spiro, why didn't you tell me?" she said breathlessly.

"My blindness is still new to me," he told her. "I don't want to evoke pity. And I'm not always comfortable talking about my condition. I suppose now you understand why I did not offer to come to Kondokali. Why instead I asked you to meet me here in the town."

"I'm so sorry," she said absently. "When did this happen to you? How did it happen?"

"I'll tell you everything over coffee," he said.

They reached the café table in moments. She pulled out a chair for him to sit. A waiter approached their table. "*Yasou*, Spiro," he greeted. "*Tikanis?*"

"*Yasou*, Dimitri," said Spiro. "*Kala. Es si?*"

"*Kala.* What can I bring you, my friend?"

"*Caffe Elleniki, parakalo,*" he ordered.

The waiter withdrew.

"I'm in shock, Spiro," Gisela said under her breath. She covered her mouth with her open palm. "I don't know what to say. Or how to begin."

"Perhaps I should have told you," he remarked.

"The blindness. How long?"

"I began losing my sight about three years ago," he told her. "But that is only part of my story."

"I want to hear everything," she said.

"Of course. And I want to hear about your life, too."

"My life?" She repositioned herself on her chair. "Yes, my life has taken many turns as well. Mostly to the left, I'm afraid."

"You're not a Communist?" he laughed.

She smiled, knowing implicitly that he could not see her expression. "Nothing like that," she affirmed.

"Good!" he said. "For a moment I was afraid—"

"I should have clarified," she laughed. "I only meant—"

"That things have not always worked in your favor," he completed.

"When one is young, it is impossible to imagine life's inevitable detours," she said.

"When one is young, all things are possible. And the world is a generous place."

"Exactly."

Gisela paid particular attention to the aura she now distinguished which enveloped Spiro. A narrow, umber border outlined his physique, but immediately gave way to a pale green, translucent light; and that luminosity in turn surrendered itself to a more familiar, pervasive white radiance. To Gisela, something about this succession of colors seemed oddly inverted, though again she was disinclined to make an exact interpretation of her perception.

"My father told me that you arrived here with the American," Spiro ventured.

"It's true," said Gisela without further explanation.

"I'm curious about your situation," Spiro encouraged.

"It's not exactly as it looks," Gisela explained. "It's not that simple."

"Nothing is ever simple," Spiro acknowledged.

"Life's greatest lesson, perhaps," said Gisela with a bit of melancholy in her voice.

"So tell me," he implored.

"After my father died, I went to Spain. I needed warmth and brightness. I needed to reconstitute. And of course I met a man."

"A serious affair?" he questioned.

"His name was Guillermo. The affair was intense, but very short."

"Why?"

"We had a falling out. I went home to Rotterdam. Again, I worked awhile with Alarice. But, as always, the work was redundant. I couldn't stand it. And besides, I knew that I'd been responsible for the rift between Guillermo and me. So I went back to Malaga to find him. But he was not there—gone without word of his whereabouts. I stayed the summer on the *Costa del Sol*, doing the usual. Ah, there were parties every night, and the beach every day! Looking for company, if you know what I mean. And the drinking! And the drugs!"

"Did you become involved with drugs?" Spiro wanted to know.

"No. Coming from Holland, I knew better."

"Fortunate for you."

"Nevertheless, my sole focus was self-gratification. At the beach resorts in Spain, that is everybody's *raison d'etre*."

"It is the same at the resorts here on Corfu," he acknowledged.

"In Spain, it's at a different level," Gisela explained.

"And you enjoyed yourself there?" Spiro asked.

Gisela smirked. "At the time I thought so. But triviality always wears thin."

"And Guillermo?"

"I never found him—never learned where he'd gone—and I shortly stopped caring. I seldom thought of him."

"Excuse me, please," said Spiro, "but it sounds to me as if you were without direction or cause."

"Exactly," said Gisela. "I was acting like a spoiled child, like a total sybarite. I was a bore."

"And you realized—"

"Eventually, yes. And I decided to leave Spain. I had to leave for the sake of my survival."

"So you went back to Holland again?"

"No, not this time. Instead, I went to Morocco. I stayed in Asilah the entire winter."

"And how was Morocco?" he asked.

"Weird and wonderful."

"I cannot imagine," he said.

"Morocco is beyond imagining," she confirmed.

"So, what then?"

"I went back to Holland for a time. I needed money, you see. And working at the business was always convenient."

"And what about Seeger?" he asked.

"Yes, Doran... Alarice received letters from him periodically. That's how we kept track of him. For a while, at least. First he was in Italy. I believe he lived in Rome for two years. Then he went to Paris. Then Munich. That's when the letters stopped and we lost track of him. We figured he'd gone back to America, and we really never expected to hear from him again. I later learned that he was living in Prague and working there as an art dealer. I was in Portugal at the time, living with a Ukrainian painter named Alexi. Our relationship was on the rocks. But through Alexi's father, Vladimir, who was also an artist, I learned that there was an American guy now living in Prague who was buying paintings in Kiev and peddling them throughout Western Europe. That guy turned out to be Doran Seeger."

"Incredible!" said Spiro.

"Anyway, I wanted to leave both Alexi and Lagos. I didn't want to return to Rotterdam, and I'd heard that the scene in Prague was very—"

"Special..."

"To put it in the Greek vernacular, yes. So, I wrote to Doran in Prague. I mean, I didn't even know if he'd remember me. After all, it had been nearly ten years!"

"But he did remember you."

"When I arrived in Prague, he was thoroughly hospitable."

"So, how is it that you've come to Corfu together?"

"It's a long story," said Gisela. "But it all revolves around a robbery."

"I don't understand," said Spiro.

"I accompanied Doran on a buying trip to Kiev. There we were robbed. In the end, it drove Doran and his partner out of the imported art trade."

"And you?"

"As it turned out, I didn't care much for the Czech Republic."

"Why not?"

"Too serious. Too imposing. Too desperate, and too dour."

"And your relationship with Seeger? Is it romantic?"

Gisela sighed. The muscles in her face tightened.

Spiro said, "If you'd rather not talk about it, Stella…"

"It's not that. It's just that I don't really know how to answer. I mean, there was one incident. After we arrived in Kondokali. On the beach."

"Yeah?"

"I was so drunk that I barely remember it," she confessed.

Spiro laughed. "Then maybe it's not so serious after all," he said.

"It's become a bit awkward."

"How so?" he wanted to know.

"Afterward, I pretended it never happened. Or, at least that I could not remember."

Spiro grimaced. "Perhaps not a wise choice."

"At the time I felt cornered."

"But it is always best to face such issues."

"You're right, of course. And now the situation is, as I said, awkward."

"As it must be with your sister," he speculated.

"My sister?"

"He was her lover first," Spiro reminded her.

"I know that."

"Does she know about you and Seeger?"

"She knows that I went to Prague to see him. And she knows that we're here together."

"But not about the so-called encounter."

"God, I hope not!"

"Now, that would be awkward," said Spiro.

"I know that sooner or later I'm going to have to tell her something."

"Possibly not," he conjectured.

Gisela shook her head skeptically. "Alarice is very astute. She'll eventually figure out that something is going on."

"But maybe by that time—"

"Everything will be sorted out. Yes, I hope so. I really hope so. For my sake as well as hers!"

"For me, relationships have never been so casual," Spiro confided.

"And who would have thought it?" said Gisela.

"I don't understand what you mean, Stella," he said in all innocence.

"You were such a playboy, Spiro. Over the years, whenever I thought about you, I always imagined you with a hundred girl friends."

"Not so," he related. "When I failed my university entrance exam—of course you remember that—I was thoroughly humiliated. Because I knew I had the intelligence to do well, and I had squandered my opportunity. So I became very serious about my studies. Next year, I passed the exam number one! Do you believe it? Number one in all Greece!"

"You never told me that in your letters," she said.

"I don't like to boast," he chuckled.

"Come off it!" she said. "You were so full of ego!"

"You think so? I don't know. Maybe I showed that face

to mask my insecurity."

"You? Insecure?"

"What young person feels secure?" he asked rhetorically. "After all, there is still so much to prove!"

"I suspect that goes on for a lifetime," said Gisela.

"I don't know. I hope not. I would prefer to live more comfortably."

"I suppose it all depends on one's personality," said Gisela. "And one's upbringing. Do you feel strong and whole, Spiro?"

"What a question!" he said.

"Well, do you? Because I certainly don't!"

Folding his hands upon the bistro table, Spiro said, "When I tell you the rest of my story, you will know the answer to your question."

"Then tell me," said Gisela. "I want to know everything."

Spiro pushed back his dark glasses to ensure that his eyes were covered. "The death of my grandmother, Aphrodite, had a profound effect on me," he began. "I don't really know how to explain it, other than to say that I seemed to gain an understanding of my greater position and my rank—not only within my extended family, but also concerning my standing within the society. I know that my explanation is vague, but I hope you understand what I'm trying to say, Stella."

"Ten summers ago you were certainly less than serious," she acknowledged.

"I was quite immature," he said.

"You were only nineteen."

"True. But when I failed the first exam, and when my father went away to Cyprus, and you went home to Holland—and of course Aphrodite's death—I seemed to mature over night. I studied tirelessly all winter long. My mother encouraged and pampered me. And when it came time for the next exam, I was ready. This time I not only passed the exam, but, as I said, I was ranked first in all

Greece."

"So you went on to the university?"

"Yes."

"In Italy?"

"Yes."

"And how did you find life as a student in Italy?" she asked.

"At first it was quite strange. The courses were difficult, and my Italian needed polishing. And the culture was unfamiliar. Luckily for me, there were many Greeks there. We formed a community away from home, and those friendships saw me through the adjustment."

"How long did you stay in Italy?"

"I stayed six years to earn my Masters degree in statistics. Again, I graduated first in my class!"

"Remembering you at nineteen," she said, "it seems an unlikely outcome."

Again Spiro chuckled. "I'm sure it does. At nineteen, the serious side of my personality was well hidden."

"So, after graduating from the university, you returned to Greece?" she prompted.

"Yes. But I was not long in Corfu. I was obliged to do military service. In Greece, it is mandatory for all young men."

"Seems an inconvenient detour," she judged.

Spiro shrugged. "From the time we are young we understand that it is required. So when the time comes, we do not resist. In truth, we're subjected to certain propaganda from an early age – concerning the Turks, of course."

"And once you're in the military?"

"What can I say? The propaganda increases ten times. Never mind the fact that the Turkish occupation was finished more than a century ago. And never mind the fact that in modern-day Greece and Turkey we need cooperation with one another far more than we can afford to continue a useless animosity. But it is difficult, you see.

In Greece, the hatred runs very deep. And in the military it is manifest to the extreme! The captains made us march up and down, endlessly chanting, 'The only good Turk is a dead Turk!' And most of the guys felt this hatred in their bones. For me, it was different. Because I understand today's reality. I shouted the slogans as loud as anybody, but I never believed them!"

"I sometimes think that there is some awful part of human nature that enjoys combat," Gisela speculated.

"Perhaps the lizard is alive and well deep inside each of our brains," said Spiro, smiling.

"Anyway, please continue," she said.

Again, Spiro adjusted his sunglasses. "Once the basic training was finished," he continued, "military life was a terrific bore! I was posted with five other guys on Karpathos. That's an island midway between Crete and Rhodes. Not many people live there. We lived in a hotel. There was very little to do, especially in winter. All day long we drank and played cards and waited for the Turks to invade."

"And of course they never came…"

"Only the Tax Police showed up. They docked their boat in Pigadia Marina for three months. They came ashore only once, because the local businessmen, rather than pay their taxes, decided to beat up the policemen. Anyway, the police were outnumbered ten to one. I guess they left when they began to run out of food."

"And you moldered how long on Karpathos?" she asked.

"Ten months. It was interminable."

"And then?"

"To Athens for a time. Then a posting in the Epirus— the northern mountains of the mainland."

"And how was that?"

"It was winter, so it was cold and snowy."

"Not what you're accustomed to."

"I didn't much like it. But at least it was my final

posting. After my service ended, I gladly came home to Kerkyra."

"What about women?" Gisela asked. "Have there been any women in your life, Spiro?"

"Women? None after you, Stella."

"You're a liar!" she accused playfully.

"It's true!" he maintained.

"Fine! Keep your secrets if you must," she said.

"These days my vulnerability is all too obvious," he said.

"It must be difficult to maintain your confidence," she remarked.

He shrugged, as he was constrained to accepting his condition. "I can't say that it's not difficult," he confessed.

"And how did it happen, Spiro?" she asked directly. "How did you go blind?"

"Quite unexpectedly," he said with a tone of overriding irony.

"I'm sure it was a shock," she commiserated.

"Just out of the army," he explained, "it was nearly impossible for me to find a job here on Kerkyra."

"Even with your qualifications?"

"The competition is intense."

"Yes, I imagine so."

"So, I had to wait for an opening. The first year of waiting led to a second, then a third. I occupied myself with further studies, mastering many aspects of computer science. In fact, I spent so many hours in front of my computer monitor that my eyes eventually began to trouble me. Odd distortions, floating objects, flashing lights. At first, I ignored the problem, but as it grew steadily worse, I researched the symptoms. I became convinced that I was suffering from CVS, Computer Vision Syndrome. It sometimes occurs in people who spend many hours in front of a computer screen. But then my sight began to fade at the center. The progress of the condition was rapid, and I was soon left with only peripheral vision. I consulted a specialist in Athens. After many tests, the doctor diagnosed my conditions as Macular Degeneration, normally an eye condition that occurs in older people. I was told that the syndrome was not only progressive, but also that it was incurable. I was also told that I would not become totally blind, but for all practical purposes... Well, you can see the end result for yourself. I am left now with only minimal peripheral vision. I cannot read or write. Navigation is difficult—especially stairs! I trip over objects directly in my path because I cannot see them. And my education in statistics has become virtually useless—at least until a time when Greece moves away from handwritten ledgers and enters the computer age. Which is of course quite ironic, since I was initially convinced that the computer had caused my problem. But the doctor told me unequivocally that CVS played no part whatsoever in my condition. Yet he could not give me a definite reason either. So, there is another possible explanation."

"What might that be?" she asked, her brows plunging together.

"It is difficult for me to talk about," he said. He folded his arms protectively across his chest.

"You don't have to say anything to me, Spiro," Gisela allowed.

"But I must tell you!" he said. "I must tell someone."

"What then?"

"A punishment from God."

"What?"

"I seldom talk to anyone about this," he said somberly. "I don't really know why I feel as though I can trust you, Stella. But I do trust you."

"Well, I'm glad you trust me, Spiro. What is it?

He shifted uncomfortably in his chair. He fingered his empty coffee cup, and then folded his delicate hands as he entered his personal confessional. "When I was away at the university—my first year there—I encountered certain lifestyles with which I was previously not acquainted," he explained.

"To be expected," she allowed, her tone encouraging him to continue.

"When I was younger, I had certain…attractions…impulses that I did not understand."

"I presume you're talking about sexual impulses," she said.

"Of course. But I never allowed these so-called impulses any expression whatsoever. In light of social attitudes and religious taboos, it's difficult to face such feelings. Not to mention the weight of judgment by one's family!"

"It's not a crime, Spiro."

"No, not a crime. But in Greek society, nearly so! At least in my particular situation."

"In this day and age, surely—"

"Stella, you can't imagine the stigma."

"Because I'm not gay?"

"Right! So you can't really understand."

"No, I guess I can't."

"Even so, it's not as simple as that. Because I'm not only attracted to one sex."

"You're telling me that you're bi-sexual?"

"I've always liked women. You know that."

"And you've discovered that you like men, too?"

He lowered his head. "For me, it's a joy and a curse."

"And what's all this talk about a punishment from God?" she wanted to know.

"I know that it's ridiculous, but the verdict of religion weighs on me."

"You can't allow parochial ideas to torment you," she advised.

"When I was a boy, there was a rumor, or rather a commonly-held belief, that if one masturbated too often, he'd be struck blind by God."

"A silly notion maintained to foster guilt and sexual

165

repression," she determined. "Everybody does it. It's thoroughly natural."

"Of course I know that. On an intellectual level I understand all the superstitions, and all the manipulative tactics. But guilt is a hard habit to break. Especially when it's instilled at a young age!"

"I didn't realize that Greek society was so negative toward gays," she said.

"Have you observed a single homosexual here in Corfu Town? Probably not. That's not because there are none, it's because they're all locked in the closet. Nobody 'comes out' here. It would be unthinkable."

"What about the ancient Greeks, the Olympians? They were often depicted as homosexuals. Or bi-sexuals."

Spiro shrugged. "People often accept in mythology that which they cannot accept in contemporary society."

"Do you have gay friends here?"

"Yes. And straight friends, too."

"If it's so repressive here, why not go elsewhere, Spiro? Someplace where the attitude is more sympathetic, more liberal?"

"Were it not for the loss of my sight, I might. Maybe I'd go to the Netherlands. Or to Sweden. But blindness changes everything, Stella."

"Ten years ago," she reflected, "I would never have suspected it."

"Neither you nor me," he said.

"What about your parents? Do they know?"

"Certainly not my father. My mother may suspect."

"Can you confide in her?"

"Not yet. I can't risk it. Not in my condition."

"Because you're not yet able to live on your own?"

"The blindness is still too new. Whether it's a punishment from God, or the result of cruel hazard, my life is going to be very different than I once envisioned it, and I still have many adjustments to make."

She put her hand upon his shoulder. "I'm glad that you

chose to tell me," she said.

"In my situation, one comes to know who he can trust."

"You *can* trust me, Spiro. And you can count on my help, if you need it."

"Thank you," he nodded.

"Now, it's time that I return to Kondokali. Can I walk you home?" she offered.

"No need," he smiled. "I've learned to navigate these streets. And if I get into trouble, everybody here knows where I live."

Standing in San Rocco Square, and pensively smoking one Stuyvesant after another, Gisela waited for the bus that would take her back to Kondokali village. Certainly her encounter with Spiro Thromos had left her shocked; the tragedy of his blindness was overwhelming. Yet she was inclined to ponder certain corollary impressions as well: for this was the same audacious and venturous young man with whom she'd had a summer romance ten years ago; though his temerity had been replaced by humility, and his devil-may-care attitude with diffidence and uncertainty. Indeed, if his account of the past ten years were true and accurate, he'd become uncharacteristically studious, as well as far more reserved concerning his sexuality, (or according to his own admission his bi-sexuality). Gisela had anticipated only a casual reunion with an old friend, an old boyfriend with whom she'd not become estranged, nor harbored any grudge or lasting animosity; instead she'd encountered a young man far removed from the overly confident *kamaki* that she remembered. Without a doubt, fate had dealt Spiro a difficult hand to play, but it was not only her sympathy that his present circumstance evoked, it was something else: something familiar and natural and comfortable. Once reunited, ten years' time had seemed to matter little, and now, as she waited for the bus, she experienced a rekindled empathy for her former lover.

And then there was Doran to consider. Gisela's feelings lobbied for an unfettered advance, while her sense of ethics and decency tempered her enthusiasm and advised restraint. Concerning this dilemma, she was in quite a quandary. For restraint seemed to imply duplicity, and fraudulence felt nearly as awkward as the situation itself! Surely, Doran deserved better treatment. On the run, she had accepted his offer of refuge without question. But had she fallen for him on the rebound?

As Spiro had said, she would eventually have to say something to her sister. And whatever justification she might contend, it would no doubt sound hollow to Alarice, if not deceitful and scheming and miserable. Gisela did not want to hurt her sister. She loved her dearly. Whether in fact or fiction, she felt herself the benefactor of Alarice's sacrifice, which only increased her sense of guilt.

Now Spiro had entered her life again, another coal on a fire already out of control. And this entire assortment of confusing circumstances tumbling out of a failed relationship with a Russian painter who drank too much and who probably, in time, would have beaten her or otherwise mistreated her. Hell, Alexi had exploited her from the start, accepting her hospitality only to overrun her home and her life. The irony inherent in a reversal of roles did not go unnoticed in Gisela's consideration of present circumstances. Nor was she oblivious to the certainty of an eventual reckoning.

As the bus arrived, Gisela maintained her reservation as the horde stormed the open door and clamored for seats. Last onto the bus, she was forced to ride standing up and pressed against several Greek men who smelled of olives and ouzo. Even so, she was barely conscious of the ride to Kondokali, for her mind whirred along in overdrive, her emotions the fuel for regret and rumination. Disembarking in front of the Tropho Market, she walked two hundred meters to Pension Aphrodite. She'd hoped to find Doran at home, for in spite of everything she knew that his presence would give her comfort, but when she arrived, he was not inside the apartment. She took off her sweater and flopped down upon her bed. Exhausted as much from conflict as from physical exertion, she wanted only to sleep. To sleep an anesthetic sleep. For perhaps in sleep she might contact her guardian, or chance upon some previously unrecognized course of action, or make an apology, or revisit her childhood home. Gisela closed her eyes and began to count backwards from one hundred.

CHAPTER 9
WHAT DO YOU DO
WITH A DRUNKEN SAILOR

Doran had fallen in with a group of British expatriates who met each afternoon at four o'clock for drinks at the Navigator's Bar. His inclusion in the group had been encouraged and facilitated by Philbar Cullinain, the sailor he'd met casually as he sat at the bar on the same night that he and Gisela had attended the karaoke session.

Doran had encountered Cullinain on several other occasions over the course of a few weeks' time—each time sitting in a bar with a pint of beer in hand—and he'd now passed more than a few afternoons with the Overdraft's skipper and his crowd of Celtic misfits. The beer always flowed freely (nobody seemed very concerned with who was paying for what) and the *crack* was good as well. In fact, Doran found Cullinain, in his low-key and low-voiced way, to be not only witty, but also eternally curious-minded. He truly enjoyed talking with the longtime expatriate, though he largely ignored the others in the clique.

Over many glasses of beer, Doran learned the

Englishman's colorful history: a rough and tumble, pre-war and wartime childhood filled with propaganda and populated by variety show actors and comics, (friends of his mother and father), who instilled in him a lifelong love of humor; a scholarship to Eaton passed by for lack of living expenses, (his father was a plumber then earning only five hundred pounds sterling per year); military service at seventeen, and eventually a post in the elite Special Air Services branch of the British Army.

"Every Englishman on Corfu claims to be ex-SAS," he told Doran. "But they're all phonies. I can ask a single trick question, *'What's underneath the clock?'* and if I don't receive the answer, *'To be a pilgrim,'* I've caught him in the lie. Simple as that."

Indeed, Cullinain had spent time abroad in Singapore, Indonesia, Thailand, and Laos. In Indonesia, he'd been detailed as a bodyguard for Sukarno, and had conveyed to Doran that in the stupidity of his youth he'd been perfectly willing to take a bullet intended for the Indonesian dictator. In Singapore, he'd established an illegal beer-running organization to supply foreign servicemen their favorite beverage. "Which was extremely profitable," he added. While stationed in Laos, he'd confessed, with tears in his eyes, to shooting two ten-year-olds, a brother and sister. "Extreme situation," he rationalized. "Pure insanity! Innocent children carrying hand grenades. No way around it." Though Doran could plainly see that the killing of the two children weighed heavily on his conscience and was perhaps the defining moment of his life—the beginning of the end, so to speak. For though Cullinain was now easy-going, casual in every sense, one suspected that the regret he carried ate away at his spirit like maggots on refuse. Did Philbar Cullinain care if he lived or died? Doran doubted the efficacy of his façade.

"Would you fancy a sail to Agni with Dazey and me?" he'd asked Doran one afternoon.

"Where is Agni?"

"Up the northern coastline. The Overdraft makes the trip in about an hour-and-a-half. Not much there, you understand. Except the White House."

"The White House?"

"The British novelist, Lawrence Durrell, had a house there. And I believe the American writer, Henry Miller, stayed there with him before the war. Not much left from their time, anyway. But there's a marvelous little restaurant on the key. Been there forever. Lovely place to have a meal and pass a lazy afternoon. Inside, they have a collection of photographs from the thirties. Larry Durrell, his brother Gerald, Henry Miller—that crowd. Quite interesting, really."

Having had little experience with boats, the idea appealed to Doran. "I'm staying here with a Dutch woman. A longtime friend," he explained. "Perhaps you remember her from the night we met. Would it be all right if she came along?"

"Can't say that I remember her. Is she pretty?" Cullinain inquired playfully.

"To my eye, she's a knockout," said Doran.

"By all means, bring her along. We'll probably get pissed up, and somebody's got to steer the Overdraft back to the marina," the skipper laughed as he finished off the beer in his glass.

On the morning they were to sail with Phil and Dazey Cullinain to Agni, Doran and Gisela arrived at the pier where the Overdraft was docked. The light was brilliant, the sky infinitely blue, and the sea calm as glass. There was little sign of activity on the boat, and Gisela wondered aloud if perhaps they'd gotten the day or time wrong. "I'm certain he said we'd sail today at eleven," Doran confirmed.

"Looks to me like they're still asleep," said Gisela.

"I'm going to knock," Doran ventured.

A moment or two after Doran's inquiry, Cullinain

appeared looking haggard and hung over. "Right-o, mate," he croaked. "Just give us a minute, will you?"

Gisela was immediately dubious. "Do you suppose he knows what he's doing?" she asked Doran.

"He told me he's been sailing for forty-five years," Doran assured her.

"That fact aside," she said, "he looks barely able to tie his shoes."

"I'm sure he'll be okay," Doran said and sat down upon the pier to wait for the Cullinains to rise and shine. Gisela sat cross-legged beside him.

Ten minutes passed before Cullinain appeared and invited them to come aboard. "Dazey will be another minute or two," he said. "She's just now getting dressed in the aft-cabin. Would you like something to drink? Coffee? Tea? A brandy, perhaps?"

"No, thanks," said Doran as he stood on the deck and looked into the forward-cabin. The yacht's interior was down-at-heel and rather grimy from negligence, though the boat's owners obviously did not notice their own muddle.

"I'm accustomed to coffee in the morning," said Cullinain as he put a pot to boil upon the stove in the tiny galley. And once his coffee was made and poured into his cup, he spiked the brew with a shot of brandy. "Java with a tipple," he explained. "Gets the juices flowing."

Doran well knew the signs of an alcoholic; his father had drunk himself to death, and was now ten years in the grave. Cullinain was no doubt well along the same path. Though Philbar Cullinain's affable personality was not yet drowned in booze, nor thoroughly consumed by grief, nor stifled by anger: something altogether likeable remained, even shined in his eyes, and shone upon his beset face. Having long ago judged himself totally wanting, he refrained, where others were concerned, from any judgment whatsoever. He habitually accepted others as they were and offered unconditional friendship. That was his magic; that was his redemption.

"How long have you lived aboard ship?" Gisela asked..

Cullinain scratched his head. "Seven years now," he said.

"This is my friend Gisela Van Zyl," Doran introduced.

Cullinain smiled warmly and held out his hand for her to shake. "Happy to make your acquaintance, darling," he said.

"The pleasure is mine," said Gisela. "Thank you for inviting me to come along."

Cullinain waved off the thanks. "It's a beautiful day. And we're all here together on Corfu! What could be better?" As he sipped his brandied coffee, his eyes seemed to clear, his aspect to brighten. "Well, let me just see what's keeping Dazey."

But as he turned to move toward the aft-cabin, Dazey Cullinain herself came through the doorway, her hair bristled, her complexion florid, her step unsteady. A bikini top covered her sagging breasts, and a faded sarong was wrapped round her hips. "Good morning all!" she clucked.

"At last she's emerged!" Philbar announced.

"Sod off, Phil! Where's my coffee?"

He handed her a mug filled with a concoction much like that in his own cup. She took the mug in her trembling hand. "Have you done the *Times* crossword yet?" she asked.

"I've only just got up myself," he said.

"No surprise there," she said. "You didn't roll in last night until past three in the morning!"

"Pissed out of my head," he added.

Dazey turned to Doran and Gisela. "He was out last night with his friend Wolfgang Lidl."

"The old Nazi!" Philbar laughed.

"Actually, he's a retired Surgeon General in the Austrian Army," Dazey qualified.

"An absolute lunatic," Philbar laughed. "And a crackerjack sailor! Whenever he comes to Corfu, together we paint the town red!"

"Perhaps you noticed the glow this morning," Dazey said to the company, referring to her husband's common metaphor.

Doran smiled benignly, while Gisela did not know how to react to this bizarre couple. But the lack of a response did not deter Dazey Cullinain one iota. She rambled on and on about Philbar's exploits with the retired Austrian surgeon. "Whenever they're together, they're like a couple of adolescents," she begrudged. "There's simply no checking them. But don't take me wrong," she said, "I truly like Wolfie."

"He's an old Nazi," Cullinain reiterated. "But he's a great guy. And a crackerjack sailor!"

"Wolfgang knows boats, that's for sure!" said Dazey.

Cullinain turned to his wife. "Sorry I forgot to tell you, darling, but apparently I've promised these two gracious people a cruise to Agni today."

"Oh, right-o," she said, utterly unruffled by the prospect of an impromptu excursion.

"So, I guess we'd better get underway."

"Yes, it would seem so," she agreed.

"Are you sure you wouldn't like a drink?" Cullinain asked his guests. "A glass of red ink, perhaps?"

"Red ink?" said Doran.

"Local wine," Cullinain explained.

"Maybe later," said Doran.

"Right-o, mate. Then I'll just tend to a few necessities, and we'll be off," he said. Turning to Dazey, he asked, "Would you mind helping with the ropes, darling, while I turn over the engine?"

Dazey climbed the three steps leading to the deck, and then teetered onto the peer. Unraveling the mooring ropes, she tossed each one onboard to Doran, and then went aboard herself.

Philbar coaxed the tired motor, which faltered three times before ignition was finally achieved. "Off to Agni!"

the skipper proclaimed as the Overdraft sputtered out of Gouvia Marina at half-a-knot, its Popeye captain at the wheel, the first mate gone below to the galley for a second cup of brandied coffee and a crossword puzzle, and two skeptical passengers on deck, ready and waiting for who-knew-what.

Along the tree-lined coast they chugged, Gouvia Bay and Corfu Town behind them, Mount Pantocrator above and to their left, and the hazy mountains of Albania in the distance. Cullinain steered the boat as Doran and Gisela sat on deck in the bright sunshine. Graceful sailboats glided across the bay. Ferryboats the size of luxury hotels navigated the narrow straight that divided Corfu from the mainland. And the Overdraft labored like a tug past Dassia, Barbati, and Kalami. But it was a spectacular Ionian morning, and the two novice sailors were happy to be aboard. As the journey progressed, their doubts concerning the competency of the captain and crew diminished. Until they heard the sound of Dazey's singing voice wafting up from the forward-cabin. Gisela cocked her head to listen. To Doran's ear, the melody was vaguely familiar. What was it?

A Gilbert and Sullivan operetta—*Pirates of Penzance*! But the words were all wrong…

> *"I am the very model of a modern techno-journalist,*
> *With words I am a demon all the meanings I can turn and twist,*
> *My knowledge of the industry is positively minimal,*
> *In management's true function my disinterest is criminal…"*

"What the hell is that?" said Gisela to Doran.

"Shhh… Just listen!" he said with a smile on his lips.

Dazey Cullinain's invincible voice went on with the clever parody:

*"As lobby correspondent for the now defunct News
Chronicle,
In nineteen forty-five when oil and gas were economical,
I am so well equipped to give out current information,
And write about the industry in times of high
inflation!"*

"She writes about the industry in times of high inflation!"
chorused Philbar's baritone voice from the wheelhouse.

*"When I have learnt what progress has been made in
the refinery,
When I know more of offshore than a pupil in the
primary,
In short when I've a smattering of basic oil technology,
You'll say a better journalist has never worked at old
BP!*

*My knowledge of the industry, for all that I'm so
devious,
Is either non-existent or is back in decades previous,
But still with words I am so good,
The meaning I can turn and twist,
I am the very model of a modern techno-journalist!"*

*"In short with words she is so good, the meaning she can turn
and twist; she is the very model of a modern techno-journalist!"*
Philbar broke out laughing as he raised his glass. "Don't
stop now, darling!" he roared.

Dazey's head popped through the entrance to the
wheelhouse. "Did you fancy my little ditty?" she asked.

"Wonderful, darling. Truly wonderful!" He turned to
Doran and Gisela. "The woman's keen with words, you
see. She loves to write little parodies."

"All apologies to G&S," Dazey qualified.

"No apology necessary," Doran encouraged.

"Right-o, mate! They're long dead, aren't they?" said

Philbar.

"I suppose they are," said Dazey. "Then I shouldn't have a problem with the copyright, I suspect."

"Have a drink!" Philbar called out to his guests. "Dazey, pour each of our friends a glass of ink!"

"Right-o!" She descended back into the galley.

"We're all here together, off Corfu, I think... (We are off the coast of Corfu, aren't we, darling?) We don't know where the bloody hell we're going, but we're sailing. We're sailing! What could be better?"

As the Overdraft lumbered into the tiny crescent-shaped cove at Agni, Doran and Gisela stood on the ship's prow and surveyed the sublime scenery. Beyond the dock was a sandy beach that gave way immediately to a verdant hillside covered by a carpet of springtime flowers. A single, whitewashed building with a sagging tile roof and green window shutters stood at one end of the beach—the venerable Taverna Nicolas, in business continually since 1901. In front of the building itself, a patio sheltered by a mature grape arbor welcomed guests to a shady repast. Upon the hillside stood a few others buildings, one in particular more dominant than the others—the writers' former residence.

At the end of the pier, a brown-skinned man with white hair waited to take the Overdraft's mooring ropes; and as Philbar Cullinain came out of the wheelhouse the man beamed and called out a salutation: "*Yasas*, my friends! Welcome!"

Cullinain stood on the deck and began tossing the mooring ropes onto the dock. Enthusiastically, he returned the greeting: "*Yasou*, Dionysus! *Tikanis*?"

"*Poli kala! Poli kala!*" The Greek's smile was bright and broad. Obviously, the two knew one another from past visits. After the ropes were tied off, Philbar jumped from the deck to the pier and embraced his old friend.

Doran was next off the boat, and he held out his hand first for Gisela then for Dazey.

"Too long since your last visit, Philly," said Dionysus. Then he turned to Dazey, whom he also apparently knew well. "How are you, Missus?" he asked as he moved to embrace her.

"I've brought new initiates," Dazey informed him.

"Welcome, welcome," said Dionysus to Doran and Gisela. "Philly and Dazey are my special friends. So of course their friends are also my friends! Now come sit underneath the vine where it's cool, and have a drink with me." Dionysus led them over the pier toward the *taverna*.

"Yes, a drink! *Krassi* from Dionysus himself! How can you beat that?" Cullinain said to Doran.

"Today we have special wine!" announced Dionysus. "*Krassi neo!*"

"Any old vintage is good enough for us," said Cullinain. "Bottom of the barrel, so to speak," said Dazey.

"Only the best for my friends!" proclaimed Dionysus.

"You're too kind," Cullinain prattled. "Too kind!"

"*Oxi*, my friend! Only pure nectar! The best wine!"

"Right-o, mate!"

Dionysus settled the four at a table overlooking the dock, and then withdrew to bring the promised libation. Philbar faced Doran and asked, "What do you think, mate?"

"Idyllic place," Doran assessed.

Cullinain turned to Gisela. "Everything okay?" he asked.

"Stunning," she said.

Cullinain took the hint of lingering doubt in her voice to be simple shyness. He put his hand on her bare shoulder as Dionysus arrived with a pitcher brimming with new wine. "*Krassi* special!" he beamed. "Special wine for special friends!"

The wine was poured and a toast was made. "To Greece!" Philbar proclaimed.

Then food was ordered—many *mezes*, from calamari to fried zucchinis; from stuffed grape leaves to feta cheese soaked in olive oil and covered with herbs; from sardines to elephant beans in tomato and cinnamon sauce. The pitcher of wine was refilled again and again by Dionysus.

"Are you familiar with the work of Lawrence Durrell?" Dazey asked Doran.

"Sorry to say, I've not read Durrell. Henry Miller, yes. I've read Miller's book about Greece, *Colossus of Maroussi*. An extraordinary essay!"

"Oh, you must read Durrell," she implored. "The Alexandria quartet is quite eloquent. And, I dare say, quite sexual."

"As was Miller's writing."

"Oh, yes. But not done with Durrell's eloquence."

"Being British, as well as a member of the Queen's English Society, Dazey is understandably biased towards L.D." said Philbar.

From his seat on the restaurant's patio, Doran could see Durrell's 'White House' perched on a low hillside not three hundred meters from where they sat. The place was elegant without being ostentatious. He tried to envision what life might have been like for the two writers-in-residence before the war broke out and foreigners were forced to leave Greece for the sake of their own safety. Considering the presumably enduring, elemental nature of this particular locale, the decades since Durrell and Miller had resided and written and reveled here had probably meant little in the way of change.

Philbar offered his own particular corollary to Dazey's analysis: "I rather identify with Durrell's point of view that 'English life is really like an autopsy...so, so dreary.' Fleeing the icy horror of English life, Durrell's character, Lawrence Lucifer, warms himself in Greece. You know, not far from here is The Shrine of Saint Arsenius. Durrell called it his 'Place of Predilection.' There is an inscription there that reads: 'There are two birth-places: the place where you were really born, and the place of predilection where you really wake up to reality.' I spent fifty-five years in England, much of that time in the service of HRH. I gave England my youth and my sanity."

"Your sanity?" Doran questioned.

"I've told you a few details of my past—SAS and all that. And I told you what happened in Laos, too. After I returned to the UK, I had a nervous breakdown. I was locked up in the funny farm nearly two years. When I finally could look into the mirror without crying, they let me out—without so much as a word of thanks, mind you. I walked away from service with a suitcase full of Asian clothing and fifteen pounds sterling in my pocket. And a sense of shame I'll carry with me to the grave!"

"And English shame is like no other shame," Dazey added.

"I'm not so sure about that," said Doran.

"Mind you, the Yanks have managed to screw things up in a place or two!"

"A continuing effort, I'm afraid," said Doran.

"We're all here on Corfu for the same basic reason," Philbar analyzed. "To become invisible."

"Is that it?" Gisela intoned.

"You come from Holland?"

"Yes."

"A neutral country…"

"Yes. In the Netherlands, we are a tolerant society."

"But, I dare say, the tolerance is a measured one, darling. Take a critical look inside yourself. Examine your deepest motives for doing what it is that you do. Your motives for coming to Corfu. Tourists come here for sunshine and the seaside. Those who come here as ex-pats come for very different reasons. Do you know what the Greeks say about us? That the best of us has killed his own mother! And they're right! Not one of the many foreigners living here is clean. Each and every one has a boil on his bottom."

"That's quite presumptuous," said Gisela in her own defense.

"I've faced the monster inside myself," said Cullinain sanctimoniously, "so I've earned the right."

"I don't understand that kind of remorse," said Gisela.

"That's because you've yet to carry your cross to the Mount," said Dazey.

"Why take up the cross at all?" Gisela postured.

"It's not so much that you take up the cross," said Philbar. "Rather it's put upon your back."

"It's better *not* to embrace causes," Gisela contended.

"Better late than never, that is my philosophy precisely," said Philbar. "Now I prefer to drink. For obvious reasons."

"But that doesn't solve anything. And you'll only ruin your health."

"Darling, I'm already a ruin. And I drink not for my destruction but for my survival."

"It makes no sense."

"It makes perfect sense. Think about it."

"If you drink, drink, drink everyday, you'll never confront your demons."

"Right-o, darling. I don't want to confront them. I cannot possibly face them and prevail. Better to anaesthetize the lot."

"Where is your sense of hope?" she implored.

"Darling, I'm sixty-four years old. I haven't a penny in my pocket. I have absolutely no responsibilities. And I have virtually no stress. At this point, that's the best for which I can hope."

"What about you, Dazey?" Gisela asked with growing incredulity.

"Not much different really," she said matter-of-factly.

"Just a different cross to bear," Doran interjected.

"That's right."

"Then you understand all this fatalism," Gisela said to Doran.

"I think I do."

"Well, I certainly don't."

Philbar laughed ironically. "You're still young, darling. Give yourself time."

"I hope I never feel as you say you do," she said emphatically.

"Take heart," said Philbar softly. "It's not so bad."

"We're all right, we'll muddle through," said Dazey as she finished off her fifth glass of wine. Her eyes now quite glassy, she seemed to be falling asleep by degrees. Her head began to droop, as her shoulders leaned precariously to the left.

Gisela regarded Dazey's curious posture with unease. And the Englishwoman's aura had turned as well, changing from a pale shade of pink to an ominous tone of raw umber. Gisela had seen such a tint surrounding her father preceding his death, and a chill moved over her body in the midst of the warm Mediterranean afternoon.

In a matter of minutes, Dazey Cullinain lay slumped upon the table, eyes closed and mouth open, spittle on her lower lip, out cold. Alarmed, Gisela asked Philbar, "Is she okay?"

"It happens from time to time. She's okay. She'll be up in a moment, bright as a bluebird."

"Narcolepsy?" Doran conjectured.

"Very observant, mate," said Philbar.

"What is narcolepsy?" Gisela wanted to know.

"She falls asleep at odd moments," Doran explained. "Sometimes in mid-sentence."

"That's right," said Philbar calmly.

"And she's all right?" Gisela asked again.

"She'll come around any minute," said Philbar.

"It's something like epilepsy," Doran explained. "Though it's not well understood." He turned to Philbar. "Has she seen a physician?" he asked.

"She's not inclined," Cullinain explained.

"There's adequate treatment available," Doran informed. "She should really see a neurologist."

Philbar shook his head. "We're all right, mate," he said.

Doran took the assertion as a polite dismissal, though he was not offended.

True to prediction, Dazey awakened within minutes, barely aware that she'd fallen unconscious. "Right!" she said as if she were responding to some question posed in a conversation already in progress, though nobody really knew to what she was referring. Philbar patted her lovingly on the head. "You had a little *siesta*, Daze. Not to worry. Dionysus is bringing more wine. The afternoon is glorious."

"More wine?" she inquired, still feeling a bit groggy.

"*Krassi neo!*" Philbar affirmed.

"Where are we, Phil?" Dazey wanted to know.

"We're in Agni, darling. We sailed the Overdraft here for a lunch with these fine folks."

"Oh, right!" she said, regaining her cognitive balance. "Yes, I believe I *will* have some more wine."

"That's the spirit, darling," said Philbar. And he took the carafe to refill her glass.

Dazey Cullinain had gone below to the aft-cabin for her traditional after-lunch *siesta* and was fast asleep even before Philbar had guided the Overdraft out of the cove at Agni. Once out to open sea, the skipper fixed the throttle at three-and-a-half knots, and then called Gisela to the wheelhouse. "Ready to take the wheel, darling?" he asked.

"I've never steered a ship before," she said. "Are you sure it's all right?"

"No worries, darling," he assured her.

With his arm around her bare shoulder, Philbar trained Gisela's eye upon a distant beacon and instructed her to point the ship with due care and attention toward the designated focal point. "I'll check your course in half-an-hour," he said. Then he went below to the galley to pour himself a brandy, and also one for Doran.

On deck, the skipper made his way over ropes and rigging to the ship's prow. There, Doran sat looking out to sea. Cullinain handed him a glass, and then raised his own for a toast. The American raised his glass as well before sipping the brandy.

By this time it was no secret to Doran that Philbar Cullinain was somewhat prone to clever prattle, but now, in the subtlety of the Ionian twilight—*a light that had brought men more strident almost to tears for its beauty*—the Englishman remained quiet, introspective. No doubt, Cullinain felt a profound respect and reverence for the sea. All jokes and barbs aside, and the captain was certainly inclined to lampoon almost any subject or situation, he seemed to enjoy, once at sea, a freedom of spirit denied him on dry land. The Overdraft was his vehicle of solace and reclamation.

Doran shared the quietude. His inclination as well had always tended toward introspection, and the calm sea and distant shoreline and shimmering light encouraged a kind of dreamy meditation. For even as he found his presence at this particular location and time to be somewhat random, the fact remained that he'd come to accept the arbitrary as intrinsic. Indeed, that was the nature of living as an itinerant.

Once he'd emptied his glass, Philbar Cullinain broke the silence. "Normally, I find Yanks to be rather verbose," he said, "but you've not said much about your situation. Mind you, I'm not inclined to pry if you don't want to talk about it."

Doran shrugged nonchalantly. "In some respects, my history is somewhat like your own."

Cullinain listened attentively.

"I, too, worked for my government —not in the military, but in the private sector as an engineer. I was directly involved, along with a number of other engineers, in the development of the Doppler Rangefinder System. Though at the time none of us understood the eventual application of our work."

"Guidance systems for missiles," said Cullinain.

"Precisely."

"So-called *smart bombs*. Cruise missiles and Chimney Sweeps and the like."

"Yes. But, as I said, we didn't know it at the time. The project was fractioned beyond recognition. Eventually, all the engineers involved began comparing notes. Once that happened, it became obvious. Of course we understood the implications. We understood as no one else understood the ominous power of the weapons we were designing. That brought personal politics and philosophy into the mix. Some of us recoiled. But of course it was too late."

"The Genie was out of the bottle…"

"So to speak."

"And your conscience bothered you?"

"Somewhat to my surprise, yes. But I was naive."

"Governments tend to count on naivety when it comes to their more nefarious intentions."

"As your own experience has taught you," said Doran.

"So you felt co-opted…" Cullinain speculated.

"And trapped," Doran added.

"You wanted out…"

"Yes. But there was a guard at the door. Not literally, you understand. But the pressure was intense. Nobody said you couldn't leave, but it was understood by everybody that we were involved in a very sensitive issue."

"The devil had you by the balls…"

"So to speak."

"So you stayed on…"

"Until the night the bombs fell on Baghdad. That was the breaking point for me. All night long I puked into the toilette as CNN narrated the carnage."

"Your work on display, so to speak."

"In all its awesome power, for all the world to see. And to fear!"

"A golden opportunity for your president," commented Cullinain.

"Of course the so-called spin was quite different, wasn't it?"

"Wars need a righteous cause."

"And the so-called defense of Kuwait provided one."

"Of course there was more to the story. We can only speculate about underlying motives."

"To me, the precise motives were irrelevant. Because I knew what was happening at ground zero. On TV, it looked incredibly clean, surgically precise. F-16 and F-17 pilots, smiling like vampires, took off on their sorties. We were the good guys, we were reassured, and nobody was going to get killed—at least nobody from our side. Back home we saw simulations that looked more like computer arcade games than real war. Think about that for a moment. It washed everybody's hands, didn't it? But I understood, as few others could, the real consequences. I knew that many innocent people were dying horrible deaths by an enemy they couldn't even begin to fathom, an enemy they couldn't even look in the eye."

"I understand what it means to reach that breaking point, my friend. Justification is no longer possible."

"As I said before, I was quite naive. But I was not without conscience. Something drove me to walk away from the madness. I came to Europe without direction. I never intended to stay, but one thing led to another. I fell in love. With Gisela's sister!"

"I had no idea," Cullinain chuckled. "How incredibly awkward."

"That affair ended long ago," Doran explained.

"A good thing it did, I suspect," said Cullinain.

Doran took out a pack of cigarettes and lit one before continuing his explanation. "At any rate," he went on, "I drifted from place to place, not necessarily moving towards anything positive as away from something negative. Eventually, I wound up in Prague selling art."

"A more benign occupation, I suspect."

Doran nodded. "I was in business there with a very

enterprising Columbian woman, but a robbery finished the business."

"Fate often plays cruel tricks," said Cullinain.

"I suppose that depends on how you look at it," said Doran. "In the end, the demise of our business in Prague is what brought me back to Corfu. A twist of fate, and Gisela's sudden presence in my life, which was in itself quite unexpected."

"The gods are playing penny-ante."

"As always," said Doran.

"So, what's your status now, mate?"

"Personal or political?" Doran asked.

"I was referring to your political status."

"Somewhat precarious, I must admit."

"A man without a vocation, a rebel without a cause…"

"More immediately, a man without a country."

"Then you've not been back to America?"

"Not for ten years," said Doran. "And my passport is due to expire soon."

"Can't you simply renew it?"

"It's not that simple. Apparently, I have to touch the soil. Literally, that is."

"And you have no desire to go back. Even for a short visit."

"None whatsoever. I've broken my connection. That's my coping mechanism."

"You're speaking of course about the guilt."

"Yes.

"I understand."

"After ten years in Europe, I have a life here. I'm renewed, so to speak."

"But not in the eyes of your government…"

"I hope they've written me off once and for all."

"They tend not to forget," said Cullinain. "Especially considering your former profession. I'm sure you're on some list of possible subversives."

"No doubt. But that's their game, isn't it?"

"The one you now refuse to play."

"Right."

"I understand. It's the same with me, you know. But achieving political anonymity is not so easy."

"I may be about to find that out."

"Concerning your passport?"

"Yes."

Cullinain stroked his prominent chin in thought. "There are dozens of guys living aboard boats in Gouvia Marina trying to maintain their anonymity. But maybe there's another way, my friend."

"Another way?" Doran was all ears.

"My SAS buddies have certain connections. These guys have a way of getting things done. Of doing the impossible."

"I'm not sure where you're leading me," said Doran.

"How would you fancy becoming a British subject?" Philbar asked.

Doran smiled at the prospect. "It might have certain advantages," he conceded. "But I'm not exactly sure of the etiquette while standing before the Monarch."

Cullinain smiled. "I can't make any promises," he said, "but I'll talk with some people I know. Mind you, I won't allude to specifics."

"Probably a good precaution. I've learned not to draw attention to myself."

"Let me see what I can learn. When does your passport expire?"

"A couple of months out," said Doran.

"Oh, I see. Not much time then. Let me see what I can do for you. No promises, of course."

"I appreciate your effort," said Doran. "Though I'm not certain I'd accept a falsified document even if it were available."

"I'm not talking about a falsified passport," said Cullinain. "I'm talking about the genuine article. Everything legal." He rubbed his hands together. "As I said, sometimes these guys in SAS, the older guys who have seen it up and down and in and out and every which way, can untie impossible knots, only to pull the strings to their own favor. I'll put out the word, and then we'll see what's possible."

Doran nodded his thanks.

"Now I must take a moment to make certain that that dear girl you've brought along has kept us on course. No point traveling in circles. Right-o!" He stood up, staggered a moment from a full day of drinking, and then made his way over the deck to the wheelhouse.

The sun had now set and the air had turned cool, though Doran barely noticed the chill. He was absorbed by the fact that, since coming to Corfu, he'd had two separate offers for help concerning his soon-to-expire passport, each one, as it were, proposing to deal with the situation, as the French called it, '*au noir*,' or under the table. The American Consul in Corfu Town had advised him simply to go back to the States, renew his passport, and then return to Europe, if he so chose. No doubt, that approach represented the path of least resistance, yet something inexplicable seemed to block that course. In his mind, *Statelessness*, a circumstance that was at least inconvenient, if not threatening, commingled with *weightlessness*, one that was more or less desirable in a strictly metaphysical sense. The so-called crime of becoming cosmopolitan failed to impress him. He'd played the role of pawn once and had thankfully found the courage to reject it. And whether he wound up officially American, or Greek, or British concerned him little. Such designations were for the benefit of those who found them important and necessary, categorically!

As a bit of fog crept over the water's surface at dusk, and as the beacon by which the novice steered was no longer visible, the captain had decided that he should personally guide the Overdraft into Gouvia Marina. Which was fine with Gisela. She'd had her fill of piloting anyway, so she joined Doran on the ship's prow.

And having risen from her nap, Dazey stood beside her husband in the wheelhouse. Studying the couple through the glass of the windscreen, Doran concluded that her particular sadness, or grief, though not explicated or specifically defined, was as obvious as Philbar's.

Referring to the seascape, Gisela remarked, "It's quite beautiful, isn't it?"

"In an unworldly way," Doran acknowledged.

"No doubt, Philbar will guide us through the fog," she said.

"Philbar is an extraordinary navigator," Doran determined.

"Yes, it would seem so," she agreed.

CHAPTER 10
STRICTLY PHYSICAL

Modestos had requested Doran's help with an undefined project, and the willing worker waited just after dawn in the patio garden for him to arrive. Underneath the leafy canopy of the grape arbor it was cool and shady. The red bougainvillea climbed the staircase wall and wound itself round the whitewashed masonry railing. The neighborhood was quiet except for the songs of swooping swallows and wrens and finches, and the ringing of the church bells calling the older women to mass. A young Italian couple slept in the apartment adjacent to the garden, but in all likelihood they would not be awake for hours—not until the sun was high in the sky and the water at Kondokali Beach had warmed sufficiently for swimming. Theirs was a different existence than the one he presently embraced: they were on a two-week holiday from their jobs in Rome; he was now a full-fledged Corfiot, not native to the island, but adapting by degrees to his newly chosen home. And work was an integral part of any man's existence, so lending his hand to whatever task Modestos had in mind was not so much a concession as it was a part of his assimilation.

And what a glorious morning it was! The sky was cloudless, a light breeze blew off the bay, and the light was scandalously passionate. Late August, and Corfu was teeming with summer visitors whose only pursuit was that of pleasure and relaxation. Though it was a decidedly different scenario for the Corfiots themselves: this was their busy season, a time when they made the money they would need to carry them through the rainy winter months. During the summer season local businesses remained open seven days a week, eighteen hours a day. Tourism had been increasing on Corfu for thirty years now, and the schism between summer and winter was, for most, a well-established routine. Modestos met incoming ferryboats at the port to find the renters who occupied his seasonal *dhomatia*; others opened restaurants and served *mousaka* and *pastitsada* to satisfy big appetites for 'authentic' foods. There were clothing boutiques, shops selling postcards and suntan oil and beach gear, rent-a-car shops, travel agencies, and gift shops—and of course many cafés and bars. But on this glorious morning, Doran felt quite removed from all the summertime Kitsch and commotion. He was simply waiting for his friend to arrive—a friend with whom he anticipated a day of physical labor.

He lit a cigarette as he thought about the Greek. Ten years ago, just off a ferryboat from Italy, he'd met Modestos at the port, and with a simple utterance camaraderie was formed. "Come to my village; I am a good man," he'd called to Doran from behind the bars that separated the Customs House from the street. The Greek had proven true to his word. Now, ten years later, the friendship was resumed as if no time at all had passed, as if indeed they had been friends their entire lives. To Doran, such unconditional acceptance and such reciprocation were unfounded. In his native culture, and in other European cultures as well, it seemed like everything was conditional. The very idea of innate mutuality had been long ago supplanted by suspicion and avarice. What a pity, he thought! And how lucky he felt this morning to be living in Greece. To be heading off to the mountains with Modestos for a day of labor and laughter and homespun philosophy, and maybe even a swim in the sea once they'd finished their work.

As Doran extinguished his cigarette, Modestos turned up the narrow alleyway riding on his 50cc motorbike. He parked the vehicle beside the wall of the building and swept into the garden in his usual fashion—as if a catastrophe were imminent, and that by sheer energy and determination he might somehow deflect misfortune. To Doran, it seemed that he was always smoothing over rough edges that did not actually exist. But that was simply his way—an approach that might have been an ingratiating character trait for one less affable and truly good-natured than Modestos, but one that was, when personified by him, quite endearing. "Hello, my friend!" he called to Doran as he took a plastic bag from the motorbike's carrier. "*Kala?*"

"*Poli kala!*" said Doran, for he could not imagine feeling better than he felt this morning.

"Good weather again," said Takis. "Fresh this morning, but the afternoon will be hot. *Poli zesti*, I'm sure of it!"

"What do you have in the plastic bag?" Doran asked.

"Breakfast!" said Takis. From the sack he took a half-dozen ripe tomatoes, four cucumbers, a small bottle of olive oil, and a loaf of dark brown bread. "Every day I eat the same breakfast: only vegetables and bread. Everything fresh! Physical! Maybe you like to eat something, too?"

Doran nodded as the Greek began slicing tomatoes and cucumbers over the plastic bag. He tore a piece of bread from the loaf and stuffed it into his mouth, chewing wildly. Unselfconsciously, he ate the vegetables with his fingers. Olive oil spilled over his lower lip as he continued to talk with his mouth full of food. "Today I want to show you many things," he said. "But first... But first we eat. Then we go by motorbike to the mountains."

Doran, too, tore a piece of bread from the loaf, though he chewed his piece more deliberately.

"Where is the girl, Stella? Still sleeping?" Takis asked.

"Yes. Late night for her," Doran explained

Modestos nodded and chewed. "Yesterday," he informed Doran, "I spoke with my friend about your passport." He shook his head as he swallowed, not in capitulation, but with the realization that Doran's dilemma would not be easily solved. "Difficult problem. My friend told me he will try to help you, but it all depends. So, now we must wait for an answer."

"I appreciate your effort," said Doran.

Modestos waved off Doran's expression of gratitude as he stuffed his mouth with tomatoes and cucumbers and bread. "We'll see what happens."

"Anyway," Doran redirected, "that's not our mission today."

Modestos smiled with satisfaction. "No. Today we have better work to occupy our bodies and our brains."

"What do you have in mind?" Doran asked.

"Ah! I think you like too much what I show you today, my friend."

"Yeah?"

"Anyway, you have a look. Then I will tell you my idea." He smiled again as he wiped tomato juice from his lips.

Driving his motorbike, Modestos seemed to know only two speeds: full throttle and '*break now to avoid collision*!' As he accelerated, Doran was thrown back from the G-force, and he had to hold tightly onto the driver's stomach to avoid being pummeled on the pavement; and as Modestos ground the bike to a halt, Doran's chest was pressed against the driver's back, initiating a familiarity he might rather have developed in some other way. Yet it was all good fun! The wind whipped his hair and cooled his face as they sped along tree-lined roads, ascended steep grades, and maneuvered around hairpin turns. Below, the sea shone like a sapphire; while above Mount Pantocrator loomed in brooding, stark silence. They whirred through timeworn villages, past meadows of grazing sheep and goats, through deep-dark olive groves. Doran's nerves tingled as the two-cycle engine croaked and cackled, splitting the morning silence. The sea, the mountains, the forests, and the essential villages: this was Kerkyra at its best—natural, timeless, and so purely physical!

For Doran, this excursion brought to mind similar jaunts he'd taken with Modestos into the mountains—trips made ten years ago to buy homemade wine, or fresh eggs, or cheese. Such memories remained clear in his mind, as if they had happened only yesterday, as if they were now a vital part of his own constitution. Indeed, one never knew as events unfolded just which experiences might prove significant. He'd thought about Modestos during the ensuing ten years, about his character and about his way of life. He admired the man; he'd always considered him a special friend. No doubt, their experiences differed radically, yet they remained somehow related—oddly connected within time, and by physical elements.

Halfway up Mount Pantocrator, they arrived at the first stop on their expedition—an olive grove not unlike the many others that covered the mountainside. Modestos hopped off the motorbike and charged into the copse. Doran followed more deliberately. With eyes trained on the treetops, the Greek examined the condition of the unripe fruits. "*Po, po, po*," he lamented. "I hope this year to catch many olives."

"These are your trees?" Doran surmised.

"My trees, yes. This ground belonged to Elena's father. Now it is mine."

"And you harvest the olives every year?"

"As you know, I like fresh—no chemicals! Physical! But it depends on the weather. Some years are too hot. Other years, too much rain. This year I believe I will take a big harvest."

"And you take the olives to a press to make oil?"

"No need to take the olives to a commercial press," he informed. "The modern one is mechanical. It destroys the taste. For this reason, I take the olives to Argyrades. There they have a press—the *old one*! Many hours turning by horse, you understand? But this is the best way! If you like to help me, Doran, we will put out the nets together. And then… And then… Once all the tourists are gone from the apartment below yours, we will clean and store the olives there. I have many jars. In the lower apartment, we will make a factory. We can produce many, many kilos— enough for us, and some to sell at the market. Maybe you like to help me this winter, eh?"

"I guess I'm willing to put my hand to the press," he told the Greek.

Counting the profits long before they were in hand, Modestos spoke with unbridled enthusiasm. "Beginning early in November, we will first clear away the brush. Then we will put out the nets. Everyday catching many olives! But we must collect them by hand, you understand. And then… And then… We will take the olives to our factory. There, we can preserve them in seawater for twenty days, more or less. Anyway, the time is not so important, because the olives can remain in the brine for many months without damage. When we have collected enough—maybe after three or four months—we will make the oil. Ah, beautiful oil! No sediment, only clear. Strictly physical! You understand?"

"Sounds like a lot of work," Doran observed.

Modestos shrugged. For fresh food was his passion. And no amount of hard work seemed reason enough to compromise the quality of his sustenance. "*Ela!*" he directed. "Now I will show you another place. A special place!"

Back on the motorbike, they sped over twisting mountain roads, through endless groves of not only olive trees, but orange trees and lemon tress as well, finally descending into a wooded valley on the opposite side of Pantocrator. Laying the bike on its side, Modestos charged into the trees with Doran at his heels. The forest felt cool and moist, and the ground was covered with ferns that grew knee-high. Larks sang in the boughs overhead. After traveling some two hundred meters into the wood, Modestos stopped abruptly and pointed toward the treetops. "Chestnuts!" he cried. "Very tasty!

Doran scoured the ground beneath the tree where they stood. He picked up one of the fallen seeds and held it out to his guide. Smiling, Modestos took the husk from him and tore away its spiny sheath, exposing the fruit. He bit into the nut to evaluate its ripeness. Spitting out the pulp, he shook his head and said, "Not ready now. We must return after three weeks. Then we catch many kilos. In the garden at Pension Aphrodite, we will roast them over coals. Very tasty, this one!" he reiterated. "I like too much!"

The next leg of the journey took them to the west side of Kerkyra and into the mountains above Paliokastritsa. There, Doran was shown numerous berry patches, a grove of kumquat trees, and a meadow where edible greens grew wild in spring and autumn. Descending to the seashore, Modestos pointed out a fabled fishing spot where, during the right season, one was likely to harpoon enough squid and octopi to satisfy the guests at a Greek wedding reception.

It was after two o'clock in the afternoon when they reached the final stop on Takis' agricultural tour. Just behind Kondokali village, the Greek owned an undeveloped parcel of land, recently rough-tilled, on a south-facing slope. Doran knew that in Greek society the measure of familial wealth was often counted by the number of property deeds held by a particular family: the Greeks, having had little in the way of hard currency during preceding generations, bought land and passed it down from generation to generation, seldom selling what they'd managed to acquire. This ground, too, had a somewhat singular history.

Modestos sifted bits of earth through his fingers. "This is very good ground," he assessed. "Very fertile!" He tossed the last bit of soil away as he explained, "When I was a very young boy living in Kondokali village, my father, Constantine Thromos, grew many potatoes on this ground. In the hollow is a water-well; and he carried the water by hand. Below, along the road where Hotel Alexandros now stands, he had a grove of orange trees— hundreds of them! Each December, he took the oranges to the market in Corfu Town to sell. He took potatoes, too!

"You see, we had very little money—nobody had money then—but we never went hungry. Some of the men caught fish. Others went to the mainland to shoot rabbits. Still others grew vegetables. Everything physical! You understand?

"My father was a clever man. The building in which you now live was once a bakery. A big furnace— everything! My father and my mother kept a small shop in the rooms below. Every morning the people lined up in front of the shop to buy bread. With the money he made from the bakery, Constantine bought land. Many hectares...

"Of course, I don't remember these things. I was very young—only ten years old when my father went away— but my mother told me everything. She told me that during the afternoon most of the men in the village went to O. Makis' Taverna to play cards, but Constantine never wasted his time with games. He went to the town to conduct business. Or he went to the farm. Always working, working, working!"

"Paradise lost," Doran commented.

"Maybe not lost forever," said Modestos hopefully. "This ground has remained idle since my father left Corfu," he continued, "but before it is time for me to join him in Heaven, or in Hades, if that is the case, I would like to see this farm in full bloom!"

Lighting a cigarette, Doran surveyed the sublime landscape. Under a blue sky laced with diaphanous clouds, the hillsides surrounding the cleared terrain supported countless cypress, eucalyptus, and mimosa trees. Sunflowers and daisies and cornflowers grew wild near the roadside. From a neighboring pasture came a cacophonous barnyard serenade: bleating sheep, clucking hens, the forlorn sound of a braying donkey, and a rather excited, barking dog. A solitary, lost turkey waddled, unconcerned, along the gravel road. At the center of the plowed half-acre grew a single olive tree.

Accounting for the tilled ground, Doran said, "I presume you have a plan to restore the natural order?"

"It's true," said Modestos. "I would like to plant potatoes on this ground—maybe three hundred plants! But I'm growing old, and I cannot dig the holes or carry the water from the well. Too much strain on an old back."

"So you need help," Doran speculated.

"Maybe you would like to help me plant potatoes," Modestos proposed. "I will buy everything we need: tools, ammonia, special fertilizer from the sheep. Nothing chemical, you understand. I will buy everything, and you can make the holes, Doran. The ground is soft, you see? And you can carry the water from the well—only two times per week—maybe one hour's work, no more! After one hundred days, we will dig up the potatoes. Many, many kilos! We will divide the profit by two—fifty percent for me, and fifty percent for you. We can store enough potatoes for the entire winter in our factory. Or maybe you would like to sell some of them at the street market. As you like, my friend!"

"But why plant only potatoes?" Doran asked. "Why not plant many other vegetables as well?"

Strangely enough, the thought had not occurred to Modestos. "Other vegetables? Which ones would you like to grow?"

"Look around," Doran gestured, referring to the area's prolific vegetation. "I'm sure anything we plant in this ground will flourish: carrots, spinach, cauliflower, onions. Whatever we choose."

"After October, the rains will come. And then… And then… If we are lucky, we will take many vegetables. All winter long we pay nothing for food, eh?" This idea particularly appealed to the Greek.

"If we plant a variety of crops," said Doran, "we must cultivate individual gardens."

"I will buy everything we need," Modestos reiterated with excitement. "You can prepare the individual plots. Not so much work, really. Maybe two hours per day, nothing more!"

Somewhere deep inside himself, Doran sensed that this opportunity promised something quite beyond material redress. The very idea of reconnecting so directly with the natural elements seemed no less than therapeutic, and wholly appealed to him. He tossed away his cigarette and put out his hand for Modestos to shake. "Now I understand the purpose of this excursion today. The olive trees, the berry patch, and the walnut grove; the fishing spot, and finally this farm: I think we have just become partners," he said.

"*Poli kala*, my friend," said Modestos, quite satisfied. "Now, we must return to Kondokali village."

CHAPTER 11
APPARITIONS

Gisela awoke with her head upon Doran's shoulder. She did not immediately move away; instead she lay quiet and motionless as she gradually came to full consciousness. She watched a tiny spider crawl across the ceiling. She contemplated the morning light that filtered first through yellow curtains, and then through the stained glass room divider.

As she collected her wits, Gisela suddenly remembered a very peculiar dream she'd had during the night. Or was it a dream? Enveloped by the silence of night, and by its darkness, she'd abruptly sat upright in bed. The figure of a very old woman, encircled by a most surreal luminosity, stood before her. The aura surrounding the specter was by all accounts quite different than the auras she normally perceived. This light seemed to emanate from beyond the physical world—a light born of essence rather than physical properties. She blinked a number of times to clear her vision. She rubbed the sleep from her eyes.

An apparition, thought Gisela. And a curious one at that! The old woman appeared dressed in a moth-eaten wedding gown, and she held a silver-framed photograph of a young man close to her breast.

The old woman spoke: "Tonight my voice grows thin, my words fly away. My mind is havoc, and my namesake is laughing behind my back. My efforts have turned feeble, *but I am here tonight for you, my darling. Only for you!*"

Her mouth agape, Gisela wanted to ask the purpose of the visit, but her voice was paralyzed, not necessarily from fear, but by the sheer incredulity of the experience.

Looking at the photograph in her hands, the phantom spoke again: "What boy is this?" she called. "Spiro Thromos, is that you?"

"Aphrodite!" Gisela gasped.

"Yes, it is Aphrodite." The force of emotion nearly took the old woman's breath as the gods and goddesses of Olympus whirled round her head. The faded garment she wore turned to dust and fell away from her spectral body.

In the blink of an eye, the apparition vanished, leaving Gisela only her doubt. Dream or vision, the experience haunted her as she searched for its meaning.

Perhaps her nocturnal imagination had simply run wild. Yet, in retrospect, the experience had seemed incredibly real—not like other dreams she'd dreamed. She readily accepted her perception of auras that surrounded the living, so why not at least acknowledge the possibility of ethereal ones, too? Lying upon Doran's shoulder, Gisela suddenly realized that she could not feel her limbs. She tried to move but her entire body felt numb. It seemed to take several minutes for her to regain a sense of her physicality.

Doran rose from his bed, put on his robe, and went into the bathroom. Standing before the mirror, he noticed two long hairs clinging to the right side of his face. Carefully, he removed the strands and examined them under the vanity light. Each hair was six or seven inches long, dyed-red in color.

He brushed his teeth but chose not to shower, for he

meant to spend a few hours working at the farm this morning. He dressed in old clothes—torn jeans and a paint-stained shirt—and put on a pair of knee-high, rubber boots that Modestos had given him. He ate no breakfast; nor did he take his usual coffee. With shovel and hoe in hand, he set off for the farm, a fifteen- minute walk into the hills behind Kondokali village.

It was easy for Doran to feel happy and unfettered on such a sun-drenched, September morning. The route passed through the old domain of the Thromos family— one generation removed. Much of the land here had been deeded to Modestos' sister Tasoula when she married Bampis Pauli Karalampous, who had managed over the years to drink away much of his wife's fine inheritance, selling off parcels of land from time to time in order to finance a slovenly lifestyle. Much to the disgrace of the rest of the Thromos family.

Past a one-hundred-year-old barn he walked, where roosters crowed in conquest, and where goats grazed a sun-scorched pasture. Palms and cypress trees lined the roadside, ivy clung to stucco walls, and bougainvillea vines formed an archway over the entrance to the cemetery. Doran detoured into the graveyard, where he picked several ripened dates from an overburdened tree. These he ate for his breakfast. And though he did not make the sign of the cross, he left a pebble on top of Aphrodite's marble tomb—a custom he'd long ago learned and adopted from a Jewish friend. Further along the main road, he passed Tasoula's house, familiar to him because he'd spent the better part of a winter there trying to determine his future course: whether or not to pursue a parted lover; or return home to the United States; or make a life for himself on Corfu; or strike out into Europe, come what may. Torrents had since flowed underneath his bridge. Now he was back on Corfu again, passing by the very place where he'd begun his odyssey. What was one to do but travel in circles? Interesting ones perhaps, but circles nevertheless.

A rolling stone gathers no moss, and Doran's shoes were clean. The Greek way of life encouraged self-acceptance, and he was less and less inclined to resist. Here again for only a summer, he found himself caught up in the rhythms of Hellenic life.

With hoe in hand, he began to break clods of dirt. Blood rushed to his muscles; sweat formed on his brow. Under the bright sun, he worked to form three separate garden plots, then he stopped to rest. He sat upon a tree stump. He drank some water and listened to the pastoral sounds of the Corfu countryside. A crow cawed three times from a distant treetop. As Doran faced the acreage, he did not see the person on foot approaching along the gravel road.

"Nice looking garden," a voice called to him in perfect, American-style English. Doran turned to see a man in his seventies standing by the side of the road. "Except the slope is too severe. All the water is going to run off."

Though the temperature was now quite warm, the man wore jeans and a jacket. A wide-brimmed hat was pulled low on his forehead making it difficult to see his face. "So you think I should level it out a bit?" Doran asked.

"I sure would."

Doran stood up but did not approach the stranger. Instead, he strained his eyes in the bright sunlight to see the man's face. It was no use. Yet something about the stranger seemed very familiar. "Your accent sounds South Texas," Doran said.

"Born and raised," he confirmed.

"I was born in Texas," Doran offered. "Corpus Christie."

"You don't say!"

"Do you live here on Corfu?" Doran asked.

"Not many Americans living here," he said. "In fact, you're probably the only one. I'm just passing through. I heard you were here, so I thought I'd say hello."

It was something about the old man's drawl that made

the fine blond hairs on Doran's arms bristle. He knew he'd heard the voice before. It was a voice from his memory, perhaps a voice from his childhood. He made a move to join the stranger at the side of the road, but the old man began moving away. "What did you say your name was?" Doran called after him.

The old man laughed.

"Your name? What's your name?" Doran called. He suddenly felt quite light-headed.

The old man replied with an all-too-familiar, identifying conundrum: "Move quickly, son, before it's too late!"

"Wait a minute!" Doran yelled. Then he swooned and fell face-first upon the dirt.

Regaining consciousness after only a minute, Doran got to his feet and walked over dirt clods to the side of the gravel road. He looked up and down the byway for any sign of the visitor. There was none. How strange, he thought. Perhaps he'd imagined the entire incident. He returned to the tree stump and sat down to clear his head, and it was only then that he realized that during his ever-so-brief fainting spell he'd dreamed of his father, Hank Seeger, for the first time since his death.

Rising early, and feeling quite uneasy over her dream-like encounter with Aphrodite Thromos, Gisela had dressed in the silence of early morning and gone on foot to her secret garden. There she picked several oranges and sat in the shade of an olive tree to nourish herself. As always, the garden imparted its primary quality: peace. For this she was thankful, because her dream, or the nocturnal manifestation, or whatever it was, had left her nerves jangled, and her sense of clarity in a fog. She peeled one of the oranges and began to section the fruit. Juice ran over her fingers, and she tasted the sweetness. She lay back in the long grass and dared to close her eyes. Within seconds she was back in Rotterdam, at Alarice's apartment in the *Cubiswonung*. The smell of freshly made confection filled the apartment.

"What are you baking?" Gisela asked her sister.

"A crumb cake," Alarice answered.

"When will it be out of the oven?"

"It's out already. Would you like a piece?"

"With coffee, please," said Gisela.

Gisela noticed several travel books on Alarice's coffee table. Leaning forward, she began studying a map of Greece. Alarice brought the small repast.

"You really are serious about traveling," Gisela said.

"Of course I'm serious," said Alarice.

"You've never traveled before," the younger sister observed.

"All the more reason to go now." Alarice settled herself on the sofa near Gisela so they might look at the same page of the open book.

"Mother says you want me to come along," Gisela said as she sipped her coffee.

"It would be extravagant for you to have a summer in Greece before starting at the university," said Alarice.

"Papa will never allow it," Gisela said dourly.

"Mother knows how to take care of him," advised Alarice.

"I can't believe she's offering to pay my way!" Gisela declared. "What's the catch? What's going on? Did you and mother devise this scheme to keep me away from home this summer? For what reason I can't imagine."

"Nothing of the kind," said Alarice as she began paging through the color photos in the travel book. "I told mother that I'd decided to go to Greece for the entire summer. I was expecting resistance, but she surprised me by suggesting that I take you along. I admit that I was skeptical at first, but the more I thought about it, the more I liked the idea. What do *you* think, Gisela?"

"I don't know what to think," said the younger sister.

Alarice recalled the summer before she had gone away to the university at Leiden. She told Gisela that she had spent the entire time cultivating anxiety. "Don't be a dolt, Gisela!" she admonished. "Just look at these pictures! It's the opportunity of a lifetime. I wish I had traveled when I was your age."

"Why?" Gisela asked sincerely.

Alarice explained, "Once you have finished studying and settle into a job—or maybe start a family—you become absorbed, and time hurtles by. One day you look in the mirror and barely recognize the person staring back. Such things are hard to imagine at nineteen, but it's true! Perhaps you say to yourself, 'Okay, it's not so bad. There is still plenty of time. And it's not as if I were old and decrepit.' Important things are put off another year. Maybe two, or three, or ten…"

"You sound a little desperate, Arissa."

"Desperate? I don't know about that. But I'm glad I've decided to do this. Please come along, Gisela."

Gisela's gaze was distant. Had she already begun this fated holiday in fantasy? Or was it something else altogether? "We're going to Greece. Imagine that!" she said. She turned to Alarice and smiled. "May I have another piece of cake?" she said.

"Coffee too?" asked Alarice.

"Of course," said Gisela.

Together they read the travel articles that Alarice had collected.

Gisela opened her eyes to a leafy dome overhead. In the distance she heard a chorus of bells coming from an adjacent pasture. She got to her feet and walked along a sloping pathway to have a look at the flock. After a hundred meters or so, she came to a sun-drenched clearing. There, sheep grazed in luxuriously long grass. Near a fence stood the shepherd—a woman whose characteristics seemed decidedly familiar to Gisela. Her hair was nearly gray, and she stood with a little stoop in her shoulders. She wore a dark gray dress and a cardigan sweater that looked surprisingly familiar, too. Gisela strained to see the woman's face. Maude.

The breath went out of her lungs as she beheld the image of her mother standing not over pre-pubescent dental patients, as she had during the whole of her adult life, but tending a flock of sheep in Greece! What was Maude doing here? What was Maude doing anywhere in the substantive world? Around the figure shone a gleaming white aura, and Gisela's lips spread into an ecstatic smile. Her feet went running to meet her long-departed mother within the realm of this Olympic Emperyan, but as she emerged into the field, the brilliant sunshine blinded her vision. She stopped amidst the flock. Searching the perimeter of the fence where the form had stood, she saw no one. The image had been absorbed by the light of the present day.

Physical labor became increasingly difficult as Apollo's chariot crossed the celestial meridian. In addition to the rising heat and humidity, memories of his father and of his former life in the United States encroached upon Doran's concentration to the point of distraction; so he laid his tools behind the venerable olive tree that grew near the center of the garden and walked from the farm to the main road. There he put out his thumb, hoping to flag a ride to the west side of the island. It was not long before a motorist stopped to ask where he was going, and once it was established that their destinations were compatible, Doran was on his way through the groves and over the mountains to Glyfada—a place once pivotal to his fortune, a place he had not re-visited since returning to Corfu.

The ride from the farm near Kondokali village to the west side of the island was not a long one, and as the driver came over the final ridge and descended the dizzying switchbacks leading to the beach itself, the unbroken panorama of wide-open sea momentarily took away Doran's breath. Indeed, he'd forgotten just how spectacular this locale really was; no wonder it had played such an influential role in his affair with Alarice Van Zyl. Again impressions from the past occupied his thoughts.

During days spent at Glyfada Beach, visions of distant and exotic places had washed over Doran like the metered waves offshore—places like Alexandria and Istanbul. Far away were the tensions of a competitive lifestyle. Instead he heard the steady and soothing sound of the sea, the call of a bird, a playful voice. Alarice's voice!

At Taverna Loyiza Hara-Theou, their friend Diakatos-Leonidas reserved their favorite table for them each night. As the sun set over the water, they drank *Retsina* and waited patiently for a lamb roasting over glowing coals to be cooked to perfection. Chef Stefanos basted the entrée with a mop dipped in olive oil, lemon juice, and homegrown herbs, while Leonidas played a game called *Mosquito* with two of his other guests. It was a good-natured game, where the unsuspecting newcomers were forced to endure humiliating slaps on the cheek if they were not adroit enough to foil the stinger of the unrelenting mosquito, Leonidas! Everyone in the *taverna* laughed hysterically at the spectacle, as the obliging Swedish contestants grew more and more red-cheeked by the minute.

And Doran also recalled another evening spent with Diakatos-Leonidas—the evening after they'd buried Aphrodite Thromos in the cemetery at Kondokali village. Over a glass of wine at the now familiar *taverna*, Doran pondered his own fate. Back home he knew that certain nebulous forces had him right where they wanted him—in a straight jacket, his emotions frozen, talking in clichés, confined within narrow parameters. In Greece he felt free, though he was not altogether certain that he could trust himself to make the most of new latitude. Turning to Leonidas, he spoke man-to-man: "Something tells me *not* to leave Greece—to start all over again—to make Hellas my home! But I just don't know…"

"Life is short, Doran," said Leonidas.

"Maybe too short for mistakes," he said.

Leonidas laughed. "If your heart tells you to stay, then who are you to argue? You know the Greeks. They will always help you."

"It's true, isn't it?"

"*Yamas*, my friend! Now drink your wine!"

At road's end Doran thanked the driver for making a minor detour to accommodate his particular destination, and then marched across the strand in the direction of Taverna Loyiza Hara-Theou. The surf pounded upon the sand, and the sun shone brightly in the clear sky. And though it was now eleven days into the month of September, many tourists remained at the resort community of Glyfada. Approaching the entrance of the outdoor restaurant, Doran recalled the night before he and Alarice had left Corfu for a self-guided tour of Athens and the Cyclades.

"So this is good-bye forever!" Katerina, the overworked waitress, had cried.

"Not forever," Alarice consoled her. "How could we not return to Corfu? Kerkyra is part of us now."

"You do not understand," Katerina lamented. "In two weeks I return to Crete to be with my mother. This is terrible. I might never see you again!"

"We can write long letters," suggested Alarice.

Pouting, Katerina had bitten her nails the entire evening.

By midnight, Gisela and Spiro had arrived and were playing cards with the two Australians, Brandon Harrison and Matthew Niven. At an adjacent table, Doran and Alarice sat with Leonidas, talking and drinking ouzo. Leonidas shook both their hands warmly and kissed each of them cheek to cheek. "Safe journey!" he had wished them, and made them promise to visit him when they returned to Corfu.

During summer, Taverna Loyiza Hara-Theou was always crowded with customers, but by the second week of September most of the tourists had returned to their homes and jobs in northern Europe, and today only a few tables were occupied. To Doran, the restaurant looked much the same as it had ten years ago: a leafy grape arbor overhead, urns sprouting fresh basil and oregano at the entrance, old fishing nets and buoys decorating trusses, octopi drying in the warm sunshine. Doran looked around for Leonidas but saw no immediate sign of him. He moved to take a seat that looked out to sea, but before he was settled, Leonidas came out of the kitchen carrying a tray of freshly grilled fish. Their eyes met at precisely the same moment. Leonidas promptly served the meal, then laid down the tray and moved toward Doran with arms outstretched.

"My friend!" he beamed. "I knew that one day you would return to Kerkyra. What took you so long?"

"I took a wrong turn at Paris," said Doran as they embraced.

Leonidas smiled, and the sunshine gleamed off his balding head. "Anyway, you are here now. And you are well, I presume. But where is your lady friend?"

"Well, she's been living in Rotterdam ever since we left Corfu," said Doran.

"*Po, po, po!* And you?"

"Here and there."

"Back to America?" Leonidas asked.

"No," said Doran.

"Good!" said Leonidas, the communist. "I always knew that you were finished with America."

"As it's turned out," said Doran.

"So you never met up with the girl?" said Leonidas.

"We wrote letters as I flounced through Europe. But we both knew that once away from Corfu our connection was lost. The real irony is that I've returned to Kerkyra ten years later with her sister!"

Leonidas' eyes went wide. "The younger one?"

"Not so young anymore," said Doran.

The restaurateur shrugged. "I try not to look in the mirror," he confessed. "Anyway," he went on, "it sounds like a tricky business. Be careful, my friend!"

"Not to worry," said Doran. "Ten years is a long time."

"But the memory is sometimes forever," said Leonidas with eyebrows raised. He called for a waitress to bring them a pitcher of wine, and when it arrived he filled two glasses and raised a toast to his old friend. "*Yamas!*" the Greek saluted.

"*Yamas!*" Doran returned the toast.

Each took a long swallow of the cool wine, and Leonidas immediately refilled the glasses. "So where are you staying?" asked the Greek.

"In Kondokali village," said Doran.

"With Modestos?"

"Yes. Gisela and I have rented Aphrodite's old apartment."

Leonidas smiled at the paradox. "I can't believe you're staying with the younger sister!"

"A twist of fate," said Doran.

"I can only imagine," said Leonidas. "How long are you planning to stay on Corfu?"

"No immediate plans to leave," said Doran.

"On Corfu, winter is very different than summer," counseled Leonidas.

"I spent half a winter here," Doran reminded him.

"Yes, I remember. Modestos went to Cyprus and you stayed on at his sister's house."

"Until I left for Sicily."

"And that was the last any of us here on Corfu heard of you."

"I guess I should have written," Doran apologized. "But life is full of unexpected twists and turns. At least my life…"

Leonidas waved off the alibi. "What's important is that you've returned. As all Corfu's prodigals return! Do you have work here?" he wanted to know.

"Nothing specific," answered Doran. "But I've agreed to help Modestos this winter with his olive trees. And we've cultivated a small farm in the hills behind Kondokali."

"Not much of a job, my friend," said Leonidas.

"So far it's my only offer," said Doran. And then he qualified, "But the work sounds wholesome. I've never farmed before, but on some level it appeals to me."

"Then why not give it a try?" said Leonidas. Again he raised his glass to Doran, this time for luck in his farming endeavor.

Once the pitcher of wine was empty, the visit came to an end. Leonidas needed to prepare for the dinner guests, and Doran promised to visit again soon.

Walking back up the beach toward the road, Doran found a place to pause. Sitting on the sand and looking out to sea, he understood why the Mediterranean appeared to so many as an ultramarine jewel. The sea ebbed and flowed between its blue-green and violet moods.

Born of sea foam, the daughter of Zeus and Dione today immersed herself in prospect. With hair tucked neatly behind her floppy straw hat, the woman's bare shoulders were full and round. Her muscular back turned toward Doran, she too looked out to sea. What horizon did she search?

Alarice!

Caught totally off guard by the mirage, Doran found himself swept out to sea and thrown over waves, swallowed by troughs until he was once more washed ashore on the solitary island of credibility.

Uncharacteristic as such visions were to him, Doran left Glyfada feeling fragmented and confounded. He hoped to find Gisela at the apartment. He wanted to discuss his two metaphysical encounters with her, for she was presumably more inclined to the ethereal side of existence. At the bottom of the incline he put out his thumb to wait for a ride back to Kondokali village.

After leaving the secret garden, Gisela wandered along a panoramic back road that overlooked the bay and led finally to the resort town of Gouvia. There she found a comfortable seat at the Paradox Café and ordered a cool drink to offset the midday heat. Her predilection for visions—first Aphrodite at the foot of her bed and then Maude as a shepherd in a meadow adjoining Gisela's own sanctuary—had left her feeling rather unnerved. Presently, she wished only for the tangible, the mundane.

In truth, her psychic tendencies had seemed to grow stronger since coming to Greece. Her dreams were more symbolic, and possibly prescient. Auras were more obvious, and more brilliant. Now, she seemed, like it or not, to be in contact with the dead; and curious as these encounters were, she felt inclined to recoil from such morbid manifestations. For the moment, a bit of normalcy was all she wanted. A Coca-cola. A cigarette. To thumb through a fashion magazine…

Across the street, the bell at Gouvia's Orthodox Church rang with an odd timbre.

What was she going to do about Doran Seeger? While her feelings for him were no doubt profound and sincere, she felt fairly certain that she was *not* in love with him. Yet in moments of uncertainty, and in times of personal crisis, she tended to cleave to him for solidarity. Was this not love? Perhaps there was no perfect love—only aspects of love. Gisela had known its various phases: Passion, yes! Familial love, certainly yes! Platonic love, yes! But a love that encompassed every fiber of inevitability, every degree of emotion, every nuance of eternity… Anyway, love was blind—an axiom redundant in its certainty. To date, no relationship of such profundity had come her way. To Gisela, a connection so essential and so vital was certainly desirable, even as the passing of time seemed to render it more and more implausible.

Again the church bell chimed. Had someone in the

village perished, Gisela wondered?

Passing her finger counter-clockwise around the rim of her glass, and lost for the moment in thought, Gisela idly looked up to see a man moving quite deliberately up the street. His back was turned toward her, but she noted an artist's palette and a small easel strapped onto his rucksack; and as the image of the itinerant registered in her consciousness, her thoughts and emotions instantly froze, and the fine hairs on her forearm stood up as a result of some obscure, psychically generated, static electricity.

Alexi Stolaroff!

Impossible, Gisela thought to herself! Yet impossibility itself was today's predominant theme, today's imposing conundrum. Did she wish to confront her former lover? Not here. Not now. Not ever! Leaving money on the table, and quickly collecting her belongings, Gisela ventured a second look. Though the figure was now further along the street, there was no doubt in her mind concerning his identity. Stumbling down the steps of the Paradox, Gisela walked briskly in the opposite direction, determined to rekindle the relative sanctity of her home in Kondokali village.

Having returned from Glyfada, Doran sat on the small balcony outside the apartment sipping a cool drink and browsing through a copy of *Der Spiegel* left by a German tourist who had occupied the lower apartment during the previous week. Gisela was inside the apartment watching television. Doran could hear her flipping through the various channels; first Greek, then French, and finally English: CNN. He'd only begun to read an article about the German chancellor's coalition with the Green Party when he heard Gisela's incredulous exclamation.

"Something terrible has happened in America! Come inside, Doran. Quickly! You must see this!"

Doran got up from his seat and went inside the apartment. Gisela sat before the TV, her mouth wide open in astonishment. "I can't believe it!" she said.

Doran turned his attention to the screen. The London transmission, which they normally received, had been pre-empted by the American version originating from Atlanta; and there seemed to be little doubt that the CNN news team was in disaster mode. Centered in New York City, the broadcast moved haphazardly from one reporter to another, each one apparently more shocked than the last. "What's going on?" Doran asked.

At that moment the screen shifted to the image of a commercial airliner crashing into a skyscraper. Fire and smoke billowed immediately from the building. "What is this?" he asked, confounded. "Some sort of disaster movie?"

"I don't think so," said Gisela. Her attention on the TV screen was rapt.

"Some sort of Orson Wells prank?" Doran speculated.

"No, Doran, this is real! They're saying that it's an attack!"

"An attack? By whom?"

"Listen to the announcer! My God! This is terrible!"

Doran again turned his attention to the TV. The screen again shifted to the image of the airliner crashing into the building. "It's a video tape," Doran surmised.

"This is unbelievable!" said a CNN reporter. *"The first crash came at slightly after nine o'clock, eastern daylight time; now a second plane has crashed into World Trade Center II! Near the site, it is absolute bedlam—smoke everywhere, people running for their lives, people jumping from windows eighty and ninety stories up! The fire department is on the scene—every available piece of equipment, every available firefighter. Mayor Giulliani is on his way to the... Wait... I'm told we have breaking news. We're switching now to a White House news briefing.*

The screen shifted to a man behind a podium. In the background was the Presidential Seal. In a somber mood, and with measured speech, the spokesman was reading a prepared statement: *"At approximately 9:21 a.m. this morning, an American Airlines 767 crashed into one of the buildings of the World Trade Center. At approximately 9:42 a.m. a second plane hit World Trade Center II—a United Airlines 767. A third plane has crashed into the Pentagon, causing significant damage and loss of life. We've been advised that a fourth plane has crashed at a rural site in Pennsylvania. These events do not appear to be an accident. Nor do they appear to be random events. Though we are uncertain as to the perpetrators of this barbaric act, or of their motives, we can only assume that this is a deliberate attack upon the United States. The president was in Florida at the time of the attack. He has since left Florida aboard Air Force One for an undisclosed location. Vice President Cheney has also been taken to a secure location. It is important to emphasize that the government is up and running. We're dealing with the situation. We'll have more details for you as they become known. Thank you."*

Again the image of the second plane crashing into WTC… The fireball. The smoke. The mayhem.

Throughout the evening, Doran and Gisela watched the television. Each allowed his attention to be diverted only for a moment or two, (to make a sandwich or fry an egg, or to visit the bathroom), and then only when the tension imposed not only by the event itself, but by the media coverage per se, became too difficult to sustain.

"Today's date is September eleventh," said Doran to Gisela. "That's 9/11… Opposite of Europe, Americans write the month first and the day second. In the USA, 911 is the designated telephone code for *Emergency*. I wonder if the hijackers were exploiting such a subtle connection?"

By nightfall, in Greece, they witnessed the collapse of the first tower. A few hours later the second tower came down as well. Tons and tons of steel and glass and cement crumbled to the street. Smoke and dust billowed up the urban canyons of Manhattan. Injured people staggered from the debris. New York looked like a war zone, reminiscent of Beirut or Sarajevo! The human toll was overwhelming; reports estimated anywhere from two thousand to possibly ten thousand people might have been inside the two buildings at the time of impact. The actual number was of course unknown. How many might have escaped the fiery devastation was, again, pure speculation. It suddenly occurred to Doran that his friend Scarlet Ponton was presently living in New York City. He recalled that her family's apartment was located in Manhattan.

For seventy-two hours, with only minimal sleep, Doran and Gisela monitored the catastrophe. The number of confirmed casualties grew by the hour, as did the anger of the American people, and that of the civilized world. World leaders and civilians expressed sympathy and support, and outrage. Seemingly within hours, the FBI had identified the suicidal hijackers of the four airplanes: nineteen men of Arabic descent, members of a nebulous group of Middle Eastern terrorists called *al Qaida*, their leader a turban-wearing, bearded, extremist Muslim bogeyman named Osama bin Laden.

To Doran, President George W. Bush had looked at first overwhelmed, though it was not long before he'd donned a decidedly defiant mask. *"There's an old poster out west,"* he told reporters. *"I believe it says: Wanted: Dead or Alive!"* A line was being drawn in the sand of the Afghan desert.

"Cowboy diplomacy," Doran muttered to Gisela.

"It's a terrible act," said Gisela. "Somebody has to stand up to whoever did this. And it's the first duty of a government to protect its citizens!"

"But it's not quite that simple, is it?" said Doran. "Because in fact nobody undertakes a suicide mission without feeling intensely passionate about his cause. And it may be the primary duty of a government to protect its citizens, but in practice governments always protect themselves first, and their citizens second."

"I don't presume to understand the philosophy of martyrdom," said Gisela, "but whatever the cause, an act like this is intolerable!"

"That point is unassailable. But nobody seems to be

asking the essential question: Why?"

"Who cares why? Bottom line is that they have to be stopped!"

"How does a government stop a martyr? Or harder yet, a well organized, well funded group of martyrs?"

"I don't know."

"It always comes down to *us* and *them*, doesn't it? When hit, the simplistic answer is to hit back harder. But when has that ever worked? Civilized societies have to evolve beyond the Biblical mentality. Otherwise we're all going up in smoke."

Again and again the image of the second plane hitting the chrome and glass tower... The fire. The smoke. The chaos.

On Wall Street, an already weak stock market lost seven trillion dollars in capital following the attack. Mayor Giulliani, an already popular, outgoing mayor, now sang his swan song. President George W. Bush embraced the opportunity for a place in history—as well as other spoils of war, presumably. The hijackers, Mohammed Atta, *et al*, had learned to fly Boeing jets at an air school in Florida. Afghanistan's hard line fundamentalist government, the Taliban, categorically denied advanced knowledge of the incident. General Musharif of Pakistan tried desperately to control the militant Muslims in his own country even as he appeased the West. And of course the arch villain himself: Osama bin Laden! He was mute and nowhere to be found.

Again the image of the plane crashing into the skyscraper... And again... And again... And again... The more times one saw this image, the more incredible it seemed. Until it was itself unreal. Until it was itself only a bad dream from which a well-heeled culture would soon awaken...

After three continuous days of anxiety-filled observation, Doran had to will himself away from the television. He could watch only so much pandemonium. He'd not set foot in the United States for nearly ten years, and his understanding of present-day American life was decidedly behind the times; yet this event, as no other event, had reconstituted him as an American. The divorce he'd initiated ten years ago had never been finalized anyway. What he felt now was *not* blind patriotism; rather it was an expression of sympathy and concern—sympathy for those at ground zero, and concern for the families and friends of those directly involved. His sense of anxiety was far more political in origin.

Indeed, how might the American Government respond? If military action was imminent, and Doran suspected that it was, who would suffer the consequences? Mostly innocent people, that much was certain. And he was not wholly ignorant of such consequences. In fact, he understood that whatever weapons he had helped create more than a decade ago were now as obsolete as stones and spears. The American military had demonstrated its capabilities on a number of occasions over the past ten years: in Libya, in Somalia, and most recently in Serbia. All under the auspices of the UN, of course… But the devastation rendered—as well as the weaponry used to render it—were well documented, if one read the right periodicals.

For example, Level-3 Communications produced a line of attack simulators, while TRW Corporation made spy satellites that could literally see an ant on an anthill from a hundred miles up through bad weather. Northrop Grummen manufactured 'Unmanned Aerial Vehicles' that flew beyond the range of anti-aircraft artillery and were used to monitor enemy troop movement on the ground. Boeing Corporation had designed and built a high-tech 'Advanced Global Positioning System'. And that was not all…

Doran knew, for example, that a company called Ceradyne was producing, by means of advanced ceramics technology, thousands and thousands of body armor suits that were capable of stopping rounds from a .50-caliber machine gun at point blank range. Also under development were 'Directed Energy Weapons' such as disruptors, radio frequency bombs, microwaves, and lasers. And the Pentagon had already underwritten R&D for a 'Total Information Awareness System' to be used to track and cross-reference all computer records of transactions made by everyday citizens.

No question about it, today's *smart bombs* were infinitely smarter than the weapons employed during the Gulf War. And unlike his father, the first President Bush, this president seemed to possess the will to go the distance. Or at least that will existed within his cabinet. The Secretary of Defense had made that perfectly clear. As the National Symbol, the hawk had summarily replaced the eagle—once again!

Reading discussions in various chat rooms on the Worldwide Web, Doran surmised that every bellicose loony in the United States was out of the woodwork and ready to let blood. The blind rage being expressed, which curiously enough was directed not only at the perpetrators, but also at one another—was chilling to say the least. Still, there remained the question that nobody—neither Americans nor international friends and allies—seemed willing to address: Why?

Apparently terrorist cells were dispersed throughout the Muslim world and beyond—a world that was growing exponentially as Christianity decreased by degrees. These cells were well organized and well funded by sympathetic governments. And their members were desperate to the point of committing *kamikaze* attacks. Martyrdom was part of their credo. Why such anger?

One who was well informed on the pertinent issues understood that the list of abuses inflicted by the West upon the Arab World at large was both long and deleterious. The American president was no doubt ready to shoot from the hip; that was, plain and simple, good politics at home. But Doran understood instinctively that the issue desperately needed fair-minded and impartial voices to offer an alternative to war. Heavy-handed politics, and forceful tactics employed to enforce them, could not be in one breath both the cause of the problem and its solution. Was he inclined to be such a voice?

Living as an expatriate in Europe for ten years, the idea of returning to the States struck him as immediately obtuse. What could a man without means or connections hope to accomplish? More likely he would be swallowed up in the patriotic frenzy. Or co-opted by the system—again! Though he understood that if the situation became critical, he might be forced to return to the States. Henry Miller had been deported when World War II broke out because the Greek Government could not guarantee his safety. Miller's repatriation had prompted the writing of his now renowned essay, *The Air-conditioned Nightmare*. If America was too chilly then for Miller, what might it now be like for an ex-engineer who'd sold off his American account and bandied about Europe for the better part of a decade?

Doran quickly determined that martyrdom was not germane to his make-up. Nor was the sacrifice of a lifestyle hard earned and well lived. For even as the devastation and grief caused by the attacks upon the WTC and the Pentagon were monumental, they had offered Doran a rather inverse release from the guilt he felt concerning Desert Storm. Whatever the mayhem and destruction unleashed by the United States upon the Taliban and the *al Qaida* terrorists, and particularly upon the Afghani people, or upon Saddam Hussein, the current weaponry was certainly a generation beyond those he had helped to fashion. Perhaps this was a reprehensible purge, but he knew that with the first salvo upon Kanduhar, his guilt would be mitigated once and for all. And if his patriotism was somehow in question, at least his professed pacifism remained resolute. To this doctrine he would remain true as he turned the earth and tended the orchard.

CHAPTER 12
AMONG FRIENDS AND
ACQUAINTANCES

It was not until all the tourists had left Corfu at summer's end that the neighbors proximate to Pension Aphrodite truly acknowledged Doran and Gisela. Residing in a variety of houses surrounding the *dhomatia*, they invariably led ephemeral lives, and their activities were conducted in an entirely different realm than those of the summertime visitors. Though once it was determined that Doran and Gisela intended to remain throughout the winter, the outpouring of hospitality and good will was enthusiastic and inclusive.

Sitting under the grape arbor in the *dhomatia's* garden, and strumming a borrowed guitar, Doran silently inventoried the aggregate of characters he'd encountered in Kondokali's rather curious society.

Living directly across the cobbled alleyway were Mikalis and Fedra Koukourous. In his gruff voice and coarse manner, Mikalis offered Doran drinks of *raki* and told him stories, second-hand, about Corfu during the time of the Second World War. Mikalis was also a dancer: he could be seen nightly at his bar leaping over flaming clay pots to the music of *Zorba's Theme*.

Fedra Koukourous, obviously beautiful in her youth, now had the voice of a banshee and the body of a mule. She appeared one day on the steps of their balcony, her arms loaded with oranges and lemons that she'd picked from her orchard in the low hills behind Kondokali village.

In the building opposite the Koukourous' house lived Mikalis' sister Koula. Standing no more than four-and-a-half-feet tall, Miss Koula was nearly as rotund as she was high. Her offering to Doran and Gisela was a freshly made pot of chicken soup accompanied by a dish of ripe olives. It was she who had tagged Gisela with the endearing nickname, *Stellamou*!

Occupying the apartment above Miss Koula was a very secretive man called Vassilis. Seldom seen on the streets of the village, it was impossible to mistake him for someone else when he did appear, for he possessed the singular identifying feature of extremely big ears—so big in fact that one had only to refer to 'the-man-with-the-ears' and anyone living in Kondokali village would have known immediately to whom the speaker was referring. But that was not his only oddity. From his balcony he could easily see into Aphrodite's kitchen window, and it was not long before Doran noticed that he spent considerable time peering into their apartment, presumably hoping to catch a glimpse of the goddess undressed. Gisela made a point of wearing her bathrobe.

Adjacent to Pension Aphrodite lived an extended family of Albanian immigrants: two brothers, their wives, and their various children—nine people living in four rooms! For Doran, (himself a curiosity because of his nationality and because he lived with a much younger woman), and for Gisela too, (now known and referred to within the immediate neighborhood as *Stellamou*), it was difficult to determine just who belonged with whom, but that hardly seemed consequential. They were simply the

Venetti family: two men, their wives, eighteen-year-old twin girls, two teenage boys, and a sister of thirteen or fourteen years. As the two brothers, Nikos and Sotheris, worked odd jobs and fished for a living, their wives cooked and did chores. The Venetti twins, Alexandra and Ariti, were slaves to the latest fashions from Milan, as they did superfluous needlework and waited for marriage proposals. The boys were devoted, body and soul, to their motorbikes. The youngest girl, Victoria, was the only one of nine who spoke English, and she provided the connection necessary for communication.

The Greek people of Kondokali village saw one another frequently, and everyday life along Christopher Street offered a plethora of heartfelt and indispensable reunions. And once the residents of the village had come to recognize their faces, it was all-but-impossible for Doran or Gisela to walk the length of the road without being greeted by Panos the baker, or Zoe the coiffeur, or Yiannis the fishmonger. Of course neither Doran nor Gisela spoke more than elemental Greek, but that seemed not to matter: the villagers usually included them in conversations whose meanings were well beyond their understanding.

One such denizen was an old woman named Thalia who lived in a ramshackle house at the outskirts of the village. There she kept a few chickens and grew a meager crop of vegetables on a sun-hardened patch of earth otherwise forsaken even by weeds. Though obviously quite poor, and in every way an anachronism, she was always treated with respect by the more affluent and progressive members of the society. Faded and tattered were her clothes, but her eyes were bright; wrinkled was her skin, but her touch was gentle. Her snaggled tooth smile was always warm and immediate, especially towards Gisela.

Caught in a stupendous downpour one afternoon in late September, Doran and Gisela huddled, soaking wet and shivering, in the doorway of an abandoned shop. They were only a few blocks away from home, but rather than brave the elements, they chose to wait for the wind and rain to cease. But the storm was a violent one, and the rain continued to come down in torrents. Within minutes Christopher Street was knee-deep in rushing water.

As they continued to crouch in the doorway to break the wind, they saw the figure of a woman, umbrella overhead and blown inside out by the force of the gale, approaching along the flooded street. Thalia! The old woman seemed undaunted by the weather, and as she reached their position, she took off her patch-quilt jacket and placed it over Gisela's bare shoulders. "*Xrio!*" she exclaimed. "Cold!"

Gisela tried to refuse the kindness and pushed the jacket back to her. Declining the gesture, Thalia remained adamant. "You take, please!" Reluctantly, Gisela conceded.

Once Thalia was certain that Gisela was warm against the wind, she waded through the water in the street and approached the doorway to the Kumquat Restaurant.

"Ruli Ianakis!" she called out in a loud voice to the establishment's owner.

After a few moments, the burly proprietor of the restaurant appeared at the door. He recognized the old woman instantly. Cold and wet, Doran was dumbfounded as the words of their conversation flew like debris in a maelstrom; but apparently Thalia had instructed her cousin, Ruli Ianakis, to drop whatever he was doing and drive the *xeni* home at once.

Without argument or delay Ruli respectfully did exactly as the woman had instructed, donning his raincoat and putting on rubber boots before bringing his car curbside in front of the two rain-drenched strangers. Still dripping, Doran and Gisela had tumbled into the old Ford for the two-block drive back to their apartment at Pension Aphrodite.

Doran was certainly inclined to acknowledge that the Greeks, as a people, were charismatic and extremely hospitable; but there existed on Corfu a separate culture as well, a so-called *second society*. Nearly three thousand British, and a smaller but still significant number of Dutch expatriates, lived side by side with their Greek hosts, most of them living aboard small yachts anchored in Gouvia Marina.

Some of the more colorful ex-pats inhabiting the village included a thirty-something Dutch hippie known simply as Pink Pants, who lived alone aboard a thirty-nine-foot boat that he'd christened Cloud Nine, and who seemed to own not a single pair of trousers that had not been dyed pink. Philbar Cullinain maintained that Pink Pants was capable of discussing only two subjects in any detail whatsoever: sailing and himself.

Another young Brit seen often on the streets and in the bars of the village was a fellow simply called Swampy. Nobody really knew quite why he was here, (or for that matter why he was called Swampy), but virtually everybody who knew him agreed that he was an extremely diverse individual. At only twenty-seven, *Swampy* humbly claimed, among his many accomplishments, to have been a motocross racer in Spain, an expert parachutist in the RAF, a surfing champion in Bali, the substitute drummer for the Rolling Stones when Charlie Watts was unavailable, and a Certified Public Accountant.

"More like a Certified Public Liar!" Dazey Cullinain had said to Doran. Quite cleverly, she had calculated that if Swampy had really done everything he claimed to have done, he would be no less than eighty-six years old!

In contrast to Pink Pants and to Swampy, the two co-owners of the Navigator's Pub, Uwe and Clarence, were quite well liked among the community of ex-pats, though neither was exempt from the gossip of their compatriots: Uwe, the Belgian who was a half-owner of the popular bar, was supposedly wanted by Interpol; Clarence, it was said, had narrowly escaped loan sharks back in the U.K. and had been hiding out in Greece for fourteen years. Doran took the scandal with a grain of salt. Whether or not any or all of this was true was anyone's guess, but most agreed, he ascertained, that where smoke rose, fire burned.

And, of course, there was Albanian Orestos, the rather infamous Elvis impersonator! Usually dressed in white sequined pants and jacket, *Elvis* always saluted Doran as they passed on the street. No doubt, this self-crowned King of Karaoke truly fancied himself as a *hunk-a-hunk 'o burning love*! Doran grimaced at the thought that Elvis Presley might indeed be eternal.

Another curious fixture known at least by sight to every citizen of the village was a ninety-five-year-old Danish man in a motorized wheelchair called Otto. Frail as a bird and blind as a bat, Otto seemed to delight in terrorizing traffic at the center of Kondokali's only intersection. And it seemed nothing less than a miracle that this Magoo of a character had managed to reach his tenth decade without being flattened by one of Corfu's more 'adventurous' drivers. Doran himself had witnessed several near catastrophes.

Also often seen (but mostly heard) in the Navigator's Pub was a rather bigoted Brit by the name of Dennis Payne, (like Cullinain, an ex-member of the SAS, and also a former inmate at London's Wormwood Scrubs Prison), who, once he'd learned that Doran was by nationality an American, complained loudly and often that England had gone to no small trouble to export a civilized culture to North America, only to have the U.S.A. turn the tables, so to speak, some three hundred years later. It was a debate that Doran had neither expected nor relished.

"The crudest aspects of American culture usually show up in Britain straight-away," Payne admonished. "It's like a plague—or a curse—almost as if the Americans have built a pipeline underneath the Atlantic through which they export, shall we say, a profusion of untreated waste. And it's driving the British culture to rack and ruin!"

Yet, in a different context, Payne truly admired the

U.S.A. Or maybe it was the other way around…

"Honestly, it's a great country," he'd said to Doran as he bought him one drink after another. "You've got everything there, don't you? Nice homes, good cars… Chevrolet is a pretty good car, isn't it? The U.S.A. has the best of everything, and everybody in the whole world knows it!

"And Shrub's no sissy, either. He's not going to take this Arab thing lying down. Not like Bushdaddy in '91. Shrub's tougher than Bushdaddy. Honestly, Seeger, the U.S.A. is a great country!"

Doran had been willing to neither accept credit nor shoulder blame for the cumulative habits and attitudes of the American culture or the American Government; but apparently Payne felt a certain regret concerning the so-called degradation of the society in which he'd once lived. A society he openly still loved! Intent on creating a scapegoat, he'd chosen the U.S.A. Still, Doran was decidedly disinclined to confirm or deny the Englishman's analysis, for his own experience was hardly current. Nationalistic rhetoric in general seemed rather superfluous to one who'd been skipping from country to country during the past ten years. After all, people were people. Their similarities were magnanimous, their differences mostly inconsequential. Conflict was never waged over blood type; it was always about money! And power! Of course money *was* power. And these days oil was money.

"Put it all together," Doran puffed, "and *what d'ya get?*"

"Suppose you tell me," said the pompous Englishman.

"At least in one regard I think you're absolutely correct, Payne: Chevrolet is a pretty good car."

"Runs on gasoline, I believe…"

"Gasoline is a compound—a solution of hydrocarbons mixed with a sufficient number of red corpuscles."

"Quite a few cars in the U.S.A. They've got to have fuel."

For the time being, Doran was not willing to divulge

his past. "Plenty of cars in Britain, too," he said.

"Not to mention industry," said Payne.

"Greece exists on the periphery of all that stuff," said Doran. "Here it's possible to live a different way."

"That's fantasy," laughed Payne.

"Not entirely," said Doran. "Here I farm with a hand shovel and a hoe."

"Mr. Back-to-nature!"

"Call it what you like," Doran invited. "It still feels good to me. And here a tomato still tastes like a tomato!"

"Maybe you can run your car on tomato juice…"

"I don't have a car. I don't want one. I walk everywhere I go, sole to the earth, heel and toe, heel and toe. It's an invigorating connection. It grounds me. It makes me feel alive!"

"How noble of you, Seeger! But that's not going to stop Shrub. You know it, and I know it."

"I know it probably sounds trite to you, but if one person refuses to kill… If one person rejects avarice, then another, and another…"

"Sixties tripe! Get in the game, Seeger!"

"I *was* in the game. I quit the game."

Payne shook his head—not necessarily with regret. "Shrub's got the right idea," he said. "Kick the Arabs' ass and take the gas! Eighteen percent of the world's known oil reserves are in Iraq. Once he's got a foothold in Baghdad, maybe he can even bring down the House of Saud!"

"But the question remains: Who's going to do the bleeding?"

"Not you or me," said Payne smugly.

"And how convenient is that?" Doran's face was growing uncharacteristically red.

"Relax, Mr. Natural! It's just the way things are. It's the way things have always been."

"And some of us can't seem to get enough of it…"

"Come on! It's great fun. And not much risk, either!"

"That's sick!"

"Who's to say?"

"I'm the one to say so," said Doran adamantly.

"So plant your pacifism on your little patch of dirt, Seeger, and see what grows there!"

Already Doran had fertilized his winter garden with sufficient guilt. This he knew. But self-reproach was not the only humus he'd used: other sentiments as well fed the earth he now tilled. And, as Modestos had told him, it was good ground indeed. Fertile ground…

Late October, and summer had turned to autumn—*Small Summer*, as the Corfiots called it. Many of the shops that catered to the tourist trade were in the process of closing for the winter; and the jewelry merchants and souvenir hawkers and rent-a-bike dealers were looking forward to a winter filled with card games and fishing and family gatherings. The village children had returned to school. The ex-pat sailors that lived aboard yachts in Gouvia Marina were preparing for the annual end-of-season regatta.

Doran, too, had abandoned the more trivial pursuits of summertime. Instead, he absorbed himself in the labor of farming: tilling soil, roping off garden plots, fashioning furrows, and spreading sheep dung. He'd also gone several times with Modestos to the forty-tree grove below Pantocrator, mostly to assess the progress of the ripening olives, for it was not yet time to put out the nets that would eventually catch the fallen fruits.

"Beginning in mid-November, the winter rains will come," Modestos told him. "For this reason we must be ready to sow the seeds. On Corfu, it is possible to grow many vegetables during winter. Whatever you like. You select. This winter we pay nothing for food!"

Doran assured his benefactor and partner that he was making excellent progress preparing the ground that would support their winter garden.

"And then… And then…" Modestos' exuberance for such wintertime activities was transparent. "And then, after forty or fifty days, the weather will change," he told Doran. "The wind will blow from the north instead of the south. For this reason we must put out the nets during November, so that when the wind changes direction and moves the branches we can catch the olives as they fall from the trees."

On a clear morning, Doran dressed in work clothes as Gisela slept. The routine he'd come to practice entailed a fifteen-minute walk into the low hills behind the village. He particularly liked the early morning light, and birdsong provided a sound track for his meditation. Having nearly finished the preparation of the garden plots, today he meant to clear away brush in the vicinity of the old water well so that he might assess the possibility of creating a gravity-flow irrigation system. If the rains came late, or came not at all, the success or failure of the crops would depend upon his ability to bring enough water from the well to the fledgling plants. Donning his straw hat, and picking up his hoe and shovel, he smiled to himself at the new application he contemplated for his engineering skills.

As Doran stepped onto the small balcony, the Ionian light hit him square in the face. With his free hand he shaded his eyes and waited for his vision to adjust to the brightness. And as he moved toward the whitewashed staircase, he naturally surveyed the *dhomatia's* patio. There the figure of a woman stood in the shade of the arbor. Her presence took him by surprise, and he squinted against the sunlight to see her face.

"How's it going, Seeger?" the woman called up to him.

The voice was not only familiar; it was unmistakable. Doran was dumbfounded. "Scarlet Ponton!"

"Surprised to see me here?"

"You might say that," he laughed as he laid down his gardening tools. "What are you doing here, Scarlet?"

"Last week, in New York, I was talking to Basso on the

telephone, and we were wondering just how you're getting along. Vasil suggested that we pay you a visit."

"Basso?"

"He's arriving tomorrow from Prague," Scarlet informed.

"I'm flabbergasted!" said Doran as he moved down the staircase.

"You ought to know me by now, Seeger. You should know that I'm likely turn up anywhere at anytime."

"But when did you arrive, Scarlet?" Reaching the bottom of the staircase, he kissed her cheek as a gesture of welcome.

"Early this morning. Yesterday I flew first from New York to Frankfurt, and then I caught a red-eye charter flight to Corfu. At the airport I told the taxi driver to take me to this village. I must have murdered the pronunciation, but I finally made him understand where I wanted to go. It was barely light when he dropped me off in front of some English-style pub up the street."

"The Navigator's Bar," said Doran.

"Of course, all the shops and restaurants were closed, so I wandered around the village for a while until some guy came along and asked me if I needed a room. Imagine that!"

"Happens all the time around here. The Greeks are a very hospitable people."

"Anyway, I told the guy that I was looking for an American man about fifty years old who was probably staying with a younger Dutch woman. The guy seemed to know immediately whom I was talking about, and he pointed out this house to me. Since it was still an indecent hour, I decided to wait here on the patio until I saw somebody moving about."

"And Basso's arriving tomorrow?"

"That's how we planned it."

"I can't believe this."

Scarlet shrugged. "So, do you know a place where we

might stay?" she asked nonchalantly.

"Of course I do. The apartment below mine is vacant. The owner is my friend. I'll contact him and have him bring a key."

"How convenient," said Scarlet.

"And Basso's coming, too?"

Scarlet smiled playfully.

"You're wicked, Scarlet."

"So I've been told."

"How long are you staying?"

Again, the Colombian girl shrugged. "Whatever…" she said.

"No return ticket to New York?" Doran asked.

Scarlet shook her head. "I'm not going back there," she said. "Leaving Prague and going to New York was a mistake. And ever since nine-eleven…"

"No kidding! What's it like there, anyway?"

"New York?"

"The U.S.A. in general."

"Up tight. Angry. Scared. You name it."

"I've been watching CNN."

"I was right there, Doran. Ten blocks away at the time."

"On TV, it looked like a war zone. It must have been hideous."

"You can't even begin to imagine. I saw all the television coverage, too. But being right there was something else. No way to get it all on TV. The noise, the panic, and the smell!"

"I tried to call you. Several times. To make sure you were all right. I never got an answer."

"Everything went crazy. Nothing worked. People were walking around like blithering idiots, talking to themselves, crying, and praying. It seemed like the end of the world."

"Probably was—at least as we once knew it."

"Who knows? I'm just glad to be away."

"From New York?"

"From the insanity. The response is not going to be pretty."

"I thought Bush looked scared. Like he knew he was in way over his head."

Scarlet considered his analysis as she took a seat at the table on the patio. Doran sat down as well.

"Maybe for the first day or two," she said. "But then I'm sure that the good old boys got hold of him and gave him a sound shaking. Somebody very high up whispered in his ear, 'Wake up, Georgie! This is your big chance. Get tough! Finish the job your dad started. Don't worry, everybody with any real power will back you.' And he changed overnight from a wimp into a warlord.

"And the American people are waving their flag like you wouldn't believe. Their teeth are bared, and they're ready to kick some ass.

"Don't get me wrong, Seeger," said Scarlet. "I'm certainly not condoning what the terrorists did. But I believe that there's an extremely passionate motive behind such a desperate act."

Doran conjectured: "I'm sure that many people in the Arab world feel co-opted by Western policies. Especially concerning Israel. No doubt the seeds of what happened in New York and in Washington D.C. were sown long ago."

"I wouldn't proclaim that point of view too loudly in the States," Scarlet cautioned. "You'd likely be crucified on the cross right next to bin Laden."

"I'm not naïve, and I'm not a Utopian. But I still believe that descent is not only an American right, but sometimes a duty," Doran contended.

"What universe are you living in, Seeger? After nine-eleven, everything's changed. Everything!"

"I might have to go back there," Doran told her.

"Why? This place seems okay," she observed. Then she asked, "Things not going so well with Gisela?"

"It's not that," he said. "Anyway, I can't even discern

what's going on between Gisela and me. Tried a bit of romance, but that proved to be a disaster. No, my problem is a little more serious than a tentative love affair. The truth is that my passport is about to expire," he explained.

"Why not simply apply for a renewal?" Scarlet asked.

"Not that simple. Some archaic law says that I have to kiss the ground once every seven years. I've not been back for almost ten."

"What are you going to do about it?"

"I've made some inquiries here on Corfu, and I've got a few people working on it."

"Something under the table?"

"I don't really know precisely what these people have in mind. To date, nothing's come of their efforts. Maybe nothing will come of them. I simply don't know."

"How long before it expires?" Scarlet asked.

"Not long."

"Maybe you ought to get back into the Czech Republic while you're still able to cross borders," she suggested.

"Is that where you're headed?" he wanted to know.

"After I leave here, yes."

"I don't think I'll be going back to Prague," said Doran. "Something important seems to be happening here to me—something very elemental. It's not easy to put my finger on it. I seem to be on the verge of finding out something important, something for which I've searched for a very long time. Except I never really knew that I was searching. Or that something was even missing. Are you following me?"

"I'm not sure. But we'll have plenty of time to talk, Doran. And Basso's coming tomorrow!"

"Kondokali's not seen anyone like Vasil, I'll guarantee that!" said Doran.

"That's because there is nobody like Vasil," Scarlet laughed.

"Plastic People of the Universe," Doran uttered.

"They're more popular than ever in Prague," said

Scarlet.

"No accident," said Doran. "Basso is very creative. And very intense."

Scarlet nodded. "Where is Gisela?" she asked.

"Upstairs sleeping."

"Is there someplace we might have breakfast?" she asked.

"Sure," said Doran. "If you wait here, I'll change clothes. Then I'll take you for coffee and scrambled eggs."

"Can I leave my bags here on this patio?" she asked.

"Of course. Nobody will take them."

"Are you sure?"

"Trust me," he said.

"Okay. But don't be too long. I'm starving," she said.

Doran went back up the stairs and into the apartment to change out of his farming clothes into more appropriate dress.

By mid-afternoon, Modestos arrived with the key to the lower apartment, and Scarlet was made to feel at home. Next day, Vasil Basso arrived from Prague, and he too took up residence at the *dhomatia*.

Doran spent most of his time with his old friends, showing them around the village and the marina; but Gisela was not particularly inclined to join the threesome. Instead, she kept mostly to herself, reading, writing in her now prolific journal, visiting the secret garden, and swimming at Kondokali Beach. For even in late October the water was warm enough for bathing. And so late in the season, one might well enjoy the calm of a tourist paradise now all but abandoned by visitors.

Gisela hired a bicycle one day and pedaled uphill to the lookout at Kommeno. From such an elevated vantage point Gouvia Bay spread out before her, its blue Ionian waters glimmering in the perfect sunlight: two tiny, uninhabited islands defined the foreground of the seascape; and the faraway mountains of Albania, shrouded in the dusty haze of autumn, provided a backdrop. From her position upon this precarious escarpment, the twin fortresses that dominated the outline of Corfu Town were visible on the eastern peninsula.

Ten years after her first visit, Corfu had again cast its indomitable spell on her. This time, she suspected, in a far more permanent way. Yet, here she remained essentially alone. For she had come to realize that the possibility of a romantic relationship developing further between herself and Doran Seeger was unlikely, if indeed it was not already a dead issue. Considering everything, perhaps that was for the best. A potential conflict with her sister was thus avoided; and by nature, Doran was every bit as much a loner as she. They were like the two tiny islets that lay offshore, visible from Kondokali Beach, or from Corfu Town, or from her present position on this particular promontory. How curious, she thought, that she had now lived on Corfu an entire summer and still she did not even know their names.

These were her thoughts as Doran reveled in the warm company of two tried and true friends.

Though the next day Gisela was implored by Doran and Scarlet and Vasil to come along as they joined Philbar and Dazey Cullinain aboard the Overdraft to sail in the end-of-season regatta. The course they'd charted lay around the same two tiny islands that Gisela had so personalized the day before. Gisela consented to join the party, and the exclusive threesome now became an inclusive foursome.

The day dawned perfect for sailing, and they arrived at the dock around eleven in the morning. Philbar was onboard the Overdraft, tightening knots and readying the sails.

"Prepare to repel boarders!" he called laughingly to Dazey, who was below drinking her morning brandy and working on her daily crossword puzzle. Doran introduced his friends to Cullinain as they stepped onboard the yacht.

On tired and shaky legs, Dazey Cullinain climbed the

steps leading from the forward-cabin to the wheelhouse. She groaned and wheezed as she reached the top step. Her hair was disheveled and her clothes seemed to sag over her emaciated frame. She greeted Doran and Gisela as old friends before being introduced to Scarlet Ponton and Vasil Basso.

"They're predicting a Force One for this afternoon," she observed gaily. "Rather perfect for a sail around the bay, I should say!"

"Any day is a good day for sailing!" proclaimed Philbar.

"How many boats will be sailing in the regatta?" Scarlet inquired.

"Nearly one hundred, I presume," answered Cullinain. "And not one sound from an internal combustion engine!" he added with satisfaction.

"Would anyone care for a libation?" Dazey asked. "We've got 'ink' or brandy. Mind you, it's not very good brandy. Nor is it very good wine. But then it's alcohol, isn't it?"

All four passengers mumbled their thanks and accepted a shot of brandy. "Why not?" said Philbar Cullinain. "Good to grease the wheels!" He laughed heartily as he took up his own glass and swallowed the remaining brandy it contained.

Gisela and Scarlet found a seat at the ship's prow, while Doran spoke with Basso near the stern.

"What do you think of Corfu, Vasil?" Doran asked.

"First impression: very beautiful!" he assessed.

"Along the west coast the sand beaches stretch a full kilometer," Doran informed.

Basso nodded as he sipped the brandy.

"And the north coast is quite stunning as well," said Doran.

"But you didn't come here for the scenery, did you Seeger?" said Basso.

True to character, Vasil had cut right to the quick. "No, I did not come here for the scenery," Doran admitted. "I came here for quite a different reason."

"I must tell you, Doran, that when you left Prague to come to Greece, I thought you'd lost your mind."

"Why?" asked Doran.

"It's rather backwards here, isn't it? People riding around on donkeys, beating their wash on rocks at the river, fishing for their supper from little boats with nets and spears…"

"As you can see, Vasil, it's not quite that primitive."

"I guess not. Nevertheless…"

"Of course Greece is very beautiful. And the weather is fine year around. But it's far more than that. There's just something about the people here. I mean, even if the terrain were grotesque, I would return again and again. For the people!"

"And does Gisela play a role in your decision to live here?"

"Our relationship is not what one might think," was all Doran had to say about that. He lit a cigarette and offered one to his friend the Czech musician. "What about you, Basso? I must say that I'm surprised to see you here."

"When Scarlet telephoned me from New York with the idea of meeting her here," he began, "well, let's just say that I wasn't particularly keen on the idea. But as we talked about old times, and about the fact that we were all now miles and miles apart, and particularly about how we missed one another…"

"You mean you and Scarlet?"

"Yes."

"All the time I lived in Prague, I thought the two of you merely tolerated one another."

"Funny, that's the way I always perceived it too."

"And has it's turned out to be something more?"

"Apparently so," said Vasil. "Imagine that!"

"And the two of you have some sort of understanding?" Doran searched.

"Something along those lines seems to be developing,"

Basso explained.

"I would never have thought it possible," said Doran.

"Nor would I. But it is what it is."

"So, what's next?" Doran asked.

"We thought it might be a good idea to meet here. Not only to visit you, Seeger, but to encounter one another on a more neutral terrain. We decided that we did not want the roles we'd come to play in Prague to intrude upon our reunion. So we decided to meet here first. If all goes well, we'll return to Prague together. Then we'll see what happens."

Doran certainly knew that a particular setting could be more or less influential when it came to sustaining or undermining a relationship that had its roots in that locale. "I wish the two of you all happiness and good fortune," he said to Basso.

"Come what may!" said the musician as he raised his glass.

By this time Cullinain was ready to set sail. He guided the Overdraft out of the harbor and took his place along the line of yachts waiting to race across the bay, around the islet known as Lazaretto, along the northern coastline of Kerkyra, and finally back to Gouvia Marina. Though the distance was not particularly far, he predicted that the journey would take the entire afternoon. "All the more time to get good and pissed up!" he proclaimed. "We've got plenty of 'ink' and plenty of brandy. So fill your glasses, mates. Let the regatta begin, for we don't give a damn to win!" He blew the boat's horn loudly, which drew a stare from the crew aboard the yacht poised next to the Overdraft.

Sitting in the sunshine at the ship's prow, Scarlet observed to Gisela, "Doran looks happy here. Very happy!"

"No credit to me," said Gisela.

"What do you mean?" Scarlet wanted to know.

"It's a long story."

"But I thought—"

"That we'd fallen in love? That we'd come to Corfu as a couple?"

"Exactly that!"

Gisela shook her head. "The truth, Scarlet, is that it was never that way. Back in Prague, I thought it might develop that way, but it never really did. Sometimes we draw close, only to repel again. Doran is a loner by nature. So am I. We each need a lot of personal space. And of course a significant conflict stems from Doran's affair with my sister ten years ago. All in all, it's a little too much. At first we talked about it—or tried to talk about it. Not much luck with that. Our relationship has become mostly silent. Don't get me wrong, we like each other well enough. I think we even wonder what it might be like if we were able to draw really close. But we can't seem to bridge the gap. I think we've both come to accept it."

"I think I've fallen in love with Basso," Scarlet confided.

"Does he feel the same way?" Gisela asked.

"Yes, I believe he does."

"That's wonderful, Scarlet."

A glow rose to Scarlet's cheeks. "But it's absurd, really. I mean, we've known one another for years. Ever since I first came to Prague. And all that time we pretended only to tolerate one another. It was only when I went to New York that we discovered how much we missed each other. Isn't that crazy?"

"When it comes to love, who's to say what's crazy?" said Gisela.

"I don't want to sound too invasive, Gisela," said Scarlet, "but you've had a number of lovers, haven't you?"

"That depends on how you're counting," said Gisela.

"You know what I mean. It's just that I don't have much experience when it comes to serious affairs of the heart."

"You surprise me, Scarlet," said Gisela.

"I'm telling you the truth," she emphasized.

"I can't give you any advice," said Gisela. "Because each circumstance is different. Anyway, when it comes to relationships with men, my rate of success leaves something to be desired."

"You seem much more experienced than me," said Scarlet, still looking for encouragement.

"Just follow your heart," said Gisela. "In the end, that's all anyone can do."

Blue waters punctuated by whitecaps, a few billowy clouds coming over the southern horizon, verdant hillsides surrounding the bay, a hundred or more white sails unfurled in the sunlight, the sound of the spurge splashing against the hull: this was the scene as the Overdraft made an arc around the Island of Lazaretto. At the helm, Philbar Cullinain was in a seaman's reverie; Dazey meantime kept everyone's glass filled with wine or brandy, particularly her own! Gisela felt a bit uneasy as she considered the insipid gray aura that surrounded the captain's wife. Scarlet felt a little sea sick and concentrated her attention upon a fixed point on the horizon. Doran and Basso drank without inhibition as they reminisced over old times spent together in Prague. The Overdraft was a worthy vessel, though hardly a speed demon. Of course nobody cared to place high in the regatta. The cruise was solely for pleasure, truly a boatman's holiday!

Following the regatta, dinner was next on the agenda for the ad-hoc sextet of weekend sailors, and they arrived together at Restaurant Pericles just after dark, their faces full of sunshine, their hair windblown, and their appetites eager. On the steps leading to the patio, they were welcomed by Pericles himself and seated at a large, round table under the boughs of a mature eucalyptus tree. A string of colored lights made the atmosphere festive, and two pitchers of village wine were drawn from the cask even before they'd settled themselves around the table.

Taverna Pericles was a venerable establishment—one of Kondokali's oldest, dating back to 1901—and its reputation for fine food and generous hospitality insured that there was seldom an unoccupied table. Tonight was no exception. The restaurant was filled to capacity with sailors from the regatta, as well as regulars from the community at large. Happy Greek music came from speakers mounted on the outside wall, and the waiters dashed in and out of the kitchen carrying trays filled with plates of sumptuous foods: sea bass and octopus; *Sofrito* and spaghetti; and of course the house specialty, *Drunken Rooster*!

"My friends, tonight is a special night!" proclaimed Pericles.

"On Corfu, every night is a special night," boasted Philbar Cullinain, laughing.

"Smart man!" said Pericles, his subtle expression reiterating the obvious.

"Pericles, did you watch the regatta today?" Dazey Cullinain asked the host.

"Of course!" he said. "I watched from Kondokali Beach. A good place from which to view it—I could see everything."

"Then of course you're aware that the Overdraft placed first without serious competition," joked Philbar.

"No, I was not aware of that," Pericles played along. "Congratulations! What was the prize?"

"Dinner for the captain and the crew at Taverna Pericles," said Cullinain.

"Oh, I see. Then, everybody who sailed in the regatta must be a winner tonight!" Pericles was of course referring to the fact that there was not one empty table in his restaurant.

"Right you are, Pericles! Everybody's a winner tonight!"

Pericles filled each glass with wine, and he filled a seventh glass for himself. "*Yamas*, my friends!" he said raising a toast. "Enjoy your dinner," he implored. "And may you also enjoy each and every day of your lives!"

"*Yamas!*" they proclaimed in unison.

At the table, Philbar Cullinain retained the role of captain; and though the table was round, somehow it seemed that he declared for himself a position at its helm. Sitting together to his left were Scarlet and Basso. Doran sat at his right hand, and Gisela sat next to Doran. Dazey Cullinain occupied the place directly opposite her husband.

Over drinks, Philbar was telling the story of Ugly the Parrot, a budgie so grotesque that even his owner could hardly bare to look at him. Ugly, it seemed, had not a single feather. He was totally bald, explained Cullinain. And if he did chance to grow a feather, he immediately plucked it out. But Ugly had another curious trait, Cullinain related. Whereas most parrots loved to have their coxcomb scratched, Ugly, it seemed, had a slightly different preference. Whenever somebody approached his cage he would lean forward and present the would-be admirer his naked eyeball. "That bird loved to have his eyeball scratched!" Cullinain roared.

"You're just making that up," said Scarlet.

"True story," Philbar verified. "I saw it myself on the BBC. Ugly the Parrot! Can you imagine it?"

As Philbar told his ludicrous story, Gisela watched Dazey Cullinain with great interest and concern. The dull gray aura that Gisela had earlier perceived had grown yet darker, and now the woman's eyelids had begun to droop as well. The look of utter exhaustion she revealed seemed, to Gisela, quite out of proportion for the circumstance. Gisela hoped that Dazey was not ill. She hoped that a hearty meal would revive her spirit.

With ample fanfare, Pericles himself served the meal: *taramousalata* and trout salad as an appetizer; stuffed squid with roasted potatoes as the entrée; fresh watermelon for desert. Glassful after glassful of village wine was poured, and when the pitcher was empty, an attentive waiter immediately refilled it.

Remaining after dinner at Taverna Pericles were several persons well known to Doran and Gisela, and to Philbar and Dazey Cullinain as well. At an adjacent table, over shots of ouzo, Pink Pants held court with the rag-tag crew of his sailing vessel. Also present were Swampy and his girlfriend Pamela. Ninety-five-year-old Otto swapped stories with the retired Austrian Army Surgeon General, Wolfgang Lidl. Dennis Payne, (ex-SAS and ex-con), chatted up a recently arrived Russian immigrant named Tanya, and Kondokali's infamous transsexual, Kylie Teetlebaum, flitted from table to table. (Cullinain had often told the story of how Kylie had gone to a Greek doctor seeking much needed hormones, which were simply not available in Greece, so the doctor had suggested a certain vaginal lubricant because the compound contained similar hormones; and how, having procured the ointment, Kylie had telephoned his mum back in the U.K. lamenting, 'What in Heaven's name am I going to do with this bleeding salve? I've not yet got the proper orifice!' To which Kylie's mother had so demurely replied, 'Well, I suppose you've got to stuff it up your bum, love!'). No doubt, Philbar Cullinain was unmatched when it came to the telling of a tale, and the entire table of six was in fits of laughter over his off-color narrative as Spanos Bouranos arrived with pomp and bravado at the *taverna*—the same Greek with whom Gisela had flirted on her first visit to the Navigator's Bar, and who had taken every opportunity since to flirt with her. In his hands he carried both a bouzouki and a guitar.

Once the dishes had been cleared away, and the after dinner drinks served and then replenished, Spanos and Pericles took positions on bar stools near the doorway that led to the kitchen. In his hands Pericles held the guitar; Spanos fawned over the bowl-shaped bouzouki. As Pericles struggled to tune the six-string, Spanos plucked out Eastern-sounding melodies on his bouzouki, the staccato notes exploding from his instrument like popcorn in hot oil. Finally, Pericles was satisfied that the guitar was well tuned. He strummed a resounding chord, and Spanos regarded his partner with a grin that could have lit Christopher Street at midnight. Again, Pericles strummed the defining chord, and this time Spanos let out with an extraordinary vocal note that in all probability could have been heard in Beirut. The voluminous note continued for more than a minute, as the singer grew more and more red-faced. And when he was finally out of breath, together the duo launched into a rendition of *Zorba's Theme*, which by now was well recognized as the 'popular' Greek National Anthem!

"My God!" said Gisela referring to the singer's spontaneous display of unbridled passion. "I didn't know that so much happiness was left in all the world!"

The Greek patrons knew the words to each and every song and boisterously sang along with one number after another; while Pericles' wife Sofia danced on a tabletop, snapping her fingers and stomping her heels. Mickey and Delila Stanford, British pensioners from Kent, sat front and center before the impromptu performers. Though landed on Corfu for a semi-permanent holiday, Mickey maintained all the reserve of his former profession, that of a prestigious solicitor, while Delila played the role of a delightfully blond, dithering butterfly, quite unaware of her age. Together, they tried in vain to clap their hands along with the ever-faster rhythms of the Greek songs, a spectacle that brought snickers from anyone who watched them.

As the merriment of the evening gathered momentum, Dazey Cullinain faded by degrees. Leaning increment by increment toward Gisela's shoulder, the narcoleptic resembled the cockeyed mast of a well-weathered boat, nearly capsized. Noticing Dazey's condition, Doran eyed her ever-boisterous husband inquisitively, who said simply, "No worries, mate. We're all right." Dazey continued her top-heavy descent; eyelids tiring, complexion pallid, lips parted. Finally, she laid her head upon Gisela's shoulder, any trace of consciousness quite vanquished.

Alarmed, Gisela placed her hand upon Dazey's cheek. The skin was cold as stone. She touched the inert woman's neck, feeling for a pulse. She found none. Then she put her palm over Dazey's breast, and felt not the rise and fall of her chest. Assessing the lump of flesh now pressed upon her body, Gisela determined that Dazey's aura was fading like a landscape at twilight.

"Um…Doran!" she said under her breath.

He leaned close to her face to hear what she had to say.

"Um…I think she's dead."

"What?"

"I think she's dead!"

"No, she's just drunk."

"Um…Doran, I think she's dead!"

Gisela's insistence finally elicited his attention. Doran put his hand on Dazey's cheek and felt the icy intrusion of her mortality. "Oh, shit!" he said. He looked round the table. Engrossed in the revelry, nobody had yet noticed the critical nature of the situation. "Whatever you do, don't move!" he told Gisela. "She might topple over."

Gisela's eyes were wide with tension. A lump came into her throat. "Do something!" she commanded in a whispering voice.

"Okay. Give me a minute." Doran leaned toward Cullinain and conveyed the news.

Philbar regarded Doran with an incredulous expression, not quite understanding the immediacy of the situation. "What's that you're saying, mate?"

With all the tact and somberness he could muster, Doran repeated himself. "I believe that Dazey has passed away in her chair," he said.

Confused and a bit dazed, Cullinain stood up automatically. He moved round the table to where his wife lay slumped on Gisela's shoulder. Laying his hand tenderly on her head, he coaxed, "Come on now, Daze! We're all right…"

But of course Dazey was not all right; she was indeed quite dead. Dead as a result of her own vices. Dead perhaps from irreconcilable grief, or from undisputable displacement, but dead nevertheless. As the realization of what had happened spread through the crowd, the music abruptly ceased. Pericles put aside his guitar and jumped off his stool to lend assistance. Sofia telephoned for an ambulance, and the gathering of merrymakers dispersed onto Christopher Street murmuring their disbelief and their regret.

Three days later, a funeral was held at the Anglican Church in Corfu Town. Doran and Gisela attended the service, as did the many friends and acquaintances of the deceased. Following the memorial, Dazey Cullinain was buried at sea at the request of her husband, and a plaque was placed on the wall near the bar at the Navigator's that read, "To an English Dazey: May she bloom eternally in Heaven!"

On All Hallows Eve, Scarlet and Basso left Greece to return to Prague, fully intending to explore the relationship they had so long denied. Doran put his arms around Scarlet and hugged her deeply. "Thank you for caring about me enough to come to Greece," he told her. "You are a true friend!" Patting Basso on the back, he said, "You're a lucky man, Vasil. I still don't know exactly what it is that she sees in you, but whatever it is, don't argue. Scarlet is an extraordinary woman. I wish you both every happiness!" And Doran further implored his friend, the rock musician and poet, "Once you're back in Prague, should you see Havel sitting in the Café Slavia, please give him my fondest regards." Basso laughed but promised to convey Doran's greeting to the Czech president.

On All Soul's Day, Gisela retreated to the secret garden. There she wrote a long eulogy to Dazey Cullinain in her journal, which she later posted on a bulletin board at the *Navies*. Doran paid Cullinain a courtesy visit on board the Overdraft, but the Englishman was too drunk even to take consolation. So Doran left his friend alone in his grief and walked out of town to the one place that he himself might feel consoled, the winter garden that he'd cultivated in the low hills behind Kondokali village.

CHAPTER 13
THE FARM

By November there was still no sign of rain, which put Modestos in a quandary, if not an outright panic. Doran had constructed a gravity flow irrigation system using split bamboo poles to bring water from the well to the various garden plots, but the autumn drought and the unseasonably warm weather had rendered the well all but inadequate for the purpose of watering any seedlings they might plant. For the time being, the ground remained barren.

"If the rain does not come soon, everything will be destroyed!" Modestos feared.

"Of course the rain will come," Doran consoled him. "Until then, we will bring what water there is in the well to the furrows via the gutters that I've laid out. I know it's not enough, but it will just have to do for now."

Modestos remained doubtful but not without hope. "Perhaps we can save some of the vegetables, but in the end we will need the rain," he concluded.

Doran could not promise to affect the weather, so in the absence of storm clouds, he implemented the watering system that he'd painstakingly engineered and built. Day after day, the sun continued to shine; nevertheless, the seeds germinated, and three weeks after the first planting, sprouts appeared. Particularly successful was the crop of *kukia*, a bean similar to a lima that matured inside a long sheath. Also prolific was the planting of spinach, as well as other greens such as lettuce and endive and chard. Roots such as potatoes and carrots had a much longer germination period, as did the crop of celery, so their eventual success or failure was left, for the time being, in the balance. They had also put out onion sets and garlic bulbs; these could survive for a time without much water, so the absence of rain posed them little threat in the short term. The tomato plants and pepper plants and cucumber vines needed the most water, so an appropriate measure was diverted to them along Doran's makeshift aqueduct. The melon patch was left to the mercy of the gods.

On days when no work was required at the farm, Doran and Modestos visited the mountain olive grove on the slope of Pantocrator. There they cleared brush, pruned suckers from the base of each tree, spread powdered ammonia, and laid out the nets that would eventually catch the ripened olives as they fell from the boughs. In the various mountain villages, they collected bottles and urns in which they would eventually store the pressed olive oil.

And each trip down the mountainside involved an impromptu detour, because Modestos knew exactly where to find anything edible that grew naturally on Corfu: pinion nuts, wild greens, berries, kumquats. He knew where to collect snails, and he knew where to fish for sardines. The several empty canvas sacks he brought along in the back of his car, or in the carrier box mounted on his motorbike, always returned filled with one edible substance or another. They often stopped at public wells to fill containers with the sweetest-tasting water available on Corfu.

And there were also side trips to the homes of peasant

farmers, or gamekeepers, or vintners. Modestos was compelled to buy the purest food: freshly-churned goat cheese, the sweetest honey, homemade wine, and the freshest eggs. Corfu was a cornucopia of delectable treats, if one knew only where to harvest them. In that regard, the Greek acted as Doran's mentor, though not without ceremony. For the earth's bounty was Modestos' foremost passion, and he delighted in sharing his fervor with his American friend.

Modestos possessed boundless energy; one chore or another forever occupied him. Perhaps that was the reason he seemed to be growing slimmer by the week. Doran remembered all too well the Greek's former stature. Indeed, there was a time when Modestos' appetite had been voracious. Nobody could eat like Takis ate. These days, however, his appetite had waned, and his intake of food was sparse, to say the least. For one so single-minded concerning the procurement of fresh food, he seemed to exist primarily on the weeds he collected from various pastures, boiled limp in a pot, and eaten with only lemon juice for seasoning. To Doran, he appeared to be preoccupied with some unspecific inner balance, strictly physical in nature. Just what his obsession was, Doran had no clue. And though he remained a bit concerned over Modestos' loss of weight, his friend's diminishing physique was not Doran's only apprehension.

"Yesterday morning, at the farm, I saw a snake," Doran told Modestos one afternoon. Atop the gas stove in the lower apartment, the Greek was boiling a rancid stew composed solely of various wild plants he'd picked in an open field.

"A snake?" The Greek's interest was piqued for the moment, and he left his lunch to simmer over a low flame as he confronted Doran through the open window of the kitchen.

"Yes," Doran confirmed. "It was about five feet long. Black with orange rings."

"Where did you see it?" Modestos wanted to know. He was obviously tense at the subject.

"Near the old olive tree at the center," Doran conveyed.

"This one is very dangerous," warned Takis. "You must get it out of the garden at once!"

"Why me?" asked Doran.

"Because it is your snake," said the Greek.

"My snake?"

"Yes, it is your snake."

Doran paused, and then he said, "How do I get rid of it?"

"Lucky for you, there is a remedy," said Modestos. "It involves burning rubber."

"Rubber?"

"Yes. First you must acquire some rubber. Then you must place the rubber in a circle around the tree. You must burn the rubber for twenty-four hours continuously. After you do that, the snake will be gone!"

"You don't say!" said Doran.

"Snakes hate the smell of burning rubber."

"Who doesn't? I guess I'd better take care of it," said Doran.

"Do it as soon as possible," the Greek advised. "The snake is very clever, and he will appear when you least expect him. Once he strikes, it is too late."

Without delay, Doran went to the little bicycle shop on Christopher Street run by Alexos Maniakis. There he requested from the mechanic several old bicycle tires. Alexos did not ask why Doran wanted the spent tires; he knew that there was a snake to be vanquished.

After preparing a bedroll and a light supper, Doran carried the tires to the farm. Around the circumference of the old olive tree he cleared away brush before laying out the rubber. He did not encounter the snake, but he did locate the hole in which the creature probably lived. When the circle was made, he lit the first of the tires on fire.

255

Black smoke billowed into the clear evening air. He lit the second tire, then the third. Once he'd set each of the tires ablaze, the old olive tree was engulfed inside a cylinder of oily black smoke. A putrid smell enveloped the glen, and a murky haze spread over the face of the nearby hillside.

Doran sat upon a mound near the lettuce patch to eat the sandwich he'd made for his dinner. He watched the tires burn and smolder, but there was no sign of the infernal serpent. The Biblical implications of his task struck him as mildly comical; nevertheless he was disposed to follow Modestos' instructions to the letter.

Immersed in the allegory of the situation, Doran questioned the express nature of his personal temptation, only to find that each manifestation existed at a critical juncture. He habitually mistrusted the emergence of his deeper sentiments. He denied that which he knew in his heart to be true and whole. He was prone to reject simplicity in favor of forged complexity. Too often he turned a blind eye on beauty, or failed to respond in kind to goodwill. He tended to accept the idea that the bitterness of greed and distinction was inevitable, while the sweetness of charity and inclusion was but a mythical or bygone State of Grace. Were such fixed attitudes to be his Achilles' heel? Were the inevitable results of denial to be the legacy of modern culture?

Twilight descended as the last rays of sunlight faded upon the mountainside. Still, the bicycle tires belched the black smoke so characteristic of a petroleum fire—an intractable blaze whose source was nothing less than the decomposed remains of reptilian flesh, concealed underground for eons, drilled from the earth by eager entrepreneurs, distilled and then refined, formed at a factory into pliable loops, and finally mounted upon the amalgam wheels of a boy's conveyance. Over this particular resource the world was currently embroiled in brutal competition. Doran concluded that the application for which he'd delegated these scraps of rubber was if not more noble, then at least more benign.

As time hung upon eternity's horizon, Artemis waiting just beyond the midnight mountain silhouette, Doran lay upon his blanket. He lay with his back pressed against the earth, his body acting as a conduit to deeper mysteries. He contemplated the chiaroscuro of a nearby tree, the pinnacle of a distant mountain. Shapes and manifestations were but projections of something much more significant: indeed, something at least temporal if not truly cosmic.

Sometimes one becomes acutely aware that he is teetering upon the precipice of a pivotal moment in his life, Doran mused. If one is vigilant, Greece is full of such moments—moments when the night sky is clear and the stars are dropping into the sea, moments when one unexpectedly meets a stranger and his donkey at midnight on a dark road in the midst of an undulating grove. The ephemeral man walks slowly and a little stooped over, as he carries upon his shoulder a faggot of freshly clipped herbs gathered tenderly this night in selene shadows.

For Doran, the sense of longing induced by such images, once bittersweet, had grown by degrees into something far more vital, if still not quite tangible.

Before dawn he awakened to the crowing of a cock. His blanket was wet with dew, and he felt chilled to the bone. The acrid smell of burning rubber still permeated the air, and his lungs felt heavy from having inhaled the smoky residue of the smoldering tires. Stiffly, he rose to his feet and moved toward the tree so that he might inspect the remains of each fire. Crouching close to the ground, he determined that only a blackened, oily residue remained at each burn site. The conflagration was complete, but had it served its purpose? It appeared that Artemis, the lovely lady of the woodlands and protector of small and helpless creatures, was less inclined to save the serpent than she had been to rescue poor Iphigenia; and Doran concluded that the snake had indeed been cast out of the garden. He waited there until daylight to make certain that the fires posed no danger of spreading to the nearby brush.

Six months had elapsed since his move from the Czech Republic to Corfu, and the rather limited funds that Doran had brought with him were now running critically low. The answer to his dilemma concerning money was not at once obvious, for even though he worked nearly everyday with Modestos at the farm, or at the olive grove, hard cash was not included as part of the trade-off. Still, Doran was not inclined to panic. He'd been hard up for cash on any number of occasions during his ten-year itinerancy, and something always turned up—not always in a timely fashion, nevertheless always in the knick of time.

He knew, for instance, that the Overdraft was due to be craned out of the water for maintenance, so maybe Cullinain would pay him something to help with the anti-fouling procedure. And that way he could spend a little time with his friend, to lend his support, as well as keep an eye on him. For he knew well that Philbar was prone to drink too much under normal circumstances, and Doran wondered just what condition the recent widower had put himself in during the days after Dazey's death.

And with Scarlet now back in Prague, he knew that she would likely be hatching one money-making scheme or another; and he further knew that if he were so inclined, she would welcome him unconditionally as a partner.

Meanwhile, the days remaining until his American passport expired fell away like the autumn leaves of a once-abundant deciduous tree. Still, he made no effort to return to the United States. For here on Corfu, Doran had begun to feel something quite special. Indeed, it was a reaction quite different from anything he'd ever experienced in the past. He might have been inclined to call the feeling spiritual, though he was hardly disposed to think in terms of revelation. Yet this so-called revivification seemed to be growing by the day, and understand it or not, he knew that under no circumstance must he do anything to compromise either its efficacy, or its eventual expression. Such a manifestation, if it were indeed to crystallize, seemed to supersede the question of nationality. This was something different—a rite of passage—one for which he'd searched, though sometimes blindly, for many years.

Besides, the American president was already bombing Afghanistan, supposedly trying to smoke out bin Laden, or depose the Taliban, or something more clandestine, and perhaps diabolical. Doran wondered just what President Bush proposed to do with bin Laden should they actually catch him. Cut off his head and parade it through the streets of New York City?

And then there was the curious incidence of anthrax contaminations: tainted letters showing up at major news networks, or at post offices, or at the Capitol Building. Payne was convinced that the anthrax-laced letters had nothing whatsoever to do with international terrorism: it was an inside job start to finish; he was convinced of that. Payne's analysis notwithstanding, the propaganda machine had obviously been well oiled, with CNN as its mouthpiece, and accusations and allegations were flying about like debris in an international windstorm. In America, the political and social landscape seemed to be dominated by a cult of fear. So Doran was inclined to remain in Greece. To wake each morning and encounter the simple beauty of the sun, the sea, and the mountain. To confront the challenge of everyday existence with the goodwill of his friends and neighbors. Come what may of political intrigues, their complications and their consequences.

Two days before Thanksgiving, Dennis Payne sought Doran out and invited him to a Thanksgiving Day meal aboard his boat, the Silver Vixen. Quite surprised by the invitation—not only because of its source, but also because of the stated occasion—Doran accepted Payne's offer. "Bring Philly along if you like," Payne told Doran. "He's probably not had a good meal since Dazey passed away."

"Right!" said Doran. "I'll be sure to bring him. What are you cooking?" he asked sarcastically.

"Ah!" said Payne. "I think you'll approve of the menu. I'm making sweet and sour turkey. Malaysian style!"

"We'll be there with bells on," said Doran.

"Just bring your appetite," said Payne. "And plenty of booze!"

On the fourth Thursday of November, Doran set out for Gouvia Marina. On his way there he stopped at the *cava* and bought a half dozen bottles of *Mavrodaphne*, a fortified red wine made in the Greek city of Patras that strongly resembled Port. And before making his way to Payne's boat, he stopped at the berth where the Overdraft was docked to call for Philbar Cullinain.

"So, this is your first Thanksgiving Day dinner," Doran joked to the Englishman.

"A day not indicative of Britain's finer moments," said his friend.

"I suppose not," said Doran, smiling.

Together they made the short walk along the quay to the berth where the Silver Vixen was moored.

When they arrived, Payne was already at work in his galley preparing the meal. The aroma from his Malaysian-style cooking was pervasive, and both Doran and Philbar looked forward to a diversion from standard Greek fare. The host welcomed his guests aboard his boat and poured a round of drinks. Doran and Philbar sat at the table in the Vixen's forward cabin, as Payne remained at his stove to test the rice and sample the sauce. Cullinain was the first to raise his glass as he directed a toast to Doran. "Cheers!" he said. "And Happy Thanksgiving!"

"And God save the Queen!" said Doran.

They drank the wine in a single swallow, and Payne immediately replenished their glasses. Then he busied himself dishing out portions of rice and Malaysian-style, sweet and sour turkey; and as he served the meal he initiated the inevitable repartee.

"Looks like Shrub's pulling out all the stops," he commented of the bombing raids underway in Afghanistan.

"Spending future social security funds to level mud huts," said Doran sarcastically.

"They'll never catch bin Laden," commented Cullinain.

"Of course they won't," said Payne. "They don't want to catch him. If they caught him, they'd have to put him on trial—probably in an American court. Imagine how that would raise the ire of the Arab World. No, they don't want to catch him. Though I'm sure they wouldn't mind killing the S.O.B."

"He's gone into hiding. And he has plenty of money behind him. They'll never find him."

"In the end it makes no difference," said Payne. "Because bin Laden serves Shrub's purpose quite well. He gives him an archenemy, a bogeyman to hunt down. Have you seen his image? In every way he looks the part of a crazed fanatic. I'm sure he scares the hell out of the average American. Not only do they not want to catch him, they don't even want to find him. It's much better for Shrub if he remains at large. Now, deposing the Taliban Government, that's another matter…"

"Their oppression of women is well documented," Doran observed.

"Not only women," said Cullinain. "Many pro-Western or pro-secular journalists, teachers, and clerics have simply disappeared. No doubt, they faced the firing squad."

"Shrub's got the right idea," Payne maintained.

"But imperialism is not the answer," said Doran. "Being British, you should certainly realize that."

"There's no denying the fact that England lost its empire," said Payne. "Maybe we can hang onto America's coattails as they forge a new one."

"Blair's nose is already three shades of brown," said Cullinain in disgust.

"He follows Shrub around like a poodle. And he's not unwilling to do some of the dirty work in return for a bit of the booty!"

"But in the end it's always the same, isn't it?" said Doran. "Innocent blood is spilled, impossible promises made, and the gentry divides up the spoils."

"Yes!" said Payne emphatically. "That's the game!"

"And a sick game it is!" said Doran. The American was a bit surprised by the intensity of his own conviction, though lately he found himself taking stands to which he'd previously paid only lip service.

"Working in the SAS, I've seen it a hundred times," said Payne. "So has Philly."

"Doran's seen it too," Cullinain told Payne. "He used to work in the American defense industry."

"You don't say!" said Payne, surprised by the revelation.

"In the private sector," Doran qualified.

"It's all the same machine," said Payne definitively.

"Yes, you're right about that," Doran allowed.

"What were you working on?" Payne wanted to know.

"Guidance systems," Doran said softly. "The Laser Doppler Rangefinder."

"Ah! The Cruise Missile! Sinister little bugger!"

"Payne, you're a master of understatement," said Doran. Then he detailed the capabilities of the weapon in question: "It can be launched from a carrier offshore, and it's capable of flying a hundred miles or more over open terrain before reaching a city. Once it arrives, it can fly at low altitude down a major thoroughfare, turn left at a prescribed intersection, then turn right and circle a cul-de-sac in order to find its target: a traffic cop at a specific intersection... Once it locates the cop, it can fly down his pants, and then right up his A-hole!"

"Bloody terrific!" said Payne. "Here's to American

know-how!" He raised his glass, but neither Doran nor Cullinain chose to endorse his sentiments.

"Why did you leave the SAS?" Doran questioned the bellicose host.

"I was getting too old. I was living on borrowed time, so to speak. I knew too many people. Too many people knew me. The military pension was all well and good—no complaint there—but I needed to make some real money. I had offers… In the private sector."

"I'll just bet you did!" said Doran, knowing well that, country-to-country, and government-to-government, the game was played by the same rules throughout the Western world.

"I'm not stupid, Seeger," said Payne. "I see the other side of the story. But I also know that there's nothing I can do about it, even if I wanted to. I've simply chosen to play for the winning team."

"The team that you *presume* will win out," Doran challenged.

"Get serious, Seeger! Shrub's going to depose the Taliban and install a puppet government, even if he leaves the Afghan people to freeze and starve next winter. And then he's going on to Baghdad. The UN is inconsequential. And if Saddam resists, as of course he will, the American bombers will level the place. Let's not forget that *somebody* tried to assassinate Bushdaddy in Kuwait after the Gulf War. Shrub's got an axe to grind."

"And then there's the oil…"

"Yes, the oil! Let's *not* forget the oil. Eighteen percent of the world's known reserves. No small prize!"

"None of that is going to stop terrorism."

"Fuck terrorism! This is *not* America's war on terrorism. That's only the ad campaign. This is a war—no, it's not even a war—it's a military exercise designed to subjugate a region—a region rich in resources! Wars are never fought over ideology; they're fought over money. Money and power!"

"Try telling that to the relatives of those killed in the WTC bombing. Or to the rest of the American people, for that matter."

"Shrub doesn't give a fuck about that. As you say, the First World aristocracy maps out the agenda. All very covertly, you understand. Secret pacts, money laundering through Swiss bank accounts, phony do-good organizations, like the IMF and the World Bank... It's gargantuan in scope, and equally nebulous. But, hey, that's politics!"

"It doesn't have to be that way," said Doran with minimal conviction.

"What are you talking about, Seeger? It *is* that way! Every single politician who is even remotely connected with the Western governments is sooner or later corrupted. Whether by avarice or by default!"

"What about Havel?" Doran proposed.

"Who?"

"Vaclav Havel, the president of the Czech Republic."

"A fine playwright, and a courageous dissident. But he's a sissy of a politician."

"Because he holds true to his convictions?"

"No. Because he's got his head up his bum when it comes to seeing reality. Like so many old-style European politicians, he's an ostrich. Simply put your head in the sand and a particular problem doesn't exist."

"But surely there's something to be said for true civility," Doran maintained.

"Antiquated thinking," said Payne.

"Then perhaps I'm an anachronism," said Doran.

"If that is your choice..."

By the time the dinner was eaten and the debate concluded, Philbar Cullinain had drunk two glasses of wine for every one consumed by Doran or Payne. He slumped in his seat, his eyelids heavy. "Maybe I'd better take him back to the Overdraft and put him to bed," Doran suggested.

"Phil's okay," said Payne. "And so are you, Seeger."

Doran regarded his host with curiosity. "In the past, I was simply a square peg trying to fit into a round hole. Though curiously enough I didn't even realize it at the time. Now I do. So I'm just trying to find a quiet corner in which to exist—a rock to crawl underneath when the shit hits the fan—a place inside myself that isn't somehow fouled—a glimmer of light, a bit of civility, a trace of hope."

"I may embrace an opposing point of view, Seeger," said Payne, "but I wish you good luck. And most of all, I wish you peace."

Payne helped Doran hoist Philbar Cullinain onto his feet. Together they dragged him up the steps to the wheelhouse and then onto the pier. "Can you manage?" Payne asked Doran.

"Yes, I think I can," he said.

With December came the rains—a bit late in the season perhaps, but welcome nevertheless. Rains to replenish the earth. Rains to wash clean the sins of mankind. The prevailing wind blew not from Africa over the Mediterranean, but out of the polar north, dusting the high mountains of Albania with a white cap of snow. For days on end gray skies remained unbroken over Kerkyra.

Doran woke each morning not to the sound of birdsong, which was customary in summertime, but rather to the flapping of sails and the clanging of rigging being blown about by blustery weather. Or he woke to the tolling of the church bell announcing a death in the village that had occurred overnight. Without fail, though, he was up and about before the light broke over the landscape. To take the chill out of the air, he would light the gas-burning heater that he'd bought with the last of the money he'd brought with him from Prague, and he would dress in darkness so as not to wake Gisela. Then he would brew coffee as he smoked his first cigarette of the day. And before he'd finished drinking his coffee, he would invariably hear Modestos outside in the garden calling his name, "Doran! Doran!"

Together they would drive to Takis' grove below Mount Pantocrator in order to harvest the recently fallen olives from the nets that covered the ground beneath each tree. Then, with their cache of olives stored in the trunk of Takis' car, they would return to Kondokali village, to the *dhomatia*, where they would clean and process the olives in their makeshift factory, separating fruit from stem, and preserving the still-hard olives in buckets filled with seawater.

Or, if they chose not to work at the olive grove, they would walk side-by-side to the half-acre farm in the low hills behind the village, Doran carrying a shovel over his shoulder, and Takis carrying a rake or a hoe. As the sun rose over the horizon, they were often hard at work, weeding furrows, or carrying water, or planting a new crop.

But as the month progressed, the weather turned unseasonably cold. The scent of olivewood smoke permeated the air each morning and each evening. Everyone in Kondokali village, it seemed, had a comment concerning the abnormal weather. Mikalis, for example, informed Doran that he'd not experienced such cold temperatures on Corfu since 1948. He was precise about the year. Minas, the bookseller, told Doran that he'd never seen snow, but he was convinced that if the cold weather continued until the Christmas holiday, he would see it this year.

And as it turned out, Minas was correct. At eleven o'clock, on Christmas Eve Night, snowflakes began to fall from the sky. Many of the neighbors living near the *dhomatia* came out of their houses for the event. Their enthusiastic shouts could be heard in the street. Doran and Gisela looked out their window, not in amazement as the Corfiots did, but rather with due amusement. The entire meteorological catastrophe lasted all of twenty minutes, with not a single snowflake sticking to the ground. Still, the weather remained uncharacteristically cold, and damp as well. Not exactly ideal conditions for raising vegetables, Doran understood. And Modestos was beside himself, literally frantic at times with concern for his olives and for the crop of vegetables planted at the farm.

"Something goes wrong with the weather! I don't understand it!" he lamented. His opinion was that pollution from factories and cars in the developed nations of Europe, and particularly in America, was responsible for the climatic shift that they were experiencing on Corfu. He was quite adamant in his concern. "If the cold weather continues," he fretted, "everything will be destroyed!"

So together they covered the vulnerable sprouts and hoped for the best. And as a result of their vigilance, not a single plant died from frost, though the vegetables did appear to be stunted by the chilly weather, as were the olives. They failed to ripen in a timely fashion. Though the harvest was certainly not lost altogether.

For Doran, the crop of vegetables planted at the farm was more than a hobby, though something less than a true vocation. Yet there was no denying the fact that he'd come to feel a certain responsibility when it came to maintaining the crop. His effort to that end was both dedicated and painstaking.

Modestos, on the other hand, seemed to view the eventual success or failure of their effort as critical to his survival, which in purely physical terms was hardly the case. Yet he reacted to each setback with desperation, a response that to Doran seemed out of proportion with any conceivable consequence. His many charming qualities notwithstanding, Takis was and always had been a nervous mouse. This Doran acknowledged, though his friend's elemental good nature was time and again compromised by the meager results of their combined effort.

Doran became increasingly concerned for Modestos'

physical state: his once voracious appetite had waned for no apparent reason, and the Greek grew thinner and thinner as the weeks passed. If one took notice, his diminishment in stature was rather alarming. But what might one expect? After all, the man chose to subsist on weeds and olives and cucumbers. To Doran, his self-imposed starvation was indeed baffling. Until one day he clandestinely observed Modestos sitting at the worktable in their improvised factory drawing blood from his fingertip. The Greek smeared the droplet onto a piece of tape, and then dipped the strip into a readymade solution. He waited thirty seconds before removing the tape from the liquid to compare its color against some sort of analytic keycard. To Doran, the Greek's outrageous eating habits, as well as his obsession over the success of their farming effort, suddenly made sense. Modestos was diabetic, and rather than take insulin, he'd determined to affect his own cure. Out of respect Doran did not presume to intervene. For all he knew, the Greek understood something that Western medicine, in all its pompous confidence, had failed to recognize.

In turn, Doran's own diet presently left something to be desired. Without money, he was reduced to subsisting on a cache of staple foods he'd been careful to stockpile: rice and legumes, soup stock and noodles. He harvested green onions and garlic from his garden, as well as spinach and radishes. He made periodic trips to Gisela's secret garden, as well as other locations he'd discovered, to pick oranges and lemons. He collected chestnuts and snails. He was happy to accept any gift of freshly caught fish, or recently dressed rabbit. He even tried some of Takis' boiled weeds, though after one taste he declined that delicacy a second time. To say the least, his material life here on Corfu was anything but glorious, though he wanted not for necessities, and in many ways he derived great joy in taking his living from the earth. And of course he understood that anyone from his own culture—or from any modern culture throughout the world—would have considered such an existence to be absurd, but he failed to care what those in so-called better circumstances might think. He was happy to live where he lived, to work as he worked. Here he had friends—simple people living simple, honest lives. Here, his conscience was clean. On one hand, he found his poverty to be ludicrous; on the other hand, it seemed to facilitate his very salvation.

On Christmas morning, there was a knock upon his door. Gisela was still in bed, and Doran was not expecting visitors. Still in his bathrobe, he answered the summons. Standing on the balcony were two Greek girls, perhaps ten or eleven years old, who asked sweetly if they could sing to him of Christmas. A smile spread over Doran's lips. He invited the girls to come inside and directed them into the room where Gisela lay sleeping. "Sing to her," he said to them.

One of the girls produced a small triangle, which was the sole instrument intended to furnish their accompaniment. She looked dubiously at Doran, who in turn nodded his approval. The accompanist struck the triangle, and the two launched into a happy little carol, exalting the coming of the Savior.

Gisela opened her eyes in sleepy surprise, as well as embarrassment. But she seemed charmed by the spectacle of the two children openly sharing their happiness in song. She smiled at Doran, as if to ask where in the world he'd found these two little angels. He feigned ignorance as his expression mirrored her look of sublime satisfaction. And when the song was finished, he made each girl a cup of cocoa to drink before they continued their musical proclamation of joy.

On Christmas Day, Doran and Gisela were invited to dinner at the Thromos home in Corfu Town. When they arrived just after noon, the atmosphere was relaxed rather than festive, and everyone except Elena, who was in the kitchen preparing the meal, sat in the parlor and watched

CNN.

As Modestos half-watched the TV commentator and smoked a cigarette, Doran observed that his friend looked overly tired and a bit distracted, a state seldom seen and quite unlike his normally buoyant attitude. And once again, Doran noticed how thin his friend had grown. Knowing well Modestos' vigorous nature, Doran felt concerned by his friend's obviously diminished physique, and also by his apparent fatigue.

From the corner of her eye, Gisela regarded Spiro, who squinted in vain to see the TV screen. She pitied him for his infirmity. How unfair fate had been to this young man who had first struggled to find himself, and then applied himself diligently to his studies at the university, only to have his future obscured by an untimely blindness. During the past few weeks, Gisela had speculated endlessly concerning his future. She sincerely hoped that someone with devotion and patience would be there to help him navigate the darkness.

When Elena announced that dinner was served, everyone moved to the dining room and took their seats at the table. The meal was plentiful and diverse, if not extravagant: a fish row salad, or caviar, (known to the Greeks as *taramousalata*); tomatoes and cucumbers and feta in olive oil and vinegar; roasted pork and roasted chicken; cheese pies (*tiropita*); spaghetti in tomato and cinnamon sauce; fried *aubergines*; and several varieties of cheese. Two pitchers of *Retsina* were laid out, as well as a pitcher of spring water.

To Doran's satisfaction, Modestos eagerly stuffed a napkin inside his collar and filled his plate with a variety of foods. He began to eat voraciously even before everyone else was fully served, and he quenched his thirst with several glassfuls of *Retsina*. Indeed, this was the man that Doran remembered—the robust man who, no matter how much he ate, had never seemed to get enough food to sustain the energy needed to conduct his surfeit of affairs.

But Doran was also well aware that Modestos had long suffered from a stomach ulcer, not to mention the more recently revealed, if still not advanced, condition of diabetes. At sixty-four, Modestos looked to be no more than fifty; and normally he had the vitality of a teenager. Yet his recently diminished figure somehow seemed to contradict that personality. As far as Doran was concerned, there was simply something incongruous between Modestos' attitude and his current physical stature. Nevertheless, the Greek seemed to be in old form for the Christmas Day dinner.

Contrary to his father's more aggressive table manners, Spiro sat beside his mother so that she might help him to fill his plate with the foods he desired. Gisela watched with some anguish as Elena arranged her son's repast upon his plate in an obviously predetermined and well thought-out array. So obvious to Gisela were the difficulties imposed by Spiro's blindness, and her heart swelled from sadness at his imparity. And even as she watched the pathetic scene of a mother helping her blind son, Gisela could not help remembering that this was indeed the same young man, then absolutely vital and audacious, with whom she'd been in love ten summers ago.

To Gisela, that recollected image seemed quite removed from the young man now sitting at her side. Indeed, her memories were of another time, if not another place, and circumstances had changed. Yet certain aspects of their so-called connection remained the same— important elements, the ones for which there were no specific definitions, and certainly no words! Spiro's youthful bravado had turned into humility. Perhaps a result of his sudden blindness, or maybe the effect of simple maturation. In Gisela's estimation, whatever the reason for his change of attitude, it was a welcome transformation. Though, undoubtedly, the price of such a conversion had been altogether too high. Heartsick, Gisela watched as Elena directed Spiro's fork to the various foods on his plate.

After the meal was finished, American whiskey was offered as an after dinner drink—a custom observed only on special occasions. Doran and Gisela accepted the courtesy, and Modestos also indulged in the libation. Though once a toast was made and the Jack Daniels consumed, Modestos excused himself rather abruptly and retreated first to the bathroom, and then to his bed. Apparently, the heavy meal, along with the wine and the whiskey, had seriously irritated his stomach ulcer. His retreat was a reaction with which Elena and Spiro were well acquainted, though Doran found the immediacy of his friend's distress to be quite alarming.

Elena cleared the table, as Doran and Gisela smoked after-dinner cigarettes. Spiro asked Gisela if she might assist him in reading certain pages on an Internet Web site that was of particular interest to him. She agreed, and they repaired to Spiro's bedroom, where his computer was located.

Indeed, the party had dispersed abruptly, but Doran was not disconsolate. As Modestos lay in his bed, and as Spiro and Gisela surfed from one Web site to another in the privacy of Spiro's bedroom, Doran tried to make conversation with Elena, but her poor command of English, and his rudimentary knowledge of Greek, soon rendered their conversation mundane at best. So Doran lounged in the salon as Elena finished washing the dishes.

The television was still tuned to CNN, and Doran listened to a previously taped interview with the American Secretary of Defense. The Secretary was describing certain military objectives to the interviewer, Wolf Blitzer—operations that, to Doran's ear, sounded both calculated and cold-hearted. The expatriate considered the probable implications of what he was hearing. The level of U.S. involvement in the political affairs of a destitute nation located in south-central Asia certainly seemed to defy the all-too-simplistic rationality of retribution. Considering remarks made by the president himself, and also those made by members of his cabinet, as well as statements made by high-ranking military planners, Doran seriously questioned the administration's sense of vision. After the attack upon the WTC, (and more symbolically upon the entire financial foundation of the Market Economy), President Bush, spouting cowboy rhetoric and shooting from the hip, had targeted bin Laden and his *al Qaida* network as America's archenemy, and further characterized himself as the country's savior.

In contrast, Doran considered the Czech president, Vaclav Havel. He envisioned the young dissident confined in a wet prison cell, his lungs rotting from pneumonia, still holding fast to his convictions! As a political prisoner, Havel had written countless letters to his wife Olga, documenting his thoughts, his reflections, and his hopes and visions for the future of not only his own country, but for the cause of freedom-in-practice and decent government worldwide. Doran had read those letters, as Havel had later published them in a book. Of course Havel was a dwarf among giants on the stage of world politics. Nevertheless, he represented honesty and decency in an arena of gladiators, warriors who seemed to care little who suffered as a result of their pursuit for ever-greater wealth.

Doran knew, for example, that half a million Iraqi children under the age of five had died needlessly during the past decade as a direct result of sanctions on food and medicine first imposed and then maintained by the American administration under the umbrella of the UN. What sort of justice was that? The innocent suffered and perished as elitists in the West salivated and sharpened their teeth in anticipation of the next big bite. Doran was given to speculate that the political events in question might well set in motion the beginnings of a global realignment—one that could possibly be played out through countless and brutal regional conflicts, or perhaps, eventually, through a single worldwide conflagration: West versus East; Christian versus Muslim. Doran hoped only for a peaceful parity, a tolerant co-existence. It was just such an attitude that he tried to practice in his everyday affairs. Which in the end was all one could do. Because such political intrigues, Doran understood, had long ago eluded the comprehension of common people in all societies; the so-called silent majority had been circumvented by a more privileged, if still quite nebulous, class of sycophants.

Thanking Elena for dinner, and informing Gisela that he was returning to Kondokali village, Doran left the Thromos' apartment and walked the short distance to the taxi rank near the Liston. In late afternoon on Christmas Day, Corfu Town was nearly deserted; and fifteen minutes after telling the cab driver his destination, Doran was back inside his own apartment. He passed the remainder of the afternoon reading and napping; and when Gisela still had not returned by eight o'clock, Doran decided to visit the Navigator's Pub for a drink and some company.

Indeed, the wintertime life in Kondokali village, and on the Island of Corfu in general, went on in dramatic juxtaposition to the frantic and openly sybaritic lifestyle of summertime. The indigenous culture cast off the accumulated tension imposed by a summer long invasion of pleasure-seeking visitors and concentrated instead upon its fundamental vision of society. Each morning the aroma of freshly baked bread wafted through the village; and each evening the smells of roasting meat tempted the pallet of anyone fortunate enough to pass an open kitchen window. Village fishermen rowed out into Gouvia Bay, spearing squid and octopi under the light of a full moon at midnight. Hunters returned at mid-morning with their quarry from pre-dawn forays into the mountains. Gypsy peddlers sold hand-embroidered linens off their three-wheel carts. And the village marching band gave out-of-tune concerts at midday on Sunday in the courtyard of the

Orthodox Church if it was not raining. In wintertime, the Corfiot lifestyle reverted to a timeless simplicity, where all things, it seemed, were pure and wholesome and good.

Doran and Gisela spent New Year's Eve together at the Navigator's Bar amidst Corfu's entire colony of British ex-pats. The drinks flowed unendingly, and a buffet supper was provided as well. Karaoke was sung until each singer had had his chance to sing, and Philbar Cullinain, wearing a ridiculous, shoulder-length wig with pink curls, did a rousing rendition of *Flower of Scotland* as everyone in the pub danced in a line around the room. *Auld Lange Syne* was belted out to a marching beat on two different occasions: first when the clock struck twelve in Corfu; and a second time at 2:00 a.m. as the new year dawned in the U.K. The party lasted until the final reveler had left the bar shortly before dawn.

With the New Year, the weather turned even colder. Each night the wind howled from the north, as the temperature plunged to two or three degrees Celsius. Snow deepened on the distant mountaintops in Albania. Nobody on Corfu could remember such cold temperatures, and it was indeed questionable whether or not the crop of vegetables at the winter garden could withstand the near freezing nighttime temperatures; though so far the leaves had not blackened or withered.

After three continuous days of cold rain, the sun shone quite unexpectedly one morning in mid-January, though it was still chilly. Dressed in a warm jacket and gloves, Doran stepped onto his balcony just after eight o'clock. With a canvas sack in hand, he was on his way to the farm to harvest a few onions, a bunch of carrots, and a portion or two of *kukia* beans. In the frosty morning air, he could see the vapor from his breath.

But as he descended the stairs, he looked up to see a stranger standing in the garden. Dressed in a parka and a knit cap, a man in his early forties smiled warmly and greeted him with a question: "Are you Doran Seeger?" The stranger's accent was decidedly American.

"Yes," he said. "Who are you?"

"Harry Black," he answered. "But everybody calls me Black Harry."

"Black Harry?"

"Never mind that. Pericles told me that there was another American living in Kondokali. He pointed out your house to me. I come from Vermont," said Black Harry. He took off his cap and ran his fingers through a full head of curly black hair.

"Not many Americans here," said Doran.

"Twenty years ago, I stayed a year on Corfu. No Americans here then either. I lived with a group of monks at the monastery on top of Pantocrator. Corfu seems to have changed a great deal since those days."

Doran nodded, though of course he could not confirm Harry's assessment from personal experience.

"Back then there were no paved roads. The locals got around on foot or by donkey. I was rather shocked to see resort hotels and modern supermarkets."

"I came here only six months ago," said Doran.

"From the States?" asked Black Harry.

"No, I came here from the Czech Republic," Doran explained. Even though the stranger's parka engulfed his body, Doran could see that his shoulders were broad, and his frame substantial. "Why have you returned to Corfu?" Doran asked.

"Actually, I'm on my way to India. I'm a writer, and I'm working on a book about India's present-day holy men. This will be my sixth trip to Sikkim Province."

Doran moved down the staircase to join his visitor in the garden. "India seems light years away from Corfu," he said, scratching his head.

"India is infinitely fascinating."

"I'm sure it is…"

"My flight leaves from London in three weeks. So in the meantime, I thought I'd revisit my past. Corfu is lovely as ever! I'd forgotten what a garden it is here."

"Where are you staying?" Doran asked.

Black Harry put down his knapsack. "That's why I've come to see you," he said.

"How can I help?"

"Pericles thought you might know of a place where I could stay."

Doran considered the stranger's request. "Yes, I do know a place where you might stay," he said. "But I'll warn you, it's pretty basic—clean room, a bed, shower down the hall."

"Basic is fine with me," said Black Harry

"The *dhomatia* is about a half kilometer's walk from here. I was headed in that direction anyway. Would you like me to take you there?"

"If it wouldn't be too much trouble," said Black Harry.

"No trouble at all," said Doran.

A short walk into the low hills behind the village led them to Tasoula's *dhomatia*. With Black Harry at his side, Doran knocked on the door. No answer. He called out her name, loudly. Still, no one appeared. Just as they were about to leave, Tasoula's husband, Bampis Pauli Karalampous, opened the door. Through bloodshot eyes, the Greek regarded the two foreigners. "*Yasas!*" he said.

"We're looking for a room," Doran told Tasoula's husband.

A bit unsteady on his feet, Bampis Pauli Karalampous came out of the house. Considering that it was only nine o'clock in the morning, he looked rather haggard, beaten. Through puffy, squinting eyes, he assessed the two Americans. "My wife takes care of that," he told them, "but she's not here now." He sniffed the morning air through a bulbous, reddened nose. "She's at her chicken coop gathering eggs and feeding the chickens. She'll be back in half an hour."

"Do you mind if we wait here for her?" Doran asked.

"As you like," said Bampis Pauli Karalampous. Already

drunk and thoroughly disinterested, he went back inside the house, as Doran and Black Harry sat on a sunny patio to await Tasoula's arrival.

"So, how long is it since you've been back to the States?" Black Harry asked.

Doran found Black Harry's inquiry to be somewhat forward, or invasive; nevertheless, he replied, "Nearly ten years."

"That's a long time," said the writer. "Don't you miss home?"

Doran fidgeted a bit. "In the end, it all comes down to where you feel most comfortable, doesn't it? I've adjusted to the European lifestyle, and sometimes when I encounter Americans, they're the ones who seem foreign to me."

"After living in Europe for ten years, that's understandable," said Harry.

"I presume you've traveled quite extensively," said Doran.

"I'm always on the move," Harry confirmed.

"Vermont is your home base?"

"Yes, when I'm in the States. Which, these days, seems to be infrequently. The truth is that I can't afford to live there all the time. Too expensive! As a writer, I'm not famous. These days you have to be famous, a celebrity. It's not like the old days—like it was for Hemingway or John Steinbeck or Norman Mailer or some of the others—you know, the literary guys. These days it's all about fast money.

"My royalties keep me going; that's all. And not in grand style! When I'm in the States, I moonlight. I work as a caretaker for elderly people. If I find just the right situation, it provides me not only a little work, but also a place to live and write.

"And I travel a lot! The Caribbean, South America, the Azores, and India. I satisfy my wanderlust and have something to write about too, and the money goes a lot further living in the 'developing' world.

"But artists have always been outcasts in America. We just don't have the killer instinct needed to compete. Bill Gates is an American icon, not Truman Capote. And the competition is tougher than ever. Not on an artistic level—that's become strictly banal. No, I'm talking about money. Because living in America is all about making money. The more you make, the higher your status. With status comes comfort and privilege. You don't have to be smart. You don't have to be ethical. You just have to be rich. If you don't have money, you're scum. And in America scum is quickly washed down the gutter."

"You paint a pretty brutal picture," said Doran.

"It *is* brutal! You've been away ten years, Seeger. Believe me, you wouldn't know the place."

"Really?"

"It's very different than it used to be. Especially since September eleventh!"

"I see things on television…"

"Yeah, but you can't begin to imagine the impact of that single event. The government has the people scared shitless of the Arabs. Not to mention one another. And everybody seems quite willing to trade basic freedoms for a little pseudo security. Sad to say, the voice of dissent is all but silent. Anyone with a contrary point of view is watching what he says—aloud, in print, on the telephone, and on the Internet."

"Europe is altogether different," Doran proposed.

"Pardon me, but I notice that Greeks are spending Euro-dollars these days, not drachmas."

"I'm not talking about economics," said Doran. "I'm talking about civility."

"Shit! When it comes to civility, the Greeks wrote the book. They invented Western civilization. The only problem is that while the Greek society took a fifteen-hundred-year nap, the rest of the Western world convoluted most of the precepts. And look what you've got now! Greed. Corruption. Insolence. In First World

279

countries, real civility is dead as a doornail. Particularly so in America! Now India is an entirely different story."

"Really?" said Doran.

"In India, it's all a matter of amplification. We're talking about a sub-continent of a billion people—a cultural stew that's been brewing for ten thousand years. That's twice as long as the Greeks, if you can even equate modern Greece with the ancient civilization. And I'm not so sure that you can. That's five times longer than the Romans, whose civilization fell seventeen hundred years ago. And when it comes to modern-day Babylon—and I think we both know what we're talking about—the Hindu culture is some fifty times older. It's like making wine: the longer you ferment the mash, the stronger the alcohol content; and the longer you age the wine, the more subtle the bouquet. And it doesn't seem to matter on which level of existence you focus, material or spiritual. Just like their cuisine, the cultural ragout is piquant. Yet it is also subtle. The disparity is stunning; the anomalies impenetrable. Each situation poses an impossible question, and there's no way out of the fun house unless you solve the Great Conundrum."

"And what might that be?" Doran asked.

"Ah! The million-rupee question!" Harry turned to face Doran and leaned closer to make his next point. "The really crazy part of it is that, try as I might to maintain my skepticism, or my objectivity—call it what you will—the more I'm given to rapturous leaps of faith. I can't seem to help myself. In India, enlightenment actually seems reachable. After meeting the Rimpoche, and being taken into his confidence, I'm hooked."

"Are you sure you're not being used?"

"The man asks nothing of me, nor anyone else. When he visits a village, the people shower him with gifts, which he in turn passes along to others at his very next stop. Everything moves through him. He's not a receptacle; he's a conduit. When I'm there, I'm simply with him—almost as if it had been pre-ordained. And when I return after having been back to the States, or to the Azores, or to Peru—it doesn't seem to matter how long I've been gone—I'm treated as if I'd left only yesterday. Everything is casual. Nothing is required. I keep waiting for the catch. So far, no catch. I'm convinced that Rimpoche is simply what he seems to be: a holy man. That's the only way I can make sense of his existence. Or my own!"

"The Great Conundrum…"

"It surely doesn't fit in with our Western way of thinking. Which to me is what makes it so credible!"

"For me, spirituality is personal. I have to take things in small strides. Otherwise I'll drown in the labyrinth. That's just the way I am."

As Tasoula came walking up the driveway carrying two-dozen eggs in a bowl made from the skirt of her well-worn apron, Doran stood up to greet her.

"*Yasou*, Tasoula! My friend Harry is looking for a room."

"*Yasou*, Doran. *Yasou*, Harry. How long you want to stay?"

"Two weeks or so," Black Harry answered.

"Come with me," Tasoula beckoned. "I have nice room for you."

The two men accompanied her up a flight of stairs, where she flung open a set of double-doors to reveal a large room with a double bed, an armoire, and a writing desk. "Toilet and shower down the hall," she explained.

"How much per night?" Harry asked.

"Winter price: ten euros," she said.

Harry nodded.

"I bring clean towels," said Tasoula to conclude the agreement, and she left Doran and Black Harry alone in the room.

"As you can see, it's not luxurious," said Doran.

"It seems okay. Thanks for bringing me here, Seeger."

"I guess you'll want to get settled now," said Doran.

"What's to settle? I'll just throw my pack in the corner and chain my laptop to the bedpost. *Voila*, I'm settled!"

Doran put his hands on his hips. "When I met you this morning, I was on my way to my garden to harvest a few vegetables, so I guess I'll be going there now."

"You've got a garden here?" Harry asked.

"Along with a friend of mine—Tasoula's brother Modestos. We've planted about half an acre. Various vegetables. It gives me something to do during the winter months."

"Mind if I tag along?" asked Black Harry.

"Suit yourself," Doran said.

Together they walked the short distance to the side road that led into the low hills. Moving through the trees along the unpaved byway, they were regaled by the splendor of the sunny morning. On a nearly barren hillside, a small herd of goats grazed somewhat nervously. Ahead, turkeys and hens pecked at the gravel, and then scurried out of the way as the intruders approached. Watchdogs barked out a warning to their owners; donkeys brayed, roosters crowed.

Arriving at the site of the winter garden, the two men paused to survey the now well-established, south-sloping farm. Since early morning, the sun had warmed the air somewhat, though a bit of fog still lay close to the ground, and moisture could be seen upon the leaves of Doran's spinach plants. Together they trod over the pathway leading to the various garden plots.

"Quite an operation, Seeger!" complimented Black Harry. "Though some of the crops appear to be rather sparse."

"It *is* January, Harry."

Harry bent over to examine a row of celery. He ran his hands through the leafy tops then sniffed his fingers. "Smells fragrant," he commented.

"Celery is slow to mature," Doran explained. "But have a look at this crop of beans."

Black Harry approached the bean patch where Doran stood. "Christ!" he exclaimed. "They're twelve inches long!"

"They're called *kukia* beans," Doran explained. He picked one of the pods from a vine and shucked its sheath to expose the tiny beans inside. He held them out for Black Harry to inspect. Harry took the beans in one hand and the pod in his other hand as Doran moved further into the bean patch.

It was obvious to Doran that Modestos had already visited the garden this morning to pick some of the ripened *kukia* beans. Lately, Doran knew, his friend had taken to eating the beans raw for his breakfast; which in itself was concerning, considering the fact that Fedra had cautioned Doran that the *kukia* beans *must* be thoroughly washed and twice boiled, otherwise they were poisonous. Doran had quickly informed Modestos about Fedra's theory of toxicity, but apparently Modestos gave it no credence. His choice to ignore Fedra's warning had proved ill advised, however, as over the course of the past few days Modestos had developed a malevolent skin condition on his face. And even with Betadine smeared over his lips and around his mouth, Modestos continued to deny that eating the beans raw was in any way the cause of the problem.

Obviously impressed by Doran's irrigation system, Black Harry called out, "This is some aqueduct, Seeger. Did you design and build it yourself?"

Doran nodded as he moved to an adjacent plot and pulled up several shiny radishes. "Back in the States, I was an engineer," Doran related.

"You don't say! What kind of engineer?"

"I designed smart bombs," said Doran somewhat cautiously.

"Ah! So that's why you're here on Corfu…"

Doran was immediately unsure why he had revealed the details of his past so nonchalantly. "Indirectly, perhaps."

"And maybe you know something you're not supposed to know?" Black Harry speculated.

"I doubt that," said Doran.

"Or perhaps somebody's looking for you?"

"I don't think so. Unless you're with the CIA, Harry?"

"The CIA? Me?" Black Harry laughed. "Don't hang that albatross around my neck. I'm exactly who I say I am. I'm a writer."

"And I'm not trying to hide from anyone," said Doran. "I'm simply planting seeds and growing vegetables."

"In all seriousness, Seeger, why would somebody with your skills and talents want to give up a good job in the States—presumably with the Department of Defense—to retreat to such a backwater?"

"I never worked for the Department of Defense," said Doran. "I worked as a consultant in the private sector. Anyway, Harry, my decision to leave the States and live as an expatriate was more a matter of coincidence than conscience. Though maybe that's changed over the years." Doran bit into one of the radishes and smiled.

"So maybe you're cultivating something other than vegetables on this ground?" the traveler proposed. "Something spiritual, perhaps?"

Doran stopped to consider Black Harry's proposition. Perhaps the winter garden did indeed generate something more significant than greens and tubers. And maybe the garden's rich soil was but a manifestation of the fertile ground within his soul. Such a projection defied any known scientific perspective to which Doran had ever ascribed, but lately he'd become aware of an unaccustomed yet benevolent feeling—one quite unspecific as yet—that seemed to germinate from a variety of seeds sprayed over the field of his everyday experience.

"Help me harvest some of this spinach," said Doran to Black Harry. "When we get back to my apartment, I'll treat you to a fresh salad for lunch."

Together they picked fresh greens in the mid-morning

sunlight.

During the course of the next two weeks, Doran met with the American writer several times. It was not only the fact that Harry Black was an American, but also his inclination to ask penetrating questions, that motivated the expatriate to seek out his company, and to cultivate his opinions and insights.

On a nearly perfect morning near the end of January, the two men sat at an outdoor café in Gouvia Marina sipping espresso and eating toast. In the picturesque harbor, the yachts owned by the many expatriates, as well as those leased by the various charter companies during the summer tourist season, were anchored in idleness. Flags of many nations fluttered on the masts. A warm breeze blew from northern Africa over the Mediterranean, and the temperature hovered near seventy degrees Fahrenheit. The water in the harbor was dappled with rays of sunlight, and the open sea beyond the harbor's buoys reflected an unblemished sky. Further in the background lay the northern isthmus of Kerkyra, the denuded summit of Mount Pantocrator crowning its still verdant incline.

"So, how is it that you became so caught up in the spirituality chase?" Doran asked as the two men looked out at the sublime scenery.

"I suppose I've always felt a need to penetrate beyond the obvious," said Harry in all honesty.

"Concerning enlightenment, I'm an inchworm," said Doran.

"Bit by bit," acknowledged Black Harry.

"I have no answers; only questions. Anyway, I think questions are more important than answers. Conclusions are too conclusive."

"That precludes belief in an absolute truth," said Harry.

"As human beings our mission is to try to impose order on the universe, but in the end, entropy necessarily wins out. My garden is an attempt to impose order. But there are a million variables. What if it doesn't rain? What if it rains too much? What if my plants are infested by parasites? Or blight? Or what if they are trampled by a herd of stray goats? I can try and try to impose my own sense of order on the world, but in the end chaos rules the day."

"You know, India is populated by a billion such inchworms, those who are the offspring of countless others, and a multitude before them. There is little hope of any sort of order ever settling over that culture—at least not in a material sense. So they seek something different, something more intuitive. They've been doing it for centuries. The Great Conundrum!"

Doran smiled. "Call it whatever you like," he said. "All I know is that I can't chase after tangibles anymore. Because once they're in hand, they immediately lose their value. That's if they were ever real in the first place. I'm gathering something quite different. I'm gathering stones on the beach. I'm gathering the fruit nobody else seems to want. I'm picking up people's cast-off junk out of the trash and turning it into *objets d'art*. I'm taking the tiniest splinter of an idea and putting it under a magnifying glass. I'm turning overlooked details into exponents."

"You prefer to lose yourself in dirt… And in minutia… And in obscurity…"

"For me, it's much easier to reform my consciousness by means of the microcosm. Sure, I understand quantum mechanics, but my hands are happy in dirt. Does that make any sense?"

"About as much sense as a man loving his mother."

"Affirmation is always nice, Harry. Thanks."

"Don't mention it," said the writer. "I guess we're simply two atoms that have randomly collided here on the big Corfu molecule. Want another coffee?"

Black Harry remained on Corfu the entire two weeks leading to his departure for India, and the foundation of

Doran's friendship with the American writer was set in their many talks and encounters. Black Harry took Doran on an excursion to the monastery on Mount Pantocrator to visit the monks with whom he'd stayed twenty years before; and indeed many of the monks were still in residence at the monastery, and they remembered Black Harry as if he'd left only yesterday. The reunion was enthusiastic and heartfelt. And Doran was intrigued by some of the aspects of the monastic life lived by the Brothers.

On another occasion, Doran took Harry on an outing to Glyfada Beach. There the shore was quite deserted, and the two men swam naked in the cold waves that rolled over a wide-open sea and broke upon the golden shoreline with a resounding clap. As the sun began to set upon the aquatic horizon, they built a campfire on the beach from collected driftwood, and talked until well after dark when the seaside chill finally began to penetrate.

Back in Kondokali village they ate and drank at the Navigator's Bar. Black Harry's taste for the company of Englishmen was somewhat less than Doran's, so they took refuge at Doran's apartment for drinks of Metaxa, a game of chess, and yet more conversation.

Two days before Black Harry's scheduled departure, Doran was committed to go with Modestos to an old-fashioned olive press in the southern village of Argyrades. Doran had invited Harry to come along, because Doran and Modestos needed all the help they might enlist in filling the many containers with the pressed oil. Into a rented van they loaded various vessels: ten-liter bottles, tins, urns, jugs, buckets, empty jars—whatever other receptacles they could find. Once the containers were loaded into the van, there was very little room for the three human occupants, nevertheless they squeezed themselves without complaint into the two front seats, shoulder-to-shoulder and hip-to-hip, and set off on the forty-minute ride to the ancient mountain village where the old-time press was located and still in operation.

"Yesterday, I transported the olives by truck to the press," informed Takis. "Many times I drove from Kondokali village to Argyrades village. *Po*, *po*, *po*," lamented the Greek. Indeed, he looked quite tired from the previous day's labor. His mouth remained swollen from eating uncooked *kukia* beans day after day, and he continued to lose weight. His body was now a shadow of its former stature. Nevertheless, Modestos managed to maintain his enthusiasm concerning the pressing of his harvest.

"Very important to press the olives by stone," he declared. "This way the degree of the oil is not compromised. Very important to handle the olives properly at every stage of production. You understand?"

Doran had heard it all before. Many times. Though Black Harry was thrilled to be part of the adventure. And why should he not be? He'd been spared months of labor, picking thousands and thousands of olives out of the nets, screening away twigs and leaves, and washing each and every fruit by hand. He'd not transferred bucketful after bucketful of olives into like containers of seawater, and he'd not listened to Modestos' seemingly endless diatribe concerning the medicinal benefits and other special properties of not only olives in general, but of Corfu's olives in particular. Involved as he might be in the island's agriculture, Doran knew he would never fully share his partner's unbridled enthusiasm for olives. In all probability nobody could. Yet he did feel the pride derived from having undertaken such elemental work, and having done it to completion.

In the Village of Argyrades, the old olive press was located on the square in front of the Orthodox Church. It had been there as long as anyone alive could remember, and it was to this particular press that the local farmers brought their crops to be processed into the purest olive oil found anywhere in the Mediterranean region. Two huge stone plates upon a timber scaffold, driven by a workhorse on a yoke, ground the olives, pit and all, into virgin oil. The mash collected on the bottom of the barrel, as the oil spilled generously from three separate spigots near the bottom of the press. Well in advance, Modestos had requested the services of the pressman and his press, and as he arrived with his two American friends, the rustic Greek who owned and operated the venerable machine welcomed them warmly. "*Yasas*! *Kali su mera*?" said Cosmos Karamousakis.

The pressman helped the threesome unload the various containers from the van, and when the vessels were divided into three groups, and several containers placed near each spigot, the olives harvested from Modestos' trees were dumped, bucketful after bucketful, into the press. Modestos positioned himself before one of the three spigots, as Doran and Black Harry each did the same. Cosmos drove the old nag round and round the press, turning the massive stone wheel on seasoned wooden gears, and the oil began to pour generously from each spigot. As each vessel was filled with golden liquid, it was quickly corked and put aside, the next bottle being placed underneath the spout so as not to lose a single drop of oil.

For olive oil was not only Kerkyra's most essential cash crop, it was indeed the one substance that lubricated Corfiot society at large. And the process used to press the olives into oil, it seemed, was every bit as important as the substance that was eventually derived. Modestos knew, as did other Greeks, that the continuation of such rituals was by nature as nourishing to the body of the culture as was the substance beneficial to one's physique.

Though midway through the process of pressing the olives, the old nag stopped dead in her tracks, stubbornly refusing to move another inch. Frustrated and flummoxed, Cosmos coaxed the nag to continue her circular trek, but still the animal did not proceed. Modestos grew irritated, because he was paying the pressman for his services by the hour. "If the horse refuses to work, you must beat her until she moves!" he implored the pressman.

Cosmos declined the suggested cruelty, only shrugging his shoulders in resignation. He knew well the disposition of his horse, and he seemed ultimately willing to wait out the nag's tantrum. Modestos, on the other hand, grew cross as the minutes passed. Finally, he jumped up from his post in front of the spigot and positioned himself directly behind the horse. He placed both hands upon the haunches and tried desperately to push the animal forward, but the horse did not move, which only enraged the Greek and amused the two Americans. He swore at the horse. He pounded his fists upon its rump. He pushed with all his might as the animal stood fast. A look of supreme irritation and boredom shone in the nag's eyes, as the angry Greek crossed himself in desperation. "What's the hurry?" Doran laughed. "The horse will move when she's good and ready to move. And not before!"

But Modestos was hardly willing to surrender control of the situation to a dumb animal. Again he placed his palms on the horse's ass and pushed with all his strength. The nag whinnied, mocking the Greek's impatience. Both Doran and Black Harry were laughing hysterically at Modestos' desperate effort to make the animal move, as was Cosmos Karamousakis. "Take it easy, Takis!" Doran implored him. "Don't bust your gut trying to move the old nag!"

Modestos, now feeling as stubborn as his nemesis, ignored Doran's warning and continued to push and prod the animal. He grew more and more red-faced as the horse resisted his effort. The Greek dug his heels into the dirt and heaved his body forward, snorting like a livid Pegasus. His tensile legs drove forward, yet not one inch of distance was made. "One thousand kilos of stupid!" he spat as he stopped to catch his breath.

Both Doran and Black Harry sat upon the ground laughing over the Greek's ridiculous obsession, even as

Cosmos petted the horse's mane and muzzle. With a knife, the pressman split an apple in half, feeding one portion to the horse and offering the other portion to Modestos. Suddenly realizing that he'd radically overreacted to the situation, the Greek smiled in embarrassment at his own imprudence. He accepted the piece of fruit and took a big bite, but as he began to chew the apple, he doubled over in obvious pain, his arms wrapped round his middle. He gasped for breath before falling backwards onto the ground.

So unexpected was his reaction that all three observers were momentarily dumbfounded. But as Modestos lay on the ground, writhing in pain and fighting for air, it became apparent that he was in serious trouble. Doran rushed to his aid, as did Black Harry and Cosmos Karamousakis. "What's wrong, Takis?" Doran demanded.

"Pain! Pain!" cried Modestos.

"Where is the pain?" Doran wanted to know.

"Fire in my stomach," gasped the Greek. "Give me water!"

Cosmos rushed to get a canteen, but Doran stopped him. "No water!" he blurted. "*Oxi nero!*"

"What's wrong with him?" Black Harry wanted to know.

"I'm not certain," said Doran, "but I believe his ulcer is bleeding."

"Shit!" said Harry. "What should we do?"

"Help me get him into the van," advised Doran. "We have to take him to the hospital."

"All the way in Corfu Town?" Harry asked.

"It's the only one," said Doran. "Now give me a hand!"

As the two men lifted Modestos into the van and laid him prone upon the bed of the truck, the Greek squirmed at their touch and moaned in pain. He might even have resisted their ministrations if he'd had the strength, but he was white with anguish and weak from his affliction. "Take me to my home," he implored his caretakers. "After a short rest, I will be well again."

Doran knew better. He could easily see that his friend was in deep distress. "Not a chance, Takis. We're taking you to the hospital."

"Not the hospital!" Modestos protested.

"Don't be ridiculous!" Doran barked. "Your illness is critical. You must go to the hospital immediately!"

As Modestos was in no condition to argue, he lay back in resignation as Doran shifted the van into gear and drove off at breakneck speed in the direction of Corfu Town.

CHAPTER 14
NARCISSUS AND ECHO

The annual celebration of Carnival had come late this year, due partly to the circumstance that, according to the lunar calendar, Easter did not occur until the first Sunday of May; but more directly because, just as the pre-Lenten festivities were about to commence, the archbishop of Corfu had died unexpectedly and somewhat mysteriously in his sleep. At least that was the rumor circulating the entire island—a rumor that reached not only the Corfiots themselves, but also the resident foreigners.

Fedra Koukouros, for example, had informed Gisela that the archbishop, though politically powerful and outwardly respected, nevertheless had quite a nefarious reputation, which derived from the widely held belief that he used his influence to import young Romanian and Bulgarian girls for the purpose of his own pleasure. His corruption had been long endured by the Church, and tolerated by Corfu's denizens; though if one listened to the whole host of hushed opinions voiced shortly after his death, it became apparent that nobody was particularly sorry that he was dead, including the Orthodox priests.

That fact notwithstanding, the archbishop's untimely death had imposed a postponement of the Carnival celebration, as it had necessitated a rather pompous funeral, which included a protracted mass at Saint Spyrodon's Church followed by a lengthy procession through the town. The body of the archbishop was sat upright in his coffin and paraded along the Liston in the back of the only hearse that would accommodate the elongated sarcophagus—a 1970 Dodge Polaris! Gisela had watched the spectacle from a seat at Café Capri on the Liston as she sipped espresso and ate a plateful of onion rings.

The following weekend—a week later than originally planned—the Carnival festivities commenced with a street party in the old Venetian Quarter of Corfu Town, which was to be followed by a massive fireworks display over the harbor near the Old Fortress. With faces concealed by colorful masks, the revelers gathered along the Liston under multi-colored lights; and as the twilight faded, music from several Greek bands inspired dancing in the cobbled street.

Gisela's own mask portrayed her as a butterfly nymph—one called Echo by Artemis herself. Such a portrayal was not wholly metaphorical, as she was inexorably drawn by the intoxicating perfume of the Narcissus flower. It was a bloom more beautiful than any she had ever seen, a strange glory of a flower, and a marvel to all who beheld it. A hundred blossoms grew up from its roots, and the broad sky and the whole earth laughed to see it, and the salty waves of the sea cried for its beauty.

Narcissus himself was a vainglorious boy who passed the loveliest of the nymphs by with hardly a glance. Now, no longer in the summer of his youth, Narcissus was captivated not by his own beauty, but rather by a reflected memory of a face once fair. Appearing on a coal-black horse out of nowhere, the Lord of Darkness had stolen the boy's sight and borne him away from the radiance of the earth in springtime to a world of obscurity. That was the sad fate of this modern-day Narcissus, a once beautiful boy who now saw only shadows—a boy whom Gisela now realized she loved and had always loved.

Though in Greek mythology the goddess Hera had spitefully punished the beguiling nymph for her fickle nature: "You will always have the last word," Hera had ordained, "but no power to speak first." So how might Gisela make the boy she had once rejected now pay attention to her?

Lost among the throng of Carnival celebrants, Narcissus called out to those now invisible who had once been his companions: "Is anyone here?"

In utter rapture, Echo called back, "Here! Here!"

His ears perked up. What voice answered his call? "Then come!" Narcissus implored.

Echo answered joyfully, "Come, come!" as she stepped forward from the multitude, her arms outstretched.

Not sensing her presence, and feeling ultimately alone within the realm of reverberation, Narcissus withdrew in contempt. "I will die before I give you power over me!" he maintained bitterly to Echo.

Feeling heartsick by his denunciation, Echo could only speak the words: "I give you power over me!"

Softening his stance and deferring his retreat, the boy looked up from the eternity of the iridescent reflecting pool and into the darkness of his own soul. "Echo, is that you?" Narcissus called.

"Yes, Spiro," Gisela said. "Take my hand!"

And as their fingertips touched an explosion of fireworks cracked high over the water beyond the Esplanade. His vision now darkened, Narcissus saw the glimmer of Roman candles in the pool of his own desire, even as Echo described for him the fleeting reflection of celestial flames over an Ionian slipstream.

A wedding was planned for June—a Greek wedding—

a three-day affair…

Modestos had recovered, after a fashion, from his illness, though his doctor had warned him that his unorthodox eating habits were taking a deleterious toll on his stomach. The doctor also prescribed medicine, which Modestos was supposed to take on a daily basis. This he stubbornly resisted, insisting instead on natural remedies—herbal treatments he'd learned during his boyhood from the village women, ones he trusted over modern pharmaceuticals.

After Gisela's engagement to Spiro, it was no longer acceptable for her to share an apartment with Doran; and to that end Modestos had enlisted Doran's help in turning the olive factory back into a comfortable accommodation in which Gisela might live until her marriage to Spiro in June. Together they scrubbed and plastered and painted; and all the while Modestos' putrid collection of weeds boiled upon the stove, as Doran cajoled his friend to take his medicine. But Modestos adamantly rejected the doctor's treatment. "I believe the natural way is the better way," he maintained.

Respect notwithstanding, Doran himself had seen his friend doubled over in pain at the olive press. Furthermore, he'd heard the doctor's prognosis, which was not good, should the patient refuse pharmaceutical treatment. "I understand your desire to treat yourself with natural medicines, but you have to be sensible about this, Takis. You've got a hole in your stomach. This is no time for experiments. Listen to the doctor; he knows what's best. I'm worried that you're going to kill yourself eating nothing but weeds everyday!"

Modestos considered Doran's assessment for a moment before commenting. "I never worry," he said.

Doran raised his eyebrows in astonishment. "Who are you trying to fool? You're an eternal worrywart."

"I may obsess, but I never worry," Modestos maintained.

"Come on," Doran cajoled.

"In Greece we have a saying about worry. It goes like this: A man has only two things in life to worry about: either he has his health or he is sick. If he has his health, he has nothing to worry about. But if he is sick, he has to worry whether or not he will get worse or get better. If he gets better, he has nothing to worry about, but if he doesn't get better, he has to worry whether he will live or he will die. If he lives, he has nothing to worry about, but if he dies he has to worry whether he will go to Heaven or go to Hell. If he goes to Heaven, he has nothing to worry about. And if he goes to hell he will be so busy shaking hands with all his old friends that he won't have time to worry!"

"This is no joking matter," said Doran.

"But I must live my life as I choose," said Modestos. "Otherwise I am already dead."

With that assessment Doran was not inclined to argue. But he did continue to worry about his friend.

"There is something else I must tell you," said Modestos.

"What is it?" said Doran as he carefully painted a window frame.

"I have an answer concerning your passport problem," said Modestos.

Somewhat surprised, Doran turned to face his friend.

"It *is* possible for you to receive a Greek passport, my friend. But there is a small problem."

"How much is it going to cost me?" Doran asked.

"The right people must be paid at the right time. Too much money, I believe."

"How much?"

Modestos shrugged. "It is impossible to say. First you pay one, and then you pay another one, and another one after that. Perhaps the line never ends. Maybe you pay too much money and never receive the passport. There is always that risk."

"It's academic anyway," said Doran. "As you know, I have no money. I have only lettuce and potatoes. I doubt they will accept vegetables in trade."

"Not likely," said the Greek.

"Then I must find another way," said Doran.

"I'm sorry," said Modestos. "I try to help, but no result."

"Thanks for your effort," said Doran. "And I'll try to remember your story about worrying."

"Good idea!" said Takis.

On a morning that promised glorious springtime weather, Doran was up well before dawn, as he was committed to selling produce from a stall at the street market in Corfu Town. Modestos had rented the stall, as well as a cargo van to transport vegetables from the farm to the marketplace, while Doran's part in the mutual venture required that he do the actual selling. He made himself a cup of instant coffee as he shaved and dressed, trying as he moved about his apartment to maintain quiet. For he knew that Gisela had come home quite late; he'd heard the taxi pull up after two in the morning, and he'd heard her voice as she paid the driver. She'd been with Spiro in Corfu Town; nowadays she spent most of her days there. Planning the wedding, he presumed. At this early hour she was probably fast asleep, and hopefully dreaming of the life they meant to create together.

Gisela's engagement to Spiro had come as an utter shock to Doran. Not that he himself had any serious intention of pursuing a relationship with her. Whatever connection they might have shared in Prague, or during their trip to Kiev, or just after coming to Corfu, had never been well defined; and as the months had passed any romantic inclination that either one might have felt toward the other had withered even before it bloomed. This circumstance Doran neither regretted, nor did he begrudge her for it. Though he certainly had to admit that he had once considered pursuing a serious relationship with her. They were of a like nature in many ways—restless, venturous, and adaptable. Yet there had always seemed to be a certain absence of honesty—not in everyday terms, or concerning the more mundane aspects of living together, but rather in terms of full disclosure. As well as he knew her, Doran had to concede that he knew her not at all.

Finishing his coffee and laying his empty cup in the kitchen sink, Doran put on his work boots and his jacket, for he was to meet Modestos just after five-thirty on the street in front of the *dhomatia*. From there they would drive to the marketplace in Corfu Town to unload the vegetables and set up the stall for business. But as he moved toward the door of his apartment, Doran noticed an envelope on the floor near his door. In Kondokali, the mail arrived rather randomly, and as nobody actually had a street address per se, the mailman simply called out names when he had mail to deliver. Apparently, Doran had been away when the postman had last made his rounds, and the letter had been deposited underneath his door in lieu of hand delivery. He took the envelope and placed it inside his pocket as he went out the door and down the stairs to await his friend's arrival.

At five-thirty in the morning it was still not light, and nobody was about on Christopher Street except the dozens of alley cats and the few stray dogs that patrolled the thoroughfare during darkness. Doran lit a cigarette then took the envelope from his pocket. The letter had come from Prague; the handwriting he recognized as Scarlet's.

15 April, 2002

Hey Seeger! What's up? I hope that this letter finds both you and Gisela well and happy.

Basso and I had a wonderful time visiting you on Corfu last autumn. Thanks for your warm hospitality. We hold you in our highest esteem, Doran. You are a true friend, and if ever there is anything that we can do for you, don't hesitate to ask.

Anyway, I'm writing this letter to let you know that Vasil and I were married on the 6th of January at the Prague City Hall. We invited Havel to the wedding, but the president apparently had other pressing business and conveyed his regrets at not being able to attend. Such are the demands of high office... Though in all honesty and seriousness, Seeger, I never would have imagined that Basso and I would wind up together. Fate is strange. Love is stranger yet!

What's up between you and Gisela? Anything? She's a hard girl to know, and probably full of surprises, I suspect. I perceive in her a great deal of courage, and a generous heart as well—attributes that compliment one another quite well, don't you think so? I wish her all my best, just as I do you, Doran.

I hope you have the opportunity and the inclination to return to Prague sometime for a visit. Our door is always open to you and to Gisela. Until then, I remain,

Your dear friend,
Scarlet Ponton

As Modestos pulled up in the rented van, Doran folded the letter and placed it in his pocket. As always, Modestos was in a hurry, and he drove away from the curb even before Doran had slammed the door of the van. In his own frenzied way, Modestos enucleated point by point the particulars of selling produce at the street market, details which Doran already well understood. Though as a result of Scarlet's letter, Doran's concentration was not trained upon vegetables, or the street market, or even upon his friend's incessant banter. Doran knew that he would likely re-read Scarlet's message at his first opportunity, for though she had not intended the letter as a query, the truth was that it had posed several questions that seemed to demand his deeper consideration.

In fact, the letter revealed his connection to two rather extraordinary women: Scarlet Ponton herself, and Gisela Van Zyl. Learning of Scarlet's marriage to Basso had energized Doran's proclivity to speculate. What if he had seriously pursued a relationship with Scarlet when he'd had the opportunity to do so? It was true that they'd both quickly dismissed the possibility of a romantic relationship. But why? Was passion always as obvious as thunder? Could passion not grow out of respect and admiration? It was widely acknowledged that passion had little or nothing to do with respect or admiration; passion was thought to be largely chemical in nature, and Doran was now disposed to wonder whether or not he even possessed the necessary elements. For him, reticence and deliberation always seemed to block the pathway to abandonment. Perhaps caution, or the fear of losing control, negated any possibility of fervent romance in his life. After all, he was now fifty years old. He'd never been married, and even the romantic relationships he counted to date had always been conditional. Retreat was always the easy way out, though it had left him alone time and again.

And what about Gisela Van Zyl? Was the situation with her not the same? Had she not come all the way to Prague to seek him out? For what reason, if not for the possibility of connecting on some deeper level now that she was older and more mature? Had he not had the opportunity to dive head first into the pool of her love? Gisela, too, was reticent concerning full commitment. Her nature, like his, was a cautious one when it came to abandonment. Of course she'd been burned more than once, so he understood why she might be reluctant to reach out for the flame of passion.

Yet she had agreed to marry Spiro, and that fact in itself posed a few interesting questions. Especially considering the young man's blindness and his confessed bisexuality. Not to mention his nationality, which undoubtedly suggested character traits that Doran imagined might appear rather backward in Gisela's eyes. Nevertheless, the marriage was on. At this point, it was hardly his place to question her directly, or to criticize. Furthermore, he realized that he would undoubtedly be seeing Alarice at the wedding in June, which invited resolutions that went well beyond present circumstances.

Yet he could not help remembering that night on Kondokali Beach when Gisela had stripped off her clothes and went running after fireflies. He could almost hear her beckoning call to run naked with her. And he remembered all too well the feeling of the fine sand on his naked body as he rolled off her in satisfaction. Now, as he recalled that fateful night, he could almost smell her scent as it commingled with the smell of the sea air. He could all but hear the locusts hidden in the leafy boughs of the eucalyptus trees as they sang their incessant song of lust. Millions of stars swirled that night in the firmament. Galaxies of pure possibility! Gisela had gathered her courage and come out of her protective shell. Why had he balked? Why had he not challenged more forcefully her denial of their intimacy the next morning?

It is said that no man is an island, Doran conjectured to himself. But, in truth, can a man be anything else? We are conceived through a union of two souls, yet we are born self-contained, alone with our peculiar nature. We might spend our entire life trying to share the most intimate details of that nature with another, yet our words are feeble tools to that end. We have our raw sentiments and emotions, and we have our sexuality, yet the sharing of such feelings is nearly always corrupted by ulterior motives. We try to be sincere. And sometimes we think we succeed. The afterglow is sublime. Though in the final analysis we find ourselves marooned once again on the island of our inability to communicate our most essential emotions, which by their very nature are not communicable. It's not our fault. It's not! It is merely the human condition. We are essentially alone. But is it enough? As Modestos stopped the van in front of the rented stall, Doran, too, found himself lost within an impossible state of narcissism.

By seven-thirty, Doran had put out all the vegetables: radishes, carrots, cabbage, celery, potatoes, melons, beans and lettuce. He'd hung a scale from one of the rafters and placed price tags in front of each crop. On a scrap of cardboard he lettered a sign in Greek, which translated: 'Organic Produce'. Still wearing a jacket, he sat on a stool in front of the stall as the sun came up, watching the other vendors arrange their stock of produce or fish. He smoked a cigarette and sipped coffee from a Styrofoam cup as the market gathered momentum.

By eight o'clock, the market was thronged with shoppers, and Doran's time was taken weighing vegetables and making change. This experience brought to mind other mornings spent working as a vendor; only his wares were different this time. Paintings or vegetables, the scene and the process remained the same.

The day warmed as the sun rose in the sky. Indeed, it would be a glorious afternoon. In the distance, Doran heard the rheumatic-sounding horns of the ferryboats coming into port. It was still too early in the season for the yearly onslaught of summertime tourists, though many Greeks from the mainland arrived on Corfu each year for the Easter celebration, as Corfu was known to have the best Easter festival in all Greece. Springtime was of course a time of renewal, and Doran was no less inclined to take part in the seasonal resurrection.

Shortly before noon, once the crowd in the marketplace had thinned and many of the vendors were storing away their wares, Doran spied Gisela walking along the queue. She was dressed quite smartly in new clothes, and her hair was freshly coiffed. In her arms she carried several packages. As she approached his stall, Doran called out her name. "*Kali mare sas, Stellamou!*"

"*Kali mare sas, philomou!* How's business?"

Doran shrugged. "I sold nearly everything," he told her.

"Splendid! Where's Modestos?"

"He's far too restless for this sort of work," said Doran. "He brings the vegetables here in a van, then he's off to God-knows-where."

Gisela smiled. "Does he take half the profit?"

"Yes. The garden is on his land. And he pays to rent the stall and the van. So I guess it's only fair that I do the selling. Anyway, I don't mind. In fact, I quite enjoy the bustle of the marketplace. So, what are you up to this morning?"

"Shopping for clothes. And for shoes! I have at least a dozen prenuptial functions coming up."

"And how is Spiro?"

"He's fine. The groom certainly has the easier part when it comes to wedding preparations."

"I imagine Elena is quite involved."

"Of course. She's really wonderful, Doran. Almost like a mother to me."

"And Modestos?"

"I don't see him much. But I suspect his major function is to pay the bills," Gisela observed.

"I see," said Doran.

"Even though I don't really need it, Elena keeps pressing money on me. Buy this, Stella! Buy that! It's almost embarrassing. But who am I to resist cultural traditions?"

"And shopping for a new wardrobe can be quite fun,"

Doran laughed.

"What about you?" Gisela asked. "Are you doing okay?"

"In what respect?" Doran asked.

"In every respect. I know you don't have much money."

"I don't seem to need much," he said without envy or worry.

"I feel a little guilty for dragging you here to Corfu, then moving off in another direction myself."

"No need to feel guilty," Doran said. "I seem to be having my own little renaissance. I may not have much, materially speaking, but returning to Corfu has brought me a peace of mind I've never known before. I'm hardly sorry to be here."

"Good!" said Gisela. "I'm happy you feel satisfied."

Doran reached inside his pocket and took out the letter he'd received from Scarlet. He handed it to Gisela as he said, "Apparently, you're not the only one who's getting married."

"What's this?" Gisela asked as she took the envelope from him.

"It's a letter from Scarlet Ponton. She and Basso got married last January."

"How wonderful!" said Gisela. She took a moment to read the letter. "I think they're perfect for one another," she concluded.

"Perhaps the are," said Doran.

"I'm surprised—" Gisela stopped for a moment to ponder her statement. "I'm surprised that you and Scarlet never…"

"Funny you say that," said Doran. "I was thinking the very same thing earlier this morning."

"Why do you suppose the two of you never…"

Doran shrugged. "Who knows? I guess it just didn't seem right at the time."

"Do you regret not having taken the relationship

further?" she asked.

"No, not really. Anyway, it's too late for that now."

"I think that maybe you do regret it. At least a little bit."

"Maybe a little bit… And maybe with you, too, Gisela."

"I'm afraid I led you on."

"Oh, no. You didn't lead me on."

"I thought about…about us. I thought about it quite a lot. Even before I came to Prague."

"Really?"

"It's true."

"But we'd not seen one another in years."

"I know. Maybe that made the thought all the more provocative."

"I never knew you had any inclination."

"Well, the truth is, I didn't. Not at first, anyway. I mean, you and my sister… And I thought you were nice, but rather simple. In a nice way, of course."

"Thanks a lot."

"But the longer I thought about you, the more I came to realize that we are very similar. In nature, that is. Don't you think so?"

"Yes, I suppose we are similar in many respects."

"But the whole thing was far too complicated from the start—too many justifications for me. I agonized over what to tell my sister, you know. And then there was that night at the beach!" she blushed.

"Yes, that night at the beach. Which you denied over and over again!"

"I couldn't help that, Doran."

"When first we practice to deceive…"

"What a tangled web we weave! I know, I know."

"We probably stopped just in time," Doran supposed.

"You were very patient with me. You never tried to push me. Or manipulate. For that I thank you. You're really quite a gentleman, aren't you?"

"I am who I am."

"No hard feelings, I hope," she said.

"None whatsoever," he confirmed. "And isn't fate strange? What a circuitous route you've taken to reconnect with Spiro. Truly, Gisela, I wish the two of you every happiness together."

"Thank you, Doran. If we ever have a child, perhaps you would consent to being his godfather."

Doran smiled. "I'd be honored, Gisela. But first things first!"

"Of course. I have a wedding to plan. And I'm late for my Braille lesson."

"You're learning Braille?"

"You bet. Elena is teaching me. It's a good idea, don't you think so?"

"Yes."

"You *are* coming to the wedding?"

"I wouldn't miss it. I've always wanted to smash plates with reckless abandonment. And I have to tell, I'm looking forward to seeing Alarice again."

"No doubt, there'll be plenty of plates on hand to smash. And my sister is arriving two weeks early to help me get ready for the wedding."

"Good. What a fun time for the two of you to share!"

"I'm glad we had this little talk, Doran.

Doran nodded. "So am I, Gisela. So am I."

Doran closed his stall and walked to San Rocco Square. He had a midday meal of *kalamari* and salad at Restaurant Rouvas and paid his bill with some of the coins he'd collected that morning at the market. Then he took the Number 7 bus back to Kondokali village, where he lay down for his afternoon siesta. Once asleep, he dreamed of planes over Baghdad—squadrons of F-16 and F-17 fighters flying sorties over the city and firing salvo after salvo at targets they could not even see, and upon people whom they would never know. He awoke covered head to toe in sweat, as dusk settled over the Ionian world. Ah, benign Kerkyra! How relieved he felt to be a vegetable farmer on Corfu!

"*Alpha, beta, gamma, delta…*"

Gisela sat at the Thromos' dining table, her fingers moving lithely over raised dots in a Braille primer.

"*Poli kala*, Stella!" encouraged Elena, her tutor.

"*Alpha, beta, gamma, delta, epsilon…*"

"Bravo! Bravo!"

Meanwhile, Spiro was in his bedroom typing like crazy on his computer keyboard. He was writing a letter to a school for the blind in Cardiff, Wales.

Gisela's engagement to Spiro posed several unique challenges. First, she was obliged to learn the Greek language, which in itself seemed more difficult than others she had learned in the past. For one thing, the Greek language had several unfamiliar characters in its alphabet, not to mention its odd-sounding pronunciations and accents. Secondly, she was intent on learning to read Braille, a writing system she'd never in her wildest imagination thought she might need to know. As well, there was the matter of conditioning herself to the idiosyncrasies of the Greek culture, of which there seemed to be many. Her cooking style would have to adapt to the Mediterranean taste; the hours she kept would necessarily conform to a culture that rose late in the morning, ate its main meal at midday, and socialized until all hours of the morning. Her more practical Dutch sensibilities would no doubt play a declining role in her everyday existence. Which was fine with Gisela. Indeed, she felt perfectly ready and willing to conform to the cultural bias of her fiancé.

Without a doubt, the news of Gisela's betrothal to Spiro had taken her sister by complete surprise. On the telephone, Alarice had paused in silence until finally prompted for a reaction by Gisela.

"This seems rather sudden, Gisela. Are you certain that this is what you want?"

"Sudden? I've known Spiro for ten years!" Gisela replied.

"More or less," Alarice qualified.

"I've never been more certain of anything," said Gisela.

"And what about his blindness? Are you sure you're up to the challenge?"

"I won't say that it's inconsequential," Gisela conveyed. "But sight—or the lack of it—does not in the end make the man, does it, Alarice?"

"I suppose not. Are you planning to stay in Greece indefinitely?"

"Spiro is applying to a school for the blind located in the U.K. So, if he is accepted, we might go to Cardiff for a while. But ultimately I'm sure we'll choose to live here on Corfu. It's a wonderful place, Arissa. If you remember…"

"Of course I remember. What about Doran?"

"He's farming."

"He's what?"

"Farming! He has a rather large garden in the hills behind Kondokali. With Modestos! They grow everything there, winter and summer. Especially in winter! Doran sells the vegetables at the street market in Corfu Town."

Alarice laughed at this revelation. "I never pictured Doran Seeger as a farmer," she said. "Nor as a green grocer!"

"He's quite different than he was ten years ago, Arissa."

"How so?"

"For one thing, he's no longer so stoic. His brighter side has really emerged, so to speak."

"Then he's happy?"

"I'd say so. But it's more than that. I'd say that he's serene."

"Yes, that's quite contrary to my remembrance of Doran."

"All the conflict he once harbored and protected seems to have somehow gone out of him. He really seems to have found himself here—in the garden."

"I'm happy for him," said Alarice. "I hope the change is a lasting one."

"I suspect so," said Gisela.

"I can't wait to see you," said Alarice to her sister.

"The wedding is June thirteenth."

"I'll be booking my ticket as soon as I can," said Alarice.

"And of course you'll be my maid-of-honor…"

"Are you going to wear a white dress?"

"Seems a bit ridiculous to me," Gisela laughed, "but I will indeed be wearing a white dress."

"A Greek wedding for my little sister!"

"It's going to be quite an affair, Arissa. Quite an affair!"

Elena offered cake and coffee as they had a break from Gisela's lesson. Together, they paged through a catalog of bridal gowns. Gisela's mother-in-law-to-be was determined to play an active role in planning the wedding. Which in Gisela's mind was probably a portent of the role she would play in her and Spiro's married life as well. Though the Greek family, in general, maintained cohesion far more so than families in her own culture. To that characteristic, Gisela was not averse. The depth of familial commitment, as well as the geniality of the Greek culture at large, she assessed as a strongly positive attribute, one that she herself was eager to embrace.

CHAPTER 15
THE EASTER PROCESSION

On Good Saturday morning, Doran and Gisela took the bus from Kondokali village to Corfu Town. From the bus stop at San Rocco Square they walked the short distance to Mustoxiodou Street in the Venetian Quarter. There the Thromos family occupied a third-floor apartment with a large balcony that overlooked the street; and from that balcony Doran and Gisela intended, along with Modestos and Elena and Spiro, to pitch clay urns and pots over the railing and into the street as the bells at Saint Spyrodon's Church chimed eleven. Indeed, this was a time-honored custom practiced by the Corfiots, and a spectacle anticipated by all, long in advance of Easter weekend.

As they arrived, Elena met them at the door. She greeted each with a welcoming smile and a kiss on the cheek; and for Gisela, she had an additional loving pat on the shoulder. Modestos and Spiro were sitting in the apartment's living room; CNN was on the television. Elena escorted Doran and Gisela into the parlor and invited them to take seats. She offered coffee and sweets as well.

Doran sat down on a chair opposite Modestos, as Gisela sat on the couch next to Spiro.

"Where are all the clay pots?" Gisela wanted to know.

"Don't worry, we have plenty. They're out on the balcony," said Spiro.

"Won't it be great fun to throw them over the side of the balcony and smash them in the street?" she said. "But I hope we're able to see others doing it, too."

Modestos turned his attention away from the TV and said, "Many people throwing pottery into the street from their balconies on Mustoxiodou. Every year the same."

And Spiro confirmed his father's opinion. "From our balcony you can see the entire length of the street. And as the buildings are four and five stories tall, hundreds of pots will be flying through the air and crashing onto the pavement. After it's finished, you can hardly walk in the street until all the rubble is swept away."

"Oh, good!" said Gisela.

Without embarrassment, Doran eyed Modestos, as the Greek lounged and watched the television. Doran was once again struck by how gaunt and frail his friend had become during the course of the winter. Not only had Modestos lost weight in his chest and shoulders, but his arms were weak and his legs were shaky. His cheeks were now hollow, his neck sinewy.

Doran turned his attention to Elena. Since Spiro's engagement to Gisela, her aspect had brightened considerably. Perhaps she had worried that her son's blindness would preclude marriage. Or maybe she knew something more than she revealed concerning his 'additional' sexual preference. But whatever the reason for her renewed sense of purpose and her revived vitality, the change was both obvious and well received. Elena doted over Gisela as if she were the daughter that she and Modestos might have once wanted, but never had.

As for Gisela, she accepted the attention showered

upon her by her future mother-in-law with good nature. Perhaps Elena was filling a void, Doran speculated, left by the untimely death of Gisela's own mother. No doubt, Gisela felt welcome and comfortable within the domain of the Thromos family, and Doran felt happy for her.

Spiro, on the other hand, appeared restless. Quite familiar with the objects in each room of the home he'd lived in his entire life, he moved from place to place with no apparent purpose in mind. He might empty an ashtray or open a curtain. He changed sweaters twice in the short time they waited for the pot-throwing ceremony to begin.

Just before eleven o'clock, the Thromos family, along with Doran and Gisela, moved onto the balcony to wait for the chiming of the bells from Saint Spyrodon's Church. As many other families had moved onto their balconies as well, anticipation permeated the atmosphere. It was a perfect springtime morning, and sunshine shone over the entirety of the Venetian Quarter. Canaries sang in their cages; dogs barked in the street; ships anchored in the harbor blew their horns. The smells of cooking wafted through the streets and narrow alleyways of the venerable neighborhood.

"I can't wait for the signal to begin," said Gisela excitedly. "I want to throw this big one first," she said, pointing to a large urn. Obviously trying hard to embrace the customs of her fiancé's culture, she invited Spiro to help her fling it over the side of the balcony.

Doran picked up a small clay pot and handed it to Modestos, and the Greek smiled benignly. Elena also held a vessel in her hands as she waited to pitch it onto the street below. Doran selected a small urn for his particular contribution to the rubble.

At precisely eleven o'clock, the cathedral bells peeled throughout the city, and the hedonistic, frenzied destruction began in earnest. Clay pots flew en masse from the heights and rained down upon the street. Together, Spiro and Gisela heaved the largest of the urns over the railing. Gisela followed its three-story descent and let out a howl as the vase shattered into shards. Elena was next to throw her pot over the balustrade, and it also disintegrated upon impact. Modestos hurled his vessel into oblivion, as Doran, too, pushed his jar over the edge of the veranda. Within minutes hundreds of clay ewers had been pulverized upon the pavement. Throughout Old Town and New Town respectively, the boulevards and side streets were filled with debris.

The clay carnage lasted only until the resonance of the eleventh chime finally faded away. As quickly as the ritual had begun, it was finished. Back inside the apartment, nobody seemed to know quite what should come next, though Doran noticed Elena tugging subtly at Spiro's sleeve; and immediately after this restrained signal had been received, Spiro invited Gisela and Doran to accompany him to a neighborhood bistro for ouzo and appetizers. Gisela was none the wiser concerning Elena's unseen gesture, but Doran could only determine that Modestos was not well and needed to rest in private. He was ultimately concerned for his friend, though he was inclined to respect the couple's wish for retreat. He enthusiastically accepted Spiro's invitation, as did Gisela, and the threesome left the apartment only moments after the pot-throwing ceremony had concluded.

Through rubble-strewn streets they walked, Spiro's white cane determining a course before them, as Gisela defined obstacles in her fiancé's path. She held tightly to his free arm, as Doran walked ahead and kicked debris out of the way. After a short distance, they reached Bistro Boileau. They went inside and seated themselves at a free table. A waiter approached immediately, and drinks were ordered.

Gisela and Spiro prattled on and on about the upcoming wedding, while Doran's thoughts whirled round his crop of vegetables, his passport problem, (which was now acute as it had finally expired), but most of all his dearest friend Modestos Thromos, whose health seemed to be declining by the day. Redirecting the conversation, Doran solicited Spiro's opinion regarding his father's well being, and the son acknowledged that his father had been losing weight steadily over the past year, and that neither he nor his mother had been able to convince him to face up to his health problems and take the proper course needed to help himself.

"I know that he's diabetic," Doran revealed.

"It is true," Spiro confirmed.

"And I know that he's trying to control the problem by eating medicinal foods."

"He does not like visiting the doctor," said Spiro. "He prefers the natural treatment."

"But is it effective? That's the question," said Doran.

Spiro shrugged in resignation. "If it were me, I would visit the doctor. And if the doctor determined that I should take insulin, I would take it. But there is no talking sense to my father. He does as he wishes."

"I, too, am not always convinced that modern medicine has all the answers, but sometimes it is not only the best answer to a particular problem, it is the only one known."

"My father holds fast to his convictions when it comes to his health, and he can be a very stubborn man. I may have a different opinion, but it is not for me to question him when it comes to his health. My mother is a vehicle to convince him to seek the help of a doctor, but in the end it is his decision."

"And then there is the question of his stomach. I know that his ulcer is acute. As you know, I took him to the hospital myself when he collapsed at the olive press."

"Again, what you say is true. He tries to take a cure by eating medicinal plants."

"I'm not so sure that he's not making the problem worse by eating weeds."

"Nor am I. In fact, my mother now refuses to clean and cook his vegetables. So he boils them himself. The smell is rancid."

"I know," said Doran. "He also cooks them in the vacant apartment. He's convinced that these weeds are his cure. But I see his steady decline. I'm certain that a doctor could deal quite effectively with each of his conditions. It's such a simple matter, if he would only consent to treatment."

"When you took him to the hospital, he had no choice but to see a doctor," said Spiro, "but I don't believe that he is inclined to a repeat visit."

"I'm growing quite worried about him," said Doran finally. "I would like to help him, but I am helpless to do anything positive."

"I feel the same," said Spiro. "In the end, Takis makes his own fate."

"As do we all, I suppose," said Doran.

On Good Saturday evening, Doran and Gisela ate *Magaritsa*, the Easter soup, brought to them in a steaming pot by Miss Koula; and shortly after ten o'clock the Thromos family arrived in Kondokali village to attend the service at the church and to walk in the subsequent candlelight procession through the village. The tiny church in Kondokali village was not large enough to accommodate all the faithful, so the gathering spilled onto the street, where the service was heard through loudspeakers mounted in the bell tower. As the hour neared midnight, the gathering in the street grew larger and larger. And as the service came to an end, the Kondokali Philharmonic Band assembled in formation in front of the church. Each villager held a candle and prepared to march in the procession, following Father Dimitrios and the other *papas* up and down Chrostopher Street. Modestos and Elena and Spiro waited with Doran and Gisela. Spiro explained the various traditions of the Greek Easter celebration to the *xeni*.

"After the procession through the village, there will be

fireworks and Greek dancing. Everybody is happy, you see, because the Christ has risen. Tomorrow, the Greek people will roast many lambs. It is the traditional Easter dinner. For the Resurrection is the most important festival, you understand," he explained.

Elena lighted each of their candles as the band began to play a dirge, and they took their places among the hundreds marching in the procession. Elena held Gisela's hand, as Doran put his arm around Modestos' waist to steady him. Spiro walked at the head of his family, his white cane tapping at the cobbled street.

The *papas* led the parade. They were followed by altar boys carrying sacred placards and icons, then by the philharmonic band. Nearly the entire population of Kondokali village followed, step by step, behind the musicians—the young and the old, the healthy and the infirmed—hundreds of candles flickering along a darkened street to symbolically light the Way of the Savior.

Those who did not march in the procession stood in doorways or upon balconies, holding lighted candles and waving to their friends and neighbors as they passed. And even as the music played by the local band was somber out of respect for the crucified Christ, the mood of the marchers was happy; for they knew from faith that the Savior would be raised from the sepulcher on the Mount of Olives in the early hours before dawn. For the faithful, the Passion was well understood, and well practiced.

Past the restaurant of Giorgos Zervas they marched, past Taverna Pericles, and past the shop of Panos the baker. They paraded past the Navigator's Bar and the Cava Golden Gate. Along the way, Modestos stumbled three times, and each time Doran had to support his weight to keep him from falling in the street. When the congregation reached the end of Christopher Street, they reversed direction and marched all the way back to the Orthodox Church. And as the *papas* reached the bend in the road where the church came into view, the bells rang out to signify the Resurrection. Fireworks exploded overhead, and rifles were shot into the air. A bouzouki band, poised in the church courtyard, began to play ecstatic music, as young men dressed in traditional costumes whirled and jumped and stomped, arm-in-arm. Everyone who had marched in the procession began kissing whoever was standing beside him. Mothers kissed their sons; uncles kissed their nieces and nephews; cousins kissed cousins; and neighbors kissed one another. Elena kissed Gisela. Gisela kissed Spiro. Modestos kissed Doran on each cheek. Smiling weakly, he said, "Happy Easter, my friend. Once again, we are all saved!"

"Remember to keep your candles burning throughout the night," Elena reminded Gisela and Doran. For this too was the tradition. She sheltered the flame of her own candle with the sleeve of her jacket. Modestos was less careful with his candle, and the flame flickered in the gentle breeze that blew off the waterfront.

Cupfuls of wine were drunk in the festively lighted church courtyard as the music played and the dancers danced, but Modestos drank no wine for fear that the fire inside his stomach might burn all the hotter. Kondokali's garrulous residents socialized as if they'd not seen one another since the preceding Easter, which of course was silly, since they saw one another nearly every day of the year.

After a short time, Modestos and Elena said good night to Doran and Gisela, for it was well past Modestos' traditional bedtime. Spiro had decided to remain at the celebration in Kondokali village, as he knew that the festivities would continue until the early hours of the morning, and he was hardly ready to call it a night. Doran kissed Elena on each cheek and wished her a Happy Easter, and then he put his arms around Modestos and hugged him tightly. He watched with concern as the couple walked toward their car, Elena's arm wrapped round the waist of her husband to steady his step.

Doran remained at the festivities with Gisela and Spiro for about an hour, but feeling like a third wheel, he finally excused himself and returned to his apartment. It was quite late anyway, and he was accustomed to rising early in order to tend his garden. Inside his apartment, he prepared for bed, thinking all the while about his friend Modestos. His deteriorating condition had been obvious for some time, but his recent decline was both profound and shocking, not to mention worrisome. Doran determined to take a firmer approach with him. The man was literally killing himself through neglect and obstinacy. And while his commitment to natural treatment was admirable, it was in this case quite futile. He simply needed to accept the fact that his problems were too advanced for him to self-medicate, especially considering that easy and effective treatment was readily available. Though Doran knew also that Modestos would fight hard to maintain his independence. That was his nature—one that Doran normally admired. But in this case it was senseless, and somebody had to make him realize the error of his ways before it was too late.

In darkness, Doran lay naked upon his bed. His window was open to the cool night air, and he could hear the continuing festivities of the Easter celebration as the church was but a hundred meters from his door. He thought again about his now expired passport. Indeed, he had become, as the American Consular had called it, a Stateless person; though it seemed highly ironic to him that he'd never in his entire life felt such a sense of belonging as he felt here in Greece, and indeed in this ramshackle village. Kondokali was a curious place, really: a village once self-contained and self-sufficient, then built up for tourism, and now in steady decline. Modestos had naturally fallen in step with the town's changing character. Indeed, the man seemed to be a mirror of the place he had lived his life. Doran, on the other hand, was rootless—as a habitual itinerant he'd all but accepted the possibility that he would never call any single place home. Though that sad perspective had seemed to change over the year he'd lived on Corfu. Strange as that seemed, he was nevertheless happy for his new perspective—even enthusiastic! He drifted off to sleep shortly after the church bells chimed three in the morning.

Only five hours later, Doran awoke to the sound of the carillon proclaiming the risen Christ. The morning was brilliant, and light poured into his room. The air coming through his open window smelled incredibly fresh and sweet. He rose and dressed to the singing of finches and wrens. Rebirth was indeed the most glorious turn in the cycle of life, and while not a confirmed Christian himself, he felt nevertheless restored—perhaps even resurrected!

He brewed coffee and ate a breakfast of toast and feta and tomatoes. He did not hear Spiro and Gisela stirring in the apartment below, so he lingered on his balcony in the morning sunlight and watched his neighbors as they came out of their houses. They were headed first to the church, and then to family gatherings, where they would roast lambs and exchange small gifts.

Having determined to spend the day on his own, Doran borrowed a bicycle from Pericles and peddled into the low hills behind the village to the location of Gisela's secret garden. Reaching the opening in the hedgerow, he stashed the bike in some shrubbery and entered her once-private domain.

Along the gently sloping terrain he walked, through the untended orange grove, light filtering through the treetop canopy. He reached the ruined house and paused there to examine the abandoned wagon that stood outside the front gate. He stepped through the front door of the house and walked over the rubble of the partially collapsed roof as he went from room to room. His mind moved backward in time, imagining this homestead in its prime. What a sublime location in which to live, Doran thought, and he wondered what might have happened to cause the owners of this property to move elsewhere. He examined the structure carefully, and found it to be strong. He assessed the condition of the window frames, as well as the shutters, which were still intact and on their hinges. And he speculated as to how he might contact the current owner of this property, for he might like to undertake its renovation, and make it whole again. Perhaps some arrangement might be struck wherein he could trade his labor in return for a place to live. A place of his own.

From the secret garden Doran rode to a promontory that overlooked Gouvia Bay, as well as Corfu Harbor. There he sat for a time and assessed his presence at this unlikely locale. It now seemed that he'd arrived here by some unspecific momentum, psychic in nature perhaps, or by some otherwise nebulous impulsion. Whatever force moved the cosmos—or the beings within it to do whatever it was that they ultimately did—Doran was here inclined to give himself up to that impetus. At any rate, there seemed to be little choice in the matter. Indeed, hazard had moved him about like a pawn on a chessboard, and by all standards of good luck—or perhaps by the grace of some Higher Being – he had landed here on Corfu, where for the first time in his life he felt truly at home, and at peace with himself.

Why not live here forever, he thought? Why not stake my claim to this ground. Certainly, I would not be the first one to find it so inspiring. Had it not been for World War II, Henry Miller might never have left Greece and gone back to the States, but he had been deported by the Greek Government because they could no longer guarantee the safety of foreign nationals—though not before the writer had visited Maroussi and found his personal colossus! And the Durrell brothers had felt no compunction whatsoever leaving England to live on this beautiful and peaceful island. Indeed, Lawrence Durrell had firmly believed that certain places touched one in such a profound and beneficent way that they literally defined not only that person's path in terms of geography, but a spiritual path as well. At one time, Doran realized, he had been reluctant even to embrace the reality of the soul, though now he had to admit that its existence seemed fundamental, if still not quite definable. But maybe specific definitions were superfluous anyway. Doran Seeger, a man who had once defined himself in terms of diminishment (subcutaneous as it were) now saw himself in terms of scale—an entity without borders or limits. When he stood on the strand at Kondokali Beach and looked across the water at the mountains of Albania, or at Corfu Town with its twin fortresses and spires and Venetian shipyard, the entire universe sometimes seemed to open up. He felt the breeze raise the fine hairs on his bare skin. He felt his lungs filling with air, and then deflating, only to fill up again. He felt his feet planted firmly on the ground—this ground! And when he looked into the clear and tepid Ionian water, he sensed his primordial past; when he gazed into the firmament, he somehow sensed his future. At any rate, these were one and the same, were they not? The past and the future: the ego and universality. Indeed, these were the elements that made up one's soul.

Just before sunset Doran arrived at the farm, a garden once sparse in wintertime, now prolific in spring. He walked among furrows of cauliflower; he thinned a crop of spinach, suddenly grown out of control. He pulled up six-inch carrots, tasted a stalk of celery, and trained a vine of cucumbers. Old Constantine Thromos had certainly had his visionary wits about him when he purchased this piece of ground, Doran acknowledged. And his son Modestos prized this land perhaps even more than had his father. After all, Doran knew that Constantine had lived out his life in Sicily after the war had claimed his eldest son, Kostos. Modestos had carried the family's torch and cared for his sister until her marriage, as well as his widowed mother until her death at age ninety-three. Modestos had always meant to farm this land, just as he'd heard stories about his father's bountiful effort here. But somehow the time had gotten away. A prolonged military service, his marriage to a city woman, fatherhood, business, a rapidly changing lifestyle for all Corfiots, the financing of an education for his son Spiro: somehow farming this ground had had to wait until his retirement, and the scope of the endeavor had then proved too much for him. So he'd enlisted the help of a willing itinerant: Doran Seeger, an American ex-engineer. Indeed, he'd left most of the work to the *xenos*. Modestos, it seemed, wanted only to see the ground come to fruition once again. That was enough for him. In effect, the farm had become Doran's project, as well as his vocation. Though both men took pride in the bounty of the winter garden.

That evening Doran ate his dinner at the Navigator's Bar. The usual collection of English ex-pats was gathered at the bar and around tables, though there was no sign of either Phil Cullinain or Dennis Payne. Doran was invited to join various groups, though he was not in the mood for company and gracefully deflected each invitation so he could sit at a corner table to dine alone. Today had been a day of deep introspection, and he was not inclined to compromise the peace such a day had imparted to him. He ate quietly and left the pub early. At home, he read awhile before going to bed just after ten.

Doran awoke at seven the next morning to the tolling of a single bell at Kondokali's tiny Orthodox Church. Totally dissimilar to the sound of the glorious Easter morning carillon, he sat up in bed abruptly and listened to the well spaced chimes; and he knew at once that someone of importance in the village had died. An uneasy feeling came over him: his chest tightened; the fine hairs on the back of his neck and on his arms bristled. Throwing back the bed sheet, he rose, put on his bathrobe, and went to the window. It was a sunny morning, and the air was fresh and clear. He could smell the scent of freshly baked bread coming from the shop of Panos the baker. The bell began to toll again, a drawn-out, ominous peal. He did not count the chimes.

He heard Gisela stirring in the apartment below, and he thought it somewhat odd for her to be up and about so early, though not unfounded. He absently thought about how he'd passed the previous day, Easter Sunday, and recaptured for a fleeting moment the peace that a day spent alone in the mountains had imparted.

The sound of the telephone ringing in Gisela's apartment drew him back to the present. He walked away from the window and lay back upon his bed. He heard drawers opening and closing in the apartment below, and he surmised that Gisela was dressing herself, hurriedly. A moment later he heard her clamoring up the steps to his flat. He sat up again as she began pounding on his door.

He rose and went to answer the door, his breath uncharacteristically short. His movements seemed to him to occur in slow motion. The sharp reality of a sunny Mediterranean morning suddenly became intangible, dream-like. And as he opened the door, Gisela's face told a desperate, heartsick story.

"What's the matter?" he asked.

Tumbling through the doorway, she went immediately inside the apartment, and Doran followed in the wake of her frantic advance. Once inside the salon, she slumped onto a chair and looked directly at him with tearful eyes. "Didn't you hear the bells? It's Modestos," she choked.

"No…" he said, still not making the connection she had tried to convey.

"Spiro just telephoned me," she said as she began to weep openly. "Modestos passed away during the night."

His throat tightened and his hands began to tremble. "How?" he croaked.

Gisela shrugged helplessly. "He died in his sleep. That's all they know for certain."

Stunned by the news, Doran said nothing as tears

welled in his eyes. There were no words to express the sudden and profound sense of loss he felt. He knelt down in front of the chair where Gisela sat and held out his arms to her. Leaning forward, she laid her head upon his shoulder. Doran drew her close, and together they sobbed for ten full minutes without exchanging a single word.

For the second time in ten years, Doran entered the small, whitewashed church with the blue dome. The first time had been ten years ago, to attend the funeral of Aphrodite Thromos, Modestos' mother. On that occasion he had sat at the very back of the church, accompanied by Gisela and Alarice. This time he sat with the Thromos family, as Father Dimitrios stood before the assemblage and chanted Orthodox verses appropriate to the somber occasion.

Elena Thromos was dressed head to toe in black. Her expression was somber yet stoic. Whatever grief she felt would be expressed in private. That was her way.

Spiro sat beside his mother, and though his vision was now dark, his eyes remained the windows to his soul. Anyone could plainly see the devastation written upon his face. He held his mother's hand throughout the service.

Gisela sat beside Spiro. She would have liked to comfort her fiancé, but consolation seemed pointless and trite. Modestos had been her friend for ten years. He had offered her comfort in her time of need. He was a man like no other she had ever met, and she herself was distraught over his passing.

And Doran sat beside Gisela. His cheeks were flushed and his eyes were red from crying. His best friend was dead. A man who had shown him through his deeds what it meant to be a truly good man. Today the world was a poorer place for his passing. And nothing anyone might say could diminish Doran's sorrow.

Beside Doran sat Modestos' sister Tassoula, also dressed in mourner's black; and beside her was her husband Pauli. Modestos' cousins occupied the row behind the immediate family and closest friends. Seated throughout the church were Modestos' many other friends, including Giorgos Zervas, Diakatos Leonidas, Mikalis and Fedra, the Venetti family, Panos the baker, and Mayor Asprouli, among others.

Modestos lay in a linen-lined casket draped with laurel branches and covered by ten miniature golden domes with ten lighted candles showing through scarlet portices. Pictures of his family had been placed near his coffin. Upon his folded hands, Doran had laid a sprig taken from the olive tree at the center of the winter garden.

As the service continued, Doran concentrated upon the face of the deceased. The expression was peaceful—one might even say fulfilled. Modestos had lived a good life, a life not rich in possessions perhaps, but a life rich in spirit. Doran's eyes moved over his friend's body to where the tender hands lay folded upon the chest. How many times had Modestos placed those same hands upon Doran's heart in an attempt to convey a feeling that his feeble command of English would not allow? Perhaps there was no truly adequate way of expressing such depth of feeling in any language, Doran thought to himself. It was simply something beyond words that on rare occasions two people might share. Doran felt lucky and privileged to have known such a man as Modestos.

Spiro had requested of Doran that he take the front position as pallbearer in the procession to the cemetery at the outskirts of Kondokali village. Doran was honored and willing to perform such a service for his dearest friend, so when the service was finished and the time came for the funeral march to begin, he stood bearing the weight of Modestos' body and coffin with tears streaming down his face.

The march was a silent one. Step by measured step, the family and friends of Modestos Thromos proceeded to the cemetery, where the deceased would be laid to rest beside his much older but long dead brother Kostos, killed by the

Nazis in 1945, and now in his grave fifty-seven years. Nearby the gravesites of the two brothers lay the body of Aphrodite, their long-suffering mother.

Father Dimitrios presided at a short graveside ceremony before the coffin was lowered into the ground. Spiro was first to shovel dirt into the open grave, and once he had performed the prescribed ritual, he handed the spade to Doran. But instead of shoveling dirt into the grave, Doran put the shovel aside. He bent down and scooped up as much earth as his hands would hold. After a moment of reflection, he tossed the dirt into the grave. Then he walked away in silence.

Once the service was concluded, the mourners lingered at the cemetery to pay their condolences to the family and to chat among themselves about the life of their friend, Modestos 'Takis' Thromos. Spiro remained close to his mother as they both accepted the sympathy conveyed by friends and neighbors. Gisela stood close to Doran, each in a state of despair.

"I should have seen this coming," she said to Doran.

"I knew he was not well," Doran said softly.

"Of course this changes everything," said Gisela

"What do you mean?" he asked.

"For one thing, there will be no wedding in June. The Greeks observe a full year of mourning for family members, so a wedding is out of the question. At least for now."

"I'm sorry," said Doran.

"I'm heartsick at Modestos' death," she said. "But I'm not sorry that the wedding will have to be postponed."

"No?"

"Things were moving way too fast for me," she admitted. "It's just so unfortunate that a circumstance like this one was needed to slow things down a bit."

"Life here on Corfu just won't be the same without him," Doran observed of Modestos.

Gisela shook her head in regret. "No doubt about

that."

And as they spoke in whispers, Doran observed Spiro moving toward them, his white cane tapping the ground to define careful steps. As he joined them, Doran said, "How are you holding up, Spiro?"

"I'm okay, Doran. But I want to tell you something."

"What is it, Spiro? Is there something you need?"

"No, Doran. I don't need anything now. But my mother and I have been discussing your situation," he said.

"What situation are you talking about?" Doran wanted to know.

"We understand that the farm where you and Takis worked together is a very special place for you."

Doran nodded, for there was no denying Spiro's assessment. "Your father loved that land," Doran confirmed. "As do I."

"Yes, I know it's true. So my mother and I want you to have that ground for your own, Doran. Only we would like for you to continue to raise your crops there. As a remembrance to my father."

Not knowing quite how to react to the bequest, Doran nodded his agreement. "That ground was meant for raising food," said Doran. "And I will honor your request. As long as I am the proprietor of that land, I assure you that it will never be used for anything except the growing of vegetables."

"That makes me happy," said Spiro.

"And I know that it would make Takis happy as well," said Doran.

Gisela put her arm around Spiro's waist. "Let's join Elena at the gravesite," she said. "She needs our support now."

Spiro nodded. But before moving off with Gisela he turned to Doran and said, "Thank you, Doran, for carrying my father to his resting place."

"I was honored to do it, Spiro."

The blind man nodded before being led back to the

gravesite by his fiancé.

Doran wished only that he could take to heart the admonishment he'd made of Spiro. For today he did not feel strong, nor did he feel whole; he felt lost, once again.

CHAPTER 16
COLOSSUS

On a warm, golden evening, ten days after Modestos' funeral, Doran walked from his apartment to the marina because he'd heard that some unusual activity was afloat concerning the Overdraft; and as he approached Philbar Cullinain's boat, he was somewhat astonished to see that the small yacht was indeed under refurbishment.

"Philly!" he called out from the wharf. "Are you on board?"

Cullinaine poked his head out of the wheelhouse. A broad smile was upon his face. "Prepare to repel boarders!" he joked. Then he stepped onto the pier to shake Doran's hand.

"I heard through the grapevine that you were working like a fiend to make this old rust bucket seaworthy," Doran quipped. "I heard you were repairing sails, swabbing the deck, polishing brass. What's gotten into you, Philly?"

"The Overdraft turned forty years old last week," the sailor boasted. "She's a good old boat."

"So you've decided to give her a makeover in honor of the anniversary?" Doran inquired.

"Not exactly, mate," said Cullinain. "I'm preparing her for a sea voyage of some significance, you see."

"You don't say!" said Doran. "And just where are you planning to sail?" he asked.

"I've always wanted to sail in the Caribbean," said Cullinain. "So, I thought I'd head first for Sicily, then to the South of France. After that I'm planning to take her to Spain, around the Costa del Sol, and port somewhere along the Algarve in Portugal. There, I'll take her out of the water for a complete refitting before heading across the Atlantic."

Doran was not only surprised by Philbar's proposed itinerary, but incredulous as well.

"You mean to tell me that you're planning to cross the Atlantic aboard the Overdraft—alone?"

"Right-o, mate. She's a good old boat."

Doran's eyes widened. "Pardon me if I seem a bit dubious," he said. "Are you sure the boat's up to an Atlantic crossing?"

"Why not?" said Philbar. "Anyway, I've always fancied seeing Barbados. Cuba, too!"

"Cuba?"

"Yeah, why not?"

"And what about you, Philbar? Are you up to making such a trip alone?"

"I'll grant you that I'm probably in far worse shape than the Overdraft," he laughed. "And an old wreck like me can't simply be refitted, mind you. But we only live once! As far as we know, anyhow. So what the hell!"

"What if you get into trouble out there?" Doran asked.

Cullinain shrugged offhandedly. "No worries, mate," he said. "We'll be okay."

"I don't know, Philbar," said Doran.

"Come on board, mate. Have a drink with me."

Doran stepped onto the deck of the Overdraft, as

Philbar went to the galley to pour each of them a glass of brandy. Together they sat on deck and toasted the sailor's upcoming voyage.

"I'm going to miss your company," Doran told his friend.

"Fine thing for you to be saying," said Cullinain. "You've been coming and going for years. You must have left a dozen or more broken hearts in your wake."

"Not the case," said Doran.

"Come on now, mate. Each of us sails his own boat, right? And if ships pass in the night, we blow our horns and salute one another. That's the way, isn't it?"

"I suppose so," said Doran. "But I'm not lying when I say that I'll miss you, Philly. I've grown rather fond of your salty face."

"Likewise, my friend. Likewise! But now that Dazey's gone, I can't just stay here and rot. There's only so many nights an old sod like me can spend in the Navigator's Bar, swapping the same old stories and telling the same old lies. A joke is a joke, isn't it? Mind you, it may be a good joke, a real belly laugh, but enough of this bullshit, I say. I need to sniff out a new pile of crap. Ha, ha, ha!" In a single swallow he downed the remainder of the brandy in his glass. He assessed the repairs that he was making on his forward sail, and he looked reflectively out to sea. "Drink up now, mate," he said. "I've got a lot of work to do before I set sail. And I've only got a few working hours left before the sun goes down."

Doran left the marina shaking his head and muttering to himself. Philbar's proposed journey was absurd; no way was the Overdraft up to such a passage. Not to mention the captain himself! But wasn't that just like Philly? To sail off into the sunset without a care. Because he loved to sail, he felt a freedom like none other when he was at sea. Better he was swallowed by the deep without a trace, or battered to bits while fighting a raging storm, Doran thought, than die the death of a pathetic old drunk in a ramshackle port town full of broken men and would-be Captain Ahabs. Anyway, one man's paradise was surely another man's hell. Philbar had simply overstayed his welcome, and apparently he was smart enough to know when to leave. Still, he would be missed. He would be missed...

On a warm afternoon near the end of May, Doran bent over a row of beets, pulling out weeds and cultivating furrows. An Exaltation of Lark sang in the treetops. Bees buzzed from flower to flower, pollinating as they went. A stray cat slunk through the broad leaves of his zucchini crop, stalking grasshoppers. He stopped for a moment to wipe the sweat from his brow with a handkerchief. The sun warmed his bare shoulders and further tanned his already brown face. He rolled himself a cigarette and surveyed the now prolific garden that grew upon this blessed ground—his ground! Indeed, the bequest of this land was no small favor; it was his lifeline. Not as much in a material sense as it was in a spiritual one. Each day, as his fingers worked the soil, he felt its energy and its richness. This earth was alive. And it seemed to impart its vivacity directly to his essence. Here he experienced a profound sense of belonging, and to Modestos he would remain ever grateful for his legacy. For although Doran was now, technically speaking, a Stateless person, in truth he had never felt more at home! And what was the definition of home, really? Certainly it was as much a state of mind as it was a locality.

Doran fervently hoped that Modestos, wherever or whatever he was presently within the cosmos, felt as whole as he did now. With a lingering bit of melancholy, he recalled the assessment of the afterlife that his friend had once made just after they'd both nearly been killed in a car crash on a winding mountain road: "Maybe we will meet again in the next life," Modestos had speculated. "Good food. No need for money. Beautiful beach. No need for clothes. What do you think?"

Lost in reminiscence, Doran had neither heard nor noticed the approach of a burly and rather unkempt man along the road that bordered the winter garden; and not until the man had called out his name did he turn to regard him. It was Dennis Payne.

"If it ain't Seeger the farmer," said Payne.

Doran dashed out his cigarette with the heel of his boot and approached his visitor. "What are you doing here?" Doran called out.

"Your lady friend told me that I might find you here," Payne revealed.

"Lady friend? What lady friend?" Doran asked.

"The Dutch girl, Gisela."

"She's not really my lady friend," said Doran. "She's engaged to somebody else."

"Your loss, I guess," said Payne. "But the truth is that I didn't come here to discuss your love life."

"I suppose not," said Doran as he stood before the Englishman. "Why have you come?"

"Truth is that I've got some papers for you to sign."

"Papers? What papers?" asked Doran.

Payne did not answer immediately; rather he took a sheath of papers from his pocket. He handed Doran a pen. "Don't ask too many questions, Seeger. Just sign here!" He indicated the bottom line.

"What am I signing?" Doran asked, perplexed.

"Just sign it!"

Doran wrote his name next to the X.

"And here, also," said Payne as he peeled back the first leaf and thrust the documents at Doran.

Again, Doran signed his name.

"Once more," instructed Payne, and Doran complied. "That's it!" said Payne. "I think we're right now."

"I suppose you now own my land," said Doran. "Or the right to my firstborn son."

"Congratulations, Seeger," Payne gloated.

"I don't understand," said Doran.

"It's quite simple, really," said Payne. "You are now an official subject of HRH Queen Elizabeth II."

"You're joking," said Doran.

"No, I'm not," said Payne. "You are now a full-fledged British citizen."

"And this is legal?" Doran asked, incredulous.

"Legal as an eagle, as you Yanks say."

"Just like that?"

"Right-o! And if you want a passport, all you need do is fill out this form and send along a couple of photos, and they'll mail your new passport straight-away."

"I don't believe it," said Doran as he examined the immigration papers. "How did you pull it off?"

"I told you before that I had connections. This really wasn't so difficult."

"I don't know how to thank you, Dennis," said Doran sincerely.

"You can buy everybody at the *Navies* a drink," said Payne.

"If I had any money, I'd be happy to do it," said Doran.

"Then maybe I'll just have a sack full of those tomatoes that you're growing."

Doran laughed. "Help yourself," he said. "Take as many as you like."

Back at his apartment, Doran again examined the documents that Dennis Payne had given him. Indeed, they seemed to be thoroughly official. Though he was an American expatriate living in self-exile in Greece, apparently he was now also a British subject. He laughed loudly, flung the papers into the air, and watched as they floated to the floor. "God save Her Royal Majesty," he shouted! "God save the Queen!"

On the first day of summer, Doran harvested the last of the vegetables grown in the winter garden. When he had finished his work, the ground was vacant and uncovered, the land itself returned again to its natural state. Once in doubt, the garden had been an overwhelming success. Not only had it yielded a bumper crop of vegetables, it had simultaneously raised the awareness and the conscience of the farmer—an unexpected but welcome auxiliary result, as far as Doran was concerned. Unfortunately, Modestos had not lived to see its ultimate fruition. That was Doran's only regret concerning the farm, for he knew that Takis would have been nothing short of ecstatic to behold the farm in all its glory.

Repeatedly, Doran saw the face of his friend in a passing cloud, or concealed within the leafy boughs of the venerable olive tree at the farm's center. He heard his friend's voice speaking to him in the song of a lark, or in the howl of a dog, or the braying of a donkey, or the banter of a rooster. When he drank water from the well, he also drank in the blood of his departed friend. And when he tasted the fruit of the harvest, he ate too the body of his benefactor. Each moment spent in the garden was, for Doran, a Holy Communion.

And after the ground had been raked and tilled, Doran saw once again the long snake that had once frightened Modestos nearly into hysterics. Doran smiled as he remembered camping overnight at the farm and burning bicycle tires to vanquish the serpent. Modestos' homespun remedy for removing the snake had failed, and Doran concluded that there was probably no getting rid of the pernicious orphidian, and that in the future he and the serpent were just going to have to learn to live together.

With no small amount of sentiment, Doran thought about his friend-in-kind, Philbar Cullinain. Philly had set his sail and gone to sea, leaving Greece forever. At this very moment he was probably sailing due west on an unalterable course to reunite with Dazey. Doran wished him well on his intrepid journey.

Then there was Gisela... After nearly a ten-year

absence in his life, she had appeared one night on his doorstep in Prague. Together they had gone to Kiev and lived through a vicious mugging. As an aftermath, she had convinced him to return with her to Corfu. For a time, he had thought that he might be falling in love with her, and she with him. But familiarity had bred caution on both their parts. Now she was committed to marry Spiro Thromos, though the wedding would not take place for at least another year. Which was fine with Doran. Because he knew that Gisela was a fickle person, not necessarily out of selfishness or egotism, but by nature. As was he himself! Perhaps Gisela and Spiro would indeed marry, and perhaps they would make Elena a grandmother. For that Doran was hopeful. Because if they had a boy child, they would certainly call him Modestos, as Greek tradition ordained, and the Thromos lineage would thereby be maintained. Whimsically, Doran imagined that the yet unborn child might come to know him as a beloved uncle: *Barba* Doran, an American *xenos*.

And as the sun began to set over the low mountains behind Kondokali village, Doran was given to assess his own character as well. His father's dying words had implored him: 'Move quickly, before it's too late…' He'd taken the message to heart, choosing not to place his stamp upon external circumstances, but instead allowing hazard to map his route. What a circuitous course he had traveled! Once a man of dissociations and distractions, he was now one of connections and wholeness. Once a vagabond, he had now come home and taken root. Deep within himself he sensed the emergence of a sensation previously unknown—a feeling both benevolent and gargantuan. What was it that Henry Miller had called it? Colossus!

ABOUT THE AUTHOR

David A. Ross was born January 6, 1953 in Chicago, Illinois. He attended William Rainy Harper College for three semesters before dropping out. After being excused from military service on a physical deferment, he moved to a remote area of northern Idaho, where he lived a subsistence lifestyle in a rustic log cabin without plumbing or electricity for more than a year. Returning to Chicago, he worked for Follett Publishers for a short time before relocating to Denver, Colorado. There he taught music for twenty-five years, wrote three unpublished novels, and worked as an associate editor for *Southwest Art Magazine* before moving first to Arizona then to New Mexico.

From 1987 through 2000, he engaged in a series of twelve extended trips to Europe, as well as several to the South Pacific. In 2001, he relocated permanently to Greece where he currently lives with his wife, author Kelly Huddleston, and works as an author, editor and Internet developer. *The Virtual Life of Fizzy Oceans* is his sixth published novel. Also to his credit is *Sacrifice and the Sweet Life*, a collection of short stories and poetry, and *Good Morning Corfu: Living Abroad Against All Odds*, a memoir.

Passion Fruit

Sandra Cuza

Published by Open Books

Copyright © 2014 by Sandra Cuza

Cover image "Orange Dreams" Copyright ©Olésea
Volta Voloshin

Learn more about the artist at
http://society6.com/volta